For My Readers

Thank you so much for picking up this book. I hope you enjoy the continuing journey of Rain and Ellie—and please keep an eye out for the conclusion of their story, *Queen of Song and Souls*, coming March 2009, from Leisure Books.

Be sure to visit my Web site, www.clwilson.com to sign up for my private book announcement list, enter my online contests, and scour the site for hidden treasures and magical surprises. I hope you linger a while to learn more about the Fey and the Fading Lands—as well as other Fey tales and C. L. Wilson novels coming soon.

I'd love to hear from you. Please, send me a Spirit weave. Or, if you prefer, you can take the nonmagical route and just e-mail me at cheryl@clwilson.com.

RAVES FOR C. L. WILSON'S EPIC TAIREN SOUL SERIES!

LADY OF LIGHT AND SHADOWS

"Released right on the heels of her impressive October debut, *Lord of the Fading Lands*...Wilson jumps back into her tale without skipping a beat, expanding her world with finesse while boldly taking her story in entirely unexpected directions. As Ellysetta comes into her own as a proper heroine, driving the story toward its breath-taking conclusion, gratified fans may find their elation giving way to anxiety, as the wait for the next volume will be considerably longer."

—*Publishers Weekly*

"I had to stop myself from reading the book more than a few times because I knew if I sat down to read a few pages, I'd end up reading dozens and lose complete track of time.... This is a book worth taking a weekend vacation solely for the purpose of reading it."

—Smart Bitches Blog

"The sequel to her highly charged fantasy debut, *Lord of the Fading Lands*, picks up right with the action, as events take a dark turn. Wilson's prose flows gracefully and is filled with evocative language that reveals the ambitious world she's creating. Fate and destiny vie with burgeoning love to place the two lovers at the epicenter of a dangerous storm."

—*Romantic Times BOOKreviews*

"One of the year's coolest—and hottest reads...Stunning."

—Michelle Buonfiglio,
Romance B(u)y the Book on LifetimeTV.com

"The situation and atmosphere were extremely vivid and it was almost like watching a movie. The characters have so much emotion and it just jumps off the pages. I loved this book....This series will be legend..."

—Night Owl Romance

C. L. WILSON

KING of SWORD And SKY

TAIREN SOUL

LEISURE BOOKS  NEW YORK CITY

A LEISURE BOOK®

October 2008

Published by

Dorchester Publishing Co., Inc.
200 Madison Avenue
New York, NY 10016

Cover art by Judy York
Cover handlettering by Patricia Barrow
Text design by Renee Yewdaev

ISBN 10: 0-8439-6059-0
ISBN 13: 978-0-8439-6059-4

Printed in the United States of America.

10 9 8 7 6 5 4 3 2

Visit us on the web at www.dorchesterpub.com.

For Lisette. Here there be tairen.

*And for Mom, because this book would not
have been written without you.*

Acknowledgements

Thanks to my wonderful dad, who didn't realize when he agreed to enter my Web site content into that little template we bought that he would soon become a master Webster, SQL guru, photoshopper, Java scripter, Flash programmer and Dreamweaver Superstar. You are my hero.

As always, thanks to my fabulous friends, critique partners, and plotting pals: Christine Feehan, Betina Krahn, Kathie Firzlaff, Sharon Stone, Diana Peterfreund and Carla Hughes. Thanks to my husband Kevin, and children Ileah, Rhiannon, and Aidan for putting up with my long hours.

Special thanks to the wonderful readers who submitted poetry in my inaugural Tairen Soul poetry contest. Congratulations to all the reader-elected winners! The winning poems are included in *King* and *Queen* (along with a few other poems I selected from those entered). Four of the winning and entered poems (or excerpts) have been included in this book: "Mages of Eld" by Michele Baird, Portland, OR; "Tairen Song" by Lynda Hendrix, Wellford, SC; "Beyond the Faering Mists" by Bridget Clark, Warrington, PA; and "Shei'tanitsa Reign" by Ariel Hacker, Monument, CO. You can read all the entered poems and the winning poems on my Web site. Thanks, ladies, for sharing your fabulous talent! And thanks to my readers for voting.

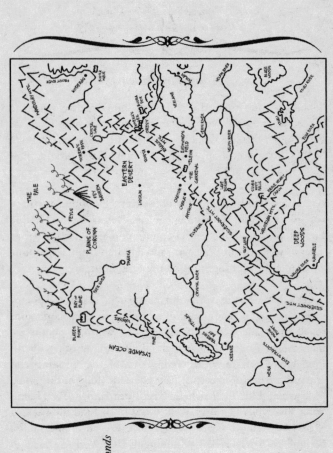

The Fading Lands

PROLOGUE

Eld ~ Boura Fell

"Two Primages and sixty of my Black Guard slaughtered, and yet somehow the pair of you survived. While my prize escaped."

In the lowest levels of Boura Fell, the subterranean fortress buried deep beneath the dark-forested heart of Eld, High Mage Vadim Maur paced the *sel'dor*-veined floor of a small, sconce-lit cell. Before him, two battered and bruised men sat chained to a pair of black metal chairs. One wore the blood and filth-grimed remnants of an exorcist's scarlet robes. The other wore shredded and stained crimson rags that had once been the silken garb of a Sulimage, a journeyman practitioner of the vast and ancient arts of Magecraft.

Vadim Maur's pacing came to an abrupt halt. Luxuriant purple robes swirled about his spare form. Long, bone-white hair slid across his shoulders, accentuating the pallor of a face that had not seen sunlight in a thousand years. One beringed hand shot out. Thin, cadaverous fingers closed around the swollen jaw of Kolis Manza, Eld's most famous and esteemed Sulimage, who had until only a few days ago served his master Vadim Maur's bidding in Celieria City.

Now, the Sulimage's sash had been stripped of its jewels of achievement, and the shredded, honor-bare swath of cloth had been tied around the man's throat to mock his once-proud status as the High Mage's most accomplished and magically gifted apprentice.

"Capture her," Vadim hissed. "Bring her to me. That was my command." Long, ridged nails dug deep into the

Sulimage's skin. "Yet you returned *empty-handed*."

"She was too powerful," Kolis protested weakly. "Not even the Primages could stand against her."

"Powerful?" Silver eyes snapped with fury, and white frost formed on every surface as the room's temperature plunged in sharp response. "Of course she was powerful! She is the crowning achievement of my last thousand years of work! The Tairen Soul I created! My greatest triumph— *and you let her slip through your fingers!*"

"What more could I have done, master? The Fey broke through our defenses." The Sulimage coughed, then groaned as his broken ribs protested. "I tried to hold them off, to give the others time to get her into the Well, but then she . . . her magic . . . just exploded. She surprised us all."

"Silence!" Vadim's free hand shot out with vicious force. Despite the High Mage's great age and increasingly frail appearance, his fist smashed hard against his apprentice's face. The heavy rings of power decorating each of his fingers amplified the force of his blow, and the crack of bone and the crunch of breaking cartilage echoed off the stone walls of the chamber. Blood sprayed from Kolis's mouth and nose. A groaning breath wheezed out of his lungs, and he slumped senseless in his bonds.

Vadim turned to the man in the ragged exorcist's robes and whipped a wavy-edged Mage blade from the sheath strapped to his waist. He snatched a handful of greasy brown hair and yanked hard, pulling back the prisoner's head and exposing his throat to the dagger's razor-sharp edge.

Pale blue eyes, surrounded by stubby black lashes, looked up at him in mute fear. Fresh blood trickled from both nostrils and the corners of the man's mouth, and vicious purpling bruises swelled on skin still mottled from earlier beatings. A pulse beat like a trapped sparrow in the man's throat, and his barrel chest rose and fell with short, rapid breaths.

The prisoner swallowed convulsively, and the skin of his neck pressed against the razor-sharp edge of the Mage blade.

Even that light touch tore a fresh slice in the captive's skin. No blood trickled from the wound. The dagger's thirsty black metal drank every drop before it spilled, and the dark cabochon stone in the blade's pommel began to flicker with ravenous red lights. The man froze in breathless silence.

Vadim's mouth twisted in a snarl. "And you, butcher's boy. Did you seriously think for even the tiniest instant that your miserable, insignificant mortal life held any value to me except as a means to capture Ellysetta Baristani?" Vadim leaned forward, letting his silver eyes turn to dark, bottomless wells of blackness sparkling with red lights as Azrahn, the sweet, powerful magic of the Mages, gathered within him.

Den Brodson, son of a Celierian butcher and former betrothed of Ellysetta Baristani, stared up into those twin pits of blackness and knew he was staring death in the face. He'd seen death before, a few days ago in the Grand Cathedral of Light, when Rain Tairen Soul had pulled a Fey blade from its sheath and smiled into Den's eyes.

Then, Den had turned and leapt into the Well of Souls to escape. Now, gods help him, he had nowhere to go.

The white-haired High Mage leaned closer still. "Your only value to me now is what small service the Guardians of the Well will offer in return for the delivery of your rotting corpse as a sacrifice."

A mewling whimper broke from Den's bloodied mouth. He'd seen the Guardians' handiwork . . . seen what they did to the dead and dying. As long as he lived, he'd never forget the high-pitched, animal screams of Eld soldiers being eaten alive when fresh blood seeped through their bandages and drew the hunger-maddened demons like wounded creatures drew thistlewolves.

Gods, he didn't want to die that way. "Please . . ."

Black eyes sparked with a sudden flare of malevolent red. The High Mage put a hand over Den's chest, directly over his heart, the fingers curved like claws so that only the fingertips touched. All five pointed nails gouged into the skin as if the Mage intended to bore through Den's chest bones and rip out his heart. The black eyes whirled. The skin where the pallid hand touched grew cold.

"No, wait! Wait!" Panicked, Den shoved his feet against the cell floor and scooted his chair back, retreating from the icy hand. The leg of his chair caught on an uneven stone, and with a choked wail, he toppled over backwards.

Pain exploded in his skull as his head cracked against the stones. His hands, shackled at the wrists, scraped hard against their metal bonds. The sudden jolt shook his entire body, and a long, narrow parcel of wadded cloth fell out of his robe's deep pocket to land beside him.

The pair of pale, hulking guards standing near the door strode forward to grab Den's chair and haul it—and him—back upright. One guard kicked the small parcel and sent it skittering across the floor. The fabric unwrapped as it went, and a handful of long, crystal-topped needles spilled out, chiming an absurdly cheerful series of tinkling notes as they rolled across the stone floor.

The High Mage went still. His eyes narrowed and lightened from nightmarish black to a slightly less terrifying shade of cold, glittering silver. Sheathing his dagger, the Mage pointed to the scattered exorcism needles. "Bring those to me," he commanded.

Both guards rushed to obey, gathering up the fallen needles and bringing them to their master. The Mage examined them closely. Most of the dark crystals topping the needles were black, but several sparkled with ruby lights.

His jaw clenched. He spun around, grabbed Den's chin in a fierce grip, and shook him, making stars whirl across Den's vision. "These crystals have tasted blood," the Mage hissed. "Whose flesh did the needles pierce, mortal? Yours? Or someone else's?"

Den swallowed the acrid bile rising in his throat. "Ellie Baristani," he groaned. "She pulled them out to stop us from taking her into the Well."

The High Mage released Den and straightened. He lifted the needles to his nose and inhaled deeply. His eyes fluttered closed. When he opened them again, the Mage smiled.

"Well, mortal, it seems you will keep your miserable life another day, after all." He untied the sash from around his waist and wrapped the needles in it carefully, then deposited the small bundle in his own deep pocket. "I do not punish those who please me, and this gift is pleasing indeed."

The shallow, relieved breath had barely left Den's lungs before his chest constricted on a new surge of panic when the High Mage lunged and his bony hand closed around Den's throat.

"Today is my gift to you," the Mage hissed. "But for life after daybreak tomorrow, there is a price, mortal." He lifted the Mage blade, twisting the black, razored edge so the light of the sconces made shadows dance across the dark metal. "Accept my Mark. Willingly bind your soul to my service. Or when the Great Sun rises, you will die a death more hideous than any you can imagine."

Den whimpered.

The Mage smiled, pressed the point of his dagger to Den's wrist, and sliced. Blood welled from the cut and slid down Den's arm like scarlet teardrops. The Mage lifted the wrist to his lips. Den flinched as a pale tongue flicked out, tasting his blood. "Answer me, boy. Surrender your soul or die. The choice is yours."

Den's hand shook. His entire body trembled. How had this happened? How had his plans gone so awry?

The Mage's grip tightened, pointed nails digging into the soft skin of Den's inner wrist. "Speak, mortal! Do you accept my Mark? Of your own free will, do you bind your soul to my service?"

Den's dreams of living in luxury in some remote part of the world, growing fat on the profits of Ellie Baristani's magic, shattered like broken glass. There would be no palatial estate. No soft-skinned, buxom serving wenches to tend his every need. No lords lining up to seek his favor. There would be no Ellie Baristani on her knees before him, kissing his feet and begging for his forgiveness, whoring herself to please him.

His eyes closed. His shoulders heaved with helpless, silent sobs.

"Yes," he whispered.

"Yes, master," the Mage's hissing voice corrected.

"Yes, master." Tears gathered in Den's throat and burned at the back of his eyes.

"Then say it. 'Of my own free will, I accept your Mark and bind my soul to your eternal service.'"

Den heard himself, weeping brokenly, repeating the damning words. Hot tears ran down his frozen cheeks. The cold press of the Mage's mouth clamped against his wrist and pulled sickeningly as the Mage sucked Den's blood from the sliced vein. Then came the colder press of that taloned hand gripping the skin above his heart. A sickly sweet aroma filled the air, overpowering, like barrels of rotting fruit. Pure, frigid ice, sharp as a knife, plunged deep into his chest. A will, heavy as stone, pressed down upon his.

He was in a black river, gasping for breath and fighting desperately to stay afloat, while a terrible weight slowly and relentlessly dragged him down. His head bobbed under. The thick, black, oily liquid of the river—so cold, so horribly sweet—enveloped him. His lungs burned as the air in them ran out and the need to breathe became overpowering. He fought, struggled, tried to kick his way to the surface, but the weight anchored him down, dragging him deeper and deeper.

His world was total darkness. No light. No hope. No hint of warmth. His lungs were on fire. If he breathed he would drown. If he didn't breathe, he would die.

His mouth opened on a deep, desperate, despairing gasp. Oily blackness flooded in, filling his lungs, filling him.

With one last, choking, weeping cry for his lost life, Den Brodson surrendered.

CHAPTER ONE

Celieria ~ The Garreval

Seven days after departing Celieria City, the Fey reached the end of the mortal world. As the small caravan of wagons and loping Fey crested the top of a last, rolling hill, Ellysetta's breath caught in her throat. A great fertile plain stretched out below, miles of land sectioned into hedgerow-partitioned fields, all greening with well-tended crops against a dramatic backdrop of majestic mountains thrusting up from the earth like a solid wall.

"Oh, Papa," Ellysetta breathed.

" 'Tis the most beautiful sight I've ever seen," Sol Baristani agreed in a whisper as he sat beside his daughter on the wagon seat, a lit match held, forgotten, over the tobacco-filled bowl of his favorite pipe.

Together, father and daughter stared in awestruck wonder at the majestic peaks filling the horizon.

At first glance, the mountains almost appeared to be a single range, but Ellysetta knew from the countless histories she'd read that they were actually two separate mountain ranges. The fierce Rhakis arrowed down from the north, nearly colliding with the stately swells of the Silvermist range. Only a scant mile separated the two, an infamous pass known as the Garreval, gateway to the Fading Lands.

Misty clouds swirled across forested cliffs and steep highland pastures of the Silvermist mountains. The clouds hovering over the Rhakis were less gentle, dark with rain and boiling into lightning-shot thunderheads as the sharp peaks continued northward towards Eld. Those soft clouds and fierce storms merged into a dense, shimmering fog that filled the pass between the two ranges, and Ellysetta gave a small shiver at the sight.

The Faering Mists. The magical barrier that surrounded the Fading Lands, impenetrable to all but the Fey.

The match Sol held over the tobacco-filled bowl of his pipe burned down unnoticed until the heat burned his fingers. "Sweet brightness!" he yelped. Hissing, he shook the match out, tossed the blackened remains over the edge of the wagon, and blew on his stinging fingers.

Ellie turned, trying to stifle her laughter as she reached for his hand. This wasn't the first time her father had seared his hands on a matchstick. It wouldn't be the last. His attention was too easily caught by some real or imagined beauty—often while he held a lit match in his hand, thanks to his fondness for his pipe.

"I'm all right, Ellie-girl," Sol protested when she took his hand.

"I know, Papa, but Marissya says I should practice whenever I get the opportunity." She held her father's hand in hers and focused on the reddened flesh, trying to block out the flood of thoughts and emotions that poured into her mind when she touched his skin.

Love. Worry. Instinctive fear, tinged with guilt. He still wasn't comfortable with the shining brightness and palpable magic of the beautiful stranger sitting beside him.

Ellie forced back the stab of pain his fear caused and tried to focus her thoughts the way Marissya v'En Solande, the Fey's most powerful healer, had shown her. Throughout the weeklong westward journey across Celieria, Marissya had spent several bells each day with Ellysetta, teaching her how to wield her own powerful healing magic.

Though Ellysetta still had much to learn, she now understood on a conscious level the basic patterns of the healing weaves she'd been unconsciously spinning all her life.

Marissya assured her she'd soon be able to summon and spin those weaves on demand, using only the amount of power needed to weave them, but restraint was something Ellie still had difficulty mastering. The powerful, hidden barriers that had kept her magic bottled up were gone now, and the weaves she'd once spun with such subtlety now surged forth at her call like a river gushing through a shattered dam.

Remembering Marissya's admonitions, Ellysetta reached down into the well of energy at her center, carefully calling forth the glowing threads of power she would need. Red Fire to draw the heat from the wound. Green Earth to heal the damaged flesh. Lavender Spirit to steal away the pain. And something else Ellysetta had discovered while observing Marissya during their lessons. A special, golden something that Marissya called a *shei'dalin*'s love, the mysterious force that was unique to Fey women. It made all the threads of the *shei'dalin*'s weave shimmer with a warm, golden cast. No Fey warrior could spin his magic the same way.

"It springs from the compassion and empathy of a Fey woman's heart," Marissya had told her. "It isn't a seventh branch of magic. We cannot separate it out and weave the *shei'dalin*'s love by itself. It's just the natural way Fey women weave magic."

"And do I weave *shei'dalin*'s love the same way?"

At that, Marissya had laughed. "Feyreisa, you do *nothing* the same as other Fey." Then, still smiling, she'd added, "I'm sure you must, Ellysetta, but when you weave, your magic is so bright, its power blinds me."

Now, holding Papa's hand in hers, she attempted to summon her magic and wield it with control and restraint, as Marissya had been trying to teach her.

She found the threads, wove them in a loose healing pattern, and with a gentle "push" of power, sent the weave into her father's hand. The push slammed out of her with the force of a hammer strike, her weave flaring with blinding brightness.

The startled jerk of Papa's body and sudden widening of his eyes made her grimace in dismay.

"Light save me," she muttered under her breath. Then, in a louder voice, she said, "Are you all right, Papa?"

Sol blinked several times and took cautious inventory of himself. When he didn't find any missing—or extra—appendages, he gave a smile. "Well-done, Ellie-girl. The finger's good as new." He held up his hand to show her.

Sure enough, the angry red burn on the tip of his finger was gone. But that wasn't the problem. She watched her father run his newly healed hand through his hair. His hand stopped in midmotion.

"Oh," he said. Sol Baristani was of the age when many mortal men began "thinning the forest," as Papa put it. Or, rather, he had been. Keeping his gaze fixed on her face, he patted the newly thickened growth of hair crowning his scalp. "Well . . . er . . . that's not so bad. Provided it's not some frightful shade of green." His brows drew together in mock concern, and he added in a hesitant, rather fearful tone, "Er . . . it's not green, is it, Ellie?"

Ellie sighed. "No, Papa, it's not green."

With a twinkle in his eye, he pretended relief. "Well, then, there you go." He laughed and grinned, and reached across to pat her hand. "You did good, Ellie-girl. You may have overdone the weave a little, but the finger's healed. Besides, what man wouldn't like a little more hair when his own starts to go missing, eh?" Thrusting his pipe stem back between his teeth, he lit a fresh match and held it to the bowl, puffing until the shreds of tobacco began to glow orange and puffs of fragrant smoke wreathed his newly regenerated headful of hair . . . and a face that had lost at least ten years of age in an instant.

She forced a smile. "*Beylah vo*, Papa." Weaving youth on mortals wasn't one of the things Marissya had taught her—but apparently the patterns were very similar to regular healing.

A happy shriek sounded at Ellysetta's right. The Fey warrior Kiel vel Tomar, his long silvery-blond hair woven into a plait, ran past with Ellysetta's nine-year-old sister Lorelle perched on his shoulders. Kieran vel Solande, Marissya's son, followed a few paces behind. Lorelle's twin, Lillis, sat on Kieran's shoulders and kicked his chest with her heels as if he were one of the Elvish *ba'houda* horses pulling the wagons in their caravan. Her small fingers clutched tufts of his thick, wavy brown hair.

Lillis and Lorelle were clad in miniature versions of Marissya's and Ellie's brown traveling leathers, which they had insisted Kieran weave for them. Kieran and Kiel had done their best to keep the children's minds off the grief of Mama's death by making each day of the trip a new adventure. The twins had taken to the idea, enthusiastically using even the briefest stops as an excuse to explore—always under watchful Fey eyes, of course, but rarely in clean, tidy places. The keepsake boxes Papa had carved for them years ago were now overflowing with treasures from their journey: small rocks, wildflowers, snail shells, bird feathers, whatever caught their attention.

Kieran cast a grin Ellysetta's way. His steps faltered as he caught sight of Sol Baristani; then his gaze shot to Ellysetta. She blushed furiously. A *shei'dalin's* ability to restore mortal youth was a secret the Fey had guarded for millennia, and she had just revealed it for anyone to see.

Fortunately, before he could say anything, Lillis tugged on Kieran's hair and bounced on his shoulders. "Faster, Kieran!" she cried. "They're beating us!"

With a final look and a shake of his head, Kieran turned away and raced down the grassy hill after Kiel and Lorelle.

Ellysetta watched them, and the tension that had been growing in her all week squeezed her chest tight. They were nearing the end of the journey. One more day, two at the most; then she would leave what remained of her beloved family to follow her new husband through the mysterious Faering Mists, perhaps never to return.

Sol patted her hand and nodded his chin in the direction of the twins. "It is good to hear them laughing again."

"Yes," she agreed. The twins hadn't had much cause for laughter of late.

"They miss their mother," Sol said. "They try to smile and laugh for my sake, but I hear them each night, crying into their pillows and pleading for her to come back."

Just that quick, Ellie's own sharp grief struck hard. Her face crumpled and her eyes filled with tears. "I miss her too, Papa." Stern as Mama sometimes was, Ellie had never doubted her love—and never loved her back with any less than her whole heart.

"Oh, Ellie." Sol slid an arm around his daughter's shoulders and pulled her close. "My sweet Ellie-girl. We all miss her."

She turned her face into his neck as she had so many times in the past and sobbed. And her father held her, as he always had, patting her back and rocking her as if she were still the small child who'd crawled on his lap for comfort after evil visions tormented her dreams.

She cried until her tears were spent and, when they were done, wiped her eyes as best she could, and begged again as she had so many times this last week, "Won't you please come with us, Papa? Rain will grant you and the girls escort through the Mists. You could live there, with us, in safety."

Sol sighed. "We are not Fey like you, Ellie. Our home is here, in Celieria. The last request your mother ever made of me before she . . ." His voice thickened. He swallowed the lump in his throat. "In the note she wrote to me before she went to the cathedral that day . . . she begged me that if anything happened to her, I'd be sure the twins were raised in Celieria, among their own kind."

"Papa, she asked you for that when she still thought I was demon-possessed and the Fey were evil. She realized her mistake in the end. Don't you think she'd realize her mistake about this too?" They'd been over this question a thousand times since leaving Celieria City. "Wouldn't she rather know the girls were safe regardless of where they live?"

"It was her last request, Ellie. Shh." He put a finger on her lips to forestall further objections. "Her wish is as sacred to me as if I'd sworn it to her on her deathbed. So long as there is a chance of the girls living here in peace among our own kind, then here we will remain. You're Fey, Ellysetta. You belong in the Fading Lands. We are mortal, and we belong here." His eyes were filled with sadness but also unwavering determination.

Seeing that look, Ellysetta knew she'd lost. Her father was the most loving man she'd ever known, but when he had that hint of steel in his eye, it meant he'd made up his mind and would not be budged. She bit her lip, stared at the hands clasped tightly in her lap, and nodded, afraid to look at him for fear the fresh tears burning at the backs of her eyes would spurt out in dreadful, graceless sobs.

She heard her father sigh again, saw him shift in the periphery of her vision. His hand, broad and bronzed and calloused from his years of woodcarving, reached out to cover hers. Love, rich and sweet and steadfast as love ever had been, poured into her through the touch, along with pride and gratitude, and a thought that rang in her head clear as a bell.

I love you, my sweet Ellie-girl. No man could love a daughter more, and no man could be prouder than I am of you. Though I will do everything I can to honor your mother's wishes, I won't risk my children's safety needlessly. If trouble comes, the girls and I will pass through the Mists. That's my oath to you.

Through vision blurred by swimming tears, she met his eyes and saw for herself the truth she could feel through the touch of his skin. It was more than she'd expected. His promise was an oath he considered as binding as the vow he'd made to his wife.

As the wagon continued its swift, smooth roll down the grassy hill towards the fertile plains of the Garreval below, Sol looked out at the majestic mountains and green fields. "This is a beautiful place," he said. "I think your mama would have been very happy here."

Ellie laid her head on her father's shoulder. "I think so too."

"The redirection weaves are up. The Garreval is secure." Belliard vel Jelani, First General of the Fading Lands, released the net of Spirit threads tying him to the dozens of Fey scouts spread in a five-mile radius around their destination. As they had all week, the warriors had cleared the caravan's path of mortals and spun redirection weaves to turn away curious locals and Eld spies.

Just over three weeks ago, Celierians and their families had lined the roads and cart paths from the Garreval to Celieria City to watch the immortal Fey run past on their annual trek to the nation's capital. This time, not one mortal would see or remember the Fey's passing.

Bel turned to find Rain staring off towards the Fey caravan, his face drawn. "Rain? Something is wrong?" Bel's hand went instinctively to his steel, his fingers hovering over the hilts of his Fey'cha throwing daggers.

"*Nei.*" With obvious effort, Rain dragged his attention back to his best friend. "Well, *aiyah*, but no different from the wrongness that has followed us since leaving Celieria. She weeps again for her mother."

Bel glanced down at his hands, away from the pain in Rain's lavender eyes. For all his power—impressive even by Fey standards—Rain could not weave the sorrow from his beloved's heart. Oh, he could have spun a rosy illusion of happiness upon her—or asked another Fey to steal her memories—but that was not the Fey way. Both honor and love bound him, and he could do only what Fey men had for centuries: stand strong for his mate and offer what comfort his love could provide.

"You should go to her," Bel said.

Rain sighed and shook his head. "*Nei*, she needs him more than me now—someone who loved her mother as deeply as she did."

Bel had known Rain too long not to hear the comment left unsaid. "Everything Lauriana Baristani did, she did for love," he reminded Rain gently. "And in the end she gave her life to save her child."

"I realize that," Rain replied, "but I cannot pretend an affection I never felt."

Bel nudged a large clump of field grass with the toe of one black boot. Lauriana had never wanted Ellysetta to wed the Fey king, and she'd made sure everyone—including Rain—knew it. "Perhaps," he finally said, "Ellysetta doesn't need you to pretend love you did not feel. Perhaps it is enough just to know you are there, loving her."

"She knows." Rain swept a sharp gaze over the valley below. "There's been no unusual activity in the last four days, and not a single person following us since we left Celieria City. I'm not sure if I should be relieved or suspicious. The Eld I knew would never let us get away so easily."

Bel took the hint. "Perhaps our decoys are working." A separate party of Fey had gone north, towards Orest, accompanied by a magic-warded wagon, so that Eld spies might think it held Ellysetta and her family.

"Let us hope so," Rain said, his face set in stone. "But let us also prepare for the alternative—and not only from the Mages. If the *dahl'reisen* learn that Ellysetta can restore souls . . ."

Ice shivered through Bel's veins. "You don't think Gaelen would—" His voice broke off in disbelief, then surged back in protest. "He is Ellysetta's *lu'tan*." After Ellysetta restored his soul, Gaelen had bloodsworn himself to her service, vowing to protect her for the duration of his life and the death that followed. No *lu'tan* would break that vow. "Gaelen is Fey once more. His honor has been restored. Do not forget, without him Ellysetta would already be in the hands of the Mages."

Rain's jaw set. "I have not forgotten. Nor do I forget that all it takes is one look at his face without that scar, and his *dahl'reisen* friends will know the truth." Of all the Fey, only *dahl'reisen* scarred, and only when they made the kill that tipped their immortal souls into darkness. When Ellysetta had restored Gaelen's soul, she'd wiped his *dahl'reisen* scar from existence. "No matter what trust you may feel for Gaelen as a fellow *lu'tan*, do not let your guard down. The *dahl'reisen* cannot be trusted, and they could attempt to use his long acquaintance with them to their advantage."

Rain's expression grew grim. Bel felt the brief surge of power, quickly harnessed, that came in response to whatever unpleasant thoughts were crossing Rain's mind.

"I think I will return to Ellysetta after all," Rain said.

He stepped back and the brief surge of power became a breathtaking flood as he summoned the Change. Sparkling gray mist billowed out in whirling clouds around Rain, and when it cleared a death-black tairen crouched in his place. The great winged cat fixed one large, glowing purple eye upon Bel, and a throbbing Spirit voice sounded in Bel's head, powerful and resonant with the rich musical tones of the tairen.

"To Teleon, brother, and tomorrow, to home."

Ellysetta climbed out of the wagon to walk the last mile across the greening plains of the Garreval as twenty Fey raced on ahead to secure their destination: the outpost built at the base of the ruins of the once-great fortress of Teleon. Lillis and Lorelle walked beside her, their small hands clutching hers.

She would always be grateful for this time Rain had given her with her family. He could have flown her straight to the Fading Lands on tairen-back, but he had not. Knowing how dear her family was to her, he'd arranged for all of them to travel together. The Elvish *ba'houda* horses, bred for endurance and speed, traveled much faster than mortal steeds; but Rain in tairen form, using magic to power his flight, could have traversed the thousand miles across Celieria in a single day.

Even though he still left small courtship gifts on her pillow each morning, this extra time with her family was his true gift to her, and she worked to sear every precious memory into her mind. Like this one: the girls tripping through the tall grass at her side, their hair bouncing with their steps. A slight breeze blowing, fragrant with the scents of mist off the mountains and warm grass waving in the wind. She squeezed the twins' small hands and watched dimples flash in their cheeks as laughter bubbled from them.

Dear gods, how she loved them. And if any harm ever befell them because of her . . .

"No dark thoughts, shei'tani." The admonishment slipped into her mind on a now-familiar weave of Spirit.

Ellysetta glanced up at the great winged black cat soaring swiftly towards her over the top of a nearby hill. *"Not so dark this time,"* she answered. *"Only a little gray."*

She could not blame him for thinking the worst. Her mind had not been peaceful since they'd left Celieria City. The High Mage might not know where her body was, but despite Rain's presence and the twenty-five-fold weaves the Fey placed around the camp each night, the High Mage had been able to find her soul more than once when she dreamed. He'd not managed to put another Mark on her, but each time he'd found her, she'd bolted out of sleep with her tairen roused to a raging bloodlust, roaring for death and vengeance.

Consequently, she'd spent most nights wide-awake and flying the moonlit skies with Rain.

"I was just thinking I'll miss my sisters when we're gone. And I can't help worrying about their safety."

"Kieran and Kiel will allow no harm to befall them." The two Fey and two hundred of their brethren would be staying behind at Lord Teleos's ancestral estate near the Garreval to guard Ellysetta's family.

Rain swooped down the side of the hill fast and hard, Changing in midflight to the black-leather-clad form of his lean Fey body. He landed running, and a brief, swift jog brought him quickly to her side.

Just the sight of him and his glowing lavender eyes made Ellysetta's breath catch in her throat. All Fey were ravishing creatures, but the legendary Rain Tairen Soul outshone them all. He was an immortal king whose unshielded Fey beauty dazzled the senses, his face a masterpiece of breathtaking male perfection, saved from prettiness by the thrust of strong bones beneath the skin and the aura of deadly promise that swirled just below the surface.

He was a Tairen Soul, the strongest and rarest of all Fey, a master of all five branches of Fey magic, capable of Changing into one of the magical, fire-breathing tairen of the Fading Lands.

He was her truemate, the other half of her soul; and when at last Ellysetta found the courage and unconditional trust necessary to embrace the darkest shadows of his soul and her own—to bare without reservation every thought, every fear, every shame and maleficence inside her—then at last their souls would join for all eternity. If she failed, their uncompleted bond would drive Rain to madness and eventually death.

Yet even knowing that, Rain's love—intense and absolute—shone from his eyes as he approached, setting Ellysetta's senses aflame. She began to tremble. *"Shei'tan"* Luckily, before Ellysetta could embarrass herself, her young sister Lillis squealed and threw herself into Rain's arms, shattering the intoxicating spell holding Ellysetta captive.

"Will you take us flying again today, Rain?" Lillis asked while Lorelle bounded up, grabbed Rain's free hand, and jumped up and down with excitement.

Ellie smothered a laugh. Lillis and Lorelle had shed their fear of Rain and his power. He had become part of their family. Which also meant he'd become a hapless male to be twined around their fingers.

Rain, in return, had learned how to relax around them and let them draw out the Fey gentleness in his heart. Though he was a man who could slaughter his enemies without mercy, with the twins he now laughed and smiled like a man who had never known darkness.

"Let us get you safely settled in your new home first, *ajianas*. Then I will take you both flying again."

Of course, he still had to work on how to say no.

"Hooray! Hooray!" Lorelle threw up her arms and danced around him in enthusiastic circles.

"Can we have a new kitty in our new home?" Lillis asked, fluttering her lashes again. "Since we had to leave Love behind."

Kieran had convinced the girls that Love the kitten, who had a terrible aversion to magic, would be miserable living in the Fading Lands or staying with them so close to the powerful magic of the Mists. They'd reluctantly agreed to leave Love behind in Celieria City in the care of Gaspare Fellows, Queen Annoura's Master of Graces.

Rain smiled. "A new kitten? I imagine Kieran and Kiel can arrange that. Perhaps one for each of you, hmm?"

Lillis strangled him with more hugs, then leapt out of his arms so she and her twin could run tell Kiel and Kieran they were going flying again, and that Rain had said they could have new kittens.

Ellie shook her head and watched them go. "One day

you will have to learn the fine line between loving adoration and slavish devotion."

He pressed a kiss on her palm. "Let me give them what gifts and freedoms I can. Their lives will soon have restriction enough. Teleos!" Rain lifted a hand to the Fey-eyed Celierian great lord, Devron Teleos, who stood beside the truemates Marissya and Dax v'En Solande, staring in silence at the place that was to be the Baristani family's new home. "How long has it been since you've been to the Garreval?"

Teleos's mouth drew down in a grimace. "I've made a point of visiting all my holdings at least once every year, but as you see, there's not much to draw me here."

Below, on the lower slopes of the Rhakis mountains, the remains of a once-great fortress rose from the tumbled rubble of silvery blue stone: Teleon, the former family seat of House Teleos. Even after a thousand years, its once-fabled beauty still lay shattered and abandoned, its Fey-spun towers and parapets crumbled, the remains covered in lichen and mosses and crowded with tufts of cliffgrass. A small stone outpost—crudely built and clearly mortal in origin—had been constructed atop a small hill at the base of the mountain, not far from the remains of what had once been a glorious gate into the walled city-fortress. Smoke curled up from a vent hole in the outpost's small central hall.

Ellysetta tried to hide her dismay. This was her family's new home?

As if hearing her thoughts, Lord Teleos said, "I feel a poor host for offering my guests so rude an accommodation." The Celierian great lord, a descendant of Rain's long-dead friend Shanis Teleos, eyed the remains of his once-great family estate with grim eyes. "Rain, are you sure the Feyreisa's family would not be better served in one of my more respectable holdings?"

Rain smiled and shook his head, his straight, silky black hair sliding over his black-leather-clad shoulders. "*Nei*, this is perfect for our needs."

"This was a place of great beauty once," Lord Teleos said in a sorrowful voice. In the days before the raising of the Mists, his family had been close friends of the Fey, and the many Fey ancestors in his family tree had left Devron and all his forebears stamped with Fey eyes, a glow to their skin, and life spans much longer than those of pure mortals. Teleon, which had once been an estate of inestimable beauty, had been a gift from the Fey to their friends and kin in House Teleos.

"*Aiyah*, it was," Marissya agreed. "I remember the terraced gardens with all their fountains. It reminded me of Dharsa."

Lord Teleos regarded the ruins of his family estate with somber eyes. "I always wished my ancestors had repaired it once the poison of the Wars was cleansed, but perhaps it's best they never did. Mortal hands could never have done Teleon justice." He sighed. "Some things, once lost, are better left in the past."

Rain made a sound in his throat that sounded like something torn between a growl and a laugh. "And some things deserve to live again." His eyes crinkled at the edges. "You did say we could make it habitable, Dev."

Teleos's brows drew together. "You mean to restore Teleon?"

"*Aiyah te nei*," Yes and no. And on that mysterious note, Rain smiled and said, "Come. I think you will find you are not so poor a host as you fear."

Brimming with curiosity, Marissya, Dax, Teleos, and Ellysetta followed Rain as he led them the final half mile to the foot of the mountains.

Near the gate of the small outpost, and stationed along its outer wall, two dozen armored Celierian soldiers stood at attention. To a man, they sported snarling tairen's-head helmets and white tabards edged with scarlet and emblazoned with the arms of House Teleos: a golden tairen rampant on a white field with a rising red sun. Pennants of white, scarlet, and gold fluttered in the breeze.

They passed through the open gate, but when Lord Teleos would have headed for the main hall in the center, Rain stopped him. "*Nei*, Dev, not that way."

Bel ran up just as the small party rounded the corner of the hall and started towards the back wall. Ellysetta turned to greet him, only to find him frowning up at the mountain towering over the back wall of the outpost. The shimmering radiance of the Mists was very bright, like a shadow made of light rather than darkness. Though mortal eyes would not see it, the whole mountainside glowed with undulating bands of magic.

Rain turned to cast a glance over his shoulder and smiled at Bel's perplexed look. The rear stone wall of the outpost lay before him. Rain took another step. The air around him rippled like water in a pond.

With one more stride, Rain passed through the wall and disappeared from view.

"Spit and scorch me," Dev breathed. He glanced at Marissya and Dax, then charged after Rain, plunging headfirst into what seemed like solid stone. The air rippled again, and Lord Teleos vanished too.

"Spirit weave," Kiel said, his eyes sweeping over the mountainside. There was no sign of Rain or Lord Teleos, only the rear wall of the outpost and, beyond that, the tumbled remains of Teleon scattered across the mountainside, tufts of cliff grass and stands of hardy mountain trees waving in the breeze.

"Scorching clever one," Bel said. "They're using the magic-shadow off the Mists to mask the energy of the weave. Not even a Spirit master would see it until he was almost on top of it."

"Well?" Kieran said with an eager grin. He held out a

hand to Lillis. "What are we waiting for? Let's go see what's behind the weave."

With a burbling laugh, she stuck her hand in his and they ran up the trampled path after Rain and Teleos. Lorelle grabbed Kiel's hand and yanked the Water master with her as she darted forward in hot pursuit.

Ellysetta, Bel, and Sol followed close behind, and when they stepped through the rippling wall of illusion and cast eyes on the sight beyond, Ellysetta's jaw dropped open in stunned wonder.

"Bright Lord save me," Sol whispered, staring awestruck at the gleaming magnificence before him. "I've never seen anything so beautiful."

"It's like a magical palace from a Fey tale," she breathed.

They were standing at the open, arching gate of an immense mountain fortress of unparalleled grace and beauty. Silvery blue stone soared high into the sky in a dazzling display of Fey artistry and architecture. Crenellated walls gave way to lush, gracefully terraced gardens bursting with trees, fountains, fragrant shrubs, and flowers. Pennants in the bold colors of House Teleos fluttered in the breeze from every tower and along the series of interior walls that ringed up the mountainside and circled the upper keep with level after level of protection and silvery blue beauty.

"Ellie! Papa! Come look!" Lillis and Lorelle stood in the center of a small grassy park nestled against the second inner wall. They laughed and danced beneath the graceful, arching branches of cherry trees as pale pink petals rained softly down upon them. Kieran and Kiel stood nearby, watching the children with indulgent smiles.

Lord Teleos stood dumbstruck at Rain's side as Ellysetta and Sol crossed the lower courtyard to join the twins. "You did it," he said. "You restored her to her former beauty."

"Not completely," Rain admitted. He dragged his gaze away from Ellysetta and the children and gave Devron Teleos his full attention. "A number of the gardens and buildings on the middle levels are still just Spirit weaves, but the walls and gates are real, and defensible, as is the manor at the top."

"Even so . . . this is an amazing feat. How did you manage it?"

"Three thousand Fey stand guard at the great war castles of Chatok and Chakai beyond the Mists. While we journeyed across Celieria, they came through the Mists to prepare a suitable home for the Feyreisa's family. And to prepare Teleon for battle once more."

Lord Teleos turned to him in surprise. "You think the Eld will strike here? With the Mists blocking any hope of entrance to the Fading Lands?"

Rain looked across the flagstone-cobbled courtyard to the lower garden, where Ellysetta, Sol, and the twins were inspecting a marble fountain of dancing maidens whose slender, upstretched fingers rained veils of clear water into a small pond.

His expression lost any hint of softness. "If the Eld come," he said, "I doubt it will be passage through the Mists they're after."

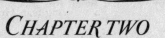

CHAPTER TWO

In sorrow, the blood-sown earth despairs,
and granite stone weeps bitter tears.
In fields once green, love lies entombed
beneath a silent lake of glass
forged in raging tairen flames,
dark with the death of dreams.
There, shades of men and once-great kings
yet battle evil's tide.
While silvery maidens softly dance and
sing of love that died.

Sariel's Lament by Avian of Celieria

Ellysetta stood on the balcony of a well-appointed bed-chamber in one of Teleon's spacious upper towers and looked up at the Mists. Several bells earlier, the lowering sun set the Mists ablaze, giving the illusion of a curtain of fire burning across the world. Now the night was deep and the Mists were a shifting, shimmering glow of multicolored radiance against the dark of a near-moonless sky.

The clap of boot heels on stone made her cast a glance over her shoulder. Still clothed in black leather and full steel, his Fey skin as pale and luminous as pearls in moonlight, Rain approached. He'd been meeting with Teleos, Bel, Kieran, and Kiel to discuss the defense of Teleon and review troop strength and dispersal in the rest of Teleos's holdings.

War was coming. No matter how some still tiptoed around the truth, all of them knew it. They only prayed there would be time enough to prepare before Celieria's borders erupted into open battle.

And though it seemed a terrible thing to ask, Ellysetta had secretly prayed that when the attack came, the Eld's first strike would come in some far-distant part of Celieria, like Orest or Celieria City, so the Fey would have enough time to evacuate Lillis, Lorelle, and Papa to safety behind the Faering Mists.

That secret prayer seemed ill-considered now. The hearth witches of the north—and there had been plenty of them living in her childhood town of Hartslea, despite the strong Church presence there—believed that wishing harm upon others would bring three times that harm to the wisher. Was hoping the first battle of a war started somewhere else the same as wishing harm upon another? Ellysetta shivered at the prospect.

"Cold?" Rain asked. His eyes narrowed. "Or have your wandering souls returned?"

Ellysetta often experienced inexplicable sudden chills, like ice spiders crawling up her spine. The chills—or "wandering souls" as Rain called them—were insignificant compared to the hideous nightmares and frightening seizures that had afflicted her all her life, and she'd always brushed them off as yet another oddity about her. Rain didn't consider the strange onset of chills as harmless as she always did.

"Nothing like that," she assured him. "Just a worrisome thought of war."

His arms tightened. "Your family will be safe. The Fey will see to it."

"I know." And she did. Kieran and Kiel would die to defend her family. All the Fey staying at Teleon would.

Rain rubbed a thumb across her lower lip, then bent his head to follow the small caress with a kiss. "There is a thing I need to do tonight before returning to the Fading Lands. I had hoped you would come with me, but perhaps you should stay here, instead, and try to get some sleep."

"No, I'm fine." She reached for his hand. "You know I can't sleep without you beside me." He was her talisman against the call of the High Mage of Eld, and she feared to fall asleep without him lying there beside her, him arms wrapped about her, protecting her from the very real terrors of the night.

"Then let's go—and bring your cloak."

Ten chimes later, they were soaring through the night skies high over Teleon. Ellysetta stretched out her arms and turned her face up to the stars. Rain spun a light Fire weave to keep her warm as the chill, thin air swept past.

Hold on. The brief command was her only warning before Rain twitched back his rounded tairen ears, spouted a warming jet of flame that lit the night, then tucked in his mighty wings and dove.

Ellysetta screamed with laughter and grabbed for the high, curving pommel of her saddle just as the unsettling thrill of weightlessness came over her. Together, she and Rain fell through the sky, plummeting freely towards the ground miles below. The moonlit sky went silvery white, and fine droplets of water misted Ellysetta's face as they plunged into a cloud bank. She caught the tangy-fresh chill of cloud mist on her tongue, drinking its bracing sweetness.

One heartbeat; two; then they burst through the clouds back into the crisp, clear darkness of the night.

Tairen wings spread wide, snapped taut, and the wild, reckless plunge became a swooping ascent. Ellysetta screamed again, a breathless, exuberant sound, and clutched the saddle tight. *Rain! I think I left my stomach back there.*

The now-familiar, chuffing sound of tairen laughter joined the rush of the wind in her ears. *Hold on again, shei'tani. This is even better.*

Flows of magic spun out to bind her securely into place, and Rain shot forward on a thrust of magic-powered speed.

The world rushed by in a dizzying blur, and with a subtle shift of his wings, he sent them spiraling into a corkscrew roll. Shadowy earth and moonlit sky whirled in a wild kaleidoscope before Ellysetta's dazzled eyes.

Another woman might have shrieked in fear and begged him to stop. Ellysetta only flung back her head and laughed in delight. Freedom coursed through her veins like a potent drug.

She would never tire of flying. The limitless joy of dancing, laughter-spangled winds, the thrill of diving through misty clouds and soaring so high she could almost scoop stardust with her fingertips: Flying was a joy so rich, it chased back all sorrows and fears. Well, she amended silently, *almost* all.

"Rain, do you honestly think when we get to Fey'Bahren, I can just walk in and spin a weave that will cure the kitlings of whatever is killing them?" That was the reason Rain had come to Celieria to find her. Unbeknownst to the outside world, a mysterious sickness had been killing unborn tairen in the egg for centuries, decimating their numbers until scarcely more than a dozen of the great cats still lived. The Eye of Truth had sent Rain to Celieria to find the key to saving them.

She, Ellysetta Baristani, was that key. Even if none of them actually knew how she was going to manage the miracle.

"I know it doesn't sound like much of a plan," he said, *"but the tairen have never let any of our healers into the lair—not even Marissya. You, however, are both a Tairen Soul and my truemate. You'll be able to enter the lair and weave healing on the kits as no other she'dalin has been able to."*

"This assumes I'll even know what weave to spin when I get there—let alone how to spin it."

"That's why Marissya will be going with us to Fey'Bahren—so she can continue your training and counsel you while you're healing the tairen. But you may not even need her help. I heard you healed

Ravel's new Fire master well enough this afternoon while I took your sisters flying."

She gave a short laugh. "Oh, yes, I healed him all right. I made that wound vanish as if it had never been."

"There, you see—"

"And I erased every hint of weariness from the last week of travel," she informed him. "And wiped clean every shadow on his soul. And filled him with such an abundance of energy that he shone like a newly minted coin and spent the rest of the day racing circles around my quintets until Bel and Ravel both threatened to pull red on him if he twitched another muscle."

There was a brief silence; then Rain said in an oddly choked voice, "Well, shei'tani, there are worse tribulations in life than healing a Fey too well." Chuffing tairen laughter vibrated in his throat.

Her eyes narrowed. He found that amusing, did he? "And when he wasn't annoying his brother Fey, he was following me around like a lovesick puppy."

The chuffing laughter changed instantly to a low, rumbling growl. Licks of flame seared the air before Rain's muzzle. "Oh, was he?" The fur on the back of his neck rose up, and his rounded ears lay back. Tairen were territorial creatures, and they definitely did not appreciate encroaching males trespassing too near their mates.

"Ha! You see? It's not so funny anymore, is it?" She ran a frustrated hand through the wind-tangled spirals of her hair. "I'm like a rultshart in a spider-silk shop. If Marissya asks me to summon a puff of Air, I call a gale so strong it knocks her off her feet. If she asks me to summon Water, I nearly flood the encampment."

"Your power is vast," Rain soothed, "and no longer restrained by the weaves set upon you in childhood. You simply need time and practice to learn how to wield it in moderation."

She sighed. "Even assuming I can learn to control my power enough to spin the right weaves, what if healing doesn't stop whatever's killing the kits?"

His right wing dipped, and he banked, wheeling back around towards the south. *"Then we go to Dharsa and start from the beginning. Perhaps you can help us discover something we have overlooked all these years."*

"Rain, be realistic."

"I am. I asked for the key to saving the tairen and the Fey, and the Eye sent me to you. To me, it seems quite clear that whatever is killing the kitlings, you are integral to making it stop. I do not doubt this, even though you do."

Rain's wings spread wide, and he sank through the sky in a circling glide, alighting on a stretch of empty field. A cradling ribbon of Air magic deposited Ellysetta on her feet while the Change swirled around Rain's tairen from in a sparkling mist.

His hands rose, long fingers threading into the wild spirals of her flame red hair, the pad of his thumb brushing across her lips and leaving tingles of awareness behind. "We're here, *shei'tani.*"

Ellysetta glanced at their surroundings. Nothing looked familiar.

"Where is 'here'?"

His eyes went dark. "This is Eadmond's Field."

The Lake of Glass stretched out for miles, its dark, glossy surface glittering beneath the dim light of the moons overhead. Mist swirled in ghostly eddies along the silent, lifeless shores of the lake, and in the scant moonlight the shifting vapors looked like spectral maidens dancing forlorn pirouettes.

Ellysetta could hardly breathe as she regarded the wide expanse of what once had been the most infamous battlefield in the history of Celieria. Here, a thousand years ago, Rain's first mate, Sariel, had been slain by Elden Mages, and in grief-stricken madness over her death, Rain had given himself to the Wilding Rage and scorched the world with tairen flame.

As they approached the southern shore of the glass lake, they passed a bronze statue set in a circle of carved stones. Her throat grew tight as she realized the bronze was a life-size replica of the doomed couple immortalized by Fabrizio Chelan's famous painting, *Death of the Beloved*: Rain Tairen Soul clutching his dead mate, Sariel, and crying out his despair to the heavens. The stones circling the statue retold the fateful battle through scenes carved into diamondine granite. Millennia would pass, she realized, before weathering finally laid to rest the story of Rain and Sariel.

Ellysetta traced the last of the etched slabs, reading the tragic conclusion of the tale she knew so well. "'Some say if you walk to the center of the lake, you can still see the Lady Sariel, beautiful as a sunrise, appearing merely to sleep beneath the surface.'" Rain's sudden stab of sorrow slapped her senses, and she gave a gasp of dismay. "Oh, Rain, I'm sorry." She'd told the tale so often to her sisters, the words had spilled out automatically. "I shouldn't have read that aloud."

"*Nei*, it's all right," he said. "I like that story much better than the truth."

She bit her lip, hating her thoughtlessness. She knew the fanciful Fey tale couldn't possibly be true. The Mages had severed Sariel's head and burned her with Fire.

"I killed millions that week," Rain added. His voice was a low scrape of sound. "Thousands of them here. Eld and their allies mostly, but even Fey and mortals and Elves and Danae who were not quick enough to flee my wrath."

Ellie knew that too. Celieria had erected smaller memorials at various points around the site in memory of all the allies of Celieria who had perished in a sea of tairen flame. The flame had rained down without cease, turning the very earth into a lake of molten obsidian glass that swallowed every trace of the armies on the battlefield.

Ellysetta left the circle of stones and went to his side.

"You must stop blaming yourself, Rain. You didn't know what you were doing."

"I knew," he corrected her. "I was simply beyond caring."

The Wilding Rage had taken him: the terrible fury of the Fey, a sweeping, conscienceless wrath that knew no mercy, no remorse, just the pitiless, relentless drive to destroy whichever enemy had spawned it.

From here, Ellie knew, Rain had flown northward, searching out the armies of the Eld and their allies, raining fire and death upon all in his path. He'd blanketed the entire nation of Eld in scorching clouds of tairen fire, leaving naught but smoldering ashlands in his wake. Even then, his Rage still shrieked for more blood, more death. He'd skimmed along Eld's eastern coast, boiling the seas with tairen flame and sinking fleets of enemy naval vessels. By the time the Fey and the tairen had finally forced him from the sky, half the continent lay in ruin and millions had perished.

"You ended the Wars," Ellysetta reminded him.

"I almost ended the world."

"But you did not. Even in your Rage, you focused the bulk of your fury on the Eld."

He would not let her cling to her illusions. "I was coming south to scorch Celieria off the map when Marissya and the others stopped me."

"Do you think you would truly have done that?"

"*Aiyah*. Gods help me, but I would have."

Ellysetta clasped both of Rain's hands in hers, feeling his self-loathing for the horrors he had wreaked upon the world. Countless innocents had died here that day, as well as the hated enemy.

"I know their names," he said. "Each and every one of them slain by my Rage—and there are so many. For centuries, I lived with the sound of them shrieking in my mind. Over time, I learned how to quiet them, but they're still there, still screaming. Anytime I let my barriers fall, I see their faces and relive their memories of the lives and dreams I shattered."

"Rain, you spent a thousand years in torment for one terrible act of madness. Haven't you suffered enough? Let them go."

He met her gaze, his Fey skin shining with a faint, silver luminescence, his eyes with their slightly elongated pupils glowing. "Ellysetta, I cannot. The torment of their lost lives is mine to bear. Only death or the completion of our bond can release me."

A misty breeze blew across the lake, cool from the night air sweeping down off the Rhakis mountains and rich with the scent of magic from the Mists. Rain looked up at the bright glow of rainbow lights that danced in undulating flows along the mountaintops. "So many lives lost on my account. Here at Eadmond's Field and there as well." He gestured to the Faering Mists. "Twelve thousand of the oldest, strongest Fey and all the tairen prides but one gave their lives to build the Mists."

"You cannot blame yourself for their deaths too."

A look came over his face that made her heart ache. "Can I not?" he said softly. "All the Tairen Souls but me were dead. I was the last, and I was wild with madness. But as the last, I was also the Tairen Soul, Defender of the Fey. Had I perceived a threat to the Fey, I would have flown again. So they built the Mists. I'm sure, in part, they meant to save the world from me, but mostly, they died to save me from the world. To give me peace for as long as they could in the hope that I would live and regain my sanity."

She felt his guilt, his silent horror. "Oh, Rain."

"How does a Fey repay such sacrifice? How can he ever be worthy? How does he atone for all the lives lost because of him?"

She captured his face between her hands. "By doing exactly what you're doing now," she assured him. "By living the best you can. By trying to save the people and the land those Fey loved. By honoring them, as you've done every day since I first met you."

"I think you look upon this Fey more favorably than he deserves, *kem'san*."

"*Nei*, I see him plainly enough." She laid her palm against his chest. "And I love the Fey I see."

When she gazed at Rain with such unwavering surety, he always saw a different reflection of himself shining from her eyes. A stronger Rain Tairen Soul, so much better and brighter than he truly was. As if, when she looked at him, she saw only the Rain he might have been if he'd never scorched the world, a good and worthy king. He longed to be that noble Fey, if only because he could not bear to diminish himself in her eyes.

"I cannot restore the lives I took or repair the dreams I shattered, but I can at least ensure that the brave friends and allies who fell here will never be forgotten. Will you walk with me while I do that, *shei'tani*?"

"Of course I will."

He led her to the shore of the lake and lit a globe of bright Fire over their heads to light the way, but when he stepped onto the dark glass, she hesitated to follow. In the Fire-light, the glass was smooth and glossy, untouched by dirt, animal tracks, or even a speck of dust. It was as if nothing of the living dared invade this sacred site of the dead.

"Perhaps we shouldn't walk on it," she suggested. "It seems a little like walking across a grave."

"Nothing of those who died here yet remains," Rain assured her. "My tairen flame saw to that. But I will spin a weave of Air beneath our feet as we walk so that we do not touch the glass."

Silvery white tendrils spun out from his fingertips, and when Ellysetta stepped out onto the glass, she slid several handspans, as if the lake were a frozen pond and her shoes were ice skimmers instead of embroidered silk ankle boots.

Barely half a manlength from the shore, Rain stopped.

"An Elvish bowmaster fell beneath my flame on this spot. His name was Pallas Sparhawk, of the Deep Woods clan. He had a mate named Celia and a son who'd seen only three winters." His head bowed. "I did not meet him in life, but I will never forget his death."

Lavender Spirit gathered in Rain's hand, spinning into a three-dimensional image of a handsome, stern-eyed Elf with nut brown hair hanging in plaits around his pointed ears. Red-orange Fire spun out in a searing weave, etching the Elf's name into the glass on the spot where he died, and below that the fallen man's clan name and country. He held his hand over the etching of the name and said, "*Las*, Pallas Sparhawk. May the world be a kinder place when next you return." The Elf's name flashed, and the Spirit weave of the Elf's image sank into the glass lake.

"I have tied the weave to the etching of Sparhawk's name," he said. "Those who draw near will see his name and his face and share a few of his memories. Perhaps they will find it in their hearts to mourn him a little."

"It is a fine tribute to him, Rain," Ellysetta said.

"Is it? There is another reason I brought you here. When you complete our bond, my memories of these folk will become yours as well. You should know, before that happens, some small portion of what that entails. You should know—" He broke off. His jaw worked for a moment, and when he spoke again, his voice was gravelly with tightly checked emotion. "You should know what really happened here that day. It wasn't the romantic Fey tale Celierians have made of it. These were good people, with lives and loves of their own. If I could spin time, I would take this day back."

She could feel the weight of his sorrow and his guilt. He knew, better than any creature alive, exactly what he'd done, the lives he'd destroyed. Until their bond was complete, she could not erase that pain. All she could do was stand beside him and try to help him shoulder the burden.

"Then let me meet Pallas Sparhawk, so I may mourn him

as you do." She stepped forward, close to the name etched deep into the glass. The moment she drew near, Rain's Spirit weave swirled in a cloud of lavender mist. The Elf's face formed in her mind, and with it came a rush of memories: the face of his wife, the love he had felt for her, the moment of his son's birth, the day he'd presented his child with his first, tiny bow, the march to battle, the friends he'd fought beside, and the final gasp of fear and acceptance as an orange wall of tairen flame raced towards him. His final thought, as the flame enveloped him, had been for his wife, Celia, and their son, Fanor.

Tears filled her eyes for the brave man lost, for the sorrow of the beloved wife and child to whom he'd never returned. "His wife and son, if they still live, should know that his last thought was of them." She took a ragged breath and wiped away her tears. "When you send the envoy to the Elves, you should tell them what you've done here and let them know their dead have not been forgotten. You should let all the allies know."

"You think they would want that?"

"I do. Even the mortals may have family members who will want to come here one day, to learn and remember as well as to mourn."

Throughout the night, they walked the lake, covering every inch of glossy black glass, creating the memorials, celebrating and mourning the lives lost, until finally, just before dawn, only the place where Sariel had died remained unmarked. It was not, as legend claimed, at the center of the glass lake, but closer to the southern end, where the Fey healing tents had been.

When Rain started to weave the same marker into the lake's surface for Sariel, Ellysetta stopped him. "For the last thousand years, her name has been linked to tragedy and death," she said. "Celierians say she sleeps beneath the glass. Why not let them have their legend, and give her a memorial that will let the world remember her as she truly was?

Why not give her something like this?" Calling upon Spirit, the one branch of magic Ellysetta could usually weave with some measure of success, she spun an image of the memorial she had in mind.

Rain regarded the Spirit weave in surprise. "Are you certain this is what you want?"

"It's what she deserves." She covered his hand with hers, and her sincerity flowed through the touch. "I do not begrudge her the love you bore for her, Rain. She brought you joy in a world of war and death, and I will always be grateful to her for that."

He drew a breath, his heart swelling with emotion so great, it nearly brought tears to his eyes. "You would have loved her too, you know."

She smiled, her eyes filled with warmth and understanding. "I know. I've loved her from the first time I read about her. Now, I think I loved her so much because some part of me knew how much you did."

He raised her hands to his lips and pressed a kiss upon the backs of her fingers. "Then let it be as you wish. Step back a little. I will need to call Fire."

He waited for her to move a safe distance away before lifting his hands and summoning his magic. Earth and Fire gathered in his body, pulsing with energy. When he had the strength he needed, the bright, swirling threads of green and red spun from his fingers, coiling and plaiting into the necessary weaves. He directed the weaves at the surface of the lake, heating the obsidian glass until it began to glow a molten, fiery red. Slowly, the glass began to rise, drawn upwards by Earth. He wove until the memorial took shape, then added Air and Spirit to finish it before slowly cooling the steaming glass with swirling gusts of warm Air.

When he was finished, the eastern sky was lighting with the first approach of dawn and the obsidian lake was no longer a solid sheet of flat glass. Instead, in the center of the southern end, on the spot where Sariel had died, a sarcophagus rose from the surrounding glass as if offered up from the depths of the lake itself. Glossy black glass set with a rich abundance of gold and gemstones formed the rounded rectangular base. Atop that base, beneath a thick layer of clear crystalline glass, a Spirit weave of Sariel lay in peaceful repose. Rain had spun the weave to show Sariel as he remembered her, a young Fey maiden as beautiful and gentle as the dawn, with snowy white Fey-pale skin, hair of blackest ebony, and lips like rose petals.

Beneath her sleeping figure—written in the four languages of the ancient allies: Celierian, Feyan, Elvish, and Danae—he had inscribed the words Ellysetta had suggested: *Sariel the Beloved. May she awaken with joy to true-mate's call.*

As Rain and Ellysetta stood together regarding the results of his weave, the Great Sun peeked above the horizon. Dawn bathed the Lake of Glass in warm light, setting the names etched in the dark surface afire like diamonds sparkling in the sun. As the sun rose higher, beams of soft, golden light fell upon the shining glass of Sariel's tomb, and the Spirit weave within shimmered and glowed, sending bright rainbows of multicolored light spilling out in a radiant aura around the tomb. Within the rainbows whirled Spirit weaves of Sariel, laughing, dancing, healing, each image filled with life and joy.

Rain's heart rose up in his throat, and the arms he had wrapped around Ellysetta's waist tightened to pull her close against him. He bent his head to press a kiss against the thick, fragrant, silken spirals of her flame red hair. "*Beylah vo, shei'tani.* Thank you for this."

No longer was the Lake of Glass a place of loss and death and hopeless darkness, but rather a memorial of peace and beauty, glistening with the golden promise of a new day.

Ellysetta turned in his arms, her leaf green eyes shining, her lips curved in a smile that filled his heart with long-forgotten joy. "*Sha vel'mei, kem'san.*" She cupped a hand to his jaw. "Take me back to Teleon so I can make a few good-byes of my own, and then let's go home . . . to the Fading Lands."

CHAPTER THREE

Celieria ~ Teleon

"Well, well, look what the tairen dragged in." Kieran vel Solande slipped a polished *meicha* scimitar into his hip sheath and turned to greet the warrior who had just passed through the Spirit weave protecting Teleon from outside eyes.

Gaelen vel Serranis paused just inside the lower bailey and let his gaze sweep across the restored estate. "Impressive."

The sounds of industry filled the air as on every level of the city-fortress Fey toiled in the midmorning sun. All Fey with enough command of Earth to make themselves useful were once again busy replacing the remaining Spirit weave buildings with real mortar and stone, while Air masters assisted in shuttling loads of blocks and wood, and Fire masters forged metal for gates, door braces, and weaponry to aid in the defense of the city.

"Greetings, Uncle. You've been gone so long, I was beginning to think a lyrant made a meal of you." Kieran made a *tsk*ing sound and shook his head. "Ah, well, hope springs eternal."

Gaelen narrowed ice blue eyes at his sister Marissya's son. "Still full of sass, puppy? Clearly, vel Jelani isn't working you hard enough if you still have breath to jabber."

"Ha. Where've you been?"

Gaelen reached out to ruffle the younger Fey's head, a deliberately patronizing gesture that made Kieran scowl and jerk away. "Not your business, youngling." It was Gaelen's turn to grin, and he took pleasure in it. "Where is the Tairen Soul?"

When Kieran just glared and pressed his lips closed, Kiel rolled his eyes and answered in his stead. "On the third level with Lord Teleos, finishing what he can before he and the Feyreisa depart."

"And the Feyreisa?"

"On the upper level, planting a memory garden for her mother with Marissya and the twins."

Gaelen nodded, then glanced at Kieran and furrowed his brows. "What's this mess?" He reached out to straighten the leather Fey'cha belts crisscrossing Kieran's chest. "You call yourself a warrior? Sloppy, vel Solande. Very sloppy."

Scowling, Kieran looked down to see what his uncle was talking about. The next thing he knew, he was flat on his back with his own Fey'cha pressed against his neck, and death was glaring down at him from the eyes of the man who'd little more than a week ago been the most dreaded and feared *dahl'reisen* who ever lived.

"Very sloppy indeed," Gaelen repeated softly, his tone a cold wind, his eyes lethal shards of purest ice. "Are you so eager to die?"

Kieran froze. Part of him was sure this was yet another of Gaelen's humiliatingly effective demonstrations of how little the current generation of Fey knew of true sword mastery. Vel Serranis had pulled one of the black-handled blades from Kieran's chest straps rather than a lethal, poisoned red Fey'cha.

Another part of Kieran feared that maybe this wasn't a lesson after all.

"Answer me, puppy," Gaelen snapped. "Are you so eager to die?"

"Are you?" Kiel growled with low menace.

That was when Kieran noticed the Water master leaning over Gaelen, two red Fey'cha pressed against Gaelen's neck and belly.

Gaelen spat out an oath, and the knife pressing against Kieran's windpipe eased back. When Kiel's blades withdrew as well, Gaelen rolled left, sprang to his feet, and glared at them both. "The Mages are at work in the north. A warrior has disappeared for days on end, and you do not know where he's been. Yet you welcome him without suspicion? You stand there like a dull-witted fool while he strips you of your own blade and threatens you with it? I ask you again, are you so eager to die?"

He expanded his disparaging gaze to include Kiel and the dozen glowering Fey standing outside the blocking weave he'd woven when he'd lunged for Kieran. "And that goes for all of you as well. Not one of you even cleared steel from scabbard before I had a blade at your brother's throat. Vel Tomar, at least, has tolerably swift reflexes . . . and good instincts." The last he added with grudging approval. He nodded at the deadly red-hilted Fey'cha still gripped in each of Kiel's hands. "Red is the right choice when you suspect the threat may be real."

Gaelen dispersed his final shield, and the surrounding Fey muttered angrily and sheathed their weapons.

"That's a good way to get yourself killed, vel Serranis," someone called out.

"By you lot?" Gaelen scoffed. "Not flaming likely. I'd have to be *sel'dor* pierced, bound, and blinded before you had the advantage. Are you the best the Fading Lands can produce? Gods save us all." Gaelen shook his head in disgust. "What is the Tairen Soul thinking to let his mate stay so long outside the Faering Mists with naught to keep her safe but a pack of untrained infants scarce weaned from the breast?"

Kieran slapped the dust off his leathers and, scowling,

caught the black Fey'cha Gaelen tossed back to him. "He was thinking to protect her family on their journey to their new home—and to give the Feyreisa as much time with them as he could before she passes through the Mists. Our scouts have been securing our path five miles in every direction. And, for your information, there have been no attacks—nor any sign of danger."

"Have there not? How lucky for you."

The sarcasm rubbed Kieran the wrong way. "Is this how you honor your oath to the Feyreisa?" he snapped. " 'Learn to get along,' she said, yet here you are again, taunting and attacking us. After she told you to stop."

Gaelen's mouth opened . . . then shut. His eyes narrowed, and he bowed his head to acknowledge the point scored. "*Sieks'ta, kem'jita'nos.* You are right. She would not be pleased." His gaze became pointed. "That you started it is no excuse."

Kieran's face froze in midsmirk.

Kiel coughed into his hand. "He's got you there, Kieran," he muttered, which earned him a frigid glare from his friend. "Well, you did," he said, then turned to Gaelen. "Since you find our warrior skills so lacking, perhaps you could help us improve them?"

Several of the other Fey stiffened in outrage.

"Are you asking me to be your *chatok*?" A mocking lift of one black brow accompanied the question.

Kieran snorted, thinking Kiel was making a joke. Only warriors of the greatest skill and most unbesmirched honor became *chatok*, highly regarded mentors of warriors. Gaelen vel Serranis, the rebel warrior who'd willingly thrown himself down the Dark Path to avenge his twin sister Marikah's murder, was the last Fey who would ever qualify for such an esteemed position.

Kiel wasn't joking. "We lost too many masters in the Wars, and of those who survived, the greatest and most experienced gave their lives to build the Mists. War will soon be upon us again, and we cannot afford to be ill-prepared. You have skills we all need." The Water master shrugged, the gesture a graceful ripple. "So, *aiyah*, Gaelen, I *am* asking you to be my *chatok* for whatever levels of the Cha Baruk you think I have not truly mastered. Will you grant me this honor?"

Gaelen was openly taken aback. "That was sarcasm, vel Tomar, not a serious offer. I have been *dahl'reisen*. I chose the Shadowed Path. I walked its bitter trails for a thousand years rather than ending my life in honor, as a worthy Fey would have done."

"That doesn't change the fact that you have skills we all need. Even the Feyreisa advised us to learn from you."

"So she did." Gaelen's lips pressed tight together. "And as I promised her, I will teach you what I know, but only as a brother Fey. I will not dishonor the *chatok* who mentored me by pretending I have the right to stand among their honored company."

"Then I will accept your instruction, and I thank you for your willingness to share your knowledge and warrior's skills with me." Kiel bowed smoothly, his waist-length, blond hair spilling forward like gleaming falls of sunlight.

Gaelen was silent for a moment, his black brows drawn slightly together as he regarded the other man. "You are surprising, vel Tomar. And I thought the world held no more surprises for me."

Kiel smiled, his eyes as blue and guileless as a calm sea. "I am a Water master, Gaelen. There is always much more to us than shows on the surface."

Gaelen laughed. "That I will grant you." He glanced at Kieran. "And you, puppy, are clearly an Earth master. Head hard as a rock. Will stubborn as stone. And so resistant to change, it will take an earthquake to move you once you've settled into place. Just like your father." When Kieran scowled, Gaelen grinned. "Ah, the Feyreisa will have to forgive me. Pricking that pride of yours is too much fun to give up altogether."

Kieran snarled.

Gaelen just laughed again and glanced at Kiel. "Where's vel Jelani?"

Kiel pointed towards a small copse of white-trunked, golden-leafed Shimmering Lady trees on the uppermost level. "Up there, with the Feyreisa and her sisters."

"*Beylah vo*, vel Tomar."

"*Sha vel'mei*," Kiel replied as the infamous older warrior raced off towards the shimmering trees.

Kieran punched Kiel in the arm. Hard.

"Ow!" Kiel rubbed his biceps. "What was that for?"

"'Be my *chatok*'?" Kieran exclaimed. "'Teach me what you know'? Tairen's scorching fire! What the Seven jaffing Hells are you thinking? You're my blade brother, and you're taking sides with the enemy?"

Kiel glanced at Gaelen's retreating form, then back at Kieran. "He's your uncle, not the enemy. Besides, the Feyreisa told us to learn from him."

"He's a *dahl'reisen*."

"Former *dahl'reisen*," Kiel corrected.

"Where do you think he's been this past week? Praying in the Bright Lord's church? He's been with *them*, the ones who walk the Shadowed Path."

Kiel's brows rose over eyes as deep and blue as the Lysande Ocean. "What difference does it make if he has? He is *lu'tan* to the Feyreisa. In life and in death, he is bloodsworn to protect her."

"You're too trusting, Kiel."

Kiel's blond brows shot up. "Me? I wasn't the one who stood there while he stripped my blade and used it against me."

Kieran's back teeth ground together. "He's insufferable."

"Admit it," Kiel said, "insufferable may be exactly what some of the masters at the Academy need to shake them up and challenge their methods, to get them thinking about new ways to train our warriors. And," he added with a smirk and a sidelong glance, "exactly what some rock-headed Earth masters I know might need as well."

"Get scorched."

Near the copse of Shimmering Lady trees that overlooked the Garreval, Marissya, Ellysetta, and the twins planted a freshly tilled flower bed with the rosebushes and flowers Lauriana Baristani had loved most. Rain's task at the Lake of Glass had given Ellysetta the idea of creating a small memorial garden: a little something of Mama to leave behind for Papa and the twins, here where Papa could sit and look out over Celieria while the twins played Stones on the lawn nearby.

Ellysetta hummed under her breath as she dug her spade into rich, dark soil and made a hole to receive the last of the fragrant pink Heartsease Lorelle was waiting to deposit. Beside her, Marissya patted into place the last of Love's Promise, the exquisitely perfumed red rose that had been Mama's favorite.

Ellie sat back on her heels to survey the work. "I think we're ready for the statue," she told Bel as the twins picked up two full watering pots and enthusiastically irrigated the new plantings. "Gently, kitlings," she advised as mud splattered on their dresses. The two looked up innocently, and she bit her lip to keep from laughing at the thick layers of dirt smeared across their small faces. Lillis and Lorelle had yet to discover the gardener's art of brushing back wayward strands of hair with a forearm rather than soil-begrimed hands. "All right, that's water enough. Come away, girls, and let Bel set the statue."

The twins stepped back from the flower bed, and Bel hefted the heavy white marble statue of a winged Light-maiden and set it down with a grunt and a thunk at the center of the semicircular garden. Though Ellysetta had allowed Kieran to carve the marble statue using Earth weaves, she had insisted that all other preparations for the garden be done entirely by hand, as her mother would have wanted.

"What do you think, girls?" Ellysetta asked as they all stood back to regard their accomplishment. A brilliant semi-circle of pink and red roses hugged the slender white trunks of the Shimmering Lady trees, and a colorful selection of fragrant blossoms and herbs filled the ground around the statue. The base of the statue was inscribed with Lauriana's name and her favorite verse from the Book of Light: *"May the Light always shine on your path and shelter you from harm."*

"It's beautiful, Ellie." Lillis and Lorelle sighed. "Papa will love it."

"I think so, too."

"I think vel Jelani set the statue crooked," a male voice declared. "You should make him redo it."

"Gaelen!" Marissya turned with a happy smile and rushed to fling her arms around her brother. "You're back." When she released him, she turned to the garden with a frown. "Do you really think the statue is crooked?"

He smiled with a tenderness reserved exclusively for his only living sister. *"Nei, ajiana.* I was teasing. I thought it might be fun to see vel Jelani heave the thing about some more."

Bel gave the former *dahl'reisen* a baleful cobalt glare while Marissya only laughed, hugged him again, and declared, *"Meiruvelei, kem'jeto.* Welcome back, my brother. I've missed you."

"I'm glad you have returned to us, Gaelen." Ellysetta reached out to take Gaelen's hands in greeting. "How are Selianne's children?" He had left Celieria City with her best friend's orphaned babies in his care, promising to take them someplace where they would be safe from the Mage Mark placed upon them.

"Safe and well and with those who will love them as you

requested, *kem'falla*," he answered with a bow. When he straightened, he frowned. "But I am not pleased to find you still here, outside the protection of the Fading Lands. Your mate is unwise."

"We leave in three bells, as soon as he and Lord Teleos have finished their discussions."

"You should not even be here. If Rain had flown you as swiftly as he could, you would already be five days past the Faering Mists."

"*Setah*." She held up a hand. "Do not scold." She reached out to pull her twin sisters close and drop kisses on their mink brown curls. "Run fetch Papa, girls. Let's show him Mama's garden." When they were gone, she told Gaelen, "The delay was on my account, because Rain knew I could not bear to be parted from my family so soon after Mama's death."

"The reason doesn't matter. You should be behind the Mists. Safe. And so should Marissya." He ran frustrated hands through sheaves of straight black hair. "I thought vel'En Daris had more sense than to keep you here in Celieria."

"I'm fine, Gaelen," she insisted. "Nothing has—"

The seizure came without warning.

One moment she was about to chide Gaelen for his pessimism; the next she was writhing on the flagstones, shrieking in agony.

The pain was instant and all-encompassing and hideously familiar. Her spine arched, spasming in red-hot pain as her hands clawed at the rock beneath her. The tendons in her body stood out like ropes of steel, and her muscles clenched so tightly they became torturous, burning bricks beneath her skin.

"*Rain! Dax! Ti'Feyreisa! Fey! Ti'Feyreisa!*" Dimly, she heard Marissya send the frantic cry for help racing across the common Fey path.

Ellysetta saw her reach out, her *shei'dalin* hands already

glowing bright with healing weaves of gold-tinted Earth and Spirit. She heard Gaelen shout a warning, but it was too late.

The moment Marissya laid hands upon Ellysetta, agony enveloped her. It didn't rush out of Ellysetta. It simply expanded to sink its venomous fangs into Marissya, filling the *shei'dalin*'s empathic senses with savage, brutal, shattering pain, as if every bone in her body were splintering, every muscle shredding, and her soul were burning in the fires of the Seven Hells. Marissya screamed and fell back, yanking her hands off Ellysetta's body in instinctive self-preservation.

"Marissya!" Gaelen grabbed her by the arms and all but flung her across the walk into the middle of the adjacent lawn, well out of reach of whatever held Ellysetta in its grip.

"Light save me." Marissya wept, her voice shaking as helplessly as her limbs. She raised horrified eyes to her brother. "Dear gods, Gaelen, I've never felt anything like that. Never." She had served on the bloodiest battlefields of the Mage Wars, Truthspoken the souls of mortals who had perpetrated acts so vile they'd made her ill to touch them, yet never felt the kind of soul-deep agony now racking Ellysetta's slender form.

"Bel, take Marissya to safety," Gaelen commanded. "I will tend the Feyreisa."

"*Nei*, I am her *lu'tan*. I will not leave her any more than you." Bel dropped to his knees beside Ellysetta's rigid body, careful not to touch her as he sent a questing filament of Spirit into her mind. He backed out again just as quickly when the wild, enraged power of her tairen sensed his intrusion and responded with a scream of fury and a flare of searing magic. Whatever was attacking her, he couldn't get close enough to examine it. *"Rain? Where are you?"*

"I am here." Rain shot over the edge of the terrace and slid down a column of Air just as Ellysetta's body flung itself into a fresh series of violent convulsions. Gaelen and Bel both leapt to catch and hold him when he lunged for Elly-setta.

"Do not," Bel hissed. "You are truemates. Touch her, and even without a completed bond, you'll feel it as strongly as she does."

A tortured scream tore from her throat, ending on a groaning rattle as the convulsions worsened, then blessedly tapered off. Ellysetta collapsed against the flagstones, trembling and gasping for air. Rain broke free of Bel's and Gaelen's grips and dropped to his knees beside her, scooping her limp body up in his arms. "*Shei'tani.*"

Her head rolled back in the crook of his arm. Her eyes opened, the pupils lengthened to catlike slits, the green irises radiant and glowing. "Rain." Her hand clutched his arm and then began to shove at him in frantic desperation as she tried to wriggle free of his hold. "Let me go. Quickly, before it starts again."

"I won't. Whatever this is, I won't just stand here while it tortures you." He would not release her, and no matter how hard she tried to break free, her slender body was no match for his strength.

"*Teska*, Rain! Please." Already the pain was back, another brutal lash of it. Her body went rigid. Her jaw flexed, and her neck strained so hard each breath was a victory. This was going to be as bad as any seizure she'd ever had. And with Rain touching her skin to skin, he would feel her shattered emotions as if they were his own.

Rain's jaw clenched like an iron vise, the tendons in his neck standing out. "Tairen's scorching fire!" The backlash of his pain redoubled her own, and she screamed.

Gaelen and Bel dove towards them in a desperate effort to pull them apart.

"Let go, Rain, scorch you!" Gaelen snarled as Rain fought him off. "You're only making it worse—can't you see that? She's feeling your pain too. You're building a harmonic. Marissya!"

His sister spun a compulsion weave and thrust it into Rain's mind while Gaelen and Bel worked to pry Ellysetta free of Rain's arms. The weave reached enough of him that his grip loosened for an instant. Bel yanked Ellysetta free, and Gaelen wrestled Rain to the ground, pinning him there until some measure of sanity returned to his wild eyes.

The moment it did, Rain shoved Gaelen away and scrambled to his knees, crawling to Ellysetta's side. Her eyes were wide and frightened, her body shaking violently.

"Get . . . Papa." Each word was a hard-won fight. "He knows . . . what . . . to . . . do . . . *ahhh!*" The last word died in a wail as fire ripped through her and the world dissolved once more into shrieking agony.

Eld ~ Boura Fell

Muscles bulged in the burly Eld guard's back and thick arms as he swung the heavy *sel'dor* war hammer he called Boraz, the Bone Grinder. The hammer strike landed with a meaty thud and the loud crack of breaking bone.

Hanging from chains attached to the barbed *sel'dor* shackles clamped around his wrists, Shannisorran v'En Celay gave a guttural roar of pain as his right hip shattered. His body writhed, and the tremors sent arrows of fire shooting through him as splinters of bone tore through bruised muscle. The pain was devastating. Already it had gone far beyond his ability to contain. He'd felt great, searing arrows of it blast down the link the Mage's evil magic had unwittingly forged between Shan and Ellysetta Baristani, the daughter he'd not seen since her birth.

"How did you do it?" Across the room, High Mage Vadim Maur watched Shan's torture with icy eyes. "How did you and our lovely Elfeya manage to hide your daughter's magic from me?"

Shan sucked air into his lungs as he struggled to separate himself from the agony engulfing his body. He coughed and groaned as a fresh bout of pain racked him. His torture had begun with a simple but brutal pummeling before advancing to the hammer blows. Several of his ribs were broken, and with every breath, blood pooled in his mouth. He spat a mouthful of it on the ground.

"I know you engineered her escape, and I know you somehow bound her magic so I would not detect it."

Shan tossed back the strands of matted black hair covering his eyes. The guard had shattered Shan's ankles first, then his kneecaps, and now the first of his hips. He still had seven major joints to go, and he knew Maur wouldn't leave one of them whole whether he answered or not. He lifted his chin in a gesture that Elfeya had always bemoaned as a sure sign of his intractability and fixed unblinking eyes—a predator's stare—on the High Mage.

Maur's teeth clenched for a moment. Then he gave a cold smile. "Lord Death." He sneered the nickname Shan had earned many centuries ago, before finding his truemate, when he'd been the deadliest Fey warrior ever to walk the Fading Lands. "So arrogant, even now. I have not forgotten how the pair of you tried to help her escape my Mark in the Solarus. You failed, you know—I Marked her again—but you'll still spend the next thousand years begging me for death as a reward for your efforts. You and Elfeya both." He gave a short nod.

The guard swung his war hammer again.

The chains rattled as Shan's body jerked and shuddered from the force of the blow. His scream echoed off the black stone walls. *Pain is life*, he reminded himself, silently reciting the litany he had taught his *chadin* at the Academy in Tehlas. *Fey eat pain for breakfast. We jaff it on a cold night just to keep warm.*

"Strip the flesh from his back," Maur ordered coldly. "Use the Fire whip. I don't want him bleeding to death, just close enough to it to make his mate eager to please me."

Shan's vision blurred as the guard circled around him,

the Mage's favorite Fire-tipped whip clutched in his meaty hand.

The first blow seared him to his soul. He writhed as flesh ripped and scorched. He reeled as the shattered bones in his legs scraped and shredded his flesh from the inside out. *Ah, gods have mercy.* Maur just might break him this time.

"*Shei'tan.*" Elfeya's voice, warm as a summer sun on the shores of Tairen's Bay, washed over him. "*I am here, beloved. I am with you. Together, we are strong.*"

With an ease that would have driven Vadim Maur wild with rage had he known of it, Elfeya slipped into Shan's mind, circumventing all the dark weaves and *sel'dor* and black witchery the High Mage had employed to keep them isolated. She was there, with Shan as she had been since the day of their bonding, an inextricable part of his soul. His strength, his blessing, his greatest weakness. "*Leave me, Elfeya. Shield yourself. I cannot bear for you to suffer.*"

"*Nei, never. I will not let him break us. You are Shannisorran v'En Celay, the greatest champion the Fading Lands has ever known. You are a warrior of the Fey, and I am your truemate, a shei'dalin of great power. This Mage may hold our bodies, but he has no command over our souls.*"

The second whipstroke shredded the flesh off his back. He flung his head back and screamed himself hoarse.

"*Shan! Stay with me. Focus on the sound of my voice, beloved.*" When he didn't respond, her tone grew sharp as the Mage's whip. "*Speak to me, Fey!*" she barked. "*Who are you?*"

She'd spent too many years of their life together eavesdropping in his mind as he drove his *chadins* to the end of their strength, then commanded them to eke out more. She was such a fierce, brave blade in her own right, his equal in every way. And she was right: Fey did not surrender, not to fear, not to pain, not to despair. They fought until their hearts burst in their chests. "*I am warrior,*" he gasped. "*I am Fey.*"

"*Kabei! And what is a warrior of the Fey? Tell me! Shout it out!*"

The whip ripped a third stripe off his back, but this time his choked scream was not a mindless howl. This time it was a declaration of defiance ripped from his aching throat, each word a rasping challenge. "I am the steel no enemy can shatter." He thrust his chin out, met Maur's vile silver gaze, and snarled through gritted teeth, "I am the magic no dark power can defeat."

The High Mage smiled.

As the fourth lash fell, pain blinded him. He focused his mind on Elfeya's warmth and forced the cry from his burning lungs. "I am the rock upon which evil breaks like waves. I am Fey! Warrior of honor! Champion of Light!"

Shan sagged in his chains as the torment enveloped him in a hazy cloud of mind-numbing pain. He clung to consciousness and sanity by a thread, the words he'd just cried so defiantly repeating in his mind again and again, punctuated by the sound of Elfeya's quiet weeping.

An icy breath blew across his face, soft and taunting. "You will rot in darkness, Fey, while your mate serves my pleasure and your daughter surrenders her soul."

The mad sentience in Shan's soul roared with fury. Across the link that bound him to his child, her own beast screamed back in wild Rage. The next moment, a vast bolus of power blasted across the link, rushing into his broken body, searing him with a painful jolt. His beast seized the power, using it to feed his Rage. Shan's vision turned to black shadow lit with vengeful red sparks. "Not if I rip you limb from limb and feast on your bloody bones, Eld maggot." He lunged for the Mage, teeth bared as he cried, "*Ve sha Desriel!*"

He saw the war hammer swinging from the corner of his eye. The Mage cried, "Don't kill him, you idiot!" Pain smashed into his skull. Shan's body went limp as consciousness fled.

Sol clutched his daughter's body, rocking her as he had so many times in the past, singing the songs that had soothed her as a child. Blazing twenty-five-fold weaves of power formed a visible dome of magic around them. A five-fold weave had done almost nothing to ease her suffering, but the twenty-five-fold weave had at least dulled the pain enough that she was no longer screaming and convulsing.

Marissya didn't know how to heal her. The pain, whatever it was, was not coming from any wound to her body, and whenever Marissya tried to probe, Ellysetta's tairen roused with a vengeance, fierce and furious over any hint of *shei'dalin* intrusion into her mind. Rain, whom Ellysetta trusted, could not touch her without causing further pain. And Gaelen, who had suggested he spin the forbidden soul magic Azrahn to see what he could detect, had been unanimously shouted down.

Suddenly Ellysetta's spine went stiff again and her eyes flew open wide. "*K'shareth na pearson sh'verre korbay!*" she cried, her voice a ragged scrape of sound, hoarse and broken and several octaves lower than her normal tones. "*K'shafair na selltemorra sh'verre dagorren! K'shadure a daynalle pear coda la cresses! K'shafay! Shaysan lowcha! Liesse chakai!*" She shouted the last wild words, then collapsed in Sol's arms. Her head lolled back, and she began to mutter the same unintelligible phrases over and over again.

Sol raised stricken eyes to the Fey, who were standing around him in shocked silence. "All you Fey with all your power, can you do nothing? Was Laurie right about this being demons after all?"

Bel swallowed. "Only if the demon possessing her is the spirit of a Fey warrior."

"What do you mean?" Sol demanded.

"We mean she is speaking Feyan," Rain said.

"Feyan? Then what is she saying?" Sol asked.

Rain answered, his face a blank mask. "She said, 'I am the steel no enemy can shatter.'" One by one, Bel, Dax, and Gaelen added their voices to his until they were all repeating the words together. "'I am the magic no dark power can defeat. I am the rock upon which evil breaks like waves. I am Fey, warrior of honor, champion of Light.'"

"It is the warrior's creed," Gaelen said, "taught to every Fey boy who enters the Warriors' Academy to begin his training in the Cha Baruk."

With a sudden, fierce scowl, Rain knelt beside Sol Baristani and seized Ellysetta by the shoulders. "*Nal?*" he demanded. "*Nal ve sha?* Who are you? What is your name?"

Her head lolled limp on her neck. He caught her face between his hands. "Tell me!" The muted pain of her unseen injuries tore at his senses. Within his soul, Rain's tairen roused, hissing, power licking at his limbs and lunging against its restraints.

He felt the sudden wild surge as Ellysetta's own tairen leapt in answer. Her eyes flew open and fixed upon his face. The threads of their bond blazed to life. His tairen, Eras, roared with fury, sensing something else—someone else— there in her soul with them. Before he could react to the threat, Ellysetta's body flared bright with sudden power, and Rain's limbs went abruptly weak. Her pupils widened until no hint of green iris showed, and Rain reared back in instinctive shock and horror as, for one brief instant, her eyes shone pure black, filled with whirling red sparks.

"*Ve sha Desriel!*" she cried. The combined power left her on a rush. Her eyes rolled back in her head and she slumped, unconscious, in her father's arms.

"What in the Seven Hells just happened?" Dax demanded. "What was that?"

"I don't know," Rain snapped. "Something was there, inside her, something besides her tairen. I don't know what—maybe a Mage, maybe a demon. Whatever it was nearly brought out her tairen, and she can't control it yet. We need to get her to the Fading Lands. Right now." He spun a shout across the common Fey thread. "*Fey! Prepare for departure!*"

"Rain," Marissya protested. "You can't mean to send her

through the Mists now. We have no idea how they'll react to her Mage Marks, and if that seizure nearly brought out the tairen, the Mists may well finish the job."

"Marissya's right, Rain," Bel agreed. "The Mists can brutalize a Fey. She needs time to recover, to rebuild her inner barriers to keep the tairen in check."

Rain turned hard, furious eyes on the pair of them. "We don't have time. I don't know what attacked her just now, but I'll be scorched if we're going to stay around here one bell longer and give it a chance to come back. Marissya, the chime she wakes, weave peace on her. Bel, Gaelen, you two help her build what barriers she needs to keep the tairen caged and protect herself against whatever the Mists might try to do to her."

"Rain?" Sol Baristani interrupted. The woodcarver was still holding his daughter's unconscious body, stroking her hair and rocking her as he had so many times since her earliest childhood. "'Vaysha Dezrielle.' She's said that before during her seizures. Is it also Feyan? Do you know what it means?"

Rain's mouth pressed into a grim line. "It means 'I am Death.'"

Teleon was a flurry of activity as the Fey rushed to prepare for departure. As Rain had commanded, the moment Ellysetta regained consciousness, Marissya began weaving peace on her, while Bel and Gaelen helped her rebuild the internal barriers her seizure had shredded. As soon as they had finished, the Fey began marching out of Teleon.

Ellysetta, still pale and wan from her seizure, desperately tried to hold back her tears as she knelt on the shining, silver-blue steps of Teleon to clasp the twins in yet another fierce hug. She didn't want to let them go, didn't want to think of waking up to a morning when she would not see their sweet, smiling faces. But her seizure and her duty to the tairen left her no choice.

"I will miss you both," she told the twins, pulling back to press kisses on their soft cheeks and rosy lips. "I'll think about you every day—and miss you every chime. I love you so very much."

Lillis and Lorelle were crying as much as she was. "Don't go, Ellie. Stay here with us."

"Oh, kitlings, if only I could." She gave her father a pleading glance. *Won't you reconsider, Papa? Come with us. You'll all be safer in the Fading Lands.*

He shook his head. Even if Papa thought the twins could actually be happy living as mortals in an immortal land, he wouldn't betray his wife's last wishes. "Please understand."

She bit her lower lip, ashamed that she kept urging him to break his vow. *I'm sorry. I just want you all safe.*

"We'll be safe here. The Fey will see to that. And as I promised you, if there is even a hint of trouble, we'll come through the Mists."

Ellysetta dashed away her tears with the back of one hand and gave him a watery smile. "I know, Papa. I'm just selfish enough to want you three with me always."

Behind Sol's spectacles, his brown eyes glistened with answering tears. "Oh, Ellie-girl, if that's selfish, then I must confess the same sin, for I would keep you by my side if I thought you could ever be safe or happy there." He embraced her. As his arms enfolded her, the love that had been her anchor all her life flowed into her once more, filling her with its warm reassurance and strength. He cupped her face in his hands, then hugged her tight once more before stepping back. "Go, daughter. Find the happiness you deserve. And may the Light always shine on your path and shelter you from harm."

"Teleos." Rain clasped the Celierian great lord's forearm. "You guard our gates—both here and at the Veil—and you guard three treasures very precious to my mate." He inclined his head towards the twins and Sol Baristani. "Your assistance is much appreciated."

"It is the great honor of House Teleos to be of service to the Fey," Lord Teleos replied.

"The first thousand blades I promised Dorian leave the Fading Lands within the week. I'll bring reinforcements to Orest by month's end, along with that Fey steel I promised you for your own men. And, Dev?"

"Aiyah?"

Rain held the younger man's Fey gaze steadily. "My friend Shanis would have been proud to call you kin."

The great lord blinked in surprise, then said in a low voice, *"Beylah vo,* Rain. I only wish I could have known him."

"You do, Dev. You are much like him." They clasped arms again in a warrior's gesture of respect and friendship; then Rain turned to Ellysetta's family. "Master Baristani. Lillis and Lorelle." Rain shook the woodcarver's hand, then knelt and opened his arms to the twins, who threw themselves into his embrace with as much weeping regret as they'd shown Ellysetta.

"Here now, kitlings," he protested when their tears would not stop. "This is not good-bye. This is just farewell until we meet again." When they pulled back, he smiled and thumbed away their tears. "Be good, hmm? Listen to Kieran and Kiel, and try to stay out of trouble."

The twins nodded. "We will."

Ellysetta put her hand on Rain's wrist. As he led her away, down the steps towards Marissya and Dax and the waiting Fey, she kept looking back over her shoulder and waving at her father and the twins, and at Kieran and Kiel standing guard beside them.

"Promise me you'll keep them safe," she begged Kiel and Kieran one final time as Rain stepped away to summon the Change.

"We will protect them with our lives," Kieran vowed. "You have our solemn oath."

The wild, rich scent of the tairen swept over her. She closed her eyes and breathed it in, then turned to take her place on Rain's back. A series of thick leather straps lashed her into place—in case she were to have another seizure while flying through the Mists. Rain leapt into the sky, and her beloved family grew smaller and smaller as he bore her away. She twisted in the saddle and watched even when she could no longer make them out.

"You will see them again, shei'tani," Rain assured her.

Would she? Ellysetta cast one final glance back at the shrinking silvery blue towers and ramparts of Teleon. Then why did she have such a terrible, sinking feeling that this was the last time she and her family would ever be together?

Rain circled on an updraft as the Fey below approached the Faering Mists. With growing concern, Ellysetta regarded the bright glow of magic that danced in undulating flows along the mountaintops and filled the pass between the Rhakis and Silvermist ranges.

"I thought we might be able to fly over the Mists," she said.

His wings dipped and he circled in the opposite direction. *"Nei, the Fey who made the Mists safeguarded against that. If you wish to enter the Fading Lands, there is no way to bypass the Mists, no matter how high you fly or how deep you tunnel."*

"So we have no choice but to go through."

"Aiyah."

"What's it like?"

"I don't know. I've only passed through it myself once, to come to Celieria to find you. The magic of the Mists cares only who enters the Fading Lands, not who leaves."

"Celierians tell tales about hunters and shepherds who wandered into them on a foggy day and disappeared, only to reappear months or even years later carrying tales about meeting the Shining Folk inside the Mists. Are those tales true?" There were hundreds of such stories, each one more fantastical than the last. Some adventurers claimed to have joined ancient Fey in a wild hunt through misty forests; others spoke of sharing an intoxicating

meal in a crystalline hall filled with music and Fey maidens so beautiful even the stoniest heart would break to cast eyes upon them. To accept such invitations, folk claimed, was to bid farewell to the life one knew, for time passed at a different pace for those feted by the Fey, and the deeper in the mist one wandered, the swifter time passed in the world.

"I suspect there may be some truth to those tales," Rain answered. *"The ones who built the Mists would not have wanted to hurt innocents—but neither would they have wanted to allow those innocents to be used against the Fey."*

But what of not-so-innocents? Shepherds and hunters might escape with lost time the only price for their transgression, but others were not so fortunate. She'd heard of entire armies that had disappeared into the Mists, never to be seen again.

Below, the marching Fey narrowed to a column ten abreast, and the first rows of warriors plunged without hesitation into the shining mist. Another few chimes and it would be Rain and Ellie's turn.

Her heart beat faster as anxiety bloomed in her belly. *"How do you think the Mists will react to my Mage Marks?"*

Rain hesitated, then said, *"You are the Feyreisa and a Tairen Soul. The Mists will realize that."*

Her stomach lurched. She heard the evasion in his voice. *"But you aren't certain, are you?"*

His ears twitched, and a small jet of flame seared the air before them. *"That is why we are flying through rather than walking. Just hold tight to the saddle. I will get us through as quickly as I can."*

The last of the Fey below disappeared into the Faering Mist.

Rain banked a final time, then flew directly towards the shimmering veil of magic. Anything else Ellysetta might have said caught in her throat. The thick fog of the Mists dominated her visual field, endless white, ever-shifting, glimmering with rainbow lights.

She leaned over the front of the saddle and threaded her hands deep into Rain's tairen pelt, clutching tightly, needing the contact. *"Rain."*

"I am with you, Ellysetta."

She had one last split second, time enough only for a swift, frightened gasp of air, and then they plunged into the Mists.

CHAPTER FOUR

A hidden land, forbidden land, beyond the Faering Mists.
A people gone except in song, beyond the Faering Mists.
Where magic's spun and great work's done, beyond the
     Faering Mists.
Where Fey still dwell behind the spell that is the
     Faering Mists.

          "Beyond the Faering Mists," from the collection
          Laments for the Fey, by Avian of Celieria

The Faering Mists were not what Gaelen expected. Over the years, when he'd been *dahl'reisen*, he'd come to the Garreval on several occasions, intending to close his eyes, walk in, and let the Mists do what they would to him, but he'd never actually been able to bring himself to dip so much as the toe of his boot in. He didn't know whether it was cowardice or pride that kept him from it, and he'd never cared to examine his reasons too closely, half-afraid of the answer he might find.

His first few steps into the Mists were as bold as any he'd ever taken, and it would have surprised most of the Fey to know how much it cost him to keep that facade of bravado intact. His nerves were shaking so badly, his guts felt like quivering jelly. To his undying shame, his sister sensed his fear. Just before she and Dax plunged into the Mists, Marissya turned her head to smile back at him and whisper on a private thread, *"Do not fear, kem'jeto. A lost son of the Fey has returned. The Mists will welcome you and rejoice."*

Then the Mists had swallowed her up, and it was his turn to take the plunge. Walking next to him, Belliard vel Jelani had looked every bit as grim as Gaelen felt. The Fey's face had gone stony, and his eyes were dark, burning cobalt stars. Vel Jelani was no untried *chadin* fresh from his first levels in the Cha Baruk. Gaelen girded himself for terror.

To his surprise, the terror never came. Instead, as he took the first dozen blind steps into the mist-filled pass, a sense of overwhelming peace suffused him. It wrapped him in a shining cocoon of warm whiteness, soft and fragrant, as if he were a child once more and his long-dead mother, Briessa v'En Serranis, held him cradled in her arms.

"Mela?" he whispered, lifting his face to the whiteness. "Are you here?" Logically, he knew it couldn't be true. His parents had died one hundred years before the Mage Wars began, slain by Feraz as they returned to the Fading Lands after visiting Marikah and the first King Dorian to celebrate the birth of their son.

Was this how the Mists led intruders astray? Not through terror but through wistful memories of better times? The lure was a strong one. Long had it been since Gaelen last knew peace. He shook off the beckoning warmth and forced himself to concentrate.

Picture our home as you remember it, Marissya had advised him. *You cannot trust your senses in the Mists, so let that memory be your guide.*

He thought of the gleaming white towers and golden spires of Dharsa, of the great, towering volcanoes of the Feyls, of the waving golden grasses of the Plains of Corunn.

The home he'd always loved, lost to him these last thousand years. *Mela, your son returns.*

He walked. He did not know for how long, but gradually, the dense fog began to thin. A light shone before him, bright and beckoning, and he could make out the figures of Marissya and Dax striding across the ground at a confident pace. Marissya's presence was like a shining beacon, and all around her, the thick vapors were naught but barest wisps of white mist, as if the magic knew and welcomed her. Gaelen glanced to his side. He could see Bel now, walking beside him just an arm's length away.

The grim look on Bel's face was gone, replaced by astonishment. Catching Gaelen's eyes on him, Bel shook his head and said, "It has never been so easy to cross the Mists before."

"We are through?"

"Through the worst of it, *aiyah*. This lighter mist will fade in less than a tairen length."

"I was expecting something far different," Gaelen said.

"As was I," Bel echoed. "Usually when the Mists spit me out on the other side, Marissya must come to my aid." Even as he spoke, they heard a sharp cry, quickly muffled, from somewhere in the dense fog behind them.

Gaelen cast a glance over his shoulder and saw a line of ten Fey emerge from the thicker whiteness. Each one of them looked shaken, and two were trembling so much their brothers had to help steady them.

"I don't understand," Gaelen said. "Why them and not me?"

Bel gave a soft, wondering laugh. "The Feyreisa. She restored our souls."

Gaelen only half heard him. The mist was clearing, and before him lay a sight he'd thought he would never see again in this lifetime: the golden blaze of the Great Sun shining on the great twin war castles of the Fading Lands, Chatok and Chakai, the Mentor and the Champion, eternal guardians of the Garreval.

They had not changed in all this time. Jutting from the western foot of the Rhakis mountains, just beyond the last tendrils of the Mists, the great fortress of Chatok still stood, as proud and fierce and defiant as ever. Perfect and unchanged from his memory. Massive, hewn boulders of silver-blue granite formed concentric rings of crenellated walls and battlements surrounding a host of soaring central towers topped by gleaming steel-roofed turrets. To the south, the matching silvery white fortress of Chakai jutted out from the hewn cliffs of the Silvermist range. The mile-wide pass between the two fortresses, guarded by the great stone Warriors' Wall, was named Miora te Baloth'Liera, the Field of Joy and Sorrow, but most warriors called it by another name: Taloth'Liera, the killing field.

Before the Mists had been created, more than one terrible battle had watered the soil of Taloth'Liera with the blood of armies foolish enough to try invading the Fading Lands. Gaelen himself had wet his blades in this pass on three separate occasions.

His breath caught in his throat on a sudden surge of emotion. There, on Chatok's great forward tower called Lute'cha, Gaelen's cradle friend Lothien vel Din had died in his arms during their first battle together, pierced through the heart by a Merellian demon prince's poison spear. And there, on Chakai's ramparts, his beloved blade brother, Eilon vel Hantor, had shoved Gaelen out of the path of an Irdrhi axman's deathblow, only to fall, his spine cleaved in two, in Gaelen's stead.

And finally there, less than three tairen lengths from where he stood now—just beyond the massive steel gates at the center of the crenellated mile-long stone wall connecting Chatok to Chakai—Gaelen and six thousand of his brothers had thrust red Fey'cha in the bloody soil of Taloth'Liera and cried, "*Bas desrali lor bas tirei!*" We die where we stand! And to a Fey, they had stood and fought and held the pass when even stone walls and steel gates failed beneath the enemy's onslaught.

Those shining gates of the Fading Lands still stood, vast and glorious, tall as twenty Fey, and a tairen length wide. And now, as Gaelen and the others approached, the massive, gleaming panels moved slowly inward, parting to reveal a land he had dreamed of for a thousand years. The land he had forsaken. The land he had spent these last long centuries protecting, even though he believed he would die without ever catching a glimpse of her beloved paradise again.

The Fading Lands, home of the Fey.

His home.

He took one step past the towers flanking the gate, a second through the broad, graceful stone arch overhead. He looked up, into the faces of a dozen Fey warriors standing on the ramparts above, half expecting red Fey'cha to come showering down, knowing he would not summon even the thinnest shield if they did.

But death did not come.

Two more steps took him past the gate, and for the first time in a thousand years, Gaelen vel Serranis set down his booted foot on the soil of his homeland.

He had faced, unflinching, the countless battles of far too many bloody wars. He'd confronted terrifying magic, fearsome enemies, and even stood firm while forces that outnumbered his, hundreds to one, charged his position. Yet with that one step, as the sole of his boot made its first slight contact with Fey soil, his battle-hardened warrior's body began to tremble. His legs shook, his shoulders quaked, and all strength fled him.

With a cry of surrender, Gaelen vel Serranis fell to his knees on the land of his forefathers.

Marissya turned, her *shei'dalin*'s radiance fully unshielded and glowing bright as a star. Love and joy and serenity caressed Gaelen's senses in lapping waves, and her smile was a balm on his soul. *"Ke tamiora,"* she said. *"Kem'jeto ruvel."* I rejoice. My brother returns.

A hand touched his shoulder. He looked up to find Belliard vel Jelani at his side.

"Welcome home, Gaelen," he said softly.

"Beylah vo, my brother," he rasped, his voice thick with emotion. Tears welled in his eyes. He didn't try to wipe them away. He simply let them fall, and the soil of Miora te Baloth'Liera drank them up, just as it had drunk the blood he'd shed here so many times in the past.

Standing at Gaelen's side, Bel understood what the older Fey was feeling. When Bel had left this last time to accompany Rain and Marissya to Celieria City, he had been so close to becoming *dahl'reisen* himself that he truly had not known whether he would ever see the Fading Lands again. The Shadows had been so near, the weight of even a few more deaths on his soul could have tipped the balance and sent him plunging down the Dark Path or seeking the desperate solace of *sheisan'dahlein,* the honor death.

But Ellysetta had restored his soul, almost as completely as she'd restored Gaelen's.

The clatter of boot heels on stone made him look up. Two dozen warriors were rushing down the tower steps, blades drawn, their faces etched in stone.

"Hold!" Bel snapped. "Stay your blades."

"Your time in the world of mortals has addled your wits, vel Jelani." With blue eyes as cold as a winter dawn and a voice to match, Tajik vel Sibboreh, the auburn-haired general of the Fey's eastern armies, approached. "He is the Dark Lord."

"He was," Bel answered. "But now he is Fey once more, and he is welcome. He has passed through the Mists, and you will greet him as the brother he is."

"Dahl'reisen are no brothers of mine." In a flash, Tajik

pulled a red-hilted Fey'cha and pressed the razor edge of the poison blade to Gaelen's neck.

Just as quickly, Bel pulled red on Tajik. Tajik's men drew their own blades in an instant, training the deadly points on Bel. Bel ignored them. "*Nei*, my friend," he advised softly, holding Tajik's gaze, "you will not do this. He is my blade brother, and we are both bloodsworn to the Feyreisa. She restored his soul. His *dahl'reisen* scar is gone. Even Marissya has laid hands upon him and declared him bright and shining."

Tajik's gaze flickered to Marissya. "*Kem'falla?* Is it true?"

Marissya nodded. "Everything is true, dear friend. Sheathe your steel. There is no evil here. Only cause for joy and celebration. My brother has returned, and Rain has found his truemate—in Celieria, of all places—and she has restored Gaelen's soul."

Tajik remained still for a long moment, absorbing Marissya's words. Then, with a final dark look for Gaelen, he sheathed his blade and stepped back. Around him, his men followed suit.

"Gaelen vel Serranis," he said, "the gods have shown you more mercy than you deserve. No matter how it grieves me to grant you passage into the Fading Lands, I will not stand in your way." His face hardened to a cold, stony mask. "But be warned: You chose the Shadowed Path before. You won't have that choice again. If you break our laws this time, I will personally escort you into your next life." His thumb caressed the scarlet hilt of his sheathed Fey'cha.

Gaelen rose to his feet. For once, there was no hint of his habitual, cocky assurance, only sober acknowledgment. "Accepted, Fey."

Tajik's cold eyes swept over Gaelen from head to toe, taking his measure. When he was finished, he grunted and turned to Bel. "Who is this Feyreisa that she should restore a *dahl'reisen*'s soul?"

Bel smiled. "Don't be so suspicious. She is bright and shining like nothing you've ever seen before. And she is a Tairen Soul."

"I don't like it," Tajik muttered.

"You don't like any change, my old friend."

Tajik grunted again. "Not all change is good. No matter how appealing it may seem at first glance." On a private Spirit weave, he added, *"And I'm not the only one who feels that way. Rumors have been flying since we received word that vel Serranis was returning with you. The Massan gathered in Dharsa this morning."*

Bel's brows shot up. *"Without Marissya or Rain?"* The Massan, the council of five powerful Fey statesmen who oversaw the domestic governance of the Fading Lands, did not convene without the *Shei'dalin* and the Feyreisen except in times of extreme need. For them to convene now—knowing Rain was on his way—was akin to declaring a lack of confidence in the Tairen Soul's leadership.

"Aiyah, without them. So you see, I am not the only one to fear this change." The faintest hint of warmth softened Tajik's stern face. "Bel, you and I are cradle friends. I trust you as I trust no other. Tell me you have no concerns—tell me there is nothing to fear—and I will believe you."

Bel had been anticipating such questions. He knew his old friend Tajik too well. The problem was that Ellysetta bore two Mage Marks. To claim no concern would be a lie, and no Fey worthy of his steel would ever lie—but neither was Bel willing to cement Tajik's doubts and fears by refusing to answer.

"Tajik, my brother, I will not give you a truth you will be able to judge for yourself when you meet her," he replied. The evasion was smooth and perfectly reasonable. "One look upon her face and you will know as I do—without a single doubt—that she is everything all Fey warriors have sworn to protect. You cannot help but love her."

The general of the eastern Fey army drew in a breath, then let it out with a nod of acceptance. *"Bas'ka*, Belliard.

As you say, so shall it be. Where is this paragon of all things bright and good?"

Bel clapped his friend on the shoulder. "Rain brought up the rear, and she is with him."

Tajik grunted. "So we wait."

"Aiyah." Bel saw Marissya break from Dax's side and hurry towards the Mists as one of the Fey emerging took three steps and fell to his knees. Now the hard part began: the waiting. For each, the journey through the Mists was different, and the passage could last anywhere from several chimes to several bells. Those on the Fading Lands side of the Garreval could only sit and wait as their brethren navigated whatever tests the shifting clouds held in store for them.

Marissya healed those whom the Mists had treated unkindly, while Bel and Gaelen walked the wall, waiting with mounting concern for Rain and Ellysetta to appear. Chimes turned to bells. The Great Sun began its descent towards the western horizon. When the last of the Fey warriors finally cleared the Mists and staggered towards the gates, Gaelen and Bel exchanged openly worried glances. The skies above the pass were clear.

Rain and Ellysetta were nowhere in sight.

Within the Mists, surrounded by a thick cloud of whiteness, Ellysetta had lost all sense of direction, all vision, all touch. She could not see even a finger's span into the dense, suffocating whiteness. She could not feel the saddle beneath her or the tufts of tairen fur clutched in her hands. Fear exploded in her belly, robbing her lungs of breath. *"Rain!"*

"I am here, Ellysetta. I am with you."

"I can't see you! I can't feel you!"

"Peace, Ellysetta. The Mists were made to confuse and isolate those who dare enter. You cannot detect me with your senses, but you can feel me through our bond. Talk to me. It makes the passing less frightening."

She couldn't imagine talking would make this better. A coldness had begun to creep over her. The white mist seemed to be growing darker, and she began to hear voices: whispers at first, a soft rumble of disquiet that grew louder as they flew. She couldn't make out what the voices were saying, but the sounds carried an undercurrent of tension, like the muffled tones of an argument heard through thick walls.

"Rain, do you hear that?"

"Hear what, Ellysetta?"

"The voices. People talking."

He was silent for a moment. *"The Fey are with us in the Mists. Could they be the ones you hear?"*

She strained her ears, trying to discern where the voices were coming from. They sounded so near, yet she couldn't pinpoint a source. The sound seemed to come from every direction, all at once. *"I don't think so,"* she said. Her heart beat a little faster. *"Whoever it is sounds angry."*

The mists grew darker still, deepening to a thick morass of shadow in which the agitated murmur of voices became a sharp exchange. She could make out a smattering of words, all spoken in Feyan.

Shei'dalin . . . Mage claimed . . . Nei! . . . tainted . . . bright . . . unwelcome . . . truemate . . . murderer . . . enemy!

Dread curled in her belly. *"Rain . . . I think they're arguing about me."*

"I will fly faster, shei'tani." The grim tone in his Spirit voice frightened her. Whatever those voices were, apparently they weren't good.

She tried to tighten her grip. She couldn't feel the wind on her face or see Rain's tairen body beneath hers. If he was flying faster—if they were even flying at all—she couldn't tell.

Now the Mists were almost black, and streaks of what looked like lightning ripped the darkness all around her, as if she and Rain had flown into the heart of a violent thunderstorm.

The sound of the accusing voices grew louder and louder. *Traitor! Shadowfolk!* Each condemning word was a crashing boom reverberating in her skull. *Tainted! Murderer!*

"Rain!" Terrified, she screamed for him, but even in her own mind, she could barely hear her own cry above the din.

Mage claimed!

Dark soul!

ENEMY!

"No!" she cried. "I'm not dark; I'm not the enemy!" She felt a terrible pressure in her chest, as if a heavy weight were settling over her. Icy cold invaded her body. "Please!" she begged. "You must believe me!"

The mist began to thin, and for a moment, Ellysetta dared hope they had passed through the worst the Mists had to offer. Then she saw what lay before her, and her tiny flicker of hope went out.

Images emerged from the mist, solidifying into a wide, green lane. Tall, majestic trees lined the avenue, and beneath the shadow of their arching branches, grim-faced Fey warriors stood with blades drawn in silent menace. They were looking at her in a way no Fey had since that first day when she'd called Rain from the sky: like death longing to slip its leash.

"Rain?" Ellysetta glanced around in sudden panic. She was no longer on his back. She was standing on her own feet in the middle of the lane. She spun in a frantic circle, searching for him, but he was nowhere to be seen. "Rain!"

"The accused stands alone for judgment," a cold voice declared. A woman's voice, rich with power.

Ellysetta's heart sank into the pit of her stomach, and fear shuddered through her. Slowly, she turned back around.

At the end of the lane stood dozens of red-veiled *shei'dalins*, backed by twice as many fearsome, red-leather-clad Fey lords. Each Fey lord had unsheathed one of his *seyani* longswords and gripped it, point down, before him. The naked steel glinted with unmistakable threat.

The thick veils of the tallest *shei'dalin* rippled, and the female voice spoke again, stern and commanding. "The accused will approach and be judged."

A powerful compulsion urged Ellysetta to walk towards the veiled women. Terrified, she fought the command. Though Rain and the Fey had declared her one of their own, her fear of how a *shei'dalin* could strip a person's soul bare had not waned. Marissya she trusted, but she wasn't about to submit herself to these unfamiliar *shei'dalins*, with their hard-edged voices. Though her body trembled from the effort it took to resist, she managed not to move.

"Who are you?" she demanded. "What is this? And what have you done with Rain?"

A roar sounded overhead, and a cloud of warm air enveloped her, rich with the scent of magic and tairen. Ellie looked up and gasped with a mix of fear and awe. The sky above was filled with tairen. Jets of flame scorched the air in great, boiling orange clouds.

One of the tairen—a magnificent, pure black creature with golden eyes and wings that gleamed with an iridescent sheen—circled behind her and swooped down in a sudden rushing dive. The great cat's mouth was open in a fierce roar, its massive fangs bared and dripping venom, its sharp, curving claws fully extended and menacing.

Her heart stopped beating. The predator was diving in for the kill, and she was its prey. For one terrified moment, every muscle in her body was frozen into place. She couldn't breathe, couldn't move a muscle even to save her own life.

Then the tairen roared again, and the fearsome blast of sound snapped her out of her paralysis. Instinct took over.

Ellie screamed and ran.

Straight into the arms of the waiting *shei'dalins*.

"No!" She cried out a protest and spun around, desperately seeking escape, but the women had moved too quickly. She was surrounded, drowning in a sea of scarlet robes. Pale, shining hands reached out. "No!" The *shei'dalins'* hands made contact. Their fingers closed in tight, unyielding grips around her wrists, her hands, her arms and shoulders. "*Nei*, please, *teska*. Let me go!" She tugged and writhed but could not break free.

"All who enter will be judged." The tall one who had spoken earlier took Ellie's face in her hands. "You will submit," she commanded, and Ellie went instantly and utterly still.

The woman flung back her veil, revealing a face of devastating beauty and eyes that burned like firebrands. All around, the other *shei'dalins* followed suit. Their power—nothing like the gentle care Marissya had always shown her—invaded her, relentless and unyielding.

Her own consciousness fought back instinctively, strengthening her protective inner weaves, trying desperately to barricade her mind against them. But they were too many, and the pressure too great. Their insistence beat at her as if the weight of all the oceans of the world were bearing down upon her, battering her shields like wild waves battering a seawall.

"Do not fight us," commanded the one who had spoken before. "You cannot win. In the end, we will have what we seek."

"Nei!" Only to Rain had she ever confessed the terrible, frightening, dark thoughts that sometimes consumed her. And she would not—could not—fling open those black, violent places to these *shei'dalins*. She was terrified of what they would find. Terrified of what might happen—to her, to them, to Rain—if they unleashed the wild, angry power that lived inside her.

"Surrender to us," the woman insisted.

The pressure grew, multiplied, became unbearable. Within Ellie's mind, the internal protective weaves Bel had helped her to rebuild—barriers to keep her thoughts private from even intentional Fey intrusion—stretched and grew thin. Behind them, the tairen shifted and hissed a warning.

"Surrender," all the *shei'dalins* commanded. "Submit and be judged." There were dozens of them, too many, and their magic was braided in a multi-ply weave of staggering power.

The first thread in Ellie's barriers snapped. The remaining threads stretched and shrieked beneath the relentless push of the *shei'dalins'* insistent will.

"Stop! Stop! You don't know what you're doing! Rain!" She screamed his name in a desperate cry.

Her internal barriers shattered.

Merciless *shei'dalin* minds poured in through the breach.

The howl of battle swept around Rain like a maelstrom, battering his senses. Screams and shrieks of the dead and dying, hot gouts of blood splashing over his face, fire, smoke, the burn of *sel'dor* peppering his flesh. His swords flashed—bright steel, stained with blood, spinning in lethal arcs. Eld, Merellians, Feraz: All fell beneath the merciless onslaught of his blades.

With sword, with fang, with claw and fiery tairen breath, he killed and killed, and with each death, a layer of heavy coldness fell upon him. Layer after layer until he was encased in ice. Still, his blades slashed and his fire burned. Still, he slaughtered.

Then it wasn't only enemies falling beneath his rain of death, but allies as well. Celierians, Elves, Danae. His own brother Fey. He saw their faces, the shock and betrayal, the disbelief. The pleas for mercy that never came.

All around, amid the gore and violence, stood the pale gray shadows of the dead, watching him with unblinking black eyes. Their bloodless mouths were open and moving, lips forming sluggish words. Mottled arms lifted. Dead fingers pointed. At him.

And then he heard the whispers. A murmur of sound cutting across the howl of battle, a low hum vibrating across his senses, felt more than heard.

Murderer. Destroyer. Thief of life.

Bringer of destruction.

He howled a denial, and the fields of accusing dead winked out.

When he could see again, he was flying over a barren, scorched land. Below him, the city of Dharsa lay in ruins, its gleaming white towers and golden spires heaps of smoldering rubble. He spun away, raced back across the sky, heading northeast to the great volcanic mountain of Fey'Bahren, home to the last living tairen pride. But when he reached it, he found fiery, glowing rivers of molten lava pouring down the mountain's sides like great fountains of blood gushing from a mortal wound. The nesting lair—the networked maze of caverns and tunnels that had been his home for most of the last thousand years—was destroyed.

Desperate, disbelieving, he flew from one end of the Fading Lands to another. Nothing living remained. Not a single blade of grass, not the smallest twig, not even the tiniest insect had survived. The Fading Lands were dead, as were the tairen and the Fey who had called this once-beautiful part of the world home.

"It's your fault, you know," a soft voice accused.

His eyes closed. He recognized that voice. He turned slowly, knowing who stood behind him, fearing what image from her life or death the beings of the Mists might have chosen to torment him with.

Sariel stood before him, slender, luminous, clad in a translucent gown of delicate dusky blue. She was so beautiful. Even among the exquisite comeliness of other Fey women, she had always been a flower beyond compare.

Ebony hair spilled over her shoulders like skeins of silk, and eyes of deep, drowning blue watched him with sorrow and regret.

The sight of her didn't rip at his heart the way it always had before Ellysetta. Now, her image only filled him with sadness for the beautiful Fey maiden whose millennia of life had been cut so short. He had loved her with every fiber of his youthful being, but that love owned his heart no longer. Rain, the mate of Sariel, had died a thousand years ago on a bloody battlefield just north of Teleon. A different Rain had risen from the ashes, born the day Ellysetta Baristani's soul had called out and his had answered. From that moment on, no other—not even the woman for whom he'd once scorched the world—could lay claim to any portion of Rain's heart or soul.

"You brought evil into the Mists," Sariel accused. "You damned us all." Her voice was soft, and throbbing with shame and recrimination. Tears filled her eyes, spilled down luminous alabaster cheeks.

"I bring no evil. I bring our salvation," he replied. "And if you meant to torment me, you chose the wrong form. Rain, the mate of Sariel, is no more. Now there is only Rainier-Eras, truemate of Ellysetta Feyreisa."

The Mists must have realized their error. Sariel's beautiful face wavered. Her body stretched and split, re-forming as a man and woman. A tall man, fierce-eyed, black-haired, unsmiling. A woman, slender and shining. Beautiful. Beloved. His parents: Rajahl vel'En Daris and his *e'tani*, Kiaria.

They were no more real than Sariel had been, but the sight of them was like a knife to his heart. The blade twisted painfully when the two of them spoke.

"You are a Tairen Soul of the Fey'Bahren pride," his father said, "sworn to defend our lands against those who wish us harm, yet you have betrayed us all." Rajahl wore an expression of stern disapproval and, worse, disappointment—a look Rajahl had directed at Rain only once or perhaps twice in his entire life, because that look cut Rain so deeply he'd done everything in his power to ensure that his father never regarded him that way again.

His mother wept. "Oh, my son, my son, better you had died than come to this."

Even the illusion of their censure seared him. He wanted to cry out in protest, but he did not. He shoved his feelings aside. Illusion gained strength only when one believed it.

"Show your true face!" he challenged the pair standing before him. "I know my parents do not live in these Mists any more than Sariel did."

"We wear the faces of those whose counsel you once sought," his mother said. "We wear the faces we hope will make you see reason. Listen to us, my son."

But even as she spoke, her image shimmered. Both she and Rajahl faded, and then it was Johr vel Eilan who stood there, the Tairen Soul who had been king when Rain first found his wings. Johr, the fearsome, granite-jawed warrior who had led the Fading Lands for eight hundred years.

When Johr had sat upon the Tairen Throne, the Fading Lands had been strong. *He* had been a king worthy of his crown: strong, decisive, unwavering, fierce. Not some untried Feyreisen who'd been handed the crown simply because there was no other to take it, but a Tairen Soul who had trained for centuries in military tactics, diplomacy, leadership. A man who had earned the right to lead both in times of peace and prosperity as well as the grimmer years of blood and battle.

To see Johr—a true and rightful Defender of the Fey—roused all of Rain's most bitter self-doubts. He knew he was not the king the Fading Lands deserved.

The Mists knew it too.

"You cast a shadow on the Tairen Throne, Rainier vel'En Daris. You are not worthy of your crown."

Rain gave a bitter laugh. "That much I will grant you.

My soul is black with the deaths of those millions I slew in the Wars. But if you banish me, who will be the Tairen Soul?"

"You know of what I speak—and of whom. You know whose dark hand lies upon her. She will cement the destruction of both the tairen and the Fey. Yet still you bring her. Because you choose self over duty."

Johr's jaw flexed, and his green-gold eyes flared with a sudden, angry burst of power. "This is not the choice of a king, Tairen Soul. You shame your crown, your steel, and the line of your forebears. She brings death to our world."

For one dreadful moment, Rain remembered Ellysetta's seizure and her black, Azrahn-filled eyes and her low, hoarse voice shouting, "I am Death."

Almost as soon as the doubt arose, he shook it off. *Nei. Nei*, he wouldn't believe that. The only death associated with Ellysetta was the foul Eld evil that stalked her, the dread reason the gods had fashioned a tairen for her mate.

He thrust out a clenched jaw. "Ellysetta is bright and shining. She is the one the Eye of Truth sent me to find—because she brings life to the Fey, not death. She is a *shei'dalin* and a Tairen Soul and my truemate. You will not speak against her."

"And when the evil she bears comes into bloom? What will you do then, Rainier vel'En Daris? How will you defend the Fey against this serpent you clasp to your breast?"

"She will not fall. We will complete our bond, and the Mage whose Marks she bears will lose all power over her." He clung to that hope, because without it he had nothing. "What else should I have done, if not bring her here? Left her out there in the world, unprotected? I did what any Fey—what any *shei'tan*—would have done. I brought her to safety."

"And endangered us all."

Rain stiffened his spine and lifted a clenched jaw. "The tairen do not agree. Sybharukai, *makai* of the Fey'Bahren pride, does not agree. Tairen do not abandon their kin. Tairen defend the pride."

A cold smile curled the edges of Johr's mouth. "Tairen also honor Challenge, for the health of the pride."

Sudden cold swept over Rain, leaving his flesh clammy and his heart stuttering with fear.

"Where is Ellysetta?" he demanded. "What have you done to her?" He spun away from the image of Johr and cried, *"Ellysetta!"*

Ellysetta screamed until she thought her throat would burst. With none of the gentleness and compassion Marissya had always shown her, the *shei'dalins* of the Mists plundered her mind, tearing into private thoughts and memories, prying loose even her most closely guarded secrets and deepest fears. She tried to rally a defense, but each time she managed to focus her will against them, they would turn those fearsome eyes upon her and her thoughts would scatter like hapless leaves in the wind.

Ruthless, efficient, they rifled through her mind, examining every memory. Her childhood in Hartslea, the seizures, the priests' declaration that she was demon possessed. Her first exorcism and the howling, bloody, violent rage that had swept through her eight-year-old mind when the long, shining needles of the exorcists had plunged into her body. They *saw* what she'd been thinking, knew how she'd dreamed of rending those exorcists limb from limb and dancing in the shower of their blood.

Ellie wept in shame and horror at her own evil thoughts. When she'd shared the awful truth of her childhood with Rain, he had offered acceptance and loving, healing forgiveness. These *shei'dalins* were not so compassionate. They dissected without mercy and left her writhing in an agony of self-loathing.

The tairen hissed a furious warning, its claws beginning to shred the last of her control.

"Please," she begged. "Please stop."

The *shei'dalins* only dug deeper, finding the memories of how she'd restored Gaelen's soul, the devastating recollection of the black Mage Mark lying like a shadow over her heart. They summoned the ghastly, shocking moment in the Grand Cathedral of Light when the Eld blade sliced and Mama's head rolled free of her body.

Heat bloomed. The first warning flare of Rage. *They hurt us.*

"Stop!" she cried, fearing what would happen if they didn't. Anger was growing inside her.

They found the memories of that terrible nightmare when she'd stood amid a field of corpses and seen herself leading the armies of darkness, slaughtering all who stood in her way. The vile, mocking claim of the Shadow Man rang in her ears: *You'll kill them, girl. You'll kill them all. It's what you were born for.*

Within Ellysetta, the coiling power gave a terrible hiss. Her muscles grew taut. Her skin burned and strained as pressure built within. *Vengeance on those who hurt us . . . vengeance for what they did . . .*

The *shei'dalins* summoned more visions, every foul, horrifying nightmare of war and death she'd ever had. Bodies torn and shredded, blood running in scarlet rivers. Only this time all the dead wore the faces of those she loved: Mama, Papa, Lillis, Lorelle, Bel, Selianne, and, everywhere she turned, Rain. In every face, she saw Rain. Rain dead. Rain dying. Rain split asunder, burning, bleeding his life out. Screaming in defiance as Mage Fire consumed him.

"*Nei!* Do not!" she cried, the words both a warning for the *shei'dalins* and a command to the destructive wildness gathering inside her.

"*Ellysetta!*" The sound of Rain's voice rang out across the Mists in speech and Spirit and tairen song, calling out simultaneously in her mind and her soul. Her heart raced, and the threads of their bond flared to life, tingling with a sudden surge of magic in response to the desperate command and raging fear in his call.

The tairen fury building inside her coalesced with sudden focus. Her hands clenched. Her eyes flamed. They dared use her to torment her mate? Ellysetta's power rose up in wild, angry waves, bright and hot.

"Rain!" She shouted his name on every pathway he'd used to call her, her voice vibrating with the incendiary roar of her tairen. *"I am here!"* Her call pierced the Mists, finding him instantly, seizing him with a searing rope of fire that blazed a path back to her.

Suddenly he was there, fierce and furious, his roar a deafening boom. Flames boiled around them with savage fury as Rain's tairen rushed to defend its mate. The avenue of trees, the *shei'dalins*, the gathering of cold-eyed Fey, all dissolved in a wall of tairen flame.

The roar rocked Taloth'Liera like a cry from the gods themselves.

One whole section of the Mists turned bright orange, then exploded in a boiling cloud of tairen fire that sent Fey warriors stumbling back. Steel clattered on stone. A great, blazing ball of light hurtled out of the dense flames. The warriors standing on the crenellated wall crossing Taloth'Liera shouted in surprise as it rocketed past.

The light plunged towards earth like a falling star. Bel raised a hand to shield his eyes and caught a glimpse of a shadowy tairen wing at the periphery of the light. His heart rose up in his throat when he realized he was watching Rain streaking across the sky, gouts of flame spewing from his muzzle—and that blaze of blinding light on his back was Ellysetta.

They landed half a mile beyond the Warriors' Wall, dust billowing up in clouds around them. Gaelen and Bel ran towards them. Marissya and Dax sprinted close on their heels, followed by Tajik and the rest of the Fey.

They all skidded to a halt when the tairen screamed and rose up on his haunches. Black wings spread wide in a show of ferocious might, and boiling jets of flame geysered into the air in warning.

When the Fey made no move to come closer, he settled back onto all four paws. Growls rumbled dangerously in his chest, and several more small bursts of flame hissed from his muzzle. The radiant figure of Ellysetta slid from his back and leaned against his foreleg. Her blinding aura began slowly to dim. Rain remained in tairen form, his tail twitching, his ears laid back on his head.

"What in the Seven Hells is going on?" Tajik demanded. "Did the Mists grant passage, or did the Tairen Soul and his mate just burn their way through?" Suspicion filled Tajik's flame blue eyes, and though his hands didn't reach for steel, Bel saw the unmistakable signs of tension gathering.

"*Las*, Taj," Bel said. "This was Rain's first time through the Mists. None of us were sure what to expect. Clearly, he had a bad time of it, but he's through, and that's what matters."

Tajik wasn't general of the eastern army because he was a trusting man. His eyes pierced Bel as mercilessly as Tajik's blades had impaled countless enemy soldiers over the centuries. "The Tairen Soul wasn't the only one to blast through with magic blazing." He nodded at the still blindingly bright figure of Ellysetta. "What stains could a *shei'dalin* bear on her soul that would set the Mists against her?"

"The Feyreisa's power is vast," Marissya interrupted, drawing the general's intent blue gaze to herself, "but she never summons it on her own behalf. Whatever torments Rain suffered no doubt roused her tairen's protective instincts. I have not seen her like this since her mother was murdered before her eyes."

The hard intensity of Tajik's gaze faltered. Outside the bonds of truemating, there was no stronger Fey instinct than the warriors' need to protect their women from harm, and the image of a Fey maiden shattered by the loss of a beloved mother roused that ingrained protectiveness with a vengeance.

"Rain will not calm until she does." Marissya edged closer. Ellysetta turned her head, piercing Marissya with a look that made the *shei'dalin* gasp and stop in her tracks. Ellysetta's eyes were pupil-less, whirling kaleidoscopes, blazing with tairen power. The *shei'dalin's* body went stiff, and for an instant an aura of bright light flamed around her.

Dax lunged toward his truemate, but Gaelen clapped a swift, hard arm around his bond brother's chest, holding him back. "Don't be a fool, Dax. Ellysetta won't hurt Marissya."

A moment later, the light around Marissya winked out. Dax broke free of Gaelen's hold and caught her as she stumbled.

Marissya took a deep breath and steadied herself before waving him off. "*Las, shei'tan*. I am unharmed." Never taking her eyes off Ellysetta, she wiped the sheen of perspiration from her upper lip. The Feyreisa hadn't hurt her, it was true, but Marissya felt as if her entire being—body and soul—had been seized, ripped open, and scoured by a merciless inquisitor.

The sensation was one Marissya knew all too well, though she'd never been on the receiving end of it. At least, never such a ruthless and brutally efficient weave of it.

Ellysetta had just Truthspoken the most powerful *shei'dalin* in the Fading Lands.

And not kindly.

Marissya blew out a breath. No wonder Ellysetta feared *shei'dalins* so much. A few chimes of that ravaging scrutiny, and even Marissya would have collapsed in a boneless puddle of shattered will and weeping helplessness. And Ellysetta hadn't even needed to lay a hand upon her to do it.

Whatever the Feyreisa had discovered—or found absent—inside Marissya apparently satisfied her, because when the *shei'dalin* stepped forward a second time, Ellysetta allowed her approach without protest.

Half-afraid that if she dared too much, Ellysetta's wild power might rouse again, Marissya quickly healed the physical effects of stress and shock and did what she could to help mend the barriers in Ellysetta's mind. The Mists had not been gentle with her. Each moment of the healing, while Marissya's consciousness was tied to Ellysetta, she was aware of the hot, angry hissing of the tairen, a violent sentience seething just below the surface.

Marissya had no desire to feel the full brunt of that power unleashed upon her.

When she was done, she pulled her hands back quickly and didn't protest when Dax snatched her up and hauled her several steps away from Rain and his truemate.

"Is she well?" Tajik stood tense, staring at the still-radiant, flame-haired woman standing so fearlessly beside the great black tairen, her pale, gleaming hand stroking its pelt.

"She is fine," Marissya assured him. "I was right. The Mists roused her tairen, but she is calming now."

The Change swirled about Rain, and the sudden burst of magic made Tajik fall instinctively into a warrior's slightly crouched attack stance, his hands on red steel.

Ellysetta's head jerked around, her eyes blazing at the perceived threat, and Tajik's body went rigid, his spine poker straight. A fierce consciousness invaded his own, spearing past all his shields straight to his core.

"Aiyah, you should fear us. We are fierce." The voice, so soft, rang in his mind with the force of a gong, leaving him trembling in its wake. *"Do not threaten us."*

She released him from his stunned paralysis, turning to face the tall, black-haired Fey beside her. Rain's eyes were blazing, power sparking around him like fairy flies. His arms caught her around the waist, and his mouth swooped down to capture hers. Unmindful of the gathered Fey looking on, he kissed her with a passion that nearly set their onlookers aflame.

"Shei'tani . . . Ellysetta . . . " His voice sang to hers in vibrant tones, shimmering down the threads of their bond and the new, fiercely blazing connection between them that hummed with wild, raw power.

Rain did not know what had happened to them in the Mists, nor at the moment could he bring himself to care. Whatever the Mists had done, whatever their reasons for it, they had brought both his tairen and hers to savage life, and in that moment of primitive wildness, when her soul and her tairen had screamed in rage and reached for him and his, the power and fury of their tairen had arced between them like searing flames shot straight from the heart of the Great Sun. Or, rather, like savage jets of tairen flame, the fire that burned all things. That thread of pure, intense power had pierced the wildest depths of his soul and anchored there.

The fiery bond thread was still there, neither extinguished nor dimmed, untamed by the others, yet braided so tight the three had nearly become one.

When the fierce radiance of their power and the wild fury of their tairen at last began to subside, the Feyreisa released her mate and turned to face the Fey. Tajik's breath caught in his throat once more. The menace of the tairen was gone, leaving only luminous, golden beauty. To look upon the unveiled countenance of any shei'dalin was to know the face of love, but with the Feyreisa, the effect was overwhelming. When her gaze fell upon him, her eyes like radiant suns, it was as if the gods themselves shone a light straight into his heart.

"She is . . . is . . ." He swallowed hard. "I have no words."

Bel clapped a sympathetic hand on his cradle friend's shoulder. "I told you she was bright."

Tajik took two trembling steps forward and fell to one knee, bowing his head. When he rose again, he fixed glowing eyes on the Feyreisa's face and gave the greeting he should have offered her from the start. *"Meiveli, kem'Feyreisa.* Welcome to the Fading Lands."

CHAPTER FIVE

Eld ~ Boura Fell

Vadim Maur's left hand was trembling.

The High Mage glared at the betraying tremors, then curled his fingers in a fist until the shaking stopped. His visit to Shannisorran v'En Celay's cell earlier today had wearied him far more than it should have. If not for the war hammer slamming into the Fey lord's skull, the blast of power that had surged from him would have caught Vadim full bore rather than glancing off his left arm. The weak shield he'd thrown up had not been enough to rob the blast of its impact, and his hand had been twitching ever since.

He should have known better than to go to v'En Celay's cell weary. And the last six days he'd spent claiming the Celierian Den Brodson's soul *had* wearied him. Most Mages who did not have the standard six years to claim a soul settled for a weaker hold on their *umagi,* but Vadim had never done things by halves. He'd taken the full power of a claiming normally spread out across six years and concentrated it into six days.

Such a reckless expense of power was not his wisest decision, but losing Ellysetta Baristani when she'd been all but his had driven him into a fury. He'd wanted a productive outlet for his rage, and Brodson's screams had been a balm to his soul. He'd also wanted complete and irrevocable control over the Celierian before using him, and since Kolis had tipped his hand in Celieria, time was quickly becoming a luxury rather than a tool at his disposal.

A knock sounded on his office door. "Enter," he called.

The door swung inward, revealing an *umagi*, who bowed and said, "Fezaiina Zebah Rael has arrived, great one."

"Send her in."

Moments later, his office filled with rich, warm, seductive scents as the beautiful, bronze-skinned Feraz witch swept inside in a flurry of colorful silken veils. "Fezai Madia sends you greetings, Chazah Maur." Zebah's red lips curved in a sultry smile as she approached his desk, but her sloe eyes were filled with an intelligence far sharper than the lush curves of her enticingly clad body would lead a foolish man to believe. Those eyes were scanning everything, missing nothing. She was the envoy of the most powerful witch in Feraz—Fezai Madia Shah, high priestess of the Blood Chalice—and Vadim knew better than to underestimate her.

"You look weary, great one," she murmured. The smooth, potent magic of her voice burned across his skin. Feraz women, particularly among the witchfolk, were a dangerous combination of exotic beauty and compelling natural sexual power. Fierce and bloodthirsty as Feraz men might be, their women held the true power.

Vadim eyed the witch coldly, ignoring the tug of her magic, and kept his still-trembling hands out of sight beneath the desk. "I am neither weary nor weak, Fezaiina, and you are wasting your time testing your power on me. As your Fezai learned long ago, I am immune to such persuasions, no matter how attractive the lure." Sex, though satisfying in many ways and useful under the right circumstances, was a distraction from the one true passion of his life: his quest for magical supremacy.

"In her last communication, the Fezai said she'd made a breakthrough that would please me," he prompted. Vadim's long association with the witches of Feraz had proven mutually beneficial in many ways, most especially in the unique spells and powers they had discovered by combining their powers, their bloodlines, and their knowledge of magic.

"*Zim.*" The Fezaiina left off her attempts to ensnare his senses and produced a black velvet pouch from the folds of her *jiba*, the wrap she wore loosely draped around her smooth curves in whispering flows of brightly colored silk. "The Fezai sends you this great gift, Chazah Maur." She opened the drawstring at the top of the bag and drew out a small, pearlescent stone, which she laid upon the parchment-cluttered surface of his desk.

Vadim leaned forward and inspected the stone visually before reaching for it. White, oval, and smoothly rounded, it was roughly the size of a peach pit and the shape of a child's skipping stone.

"And this is . . . ?"

"Magic, Chazah. Great and powerful magic."

"What sort of magic?" He cupped his hands around the stone and summoned a brief spell, but nothing in the stone responded to his flare of power. "I sense none."

"Precisely."

He scowled at her. "Do not waste my time, witch."

"Watch, great one." She bent her head, parted her red lips, and whispered a Feraz witchword. A shadow flickered in the heart of the pearly stone, like a larva wriggling in its egg. Beneath the outer layers of stone, a rune began to gleam with a brightening glow.

Vadim's brows drew together. He recognized the rune and knew its meaning only because of his dealings with long-forgotten Feraz witchcraft.

"Gamorraz?" The rune was beyond ancient, hailing from a forbidden form of witchtongue used in the blackest days of the craft, millennia ago. Gamorraz was a very powerful demon, the father of the four Guardians of the Well of Souls.

"*Zim*," Zebah breathed. "An ancient and powerful name to summon an ancient and powerful magic."

"And the purpose of this stone?"

Zebah smiled. "To open gateways, Chazah. To the Well of Souls."

He snatched the stone up off the desk and tossed it back to her. She caught it with one, swift snap of her wrist. "This is your Fezai's great new triumph? The *selkahr* crystals already do as much."

Her eyes narrowed. "You dismiss so quickly a gift whose greatness you do not begin to fathom, Chazah. *Zim*, the stones—which we call *chemar*—do what your *selkahr* does, but only in their purpose are *chemar* and *selkahr* similar." Zebah opened her fist and rolled the stone between her fingers. "*Selkahr* is very precious, we know. How much do you have to spare for such uses as gateways and portals?"

Vadim's spine stiffened at the directness of her probe. "Enough," he answered guardedly. *Selkahr* was made from Tairen's Eye crystals, and those had been in exceedingly short supply of late.

She laughed, a throaty sound. "But it is not so easy to come by." She leaned forward, her breasts pressing together invitingly, her sloe eyes fixed on his face. "*Chemar*, great one, are made from the bones of those sacrificed to Gamorraz. The stones can be manufactured at will and in great quantities. But best of all, as you have seen for yourself, the *chemar* have no magical properties until they are activated by the proper witchword. Fey wards will not detect it. No sacrifice is needed to make the stones work. You can place *chemar* anywhere you desire a portal and open the gates at will—and without using Azrahn. You can insert your armies, without warning, anywhere you so desire. The stones are consumed when you use them, but all you need do is simply drop another when you wish to open a gate again."

The High Mage leaned back in his chair. "Very well. You have piqued my interest." He gestured to the bag dangling from Zebah's wrist. "How many of those *chemar* did you bring with you?"

The witch hefted her black pouch. "Fezai Madia sends four dozen as a gesture of her goodwill."

Vadim rose to his feet, the hem of his purple Mage robes swirling about his ankles. "You will give me a demonstration of their effectiveness. Then I will decide how useful they may, in fact, be."

Zebah bowed low, but the slow, confident smile on her face when she straightened belied any implication of subservience. "As you will. It is my pleasure to serve, great one."

"What price does the Fezai have in mind for more of these *chemar*?"

The Fezaiina's smile widened, showing the pointed edges of her small, white teeth. "One of your strongest males for every four dozen stones."

Vadim's glance sharpened. "That is a steep price."

"Perhaps." Zebah lifted her dark, arching brows. "But consider this, Chazah: Your males will be returned to you when the Fezai is through with them." She shook the bag of *chemar* stones and laughed. "Or, at least, what is left of them."

Three bells later, the Fezaiina took her leave, stepping into the open maw of the Well of Souls. Four muscular, *sel'dor*-shackled men followed her, tame as sheep, their eyes downcast, their faces blank with the dazed effects of the Feraz witch's enchantment.

Vadim Maur watched them go with a twinge of regret. The four had been promising men from strong bloodlines, full of latent magic. But Fezai Madia would not have been pleased if he'd sent her less than quality in payment for her latest discovery . . . and the woman had an evil temper.

The hand holding the *chemar* pouch began to shake again. He bent a hard gaze upon it, trying to will the trembling muscles into obedience. Instead, the tremors grew more pronounced and shot up the entire length of his arm. The velvet bag filled with *chemar* dropped from nerveless fingers.

"Master Maur." A nearby guard started towards him until a snarled command from the High Mage sent him reeling back in fear.

Vadim bent to snatch the *chemar* pouch from the ground and stuffed it in the pocket of his robes. His trembling hand he stuffed in the other pocket. His gaze swept the room, noting which men had witnessed his moment of weakness. Unfortunately for them, all four belonged to Primages who had apprenticed to a Mage other than Vadim Maur. He did not have access to their souls the way he did to the *umagi* of his own apprentices.

"You four. Come here."

Nervously, they came. What choice did they have, really?

"Kneel."

Two of them swallowed and hesitated. "Master Maur?"

The fearful defiance annoyed him. "Do as I say."

Gulping, the four men knelt. "Mast—" The guard's voice broke off in a gurgle as Vadim's Mage blade swept out in one clean slice across three of the four men's necks. The fourth man gave a cry and jerked back just in time to miss the first death strike. He didn't miss the second.

From the doorway to the Well of Souls—kept open with a combination of Azrahn and frequent sacrifices to the Guardians of the Well—demons howled at the scent of fresh blood and death. Vadim left the creatures to their feast. Souls consumed by what lived in the Well could not be called back from the dead. The four would carry no tales of Vadim's weakness to their masters.

As he exited the room, he paused to tell the guard outside the door, "Contact your captain. Tell him to send more guards for the Well."

The soldier brought his heels together with a snap and bowed sharply at the waist. "As you wish, Most High."

The Fading Lands ~ Chatok

Night had fallen. A warm, dry breeze blew from the west, swirling through the long skeins of Rain's hair. He stood on the battlements of Chatok's great tower, his face turned to the north, eyes whirling with glowing radiance as he sang a message to his tairen kin in the still-distant nesting lair of Fey'Bahren.

Ellysetta drank in the vibrant notes of his song as she climbed the last few steps to join him. He had changed out of his leathers and steel, trading them for flowing robes of dusky blue velvet over a tunic of heavy lavender silk shot through with silver thread. An intricately woven circlet of beaten silver rested on his brow, and he'd transformed the golden chain and pendant holding his *sorreisu kiyr*, his Soul Quest crystal, from gold to gleaming silver.

He turned to her, still singing, and held out a hand. She took it, and he pulled her close, his arms wrapping with casual possessiveness around her waist. The folds of his robe swirled about her, warm and rich with the scent of Rain. The tension that had been coiled within him for days was finally beginning to ease. Despite the unkind welcome the Faering Mists had offered them, at last they were here, safe in the Fading Lands, only two days' run from Fey'Bahren, the nesting lair of the tairen.

"Good news?" she asked when the last notes of his song drifted away on the wind.

"Cahlah fed again today," he said. "Sybharukai says her

strength is returning. The kits show signs of improvement as well."

"That *is* good news." Ellysetta tilted her head back, a faint smile lifting the corners of her mouth. "Perhaps the Fey don't need me so much as you first thought."

His arms tightened. "Do not be so quick to discount your importance. Cahlah may be recovering, but her kits aren't safe until they break from the egg."

"So we head for Fey'Bahren tonight?"

"*Nei.*" He smiled and brushed back her curls. "Tonight, we rest and let the warriors downstairs celebrate the arrival of their Feyreisa. It's been too long since they've had cause for joy."

Together, they made their way downstairs to Chatok's massive main hall. There, a great fire burned in the center of the room, and all the warriors of the eastern army had gathered for a feast to welcome their new queen.

When she and Rain stepped onto the landing that led down into the main hall, a hush fell over the assembled Fey and all eyes turned towards her. For one brief moment, a shaft of familiar terror froze her in place—the memory of her first, ill-fated introduction to the heads of Celieria's noble houses—but then hundreds of Fey voices rose in a now-familiar cry: "*Miora felah ti'Feyreisa!*"

Bel and Gaelen, looking taller and more handsome than she'd ever seen them, approached the foot of the stairs, smiling up at her as she and Rain descended. Like the rest of the Fey, they'd exchanged their leathers and steel for flowing robes. Gaelen wore subtle shades that called to mind images of ancient, misty forests, while Bel wore a drape of cobalt blue over a tunic of lustrous silver and pewter gray. Both men regarded her with warm eyes.

"You are lovely, *kem'falla,*" Bel said with a smile.

"*Beylah vo,* Bel." While Rain had donned robes the color of dusk, he'd clad her in starlight. Her gown was sumptuous white silk beaded with thousands of tiny diamonds that shimmered as she moved. A wide, boat-shaped neckline and snug bodice gave way to full, flowing skirts that trailed behind her. A girdle of platinum links shaped like twining vines circled her waist and dripped graceful loops of *sorreisu kiyr*, the Soul Quest crystals of the Fey who'd died on her behalf in Celieria. Bel's and Gaelen's bloodsworn daggers hung sheathed at her hips. Her hair flowed unbound, curling in soft, thick spirals of flame down to her waist, and on her brow she wore a crown of stars—diamonds and Tairen's Eye crystals sparkling from the delicate platinum whorls and arches of the circlet nestled in her hair.

With Gaelen and Bel close behind, Rain escorted her to the head table, where Marissya and Dax were already waiting.

Ellysetta stopped at the sight of the five unfamiliar Fey women sitting with them. "Who are they?"

"*Shei'dalins* from Dharsa," Rain answered. "They arrived earlier this evening while we were getting dressed, along with the warriors I promised King Dorian I'd send to help secure the Eld border."

"*Shei'dalins?*" Ellysetta stiffened.

"*Las, shei'tani,*" Rain soothed. She'd told him about the *shei'dalins* in the Mists who'd Truthspoken her. "I promised Great Lord Darramon the Fey would heal his dying wife if he brought her to Teleon. These five *shei'dalins* came to honor my oath. Come, meet them," he said, inviting her to follow him.

Ellysetta followed him reluctantly to greet the *shei'dalins* and murmur what she hoped were appropriate greetings. She tried not to let her distrust of them show, but she did not sit near them either.

The feast that followed was nothing like the studied artifice of Celieria's royal state dinners, but rather a true celebration. Safe behind the Faering Mists, stoic Fey expressions softened with smiles and laughter, transforming the fierce, deadly warriors into approachable men of uncommon beauty and warmth. Laughter rang out from every corner of the room. The tables overflowed with roasted meat and a variety of tempting delicacies: cool salads, steaming vegetable dishes, fresh and honey-glazed fruits, all accompanied by pale sweet wine and crisp, cool water that made her eyes widen in surprise when she sipped it.

"This is good." The water tasted like fresh-fallen snow and sunlight, cold, sweet, and pure, with an unexpected energy that radiated through her as she drank.

"I'm glad it pleases you." Rain drank from his own cup, then set it aside. "We call it *faerilas*. It is the water of the Source, the great fountain at the center of each of our largest cities." He smiled as he sliced a nearby round of cheese into thin layers and handed one to her. She took a tentative bite. The cheese was firm, with a creamy, nutty flavor that melted on her tongue. "You may have heard of the Source. Some mortals, who misunderstood the reason for Fey longevity, used to call it the Fount of Eternas."

"The Fountain of Eternal Youth?" Ellysetta paused before her next bite of cheese to examine the water in her goblet with greater interest.

He laughed. "*Las, shei'tani.* I said misguided mortals called it that, not that they were right."

"But there is magic in this *faerilas*." She took another sip to confirm it. "I can taste it." One sip and a tingling energy filled her with renewed strength.

"*Aiyah*, but the magic will not make you young—nor keep you that way. The waters of the Source replenish magical energies and purify whatever they touch, but no more than that. The cleansing spell the Fey cast on the Velpin River does much the same, though in a less powerful way." He smiled at her disappointment and reached for a small, teardrop-shaped globe of bright green-and-scarlet fruit. "Here, taste this." He sliced the fruit with a few deft strokes of a Fey'cha blade and held out a small segment. "I think you will like it."

Ellysetta took the proffered morsel and bit into the firm, cool flesh. Sweet, tangy juice filled her mouth with bursting sweetness and trickled down the corners of her lips. Laughing, she lifted a hand to wipe away the dribbles. "It's very good. And very messy!"

"We call it *tamaris*. It is a cousin to the *komarind*, which is more beautiful to look at but no good for eating."

Her tongue was tingling. "There's magic in the *tamaris* too."

The corners of his eyes crinkled. "Magic is everywhere in the Fading Lands. Legend claims it was the great tairen Lissallukai who sang magic into this world, but after countless millennia, the *faer*—the magic of the tairen and the Fey—has become a part of this land, and we a part of it."

She took another bite and more juice spurted against her skin, but this time Rain reached over and caught the runnel of juice before she could. His finger stroked upward, scooping the nectar from her skin, then painting it across her lips with one burning stroke of his hand. His eyes were glowing.

Her laughter fell silent. Everything in the Fading Lands brimmed with magic: the Fey, the tairen, even the waters and the fruits of the fields. But for her, the greatest magic of all was Rain and what he made her feel. "Will it always be like this?"

"Like what?"

"Like magic, between us."

His eyes flared bright for a brief instant. "*Aiyah*, Ellysetta, it will. *Shei'tanitsa* bonds, once forged, will never wane. What exists between us will last to the end of time."

Eld ~ Boura Fell

Vadim Maur made his way through the sconce-lit stairways and corridors of Boura Fell to the hall that housed Elfeya v'En Celay's bedchamber-prison. As the earlier episode by the Well had proven, the weakness in his arm required immediate tending. Clearly, the powerful *shei'dalin* had not been doing her best to keep him strong and healthy. That was going to change.

He unlocked and cleared a heavily warded door. It swung inward, and he smiled at the sight of the flame-haired Fey woman chained naked to the bed within.

He had promised Elfeya and her mate torment beyond imagining for their part in hiding the truth of their daughter's magic from him and for trying to help her escape the trap he'd set for her during the Bride's Blessing. True to Vadim's word, Lord v'En Celay now lay in the depths of Boura Fell, little more than a bloody heap of shredded skin and shattered bones.

Elfeya's punishment wasn't quite as bloody—he needed her body whole enough to work the healing magic that was so useful to him—but torture wore a million faces. He sat on the edge of the bed and cupped the soft globe of her naked breast. One long, cold thumb brushed across the still-raw bruises and lash marks marring the perfection of her luminous skin.

She flinched and glared at him, her golden eyes afire with loathing.

"Your mate has had a very bad day," he murmured. "Much worse than your last night." His thumb dug into her soft flesh, his sharpened nail drawing a thin line of sweet, scarlet blood. "His tomorrow will be much worse yet if you don't heal me very well tonight. Do you understand?" He bent his head and licked the blood from her skin, savoring the tingle of powerful magic that infused it. "I can be quite cruel to pets who displease me."

Several floors below the Fey *shei'dalin*'s cell, two stocky *umagi* hauled away the bloody remains of the last pet to displease one of the Mages of Boura Fell. A ragged young girl with a mop of tangled black hair held the refuse cart steady as her companions dumped the limp body inside. Shattered limbs flopped like wilted flower stalks, the man's bones little more than pulverized dust within a bloody bag of flesh.

"Well, he didn't last long," one of the men muttered.

"Most don't once Goram gets his hammer out." The second man jerked his chin toward a door at the shadowy end of the corridor. "'Cept for him. Never seen any creature, mortal or magic, survive what he does. It's like Death himself fears to claim him."

The first man shuddered. "That's what they called him, you know. Desriel, Lord Death. Deadliest Fey ever to walk the earth . . . killed near as many as the Tairen Soul did when he scorched the world . . . only Lord Death did it with nothing but blades and magic. Even Master Maur fears him—I thought he was going to wet himself two weeks ago when all the *sel'dor* that one wears came off."

"Watch your tongue, Durm. There's ears here." The second man jerked his head towards the girl holding the cart. He cuffed her on the side of the head. "Go on. Dump this lump of flesh in the pit. Master Maur's pets are hungry. Then get up to the next level. There's more work for you there."

Cold silver eyes regarded him from beneath strings of tangled hair. Without a word, the girl pushed the heavy cart towards the refuse chute at the opposite end of the corridor. The body didn't have far to fall when she dumped it. This was the lowest level of Boura Fell, and the pit was only a few manlengths deeper.

The boneless body hit the bottom of the pit with a dull thud. Mad barking, snarling, and the scrabble of racing feet followed instantly.

The girl peered into the chute, silver eyes observing with cold interest as the pack of leather-hided, wolflike *darrokken* ripped into their newest feast. One of the beasts glanced up, its red eyes glowing in the darkness of the pit, jagged yellow fangs bared. It saw her peering down and raced for the walls of the pit, leaping and snapping barely a manlength below her. The girl drew back quickly, covering her mouth as the foul reek of the *darrokken* wafted up.

The two *umagi* had already finished and were heading upstairs. As she put her foot on the bottom stair to follow, she cast one last considering glance towards the guarded cell door at the end of the corridor. Desriel. Lord Death. She whispered the names under her breath, and ran up the steps.

The Fading Lands ~ Chatok

Midway through the meal, Marissya leaned towards Rain and murmured, "Has Tajik had a chance to speak with you?"

"No," he said. "I haven't seen him since we came through the Mists. Why?"

"Apparently the Massan convened in our absence."

Rain's hands tightened briefly on his silverware.

"What is the Massan?" Ellysetta asked.

"Not what," Dax murmured. "Who. The Massan are the five Fey lords who work with Marissya and Rain to govern the Fading Lands."

"You mean like the Twenty?" Celieria's twenty great lords, the nation's largest landholders, were the most influential men in Celieria after King Dorian, and they voted on all important matters of state.

"More like his personal council of advisers." With a slender, two-tined fork, Dax speared a slice of one of the crunchy, slightly sweet root vegetables Ellysetta had tried earlier and bit into it. "There are five Fey lords of the Massan, each mated, and each a master of the magic he represents."

"It sounds like a quintet."

"*Aiyah*, only they do not defend a single *shei'dalin*. They protect the Fading Lands."

"From what?"

Rain gave a short laugh. "For the last thousand years? From me. Or so it always seems," he added when she frowned in concern and Marissya gave him a chiding look. "We do not often see eye to eye. If not for Marissya, we would have been at one another's throats on more than one occasion."

Ellysetta glanced at Dax's mate. "Marissya serves on the Massan council too?"

"She is not just a *shei'dalin*," Dax said. "She is *the Shei'dalin*, the leader of all Truthspeakers and healers of the Fey." When Ellysetta still looked confused, he explained. "In the Fading Lands, all authority ultimately rests with the Defender of the Fey. But the *Shei'dalin*"—he indicated his mate, Marissya, with a wave of the speared vegetable—"and the Massan assist in the administration of the Fading Lands and oversee all tasks of governance that do not require the Tairen Soul's attention."

"What does it mean that they're meeting without Rain and Marissya?"

"It means there is trouble brewing in Dharsa," Rain said bluntly.

"I'm sure it's nothing," Marissya said at the same time.

Ellysetta looked between the two of them. "So which is it: trouble or nothing?"

Rain sighed. "I may have been the Feyreisen for the last thousand years, but Marissya and the Massan have been the ones leading the country since the Wars. First because of my madness, and then because I devoted all my attention to completing my Cha Baruk. The *chatok* thought the discipline of the training would help me to rebuild and strengthen my internal barriers and keep my madness in check. They were right, but the training didn't leave me much time to be the king of the Fey."

"You think some of the Massan grew too accustomed to wielding the power of the Tairen Throne themselves." Ellysetta pressed a hand against her stomach. Having only just left the political turmoil of Celieria, she'd been hoping to find a measure of peace in the Fading Lands. A fool's hope, perhaps, given that war was imminent and the tairen were dying, but still . . .

"*Nei*, Rain, do not alarm the Feyreisa," Marissya said, frowning at him. "You know it's nothing like that. Hunger for political power is a mortal affliction. The Fey have no such desires."

"The tairen do not hunger for political power either, Marissya, but that does not stop the members of the pride from issuing Challenge if they think the *makai* leading them is weak. The strongest leads; the rest follow. That is the law of the pride." There was a grim set to his jaw, and when Ellysetta feathered a hand across his, an unsettling mix of emotions roiled through her senses: tension, anger, and something that felt strangely like . . . shame.

Rain pulled his hand away to reach for his wineglass.

"The lords of the Massan are honorable Fey whose sole interest is the protection and welfare of the Fading Lands," Marissya insisted. "They would never betray the Feyreisen."

"Marissya, the lords of the Massan are warriors, first and foremost. I do not doubt their honor, but there's not a Fey warrior born who is not tairen enough to issue Challenge if he believes the situation warrants it."

"A meeting is not a Challenge, Rain, and I'm certain the Massan would not even have done that much unless something had them deeply concerned."

Dax leaned forward, arching a brow. "Something like—oh, I don't know—your *dahl'reisen* brother, the Dark Lord, passing through the Mists, perhaps?"

"Former *dahl'reisen*." Marissya sniffed. "And sarcasm does not become you, *shei'tan*." Then she grimaced and admitted to Rain, "But Dax is right. That is why I think they met. And that's why I think Gaelen and Bel should start for Dharsa first thing tomorrow. Once the Massan meet Gaelen face-to-face they will realize there is nothing to fear."

Dax bent towards Rain to mutter, "Nothing to fear, but plenty not to like."

Marissya glared at her truemate. "Dax!"

Despite the seriousness of the conversation, Rain smothered a laugh, but his expression flashed quickly to sobriety when Marissya turned her glare on him. He cleared his throat, tossed back the rest of his wine, and said, "Your idea is a good one, but I don't want Gaelen confronting the Massan without us. The four of us will leave for Fey'Bahren at first light tomorrow. Have Bel, Gaelen, and the returning warriors meet us by the Sentinels outside of Dharsa in four days. That should give us enough time to reach Fey'Bahren, let Ellysetta spin her healing weave on the kits, and then fly to Dharsa."

"Dax and I had planned to leave for Elvia after assisting Ellysetta at Fey'Bahren."

Rain twisted the empty wine goblet in his hand and shook his head. "There's no sense in negotiating with Elves before sorting out the Massan. Hawksheart will sense the disunity among us and hesitate to commit the troops we need. We'll see to the tairen first, then the Massan, and then Elvia."

After the meal, two dozen Fey took up flutes and stringed lutars to fill the night with music. And Ellysetta discovered that the warriors of the Fey sang as masterfully as they wove magic and wielded steel. The haunting beauty of their voices rose in soaring, crystalline swells interwoven with multiple complex harmonies, and made her want to laugh and weep all at once.

Following a rousing rendition of "Ten Thousand Swords," which the entire gathering of warriors joined in singing, the Fey made their way by the score to the front of the room. There, one after another, they approached the head table to greet Ellysetta and Rain, offer well wishes for the speedy completion of their truemate bond, and kneel before Marissya and the other *shei'dalins* to receive their blessings.

Ellysetta noted a large group of warriors at the back of the hall—Tajik vel Sibboreh among them—who did not join the others in approaching the front table where the women sat. The aura of somberness about them caught Ellysetta's attention and would not let go. They sang with the other Fey, but their smiles were not so frequent, and their laughter was quietly subdued.

"Rain, who are those warriors?"

Rain followed her gaze. "Those are the *rasa*. They are as Bel was before you made his heart weep again."

Ellysetta's heart contracted. She remembered how Bel had been when she'd first met him: his eyes full of shadows and pain, the careful way he had avoided meeting her gaze for more than a few brief moments at a time, the sorrow that hung about him like a shroud.

"Why are they not coming forward to receive a *shei'dalin* blessing?"

"They have seen too many battles and carry the weight of too many souls upon theirs. The *shei'dalins* cannot lay hands upon them without sharing their pain, so our women do not touch them except to heal mortal wounds."

"That isn't fair," Ellysetta muttered, frowning at the solitary warriors.

"Little in life ever is, *shei'tani*," Rain replied. "But it is the Fey way, and all Fey warriors accept that life is a dance of duty, honor, and sacrifice."

It was the one aspect of Fey culture that her heart railed against. Those men, those warriors, had sacrificed so much for their country, and ultimately, if they could not find their own truemates, they would have to choose *sheisan'dahlein*, the honor death, or they would slip down the Dark Path and become *dahl'reisen*, banished forever from the beauty of the Fading Lands. There wasn't even any guarantee a true-mate existed for them—only the hope that if a Fey were honorable enough, worthy enough, the gods would eventually create and set in his path the one woman whose soul could call his own. But most Fey died before ever seeing that dream come to fruition.

Her fingers tightened, the nails digging into her palms. Ever since she'd been small, the call to heal those in pain had been a powerful urge. Those Fey were hurting. She could feel their pain pricking her senses like small, sharp knives.

Ellysetta pushed her chair away from the table and stood.

"Shei'tani?" Rain rose to his feet as well, a frown furrowing his brow.

"I'm going to talk to them."

His hand caught her wrist. "Just talk?"

He was coming to know her a little too well. She wasn't sure that was a good thing. "Perhaps offer them a *shei'dalin's* blessing," she admitted.

"Nei, you must not touch them," he commanded. When she set her jaw, he explained on a low throb of Spirit, *"Though you mean well, your offer would shame them. You would force them to hurt you by refusing your gift, or hurt you by causing you pain with their touch. Either way, their hearts would bleed with remorse."*

Scowling, Ellysetta sat back down. She knew that if she went over to the *rasa*, she wouldn't be able to stop herself from trying to heal them. Earlier, the music and the joyful celebration had masked their pain, but now the *rasa's* torment—and her own urge to lessen it—beat at her.

"Beylah vo, shei'tani," Rain murmured.

"Don't thank me for letting them suffer."

He laid his hand over hers. "That is not why I thanked you."

Many bells after the last song was sung and the last warrior sought his bed, Ellysetta lay beside Rain, staring up at the ceiling overhead, unable to sleep. She was tired beyond measure, but she could not stop thinking about those Fey, the *rasa*. She hated the thought of their living here in semiexile without so much as the comfort of an embrace or a loving hand touching theirs to wish them gods' mercy and a safe return when they headed into battle.

No man, not even a Fey warrior trained to fight since birth, should have to watch other Fey receive the *shei'dalin* blessings and warmth he was denied.

She rose from the bed, pulled on a robe, and cast a glance over her shoulder. Rain was sleeping. The long journey from Celieria City, the magic he'd spun to help restore Teleon to its former glory, and the exhaustion of today's trials in the Mists had finally taken their toll. He hadn't stirred.

If she wanted to do this, now was the time.

She started for the door, then froze when he shifted on the bed. He would not be happy if he woke to find her gone.

He would be even less happy when he found out what she'd done.

Ellysetta stood there, wavering, but soon, the throb of the warriors' pain began beating at her again. She drew her robe more snugly about her and tightened the sash. Tomorrow she and Rain would fly to Fey'Bahren in the hope that she could save the tairen. Neither of them knew if she really could.

But healing souls was something she already knew she could do. She still didn't understand how she did it, but she could. And Ellysetta was not the kind of woman who could ever stand by and witness the suffering of another without offering aid. The *rasa* were in pain. She was going to heal them.

With careful silence, Ellysetta opened the bedchamber door and slipped through.

Downstairs, Chatok's main hall was now carpeted with the bodies of sleeping Fey. Ellysetta tiptoed through their midst, navigating the maze of booted feet and tousled heads, her robes hiked up so the trailing cloth would not brush against the sleeping warriors and wake them. A few stirred as she passed, but most continued to sleep soundly.

She started down the corridor that led to the bailey. Halfway to the massive doors guarding the keep, a strange whisper of awareness brushed across her senses. She was not alone. She stopped and turned to look down the long, shadowy corridor, illuminated by the flickering glow of candlelit sconces burning dimly every tairen length. She couldn't see anyone, not even with the added help of Fey vision.

But she could feel them. Both of them.

"Gaelen, Bel, I know you're there. Show yourselves."

A moment later, a lavender glow lit the darkness, and her two bloodsworn champions shimmered into sight.

"How did you detect us?" Gaelen asked. "It was vel Jelani, wasn't it? His weave wasn't tight enough."

Bel stiffened, his cobalt eyes narrowing. "I spun my weave exactly as you showed me," he objected. "If any imperfection existed—which I doubt—the fault lies in your instruction, not my execution."

"It wasn't the weave," Ellysetta said. "And how did you manage to hide yourselves even from Fey eyes? That was what you did, wasn't it?"

Gaelen shrugged. "A little trick the *dahl'reisen* have learned over the years. Many Eld weave Spirit too, so we've had to learn to mask the signature of our magic even from those to whom the flows would normally be visible."

"A useful talent."

The corner of his mouth curved up. "Most useful," he agreed. "It's saved my life on at least half a dozen occasions."

Ellysetta immediately thought of the men who would be leaving the Fading Lands in the morning, the ones heading north to defend the borders against the Eld. "Is this something you could teach the other warriors—the ones who are leaving for Celieria?"

"I could teach the strongest Spirit masters among them, *aiyah*, if there were time," Gaelen said. "And if they were willing to learn from one who was once *dahl'reisen*."

"How much time would you need?"

"I taught vel Jelani in just a few bells, but he was very skilled to begin with." Bel looked surprised by the compliment, then quite pleased. "The others might require more practice."

"I doubt delaying their departure a day or two will do much harm on the borders, but it seems to me that having Fey warriors trained to hide their presence even from the eyes of a Mage could save many lives."

"There is still the matter of Fey pride," Gaelen reminded her. "I was *dahl'reisen*. Even though you restored my soul, my honor remains tainted. A *chatok* should be above reproach."

"Gaelen, you have knowledge and skills the Fey need. Kieran, Kiel, and Bel were willing to learn from you. Why should the rest of the Fey be any different?"

"They served as your quintet, *kem'falla*. Their loyalty was to you. But if you recall, even they would not accept instruction from me until you ordered them to do so."

Bel interrupted, his cobalt gazed fixed upon Ellysetta. "At the moment, I am more interested in knowing what you are doing wandering the halls of Chatok alone in the small bells of the night. Where is Rain?"

Ellie blushed. This was not the first time Bel had caught her sneaking out of her bedchamber at night. "I couldn't sleep." Despite her best effort, she couldn't keep the defensiveness out of her voice. "You know I've always liked to walk in the night when I'm restless. And you told me yourself it would be safe to do so in the Fading Lands."

"It's not the walking that concerns me this time, *kem'falla*. It's the destination."

She bit her lip. Rain wasn't the only one getting to know her too well. "You will not stop me. I have to do this."

"Ellysetta, did Rain not already forbid you to touch the *rasa*?"

"He warned me they would feel shame if they hurt me; but, Bel, you were *rasa*, and I healed you without a twinge of pain."

"The glamour that hid your abilities must also have buffered your empathic senses. And you had built hundreds of Spirit weaves on top of that, which provided further protection. But both that barrier and those Spirit weaves are gone now. You will feel the warriors' pain almost as strongly as you felt Gaelen's when you laid hands upon him. We cannot let you do this."

"You're assuming that without any proof that it's true."

"I was there the night you restored Gaelen's soul," he reminded her. "I saw what happened to you, and I remember the way you could hear everyone's thoughts and feel their emotions so strongly after Marissya unraveled your Spirit weaves."

She crossed her arms. "I'm going to do this, Bel. With or without your approval. I *need* to do this."

"You're asking me—us," he corrected with a quick glance at Gaelen, "to betray our bloodsworn oaths to protect you from all harm. Tell her, Gaelen. We cannot let her do this."

For a moment, Gaelen said nothing. He merely stood with catlike stillness and regarded her from pale, glowing eyes, his face expressionless. "She is the Feyreisa," he said at last. "And we are the warriors bound by *lute'asheiva* to serve and protect her in every way we can. We do not command her, vel Jelani. We are hers to command. If she says she must do this thing, then we must help her do it."

"Don't be a fool!" Bel exclaimed. "If she wanted to jump to her death, would you have us give her a shove? Simply touching them will hurt her! You know that."

Ellysetta caught his hand, and Bel went still. His dark brows were drawn tight, his cobalt eyes glowing like blue flames in the dark. "I'm a *shei'dalin*, Bel. Whether you like it or not, pain has become an inescapable part of my life. You can't protect me from that."

"Ellysetta—"

"Shh." She reached up to take his face in her hands. "You are my friend. I couldn't love you more if you were my own brother. But I need to do this. Don't you see? It hurts me more to feel their pain and do nothing. I know I can heal them. It's the one thing I know I can do."

"But—"

"*Teska.* Please."

His eyes closed in defeat, and he gave a reluctant nod. "*Doreh shabeila de.* If this is your choice, I will stand beside you."

"*Beylah vo,* Bel."

"You want to do what?" Tajik vel Sibboreh looked aghast. He speared Bel with a glance. "And you aid her? It is madness! Not even Marissya can touch the *rasa* without pain."

"She is not Marissya," Bel said. "The Feyreisa's abilities go so far beyond what we expect from a *shei'dalin*—even from one as powerful as Marissya—there is no comparison. And I aid her because I am her *lu'tan*, her bloodsworn champion, and she says she must do this."

"*Nei*, it is out of the question. Honor is all the *rasa* have left. You cannot take that from them." The general had changed back into his leathers and steel for night watch on the wall. His arms were crossed over his chest, his fingers close to the silk-wrapped hilts of his Fey'cha.

"Vel Sibboreh," Gaelen interrupted, "how long has it been since last a *shei'dalin* laid hands on you except to heal a mortal wound?"

Tajik's jaw went hard as a rock, his eyes flinty. "Far longer than for most of them. I nearly lost my soul in the Mage Wars when my sister was taken. I serve here because I am the last of my line, and the Massan does not want to lose yet another of the ancient bloodlines."

Ellysetta stepped forward. "Then let me offer my first blessing to you, so you may see for yourself that I can do this."

"What? *Nei!* I will not. Of course I will not! It's out of the question."

She regarded him steadily, with far more patience than she was feeling. "Ser vel Sibboreh . . . Tajik . . . if another *shei'dalin* were standing right here where I am, what would she be feeling?"

"A measure of what I feel myself. Pain, torment. Despair." Shame crossed his face. "Enough to make all but the strongest among them weep, despite my efforts to keep my emotions in check."

"And yet I am not weeping. I feel your sorrow and your pain, but by far the greater wound comes from sensing your hurt and not being allowed to heal it." She shook back the cuffs of her robes and reached out to him. "Give me your hands." She looked deep into his eyes, trying to infuse her gaze with a measure of the command Rain wielded so readily. *"Teska."*

"Trust your Feyreisa, vel Sibboreh," Gaelen murmured.

"Do as she asks, Tajik," Bel added.

With obvious reluctance, Tajik lifted his hands and held them out to her. He did not let his skin touch hers. He just held his hands, hovering, over hers until she reached up to grasp his fingers.

The instant her skin touched his, a wave of pain smashed into her. The force of it caught her by surprise and actually rocked her back on her heels. *Good sweet Lord of Light! How can he bear to live with such torment?* How had she managed to heal Bel the way she'd done without feeling even the slightest twinge of pain when she'd touched him?

A rumbling growl stirred at the edge of her consciousness.

Rain was waking. Quickly, she flung up a barrier to try to stifle the pain and keep it from flowing down the bond-threads linking them together. The last thing she wanted was for Rain to discover what she was doing. He would be furious.

"*Sieks'ta, sieks'ta.*" Horror stamped Tajik's face. "Release me, Feyreisa, I beg you." The Fey general tried to pull away, but Ellysetta kept her grip closed tight.

"Ellysetta, listen to him," Bel urged. "Let go before you hurt yourself."

"*Nei*, I'm all right. Please, just give me a moment."

A hand closed around her shoulder. Gaelen. *"Is it too much, kem'falla?"* He was a cool, steady anchor of strength.

She sucked in a deep breath. *"It's worse than I expected,"* she admitted. Her back teeth were ground tight together, and fine tremors shook her limbs. Merciful gods, touching Tajik hurt! *"I don't understand this."*

"I think Bel may have been more right than either of us knew. Take what you can from me and use it to shield yourself." Along with the offer came a rapid series of instructions woven on Spirit.

She latched onto the power Gaelen offered as if it were a lifeline. As her mind processed the instructions in his weave, her body was already instinctively following the commands, absorbing a portion of his strength into her own body and allowing a little of Tajik's pain to flow out along the same path.

Gaelen gave a quiet hiss, quickly stifled. *"Perhaps you should release him."*

Ignoring him, Ellysetta gritted her teeth and tried to shake off the worst of the pain. Why was she sensing it so strongly when she never had before? Was this what most Fey women felt when they touched the *rasa*? Gods save them, she hadn't understood. No wonder the warriors were so fiercely protective of them. And no wonder the *rasa* clung to the fringes of their society and tried to avoid contact with the women of their kind.

Her kind, now, she reminded herself. One thing that awful day in the cathedral had taught her for certain was that she was Fey, not Celierian.

And she would not—could not—participate in this abandonment of the brave men who had sacrificed their own happiness and the peace of their souls defending the Fading Lands.

"Ellysetta, let him go now," Bel insisted. *"If you don't, I will call Rain."*

Her eyes flashed. Her lips drew back in a snarl. "Tairen do not abandon their kin. Tairen defend the pride. Either help me or leave."

Bel's face went blank with shock. Beside him, Tajik's did too. *Good.* They both needed a shock to jolt them out of their blind acceptance of senseless customs. They were so certain the ways of the past could never change, they did not even want to try.

Ellysetta wasn't so ready to accept defeat. These people, these Fey, were hers now. Her people. Her family. Her pride. She would protect them. She would heal their pain.

"Take her other shoulder, Bel," Gaelen snapped. "She can use the *lute'asheiva* bond to draw upon our strength and wield it as her own."

Bel hurried to comply. *"Kem'falla,* has Gaelen shown you how to—" His voice broke off, then resumed in a slightly hoarse but rueful tone. "Ah . . . I see that he has."

The moment Bel touched Ellysetta, a fresh burst of renewing strength flooded into her. She responded with the ravenous, near-desperate consumption of a parched man finding an oasis in the middle of a desert, drinking in as much of the vibrant power as she could hold, then reaching out yet again, searching for more.

It came in a sudden rush, bright and blazing. And furious.

Tajik's face went white. Bel and Gaelen both went stiff as boards. Ellysetta didn't need to turn to know the source of that power was standing right behind her.

Rain.

CHAPTER SIX

Fierce as the sun, she made shadows take flight
The Star of Chakai, who spun souls back to Light.
From "The Star of Chakai," a warrior's song of
Ellysetta the Bright

The Fading Lands ~ Chatok

"*Teska*, Feyreisa, release me. I beg you." Tajik once again began frantically trying to pull free of Ellysetta's grip, his efforts hampered by his unwillingness to use force against her. "Rain, *kem'Feyreisen, sieks'ta*. Forgive me. I should have refused. The blame is mine entirely."

Rain eyed the group grimly. "I know exactly where the blame lies." Bel wouldn't meet his eyes, and even Gaelen looked shamefaced—which had to be a first for the arrogant former *dahl'reisen*. "*Nei*, don't release her, you idiots," he snapped when the guilty pair started to step away. "It's much too late for that. Flames scorch it, Ellysetta! You simply could not listen, could you?"

"Rain—"

"Be silent." He was furious with her for sneaking out of their bed to do this—and furious with himself for not realizing she would. If nothing else, the last few weeks should have taught him his sweet, gentle *shei'tani* had a will of steel—and a head hard as a rock! When she set her mind on a thing, she would no more be diverted from her aim than a starving tairen from its prey.

His hands clamped her waist. "Finish it," he snarled. "Now, before I lose what little control I have left and rip their throats out for laying hands on you."

His knees went weak as Ellysetta drew so much energy from him, so quickly, she left him dizzy.

Connected to her, his hands upon her, he felt the flows of magic spin together with extraordinary speed as vibrant, glowing threads formed a weave so bright he could not see its pattern. The magic poured out of her, and Tajik went stiff, his eyes widening with shock as the swirling cloud of brightness enveloped him in a sparkling haze, then sank into his skin.

Eld ~ Boura Fell

"Shan!" Elfeya gasped her truemate's name.

He was slow to answer, his mental voice thready and weak. The High Mage had not let her go to him yet. *"I feel it, beloved."*

The High Mage's darkest magic had forged a connection between Shan and Ellysetta, and through her *shei'tanitsa* bond with Shan, Elfeya shared the connection too. They had used it over the years, doing what they could to help reinforce the barriers they'd placed around their daughter's magic, sending subtle thoughts and weaves that urged her to keep hidden from the High Mage.

Now that power flared anew, and both of them felt a draining tug, as if some portion of their own magic, so long locked away from useful summoning, were being siphoned off.

Just as suddenly the draw stopped and their power surged back to them in a wave. With it, like a subtle fragrance wafting through an open window, came the scent of a dear and familiar magic. One Elfeya recognized and had never thought to sense again.

A name breathed from her lungs on a sigh, sorrowful and wondrous all at once. "Tajik."

The Fading Lands ~ Chakai

"Tairen's scorching fire," Tajik breathed. When Ellysetta released him, he was trembling from head to toe. "Blessed gods. I knew it must be true—the *dahl'reisen* is proof—but still I did not truly believe." He lifted shaking hands, staring at the palms as if searching for some now-absent mark of shame. "The shadows on my soul are gone. My heart weeps again." Tears shimmered in his eyes and spilled down his cheeks. He did not even bother to brush them aside. "How is this possible?"

"I told you," Bel said, "there is no other like her in all the world."

Rain gave a warning growl. Bel and Gaelen both snatched their hands away from Ellysetta, and he drew her firmly back against him. *"You need a good shaking,"* he snapped on their private thread.

"Because I can't sit here like the rest of you and do nothing while these brave Fey suffer?" She twisted around to glare up at him, her jaw set and thrust out in the mulish lines he'd come to know and dread. *"I tried to stay away, as you asked me to, but I couldn't. I'm just not made that way, Rain. Their pain beat at me until I couldn't stand it any longer."* Her expression softened and her hands rose to cradle his face. She stood up on her toes to press her lips to his. *"Forgive me?"*

He should have stepped away, lest she think him so easy to control, but he could not deny himself the pleasure of her kiss. When their lips met, his arms locked tight around her, dragging her close against him. He filled his lungs with the sweet intoxication of her fragrance, and his mouth with the equal enchantment of her kiss.

Who was he deluding? She *could* control him. One crook of a slender finger or a flutter of those dark red lashes, and he became clay in her hands. He could attempt to stand firm, to protect her even from her own self, but in the end there was nothing he would deny her if she wanted it badly enough. And both of them knew it.

When she released him, his eyes were glowing again, but this time not with anger. *"Bas'ka. You've done your good deed, Feyreisa; now come back to bed with your mate, where you belong."* He purred the words, accompanying them with the vibrant sparks of near-visible sound that were tairen song, and watched with satisfaction as her eyelids fluttered closed. He might not be able to control her, but she was no more immune to him than he to her, thank the gods. *"Come with me,"* he urged again, filling his tones with seduction and sweet promise.

She began to sway towards him until Tajik coughed and broke the spell. Rain could have leapt upon the Fey and rent him in two for the interruption.

Ellysetta's eyes opened. The haze of desire clouding her gaze changed swiftly to a blush of self-consciousness when she realized Bel, Gaelen, and Tajik were still there, watching. The self-consciousness became a narrow-eyed look of suspicion that settled on Rain, who had never been any good at looking innocent. Too much tairen in him for that.

"Come," he said again. "It's late and we have a long way to travel tomorrow. You should get what sleep you can."

"But, Rain, I'm not done yet. I still need to do what I can for the other *rasa*."

His spine went stiff. "*Nei*. Absolutely not."

"But—"

"*Nei!*" He clutched her shoulders in a tight grip and gave her a little shake. "Do you think I did not feel what just happened to you? Do you think I will let you go through that again?"

"It hurts me more to do nothing."

"And when I kill a Fey because his hand upon you drives me mad, what will you feel then?"

"I have more faith in you than that."

"Perhaps you should not."

"Rain, please. If I can help even a little, I must at least try." *"And you must allow it."*

He glared at her. "Do you think you are the only woman of the Fey ever to feel this need? A warrior's lot is to suffer. A *shei'dalin's* is to bear it. And as your *shei'tan*, my duty is to help you bear it and to stop you from doing anything foolish"—he turned his glare upon Gaelen and Bel—"which should also be your *lu'tans'* duty, though plainly they have both forgotten it."

The pair had the grace to look shamefaced.

"Rain, no other *shei'dalin* can take away the pain like I do." She turned to Tajik. "Tajik—do you still suffer?"

"*Nei.*" His voice was hoarse, his eyes filled with wonder. "My soul is bright as a child's."

She turned back to Rain. "There, you see? How can you demand that any Fey live with such pain when you know I have the power to stop it?"

"When it hurts you to use that power? Very easily."

She ground her teeth in frustration. He was so stubborn. "I can do what no other *shei'dalin* can. I don't know how or why any more than you do, but this is the gift I was given. Surely the gods meant me to use it."

"She has a point," Gaelen murmured.

Rain shot him a hot look. The last thing he needed was Gaelen encouraging this madness. "She does not have a point. The gods gave you Azrahn, too, but that doesn't mean you should spin it. Some gifts were not meant to be used. Some gifts are too dangerous."

"All gifts come with a price, Feyreisen," Gaelen shot back.

"And sometimes the price is so high it should never be paid," he snapped. "*Nei.* I will not allow it."

"Rain, these men may soon be leaving the Fading Lands to defend Celieria—the people I begged you to defend.

They could die fulfilling the vow I urged you to make. You must let me give them what comfort I can before they go. The pain I feel when healing them is momentary. It ends as soon as their souls are restored. But if I don't do this and they die, their pain will never leave me." She grasped his arms. *"Would you have me bear the same sorrow and regret you shared with me at the Lake of Glass?"*

No matter how much Rain wanted to deny it, he knew the *shei'dalin* in Ellysetta had risen as strongly as the tairen. To sense the pain of the *rasa* and do nothing to assuage it was hurting her. It had tormented her dreams, woken her from sleep, and driven her here, prepared to endure whatever pain she must to stop their suffering.

And she'd come alone, without him, because she'd not trusted him to let her do what she felt she must.

"Kem'jeto." My brother. Bel's voice whispered on the private weave forged between them centuries ago. *"I think perhaps Gaelen and Ellysetta are right."*

"You too, Bel?" It stung to hear Bel, the most honorable Fey Rain knew, whose opinion he trusted in all things, agreeing with this madness. *"How can you suggest such a thing?"*

"Our numbers are too few. If our most experienced fighters lose their souls in the first battles, too few will be left to protect the Feyreisa and the Fading Lands." Bel's cobalt eyes were steady, filled with a mix of bleak sorrow and grim acceptance. *"She is here, in our time of deepest need, wielding a power no shei'dalin before her ever has. I do not claim to know the minds of the gods, but the pattern in this weave seems clear."*

Rain spun on his heel and put several long steps between them. The *shei'tan* in him was torn between protecting his beloved from the pain it would cause her to save the *rasa* and the pain it would cause her if she did not.

The Tairen Soul in him cast the deciding vote.

Though he wanted desperately to deny it, he knew Bel was right. The Fading Lands would need every warrior

who yet lived—most likely even the mates and truemates—
to defeat the Eld when open war broke out, but the souls
of these *rasa* were already so damaged, they would die or
fall to darkness after the first or second battle. The Defender
of the Fey could not afford to lose the oldest and most experienced Fey warriors—and, in truth, neither could Ellysetta's truemate.

Because all talk of gifts and the gods' intent aside, one
hard, simple truth could not be denied, and that one truth
canceled out every other concern.

If the Eld came and the Fey were not strong enough to
defeat them, a torment far worse than sharing a *rasa*'s pain
would befall Ellysetta.

Rain spun back around to face his truemate and her two
lu'tans. A muscle ticked in his clenched jaw. Just because
he'd made the decision didn't mean he had to like it. "Very
well, *shei'tani*," he bit out. "As you insist upon this, let us see
it done." He put a hand out.

"Wait," Tajik said. "If the Feyreisa is going to do this, I
would add my own strength to all of yours to help her." He
withdrew a black Fey'cha from his chest straps and dropped
to one knee. "Of my own free will, Ellysetta Feyreisa, I
pledge my life and my soul to your protection. None shall
harm you while in life or death I have power to prevent it."
He drew his dagger across his palm and let six drops of the
welling blood fall upon the blade. "This I do swear with my
own life's blood, in Fire and Air and Earth and Water, in
Spirit and in Azrahn, the magic never to be called. I do ask
that this pledge be witnessed."

"You are the last of your line, vel Sibboreh," Rain said.
"Will you not keep your bond for your own truemate?"

"If the gods judge me worthy of a *shei'tani*, they will ensure I meet her in my next life. For now, *lute'asheiva* is my
right, and I claim it."

"Then I will not deny you, my brother." Rain nodded.
"Your bond is witnessed."

"Witnessed," Gaelen and Bel echoed.

The blade flashed bright in vel Sibboreh's grip. He passed a hand, glowing with green Earth, over the naked blade. When he was done, the sharp glint of steel had been covered by a decorative golden sheath shaped like a sword of flame. Tajik handed the sheathed blade to Ellysetta. "Your *shei'tan* will always be your first protector, *kem'falla*, but know that I am another. Through this life and its death until I come to the world again, I am yours." He bowed low. *"Miora felah, ti'Feyreisa."*

Ellysetta stared at the sheathed blade in her hand, the third such bloodsworn blade now in her possession, then frowned at the Fey who'd given it to her. "What did Rain mean just now when he asked you about keeping your bond for your own truemate?" She turned to her mate. "Rain?"

Halfway hoping the knowledge would make her change her mind about blessing the *rasa*, Rain spread his hands and gave her the blunt truth. "*Shei'tanitsa* bond cannot form where any other holds sway. Tajik, Bel, and Gaelen have bloodsworn their souls to your service. That vow is binding in this life and the death that follows, which means there can be no *shei' tanitsa* bond for them until they are born again. A truemate's heart cannot be divided."

She swallowed and turned horrified eyes towards Bel, Gaelen, and Tajik. "You knew this, yet still you bloodswore yourselves to me? Why would you do such a thing?"

"Ellysetta, *kem'falla*, this is no burden," Bel said. "You restored our souls. Of course we pledged them to your service."

"But to give up any chance of a truemate of your own . . ."

"In this life only, *kem'falla*," Gaelen said. "We will be born to live again. Until then, we are free to accept love if we find it. The bonds of *e'tanitsa* are no less worthy and no less welcome to a Fey's heart, and for a warrior who has lived centuries unable to touch a *fellana* without causing her pain, even *e'tanitsa* love is a blessing beyond measure."

"But—"

"All great gifts come with a price, *kem'falla*," Gaelen said. "All choices come with consequence. And all Fey accept that."

"All men of honor, at least," Tajik said, giving Gaelen a pointed look. Gaelen's eyes narrowed.

Ignoring him, the Fey general cast out a hand towards the silvery white walls of Chakai on the other side of Taloth'Liera. "The *rasa* sleep there, *kem'Feyreisa*. If you still wish to bless them, I would ask you to begin with a particular two."

"I . . ." Ellysetta hesitated. She had never considered what cost her actions would have on the men she blessed. She'd thought only to stop their pain. And, all right, yes, some vain part of her liked seeing the wonder and joy on the warriors' faces when they realized the torment of all the lives they'd taken was gone. But how could she offer such healing now, knowing what price they would feel compelled to pay?

"I don't want to rob them of their hope for a truemate. It's bad enough I did that to you three without knowing it."

"Do not berate yourself for healing our souls, Ellysetta," Bel said. "The Fey number a mere forty thousand. If there were truemates to be had for us, we already would have found them."

"Yet Rain found me, and Adrial found Talisa," she pointed out. Though the ill-fated trumating of Air master Adrial vel Arquinas to Great Lord Cannevar Barrial's married daughter could only end badly—King Dorian had upheld the marriage rights of Talisa's husband, so Adrial could not claim her—Talisa Barrial diSebourne's mortal-born soul had nonetheless called a Fey's. "There could be more truemates in Celieria just waiting for their Fey to find them."

"The odds are unlikely, Ellysetta," Bel said gently. "How

many other Celierian women descend from both Fey and Elvish blood, as she does? *Nei*, the *rasa* have already lost all but the smallest flicker of hope. Most of them will perish before their next battle's end—they are that close to shadow."

Rain shifted restlessly, and a low growl rumbled in his throat. "Which will in no way reflect on Ellysetta," he said, giving Bel a hard look. "The *rasa* live and die by the gods' decree, as they always have." He gripped Ellysetta's shoulders. "*Shei'tani*, if you are having doubts, then do not do this. The Eye of Truth said your purpose was to save the tairen; it said nothing about restoring light to the *rasa*. If the pain of their presence disturbs you too much, we can leave for Fey'Bahren now, without delay."

She looked up at him, her eyes wide and troubled. "Is Bel right? Will those men die if I don't heal them?"

Right at that moment, Rain could cheerfully have put his hands around his best friend's throat and squeezed until his eyes popped. *"Bel, my brother, what flaming maggot in your brain possessed you to tell her that?"*

"I should have let her think she's stolen our hope instead?" Outrage colored Bel's voice. *"What she can do is a miracle sent from the gods. I won't let her berate herself for it. Besides, you know as well as I do how many of the rasa cling to honor by the merest thread."*

"You are supposed to protect her from pain, not encourage her to embrace it!"

"And which do you think will be worse? The pain of knowing the rasa will have no truemates in this life, or the pain of knowing they chose sheisan'dahlein or slipped down the Dark Path when she could have healed them and did not?"

"Rain?" Ellysetta shook herself free of his grip and frowned up at him. "Answer me. Will the *rasa* die in the next battle if I don't heal them?"

His lips drew back, baring clenched teeth. He wished he could lie. He would lie to her now, if he could. But he was

Fey, and Fey did not lie. "They live here, far from other Fey, because the shadow lies so dark upon them. If war comes, they will not survive it. At least not as Fey."

The admission hit her like a blow. She flinched and her face went pale. Then she caught herself, and Rain saw the reaction he'd been dreading. Her slender spine went stiff and straight. Her shoulders squared. Her jaw clenched, then lifted with a determined tilt. The small, now-familiar gestures made him want to shred things, starting with Bel and Gaelen.

Ellysetta Feyreisa had made her choice.

"Take me to the *rasa*."

When Rain held out his wrist so she could put her hand upon it, she looked startled.

"You don't need to come with us, Rain. You've already said it will be too difficult for you."

Only then did he realize how little she understood. "I am your *shei'tan*, Ellysetta. What choices you make, you make for both of us."

The *rasa*, when they heard the reason Ellysetta had come, were horrified. Like Tajik, they refused to let her touch them at first, unwilling to inflict their pain upon her, until Tajik rounded up two grim-eyed Fey and hauled them to the front of the warriors' barracks to stand before Ellysetta. They were the oldest of the *rasa*, warriors the same age as Bel and Tajik, and they well remembered the destruction of the Mage Wars.

"The Mages have returned," Tajik told them, "and war will soon be upon us. The Fading Lands will need all her sons. The Feyreisa can heal your soul so you may live and fight like a Fey whose steel has yet to taste its first enemy's blood." On the Warriors' Path, he added, *"I know it is hard, but accept this gift, my brothers, so we may live and fight together as once we did."* With grim ferocity, he added, *" I need you with me, beyond the first battle, to drench the earth in Mage blood and avenge the deaths of those we loved."*

"Mages? You are certain?" The question came from Gillan-daris vel Jendahr, a white-blond, black-eyed Fey who was a scorching artist of death with his blades. He'd lost both parents, two brothers, and a beloved *shei'dalin* niece to the El-den Mages. Not even a thousand years had been enough to dull the pain of so great a wound.

"Bel swears it. Three of them attacked the Feyreisa last week."

Gil's jaw clenched, and power sparked like stars in his midnight eyes. He dropped to one knee before the Feyreisa and offered her his hands. "May it please the gods, Feyreisa, I accept your offer of healing, that I may defend the Fading Lands and avenge the deaths of those I loved."

"What is your name?" Ellysetta asked.

He tossed back his head, sending white-blond hair rip-pling across his black leathers. "I am Gillandaris vel Jen-dahr, Master of Air and Earth and Fire, fourth-level talent in Water and Spirit, friend and blade brother of Tajik vel Sibboreh, and former *chadin* of the great Shannisorran v'En Celay." He sent a cool glance in Gaelen's direction.

"If I restore your soul, Ser vel Jendahr, will you promise not to bloodswear yourself to me in payment? Will you ac-cept my gift as just that—a gift, freely given?"

Gil's brows drew together. *"Lute'asheiva* is a warrior's right, not a gift for a *shei'dalin* to allow or deny, no matter her reasons." Gil had never been a Fey to softpaw around anyone or any subject. He was all warrior, steel strong, blade sharp, fierce in his beliefs and his willingness to de-fend them. *"Nei,* I make no such vow."

The Feyreisa's spine stiffened, and for a moment, Tajik thought she might refuse to share her gift. But then her eyes flashed and she reached out to seize Gil's hands in a tight grip. Gil's mouth opened in a soundless gasp. Light blazed around the Feyreisa, enveloping them both. Bel, Gaelen, and Rain all swore and stepped forward to lend her their strength, but before they could get close enough, Gil gave a hoarse cry. The light flared with sudden brightness, then winked out.

Gil was shaking, and the Feyreisa looked shocked and unhappy.

"What . . . ? Is that it?" Tajik frowned. Had she chosen not to heal Gil's soul after all? "Feyreisa, he is a good man. An honorable warrior, one whose death would be a loss to us all. *Teska*, heal him that he may defend the Fading Lands for another thousand years to come."

A voice, hoarse and disbelieving, said quietly, "She did." Without taking his stunned eyes from hers, Gil reached for his Fey'cha, pulled black from its protective sheath, and slit his palm on the trembling blade. The words of *lute'asheiva* spilled from his lips in a torrent. Rain, Tajik, Bel, and Gaelen called witness, and with grim acceptance, the Feyreisa took the bloodsworn blade from Gil's hand.

"I do not want this," she said.

"It is yours all the same, *kem'falla*."

"I was angry, and I was not kind." She looked up from the blade and met his eyes, dark misery in her own. "I hurt you. *Sieks'ta*. I should have used more care."

Gil rose to his feet, his white-blond head towering over hers by two handspans. "A buzzfly sting, *kem'falla*. Gone almost before I felt it." The corner of his mouth kicked up. "I suppose I deserved it for defying you. I should have remembered tairen do not take insolence kindly."

"*Aiyah*, you should have," the Tairen Soul agreed, his voice a low rumble of sound. He laid a hand on the Feyreisa's shoulder, and when she turned to look up at him, his face bore an expression of such fierce devotion, Tajik felt his own chest grow tight. Once he had dreamed of finding a woman in whose eyes he would see the Great Sun rise and set, a woman whose soul would call to his. He no longer hoped for that in this life, but now, he did dare once more to pray for such a miracle in his next.

Rain sent flows of tairen song to Ellysetta, the melody vibrant with reassurance and pride as it rippled along the threads of their bond. *"You restored Gil's soul, shei'tani. I can see you are troubled, but there is no need. Look at him. He is unharmed."*

"Is he?" She looked up, her eyes filled with worry. *"I'm not so sure. I'm not sure I'm all right, for that matter."*

"What do you mean?"

"I mean it didn't feel right, what I just did to Gil. I was angry, Rain." She bit her lip. *"He defied me and I didn't like it. I think some part of me actually meant to hurt him."*

She shifted in Rain's embrace, as if she intended to pull away, but he would not release her. *"Las, Ellysetta. Does he look hurt? Nei, because he is not. He challenged your authority. You showed him your claws. It is the tairen way."*

"Nei, it's more than that. The weave felt wrong. Like a sweetness gone sour. It reminded me of when the High Mage set his Mark upon me."

"You are imagining things." He scowled at her, not liking the implication that any part of her magic was similar to the black arts practiced by the High Mage.

"Am I? Rain, you know part of him is in me, and you know night is the time when I feel it most. What if he's using the Marks he put on me to . . . change me?" More than anything, she feared the evil High Mage would use those Mage Marks to corrupt her soul and destroy the Fey. *"What if the power I just used on Gil came from him . . . the Mage?"*

"Ellysetta, look around you. You're surrounded by the oldest, most experienced warriors of the Fey. If anything in your weave was like Eld magic, these warriors would have felt it." He reached out to brush a tumbling lock of hair from her face. *"You didn't hurt Gil; you restored his soul. Don't misunderstand. I'm not happy that you've chosen to heal the rasa—and I'm certainly not encouraging you to continue—but I won't let you see Mages every time the tairen shows its fangs."*

She drew a breath, and he could see her almost visibly pulling a veil of calm around her emotions. *"Bas'ka,"* she said. *"Perhaps you're right."*

He smiled and bent to kiss the worry from her face. His song sang notes of confidence and reassurance until the tension in her shoulders melted and she wrapped her arms around his neck and kissed him back.

Behind them, Tajik cleared his throat. "*Kem'falla*, may it please you, this next fine warrior of the Fey is Rijonn vel Ahrimor, my oldest and dearest friend. He and I were cradle friends, and *chadins* together in Tehlas. He is one of the strongest Earth masters ever born to the Fey."

"Ser Ahrimor." The warrior standing beside Tajik was the tallest and most heavily muscled Fey Ellysetta had ever seen. His eyes and hair were brown as the fertile earth of the Garreval, and there was a deep, stoic strength about him, as if mountains would fall before he did. She liked him instinctively and immensely. Ellysetta held out her hands. "Will you allow me to heal your soul?"

The Earth master gave a nod and offered his enormous hands, not putting them in hers but leaving her to make the final choice.

The only sound he made was a soft gasp when she laid her hands upon him. Whatever wrongness Ellysetta had sensed when she'd healed Gil, it did not recur, nor did touching Rijonn wound her any worse than laying hands upon Gil had done. When she was finished, he sank to his knees and spoke the *lute'asheiva* oath in a low, gravelly voice.

From pallet to pallet, barracks hall to barracks hall, she walked the silvery white corridors of Chakai, seeking out the *rasa* and offering the gift of peace for their battered souls.

Many of the warriors she approached refused her offer. Some were unwilling to inflict their pain upon her. Others refused to touch another Fey's unbonded mate. A grim-faced few declared it dishonorable to escape the suffering the gods had seen fit to lay upon them.

But for each Fey who turned away her gift, there were two or three others who did not.

Lured by the promise of confronting the Mages of Eld in battle once more—and seeing the growing number of dazzle-eyed *lu'tans* standing at Ellysetta's side—warrior after warrior stepped forward and offered his soul up for healing. Warrior after warrior wept as the peace he'd lost to war showered down upon him again. One after another, those who had been *rasa* sank to their knees and swore the bonds of *lute'asheiva* to their new queen.

Chimes became bells. The ranks of the *rasa* shrank by the score. Word of what was happening traveled across the mile-long Warriors' Wall to Chatok. The warriors guarding the silvery blue ramparts heard of it. The *shei'dalins* sleeping in their chambers woke to shocked whispers: "*Come quickly. The Feyreisa . . . she is healing the rasa!*"

Chatok emptied. Its inhabitants made their way across the wall to the white towers of Chakai to witness the miracle.

Marissya found Ellysetta in Chakai's main hall, healing the *rasa* who had laid pallets upon the floor there. Her eyes were afire, her body enveloped in a shimmering aura of golden white light. Behind Ellysetta, his own eyes blazing with restrained fury, Rain bored crumbling holes into stone with his bare fingers as he allowed Fey after Fey to lay hands upon his mate.

All the *lu'tans* were feeding Ellysetta their power now. As each newly healed Fey fell to his knees and bloodswore himself to her, she seized his strength and added it to her shining web. The glow of magic surrounded them all, bright and golden white.

Marissya stared in horror at the Fey warriors who should have been protecting Ellysetta—the same warriors who were instead crooning encouragement. "Gaelen! Bel! What are you doing? Have you lost all sense? How can you allow this madness?"

"She said the pain is manageable," Gaelen said.

"She *said*?" Her voice rose. Her hands clenched into fists.

"Gods save me from fools and men! One may have been manageable—she's so strong, even the first dozen or so might be bearable—but how many *rasa* has she healed? Do you not understand that theirs is the sort of pain that *accumulates*?"

Marissya bit her tongue to stop from launching into a furious tirade. Even though her brother and Bel should have known better—much better!—they could not feel Ellysetta's emotions. They did not know what this was truly costing her. Marissya and the five *shei'dalins* standing in stunned silence beside her did.

And so did Rain.

A familiar burst of wild power flared around him. No matter what Ellysetta may have claimed at the outset, the torment of healing so many *rasa* souls had left her empathic *shei'dalin* senses raw and throbbing, as if a gaping wound had been ripped through her chest straight to her heart. The wild fury of Rain's tairen was rousing in response to his mate's pain.

And an equally fierce anger was writhing and hissing inside of Ellysetta. The glow around her flared with sudden brightness.

The warrior in Ellysetta's grip gave a sharp cry and fell to his knees, shaking like a leaf as his hands reached for the leather straps holding his black Fey'cha. Even as he swore his *lute'asheiva* bond, she was reaching for the next Fey standing behind him.

"Sisters," Marissya commanded the other *shei'dalins*, "give me your strength." The five Fey women offered her their power without question. Neither Marissya nor the other *shei'dalins* could heal the warriors as Ellysetta was doing, but they could add their strength to hers and weave away at least some of her pain so she could continue.

Marissya wove the *shei'dalins'* power into multi-ply threads of healing and laid her hands on Ellysetta's shoulders. Sparks snapped and popped when their bodies made contact, and Ellysetta's head whipped around, eyes narrowed in threat.

"*Las*, Ellysetta," Marissya soothed. "Take what we can give. Use our weaves. Spin our strength into your own." Weaves of peace and healing flowed from her hands, ropes of Earth and Fire and Spirit, all gleaming with the warm golden glow of *shei'dalin* love. "Long have we all wished these Fey more joy than we could grant. Whatever power we have is yours to use. Heal our brothers. Make them whole once more."

Ellysetta's blazing eyes examined Marissya's weaves. Without a word, she turned back to the Fey in her grip, and Marissya's mouth opened on a gasp as Ellysetta seized the threads of *shei'dalin* power and thrust them deep into the blinding brightness of her own pattern.

"Light save me," she whispered.

"*Shei'tani?*" Dax clutched her arm.

"I'm all right. *shei'tan*. Just surprised. She is buffering me, but her pain is terrible." Quickly, Marissya spun peace and absence of pain upon Ellysetta, then swallowed and shook her head. "I can feel the pattern of her weave. It's not so different from weaving peace, except for the love. . . . Light save me, I've never felt a *shei'dalin*'s love so strongly."

That was the strength of Ellysetta's weave. Bright, unyielding, indefatigable love. Love that did not know surrender. Love that did not understand limitations or even basic self-preservation. Love that would batter itself to death before giving in to defeat.

"Dax," she said, "gather a group of Fey. Have them go room to room through the rest of Chakai. Bring any other *rasa* who wish for healing here. Hurry. Those of you who have refused her gift, get out. Now!" she barked at several of the warriors who stood off to one side, arms crossed, eyes grim and filled with suspicion. The men looked startled at Marissya's vehemence, but they'd been too long conditioned to respect her command to do anything but obey. Wordless, casting final glances over their shoulders, they departed.

"She must stop," Rain growled.

Marissya knew how hard he was fighting to keep his tairen in check. "*Nei*, Rain. *Sieks'ta*, I know how hard this is for you, but she must finish. She has put too much of herself into the weave, holding nothing back. I fear what will happen if you make her stop before she is finished." She muttered a curse. "I spent all those days trying to teach her how to weave her magic with restraint, when what I should have been teaching her was how to restrain herself instead of her magic."

Shei'dalins anchored themselves before they touched the *rasa*. Always. The pain of so much death, so many sorrows crying out for healing was overwhelming. Even the strongest *shei'dalin* risked losing herself in the torment of the one she was healing if she did not keep a portion of her soul, of her oneness, carefully blocked off, preferably tied to some other person such as a mate or another *shei'dalin*.

Ellysetta was holding none of herself in reserve. Though that impenetrable barrier still guarded her mind from *shei'dalin* intrusion, the floodgates of her empathic power were wide-open, and the shining brightness of Ellysetta's soul was pouring out upon the *rasa* like searing beams of the Great Sun's light. Even before one warrior was healed, her power was already reaching for another, drawn by the need to end the pain she felt so acutely.

All *shei'dalins*—all strong empaths, for that matter—felt a similar driving need to heal and bring peace to tormented souls. The only difference was that Ellysetta was somehow able to withstand the pain.

Not because she didn't sense it, though. Instead, it was as if she absorbed the *rasa*'s pain and transformed at least some part of it into the healing light she poured back into them.

A dull throb gathered at Marissya's temples as warriors began streaming into the hall. The *rasa* did not broadcast their despair like the *dahl'reisen*, but even well-shielded *shei'dalins* felt the echoes when a dozen or more *rasa* gathered together. That was why they lived here, by the Garreval, isolated from the women of their kind.

Gritting her teeth, Marissya spun Spirit tinged with the barest hint of compulsion. *"Ellysetta, listen to me. You cannot continue to heal each warrior individually. You will lose yourself long before you are finished."*

"Nei." Ellysetta frowned and shook her head, but gave no other sign that she realized Marissya was "pushing." Still, that frown was enough to make Marissya back off. She'd felt the hard edge of Ellysetta's power earlier today, and she wasn't eager to confront it again.

"*Las*, little sister. I can feel your need to bring them peace. But you don't need to restore each warrior's soul to complete innocence. When all the *rasa* are gathered here, the other *shei'dalins* and I will help you spread your weave over all of them at once. It may not heal them as completely as you are doing now, but it should pull them back from the shadows of the Dark Path. Later, if you must heal them fully, you can do so without putting your mate at such risk."

Ellysetta's head reared up. Her blinding gaze shot towards Rain. "*Shei'tan*, I wound you?" The fingers clamped around the current warrior's wrists flew open, and the Fey fell to his knees, shuddering as his hands fumbled for his Fey'cha belts.

Her grief and guilt swamped Marissya's senses. It was clear she had not realized what she was doing to Rain. She'd been so intently focused on the *rasa*, she'd blocked out everything else. Even Rain's torment.

"Just finish it, Ellysetta," Rain bit out. "Either stop or heal them all. But whatever you do, do it quickly."

Ellysetta pinned Marissya with a blinding gaze. The bright power in those eyes hit like a blow, soul-deep and searing. "How can you help me?"

"Allow me and the other *shei'dalins* to join your weave. Let us anchor you and help direct and disperse the threads of your magic to heal all the *rasa*, rather than just one."

Already the drowning pain of the next *rasa* had Ellysetta in its grip, dragging her thoughts, her concentration, away from Marissya. Her magic surged in powerful response, sending brilliant threads spinning around her. Ellysetta seized the warrior's hands as the searing fury of her magic poured out upon him. Like his many brothers before, he cried out and fell to his knees, trembling from head to toe and reaching with a shaking hand for one of the black Fey'cha strapped to his chest.

As he wept and uttered the vows of *lute'asheiva* bonding, Ellysetta turned to Marissya. "*Bas'ka.* Do it." She pinned the other *shei'dalins* with a blazing green gaze. "And do not dare to trespass. The tairen will not treat you kindly."

Not one of the *shei'dalins* pierced by that whirling glare doubted the Feyreisa's threat was real.

CHAPTER SEVEN

Swiftly, under Marissya's direction, the *shei'dalins* spun the threads of their own magic into Ellysetta's weave. The instant the threads combined, Ellysetta's power shot out like bolts of golden white lightning, tracing the glowing lines of magic back to the women who'd spun them. Light flashed as the *shei'dalins'* natural Fey luminescence suddenly blazed sun-bright. Their light filled the entire room, intensifying until the gathered warriors lifted their hands to shield their eyes.

Marissya gasped as she and the other *shei'dalins* fell to their knees. Ellysetta wasn't weaving *with* them. She was draining them. Absorbing their power and commanding their flows as if they were her own, just as she'd done with the *lu'tans*. Only there was no *lute'asheiva* bond between the *shei'dalins* and Ellysetta. She should not have been able to command their magic.

Yet commanding them she was.

Marissya could feel her own will falling away. The deep, strong well of her power rose in response to Ellysetta's summons, pouring into Ellysetta as quickly as it came. Marissya began to tremble. So much power . . . so unbearably bright. How could Ellysetta hold so much?

Beside her, two of the other *shei'dalins* began to sway, and their Fey brightness dimmed.

"Ellysetta . . . little sister . . . *teska* . . . you must stop. Spin the weave. Spin it now." With the last ounce of her control, Marissya wove the command in Spirit and buried it in the river of magic pouring unchecked from her body into Ellysetta's.

Later, she would not be sure whether her command worked or Ellysetta's wilding magic had simply gathered as much power as it could, but all at once, the ravenous consumption ceased. Ellysetta's weave shot out in great streams of burning filaments, spinning into a brilliant net of gold power. It enveloped the gathered Fey, swirling above and around them. Then, with a final flare of light, the magic sank into the warriors' flesh. Their bodies flashed golden bright, then dimmed to the natural silvery luminescence of their kind.

Ellysetta's power went out. Marissya and the *shei'dalins*

staggered to their feet, reaching blindly for the brace of stone walls to keep from falling.

The warriors in the hall locked shocked gazes on Ellysetta. One by one, then in increasing numbers, they fell to their knees, reaching for their Fey'cha.

"*Nei.* No more." Ellysetta backed away, her hands flung up. "*Parei.* I won't accept another bond." She turned, hands extended in a pleading gesture. "Rain, *shei'tan*, get me out of here." He was standing by the wall behind her, the stones around him a crumbled ruin, his eyes blazing purple suns in a face carved by a grim blade. *"I can feel the unhealed rasa already pulling at me again. Quickly, take me away from here to someplace I cannot feel their pain. If we stay, I don't think I will be able to stop myself from healing them, even if they refuse me."*

He surged away from the wall in a rush, power crackling around him in a swirl of multicolored sparks. Without a word, he caught her up in his arms under her knees, and an enormous thrust of Air sent them spiraling into the night sky.

They flew south until the lights of Chatok and Chakai were far behind them and the tug of the *rasa* had faded enough that Ellysetta could breathe again.

That small peace did not extend to Rain. His wings beat the sky in furious sweeps. Jets of flame shot into the air before them, sending clouds of heat and magic bursting across the shields Rain barely remembered to fling up around her.

The enraged snarl of his tairen screamed along their bondthreads, half-wild with fury over the Fey males who had laid hands upon its mate. *She is ours. Ours! Scorch the Fey-kin. Burn away their scent upon her!* The tairen's rage whipped at her, making her own tairen roar and dig its claws deep.

Abruptly, Rain put on a powerful burst of magic. A blazing cone of Fire and Air took shape around them, and they shot forward with such force, Ellysetta fell back against the high back of her saddle. Magic poured from Rain in rivers, condensing into great, powerful jets that propelled them across the sky faster than they'd ever flown before. The ground below them flashed by in a blur. Rain's tairen fell silent, the full force of its raging energy now diverted to keeping its wings held steady and tucked close to its body in a backswept vee as they shot through the sky.

Only then, without the scream of his tairen rousing her own, did Ellysetta realize the magnitude of the harm she'd done with her stubborn, selfish determination to heal the *rasa*. The barriers of Rain's control were stretched so thin, they were all but shredding. He'd kept his torment from her during the healing—or perhaps she simply had refused to see—but now she could not blind herself. Violent clouds of bloodlust and fiery Rage boiled inside him, shot through with streaks of icy fear and grim desperation as he fought to keep control of his tairen and his magic.

Horror consumed her. Oh, gods, what had she done to him? *"Rain?"*

He did not answer.

Ellysetta could still feel the furious roil of emotion through the touch of her bare leg against Rain's tairen pelt, but he had closed off their bondthreads, silencing the connection between them. *"Rain, teska. Please talk to me. I'm sorry, shei'tan. I'm so sorry."*

She leaned forward to bury her hands in his pelt, trying to weave peace upon him. Slowly, far too slowly, she felt some of the terrible Rage begin to calm.

She did not know how long or how far they flew, but when they came to a silver ribbon of river shining in the starlight, Rain swooped down, skimming the treetops of the dense forest growing on the slopes of the Silvermist mountains. Flocks of birds squawked and took startled flight. The shadows of grazing animals darted into the trees and brush, seeking cover from the predator overhead. A growl rumbled deep in Rain's tairen chest. He dove for the ground, and Ellysetta gasped as a slide of Air lifted her from the saddle on his back and deposited her in the dark woods beside the river.

I must feed. You will be safe here. Speak the command "lissi" to light the lamps. That was all he said, the first words he'd spoken to her since leaving Chakai. His voice was a ragged thread of sound. Then he was gone.

"Rain!" she called after him. *Rain!*

Light the lamps, Ellysetta, and go to the hall. I will join you as soon as I am done. In the distance, Rain's tairen roar broke the silence, followed by the frightened squeal of whatever unfortunate creature had caught his predator's eye.

A shudder rippled through her, but it wasn't caused by fear or squeamishness. The primal sound of the hunt had sent hot energy rushing through her veins. Her muscles tensed. She could picture Rain in her mind, wings spread wide, fangs dripping with the blood of his kill, a powerful, deadly predator. Inside, her own still-restless tairen growled with a hungry bloodlust that made her pulse race and her breath come fast and shallow.

"*Lissi!*" she called out, hoping to dispel the disquieting sensation. She dragged the folds of her cloak closer around her and took a hurried step forward, towards the soft lights that bloomed in the darkness.

Worry turned to wonder as she drew closer and discovered the abandoned city that emerged from the deep shadows of the forest, lit with a silvery glow. Steadying herself with a palm against the trunk of a nearby tree, Ellysetta let her stunned gaze sweep across the luminous forest treasure.

Rain, what is this place?

In the distance, she heard another terrified squeal, followed moments later by a tairen's roar. *It was called Elverial.* His Spirit voice throbbed with dark, dangerous tairen notes.

Elverial. The valley of the elves. The name seemed

entirely appropriate. The city was nestled in a deep valley between two peaks of the Silvermist range, and the buildings seemed as much a part of the forest as the trees themselves, rising from the ground in muted shades of green and brown and silvery stone, curling around the living trunks of ancient trees and flowing in graceful levels up the steep rise of the mountainside.

The place looked so Elvish, she was half expecting some point-eared bowmaster to leap down from the tree branches overhead and challenge her presence, but if the elves had indeed ever dwelled here, they had left long ago. Stone walkways led across the leaf-scattered forest floor, and statues darkened by years of neglect stood silent, melancholy guard in gardens reclaimed by the untamed beauty of nature.

A large building she assumed was the hall Rain had mentioned rose from the forest nearby, and Ellysetta followed the nearest pathway, now barely more than a trail of broken stones leading through meadows of ivy and ferns. She climbed a short stairway and passed through the open, arching doorway leading to the interior of the hall.

Within, the hall was beautiful and otherworldly, as peaceful a place as she'd ever seen. Her gasp of wonder became a deep, luxurious breath, brisk with the cool, fresh air of the forest and the tang of mist from the mountain streams tumbling down nearby waterfalls.

Overhead, fire glowed soft in silvery chandeliers shaped like blossoming vines. Soaring, open arches brought the forest into the hall, where the muted green, brown, and gold forest tones merged harmoniously with touches of color—deep purples, rich blues, and occasional bright flashes of buttery yellow and crisp crimson. A mix of Feyan script and Elvish runes scrolled in graceful whorls along the arched doorways and up the stone columns that had been carved to look like tree trunks rising from the floor, their branches holding aloft the vaulted ceiling. Tapestries and elegant furnishings still filled the empty hall, as if some caretaker or protection weave had kept away the ravages of time.

"This was my mother's birthplace."

She felt the sudden burst of Rain's Change only instants before he spoke, and she turned, heart racing, to find him standing in the doorway of the hall. Magic glowed bright around his tall Fey form, his eyes still more tairen than Fey, and despite the serenity of their surroundings, she felt her own tairen shift and tense in response.

"After I returned to sanity, I would come here from time to time, seeking peace and solitude." He had finished his hunt, but tension still swirled around him—as did a hunger his hunt had not assuaged.

Her mouth went dry. "And did you find it?" She cleared her throat. "The peace you sought?"

"A measure of it." He began to walk towards her, his steps long and deliberate, his face a gleaming pale mask that appeared carved from Silverstone, his eyes searing jewels. "More so than tonight."

Her heart slammed against her ribs, and despite herself, she took several steps back. A wall covered with a tapestry depicting elves at the hunt stopped her retreat. "Rain, I'm sorry. I didn't realize what I was doing to you . . . what toll my healing the *rasa* would take on you."

He reached her, stopping with only the barest hand span between them, not touching her, but so close she could feel the swirling heat emanating from him, the tingle of great magic scarcely contained by his flesh.

"Do not blame yourself. You made your choice, and I made mine." His voice was a low scrape of sound that combined with the steady, burning gaze of his eyes and the electric throb of his magic to make her tremble from head to toe. "I could have stopped you or simply taken you away from Chakai to a place where you could no longer feel the *rasa*'s pain."

She wet her lips. The answering throb of her own magic was rising again, quick and hot. "Why didn't you?"

"You needed to save them *from* death. I needed to save them *for* it. When the Eld strike, I will need every Fey blade I can find to defend the Fading Lands." He put his hands on either side of her head, palms flat against the wall. "I also knew you would not easily have forgiven me for stopping you. You already trusted me so little you felt the need to sneak from our bed. There are enough obstacles in the path of our bond without creating more."

"I . . ." Her voice trailed off. What could she say?

"So I allowed you to do what you felt you must, Ellysetta. I knew the price of my choice, and I paid it." His head lowered, his glowing eyes fixed upon her, holding her captive. "But there was a price for your choice too, *shei'tani*, and that must be paid as well."

A strand of his hair slipped free of his shoulder to brush her cheek, and the ends of it tickled the top of her left breast. Her womb clenched tight, sending a bolt of pleasure shuddering through her. Just that one tiny touch and she was ready to explode.

She swallowed hard. "P-price?"

"They touched you. Fey after Fey, unbonded males." The edge of his lip curled up, baring the white gleam of teeth. "You let them put their hands upon you, their scent upon you."

All the air evaporated from her lungs. "I-I . . ."

"I've done all I can to exhaust the tairen and drain myself of magic, but I can wait no longer." His pupils narrowed to slits, then disappeared entirely, and his eyes began to whirl with tairen radiance. "We will wait no longer."

Heat poured off him in waves, and with it came the heady scent that belonged solely to Rain, a complex, multi-layered aroma that combined the fresh fragrance of the Fey, the tang of powerful magic, and the rich, dark, earthy scent of tairen. He still had not touched her, yet that wave of fragrant heat enveloped her so completely it hardly mattered. She dragged a breath into her lungs, and his scent came with it, filling her nose, her mouth, her throat, permeating her body.

He lowered his head to hers, his lips hovering above her own. The bright whirl of pupil-less tairen eyes, blazing a fierce purple, held her transfixed. "Forgive me, *shei'tani*. I do not think I have the strength to be gentle."

She took a shallow gasp of breath. "Then don't be—"

Her voice broke off as his body pinned hers to the wall. Lean Fey muscle, burning with heat, pressed tight against her softer *shei'dalin* curves. He caught her wrists, clamping them over her head at the same instant his mouth captured hers in a ferocious kiss.

At the first touch of his skin on hers, the threads of their bond came screaming back to life. She cried out, but the sound was consumed by the ravenous dominion of his kiss.

Emotion and power flooded her senses: Rain the *shei'tan's* fury over allowing other males to touch his unbonded mate. Rain the tairen's driving need to claim his mate and eliminate all trace of another male's scent from her. Hunger. Oh, gods, such hunger. An ache so strong, Ellysetta nearly wept with need herself when she felt it.

All the pain and fear of the last day burned away like mist in the sun. Nothing mattered—nothing existed—except Rain and Ellysetta and right now.

"Ve sha kem'tani. Kem'san. Kem'reisa." You are my mate. My heart. My soul. He growled the words against her lips, sending them on Air to her ears, on Spirit to her mind, singing them on their bondthreads in the shatteringly vivid tones of tairen song. With hands and words and lips and teeth, he laid claim to her, declaring possession, marking her with his touch, his kiss, his breath, the scent of his skin rubbing hers with hot friction, singing to her soul.

He tore his mouth from hers, and she dragged in great gulps of air. A rapid weave held her wrists locked over her head and freed his hands to trail a searing path down her body. As he'd warned her, there was no gentleness to his touch. There was only fire, the burn of flesh on flesh, the scrape of teeth dragging down her throat and over breasts stripped bare with a wave of hot magic.

"*Aiyah*, Rain, yes. As you are mine, so I am yours." She wanted him, all of him, only hers, forever hers, from the skeins of night-black hair swirling like silk torment across her skin to the wild, whirling purple blaze of his eyes to the hot groan of breath panting from his lungs and the searing hardness of his body wrapped around her like ropes of steel.

Hands and mouths of flesh and magic moved over her body, caressing every inch, laving her in moist, erotic heat. She cried out again as his teeth closed over one taut nipple and his tongue flicked out, teasing the sensitive flesh to diamond hardness. She screamed as he bit down just hard enough to send her shuddering towards the crest of orgasm. His hand dove between her legs, fingers delving into her curls. Fire exploded, flooding her with hot moisture as the flick of his nimble fingers sent her over the edge.

Rain went to his knees before her, his mouth tracing a burning path down her belly, the flare of her hip. A deep growl rumbled in his chest, vibrating in his blood. The threads of their bond pulsed with energy. The wild, fiery magic of their newest, sun-bright thread cracked like whips of lightning in his flesh as he gazed up at her, naked, her arms locked above her head in bonds of magic as if she were one of the virginal sacrifices ancient mortals made to the immortals they once considered gods.

Trembling. Naked. Helpless.

His.

The tairen roared in triumph, and this time when the primitive, savage rush of power filled him, he allowed it. "*Ve sha kem*," he snarled. You are mine. His teeth nipped at her thigh. His fingers continued to flick and torment, her flesh already enticingly slick. The scent of her arousal filled the air with musky sweetness, making his sex swell to painful hardness. *"Bera."* Ours.

She sobbed her agreement. *"Aiyah*, Rain. I am yours. Only yours."

It wasn't enough. Not nearly enough. His hands cupped her buttocks, and his mouth dove to claim the soft, heated flesh between her legs. He held her mind and gaze locked to his and devoured her until she screamed his name and flew apart in his hands, her body shaking in helpless abandon.

He rose in one swift motion, discarding leathers and steel with a flash of Earth. His hands closed around her hips. His own hips thrust close, and the long, hard column of his sex pressed against her belly. She gasped and bucked her hips. Already his fierce hunger was calling to her again, rousing her own.

Her eyes squeezed shut, but in the darkness, her other senses only seemed more acute, and threads of multicolored light flickered against the backs of her lids. Fey vision, she realized instantly, the magic sight that did not need eyes to see. Instead of black hair and blazing lavender eyes and the graceful beauty of Elverial, she saw the glowing threads of magic that made up all things, Fire, Water, Earth, Air, and Spirit—and the blinding, burning flame that was Rain standing before her, enveloping her in fire and light.

And all around him, emanating from him and lit by threads too bright to identify, the incandescent form of a tairen spread wide its wings in a fearsome show of strength and dominance. Its eyes were the same glowing wells of power that Rain's were. As she watched, it roared, and golden red flame erupted from its mouth and swept over her.

Her eyes flew open as heat and hunger whipped through

her body. Magic and need swelled inside her, so hard and so fast her skin burned, as if stretched to the breaking point.

"Rain . . . Rain, please . . . I need—" Her voice broke off.

"What?"

She squirmed, wriggled, the ache so fierce, her need so great. But he would not relent until she gave him his answer. She cried it in desperation, "You!"

"Then take me, *shei'tani*." His fingers dug into the soft swell of her hips, lifting her high, then bringing her down hard and fast. Her legs locked around his waist, and she flung her head back on a scream of pleasure as his body surged into hers in one powerful, claiming thrust.

"Ver reisa ku'chae. Kem surah, shei'tani." The driving rhythm of Rain's hips punctuated the growled words of *shei'tanitsa* claiming, and with each hard pulse, Ellysetta cried out his name as his sex swelled inside her, stretching her, filling her.

Ah, gods, with Rain inside her, his skin pressed tight against hers, she felt his every shuddering pleasure as clearly as her own. The breath was driven from her lungs as wave after wave of heat washed over her. Fire danced behind her eyes, and searing blue-white flames mingled with a sea of billowing red-orange heat as another shattering orgasm consumed her.

Rain groaned as Ellysetta's body clenched tight as a fist around him. Her inner muscles gripped him like steel, rippling so forcefully the pleasure bordered on pain. Thought dissolved in a fiery wash of sensation, and a cry ripped from his throat as his own release tore through him. His legs trembled and he staggered back, barely staying on his feet.

A quick weave released the bonds holding Ellysetta's hands, and she slumped against him, clinging to his neck, her body still quaking. Two steps brought him to a long chaise covered in dark purple velvet, but even before he could lower Ellysetta to her rest, the tairen growled again and a shaft of re-

kindled heat speared through him. The arms holding
Ellysetta tightened as his spent body filled with renewed
strength.

Throughout the night, the tairen drove him, relentless,
ravenous, refusing to release him. Time after time, bell
after bell, with an insatiable passion that outmatched even
the night of Ellysetta's carnal weave, he staked his claim.
He took her on the chaise, on the floor, bent over a small
table, on her knees leaning back against his chest so his
hands could have unfettered access to her breasts and the
soft, slick folds between her legs. He took her until there
was no finger span of flesh she had not surrendered to
him, until her voice was hoarse from her cries and her
body so sensitized a single flick of his tongue or the
slightest breath of Air could make her sob his name and
start to shake.

Only as the darkness of night faded in the face of the
approaching dawn did the violence that had raged inside
him abate and the fierce roar of his tairen finally fall silent. And then, with a whispered prayer of thanks and a
sigh of relief, Rain collapsed on the chaise beside Ellysetta and slept.

CHAPTER EIGHT

A child's laughter fades into an endless void.
Darkness grows stronger with each passing breath.
Dreams forever haunted by nightmares untold.
Hunting the pure is all they have left.

Mages of Eld ~ by Daria vol Siar

The Fading Lands ~ Elverial

Ellysetta woke to the sound of water falling and a cool breeze blowing softly through her hair. She started to stretch, then groaned as sore muscles protested the movement.

Her eyes fluttered open. She lay in the middle of an exquisitely shaped bed made of untarnished copper scrolls, draped in soft sheets and piled high with plump pillows in rich shades of green and gold and deep purple. The bed rested at one end of an open-air, copper-roofed room that overlooked a series of frothy waterfalls spilling down the mountainside.

A cool breeze whispered into the room, carrying a scent of wood smoke and roasting fish that made her stomach growl. She gathered the moss green sheets to her body and ignored the flare of aching muscles as she climbed out of bed and walked to the open window arches to look outside.

Rain, wearing only his leather trousers and Fey'cha belts, crouched on the riverbank, roasting a spitted fish over a small log fire. He looked up at her, his expression inscrutable. "Hungry?"

Despite the excesses of last night, a fresh bloom of warmth

suffused her at the sight of his bare, shining skin, his muscular arms and broad shoulders, the lean, sculpted strength of his naked chest. "Very." And no longer just for food.

"Stay there." He slid the fish from its wooden spit onto a small platter and strode up a narrow wooden stairway that curved up from the river's edge to the bedroom. "I meant to have a meal prepared before you woke." That was when she noted the small round table and cushioned stools nestled against the far window, set with a vase of fresh woodland flowers and a pitcher of clear water from the stream.

She sat gingerly on one of the stools, and turned her attention outside to hide her faint grimace as little needles of pain shot through her sore muscles. With daylight shining on the stream and surrounding forest, she could see the whole of Elverial's peaceful woodland splendor. "This is the most beautiful place I've ever seen. It almost looks as if all the buildings grew here as part of the forest."

"*Aiyah*. Elvish architects have always had a way of blending their creations with the natural surroundings."

"You said this was your mother's birthplace."

"It was. She descended from an ancient Fey-Elvish bloodline that spanned back to the days when our two peoples were more than mere allies. We came here often when I was a boy."

She could easily imagine a young, bright-eyed Rain running through these forests, climbing trees—she glanced at the plate of roasted fish and smiled—catching fish in the mountain streams. "Why was such a beautiful city abandoned? And so abruptly? It looks like all the people just went away one day, never to return."

"They did. Most who lived here died in the Wars or the forging of the Mists. The rest eventually went to Dharsa to be among other Fey. Here. We need to leave soon, and you should eat before we go. Dax and Marissya have already set out for Fey'Bahren, and I would prefer not to stop until we've caught up with them." He stripped flaky meat from the fish and lifted the steaming morsel to her lips. A ripple of awareness shivered through her as she opened her mouth and ate from his fingers. His lashes lowered, hiding his eyes from her.

She accepted another bite of fish from his hand and frowned when he took none for himself. "You aren't eating?"

"I fed while you slept. This is for you." He handed her another bite.

She shifted her weight on the small stool, then winced as the movement made sore body parts twinge.

Rain's lips tightened. "*Sieks'ta, shei'tani.* My shame is great. I was not gentle with you last night."

She blushed and swallowed the morsel of fish. "I don't recall complaining."

"I did not treat you with the care of a *shei'tan.*"

"Rain." She put her hand on his to still his fingers from continuing to shred the fish. "I'm fine. If anyone owes an apology, it's me. I insisted on healing the *rasa.* I didn't realize what it would do to you. You tried to tell me, but I refused to hear, because I didn't want to let you stand in my way." Admitting that hurt far more than any physical reminder of last night.

His jaw set in a grim line. "I allowed it. I allowed them to touch you, allowed their pain to torment you, because I am the Defender of the Fey and I needed their blades for war. And then I punished you for it."

"You didn't—"

"You'd already been brutalized more than any mate of mine ever should be. First that seizure in Teleon, then the Mists and the *rasa.* Then me. You cannot deny it." He caught her hands, rubbing the faint ring of bruises on her wrists and scowling at the bluish imprint of his fingers on her upper arms. "I saw these on you when I woke."

She pulled free. "You did not brutalize me. I'm a little sore, yes, but unhurt. Besides"—she touched her fingertips to the reddened marks on his chest where her nails had raked like claws— "you didn't come out completely unscathed."

He glanced down and gave a dismissive snort. "Those marks are nothing."

"And these are nothing."

"They are *not* nothing. You cannot compare the two. I am a warrior and a Tairen Soul. If you broke my bones and drove a blade through my ribs, it would be no more hurt than I receive in a hard day's training at the Academy. *You* are my mate. My sworn duty is to keep you from all harm, yet I put these bruises on you." He met her gaze, his eyes so full of remorse and self-loathing that her heart broke. "I promised you weeks ago that I would control the tairen, that you need never fear it, and last night I unleashed its fury on you."

"Rain—"

"I should have stayed away, hunted longer. You were safe here. I knew better than to return, but I did nonetheless." His throat worked and he looked away, staring blindly at the mountain stream tumbling over the rocks below. "The tairen is not a gentle creature. The one time I lost control of it with Sariel, I frightened her so badly she cried for days."

"Rain." She caught his face between her hands. "I am not Sariel."

"I know that, Ellysetta—"

"Shh." She put a finger to his lips. "You've had your say; now I will have mine. You did not frighten me. Not much, in any case," she amended quickly. "And you did not hurt me. In fact, I can't think of any part of what you did that I did not enjoy." Heat bloomed in her cheeks. Her mother had raised her to be modest and circumspect, and last night, in the heat of passion, she'd done and said many things that mortified her even to remember now, in the light of day. Despite her fierce blush, she held his gaze steadily.

"So much so," she continued, "that I was hoping I might convince you to do some of it again." Now her cheeks felt fiery red, but the stunned look on his face was worth the price. "Do not forget that I am tairen too." Trying very hard to look much braver than she felt, she reached out to brush a thumb across the flat coin of his nipple. The coin tightened instantly to a small, hard point. Fascinated, she rubbed it again.

He caught her wrist and growled a warning. "Ellysetta. Do not toy if you do not mean it. My control is still far from what it should be."

The sound of his growl rumbling across her skin and the sudden flare of heat that emanated from him made her face flush and her breathing grow shallow with vivid sensory memories of last night. She moistened her lips with the tip of her tongue. His gaze fixed instantly on the small movement, and she saw his nostrils flare.

Another memory flashed in vivid detail: Rain, his head bent to her breast, glowing purple eyes holding her gaze as his tongue lapped at the taut peak, filling her with exquisite pleasure. She shivered in her seat and stifled a moan as the aching muscles of her body clenched tight and a rush of now-familiar heat flooded her.

Feeling suddenly quite daring and wicked, she leaned forward. "And what if I do mean it, *shei'tan*?" Holding his gaze, she dipped her head and, in a brazen move totally alien to the good, modest Ellie Baristani her mother had raised, she licked that hard, pointed nipple.

He rose from his seat in a flash, dragging her up into his arms as he went. The sheet she had wrapped around her body fell free, leaving her naked and laughing breathlessly in his arms.

"Just one thing, Rain," she begged. "Please, let's use the bed this time."

Much later, Rain and Ellysetta left the woodland peace of Elverial and raced across the skies of the eastern Fading Lands with the aid of magic-powered flight. They passed the Garreval and caught up with Marissya and Dax by early afternoon.

Rain changed Ellysetta's clothes to brown traveling leathers like the ones Marissya wore, and thanks to his insistence that Marissya heal her before they set out again, Ellysetta was soon loping across the rosy sand of the desert as swiftly as the other three Fey and without a single twinge of soreness. She didn't even break a sweat, despite the heat of the summer sun beating down on the desert, and they were running so fast and so effortlessly that except for the tug of gravity and the rhythmic thud of boot heels hitting earth, she could almost close her eyes and believe she was flying.

There were definite advantages to being Fey.

"I did not expect so much desert," Elysetta said as she leapt over a small, prickly deep purple shrub Rain called *kaddah.* Gone were the cool waterfalls and sunlight-dappled woods of Elverial. From the west slopes of the Rhakis as far east as Ellysetta could see there was only barren, sandy earth dotted with succulent shrubs like the *kaddah,* and an occasional, stunted tree determinedly clinging to life in the harsh environment. "The Fey poetry I've read talks about sweetgrass glades and gentle streams bordered by shade trees taller than tairen."

A much larger *kaddah* lay in Rain's path. He cleared it with an effortless leap. "Once all the Fading Lands were as you describe, but after the Mage Wars, when we lost so many of our mated women, our lands began reverting to desert."

"You think the loss of the women caused the land to turn to desert?"

"I know it did." He smiled at her surprise. "*Fellana*, the Fey word for woman, derives from the old tongue, *felah'naveth,* which means bringer of life, because when a Fey woman is with child, life literally blooms in her footsteps."

Ellysetta was so surprised, her gait slowed. Rain, Marissya, and Dax passed her, and with a burst of speed, she caught up to them. "You mean . . . pregnant Fey women can make grass bloom in the desert?"

"Technically, they make Amarynth bloom in whatever soil they tread upon. All other life is seeded from that."

"Amarynth? The undying flower?" Ellysetta had seen mention of Amarynth in the ancient tales and Fey poetry she'd read all her life. Supposedly, the flowers bloomed for a hundred years and had special magical properties. "I always thought they were just a legend."

"So they have seemed even to the Fey for most of these last thousand years. We call them the flower of life. They bloom only in the footsteps of a *fellana* who is with child."

"The gift is a great one," Marissya said, "but it can be exhausting." At Ellysetta's blank look, she explained, "When a Fey woman is with child, her gifts are the strongest they will ever be. The ground around her literally blooms with life. To share that magic, she walks the land. It wasn't so bad before the Mage Wars—Amarynth grew abundantly—but after the Wars, there were no births. The Amarynth faded. By the time I became pregnant with Kieran . . . Well, let's just say I had plenty of exercise for twelve months."

Beside her, Dax made a haggard face. "*We*," he interjected. "*We* had plenty of exercise. I measured it. Four thousand miles we walked, and that's not counting the miles spent going from house to house blessing all the other matepairs who were hoping some of Marissya's *fellana* magic would spread to them." He shook his head and rolled his eyes. "Best you and Rain pray for a sudden epidemic of fertility among the Fey before the gods shower their gifts upon you. By my reckoning, the first matepair to carry will need to run, not walk, the Fading Lands even to make a dent."

"That doesn't sound so bad." Ellysetta leapt over another

kaddah plant, spreading her arms as her body momentarily took flight. "I've discovered I like to run."

Rain smiled.

Eld ~ Boura Fell

His hand was trembling again.

Vadim Maur clasped his palms together, squeezing his fingers tight, and looked across his desk at Gethen Nour, one of the Mage's most promising former apprentices who had long ago joined the rank of Primages. "I'm sure you've heard that Kolis has recently disappointed me."

Though he tried to hide it, Gethen couldn't completely restrain his instinctive flinch. Kolis's fate had become common talk in the Mage Halls upstairs.

"He still lives," Vadim assured him. Then he smiled. "Unfortunately for him."

Gethen managed to keep his gaze steady. "I hope never to disappoint you, master."

The High Mage nodded. "That is my hope, too, Gethen. And now you have an opportunity to remind me how skillfully you can serve me." Three stripes adorned the cuffs of Gethen's blue Mage robes, only two less than those Primages who served on the Mage Council. Vadim wasn't going to make the same mistake he'd made with Kolis. This time, his envoy would be a full-ranked Mage, as experienced as he was powerful.

Nour gave a quiet cough to clear his throat. "Master?"

"You will take Kolis's place in Celieria." He eyed the younger man critically. Nour wasn't half as pretty as Kolis had been, but his body was tall and firm, his features appealing enough that he had no shortage of willing bed partners. His hair was thick and dark, his eyes a shrewd forest green. That was a plus. Queen Annoura preferred brunettes, the better to set off her own fair beauty. "Kolis's *umagi* in the court will smooth your path into the queen's inner circle."

"Forgive me, master," Nour ventured cautiously, "but I thought the Fey had left Celieria City and our plans there were uncovered."

"We suffered a setback, yes, but our work in Celieria City is not done. Dorian still sits on the throne, and after all these years, it appears he's finally grown steel in his spine. He is arming the keeps along the borders. That doesn't suit my plans. I'll take Celieria by force if I must, but I prefer to save our strength and resources for the Fey."

The Primage bowed his head. "Of course, master. When do you wish me to depart?"

"Tonight. Kolis's *umagi* will gain you entrance to the court and access to the queen. Dorian must be controlled, rendered ineffective, or removed. One way or another, I want the hand of Eld guiding Celieria's throne four months hence, before the night of the new moons."

"I will not fail you, master."

"If you do, you will do so only once." Vadim's left hand began to tremble again. The Mage rose to his feet and clasped the shaking hand behind his back. "There is one other thing, Nour."

Gethen's face settled into an expression of mild curiosity. "Master?"

"You will find a way to bring the Tairen Soul's truemate to me. Alive. *Before* she completes the matebond with him."

The Primage's jaw went slack, and for one brief moment alarm flashed openly in his eyes. He tried to rally, dropping his gaze and covering his gape with a forced cough. "Forgive me, master, but every Mage in Boura Fell knows the Fey have taken the girl through the Faering Mists. No Mage can reach her now. Such a feat is beyond even your vast power, Great One."

"We will see about that," Vadim snapped. He took a breath and forcibly calmed his temper. "I am not asking you to reach her in the Fading Lands, Nour. I'm telling you to find a way to draw her out. The girl's family has still not been found. They've not entered Orest, but the same scouts who spotted the Tairen Soul reported a powerful redirection weave spun around the Garreval. I find myself wondering why the Fey would trouble to spin such a weave if they were just passing through to the Fading Lands."

"You think the girl's family is there?"

"I think something is there, and I want to know what." Vadim opened a drawer by his desk and pulled out the black velvet bag of *chemar* left by Fezaiina Rael. "Here. I want these planted around the Garreval, inside whatever is hidden behind that redirection weave. They are like *selkahr* but have no magical signature. Leave them where they will be most useful as gateways for invading forces. If Ellysetta Baristani's family *is* there by the Garreval, find a way to bring them to me."

Nour picked up the bag and glanced inside before depositing the pouch in the pocket of his robe. "Yes, master."

"You will take my newest *umagi* with you. He knew Ellysetta Baristani and her mortal family, and he has a few scores he wishes to settle. He is eager to help you find them, and he has many ties among the rabble that may come in useful." A door opened to Vadim's left, and the thick-muscled, brutishly handsome Celierian stepped into the room.

Despite the debatable wisdom of claiming Den Brodson, Vadim Maur still felt a surge of pride at the sight of him. It took a very powerful Mage to deliver six full-strength Marks in six days, but it also took a very strong *umagi* to survive the process. Brodson had, though not easily. The Celierian's ruddy face was pale beneath its tan, his dark hair now streaked with white, and his thick muscles were still twiching from the memory of his torment and subjugation.

"This is Master Nour, *umagi*. You will serve him as you would me." Vadim held Den Brodson's gaze and summoned the icy, dark sweetness of Azrahn. "Do not disappoint me, mortal. As you know, I deal harshly with those who fail me."

Brodson's face blanched three shades whiter, and a muscle in his jaw began a rapid tic. He bowed and moved to Nour's side like an obedient dog.

"Go. You depart at nightfall. You will use Kolis's entrance to the inn. Have his *umagi* bring a sacrifice for the guardians of the Well. There must be no hint of Azrahn to alert anyone to your presence."

"Understood, master. It shall be as you command." Gethen bowed, snapped his fingers in a wordless command for the Celierian to follow, and exited the room.

When the two men were gone, the High Mage lifted his trembling hands and examined them. The shaking had grown worse again, despite Elfeya's obediently diligent efforts to heal him, and much as he wanted to, he could no longer deny the truth.

The tremors hadn't started because he'd spent too much energy claiming Den Brodson's soul. They hadn't started because Shannisorran v'En Celay landed a lucky blow. He'd been weakening steadily since the night two weeks ago when he'd found Ellysetta Baristani in the realm of dreams and tried to force his second Mark upon her. She'd fought back with a ferocity he hadn't anticipated. The Fire she'd summoned had reached across the barriers of the dreamworld and scorched him in the physical realm.

And mixed in with that Fire had been something else. Something that struck deeper than a few layers of scorched flesh.

Despite his multiple visits to Elfeya v'En Celay and the daily ministrations of her healing hands, he had yet to completely recover. He was finally coming to realize he never would . . . at least, not in this form.

Age was finally outpacing magic. The time of his next incarnation—so long postponed by Elfeya v'En Celay's impressive talents—could no longer be held in abeyance.

Death was drawing near.

Shadows rot Kolis's soul! The Sulimage's ineptitude in Celieria City had cost Vadim dearly—the price far more than Celieria's discovery of Eld's secret aggression and the loss of a valuable Fey captive.

A Mage, when the time of incarnation came upon him, needed a new vessel to house his soul. Only the strongest, most magically gifted vessel would do, because though a Mage's memories and knowledge transferred to his new body during the incarnation, his powers did not.

Over the millennia, more than one High Mage had ousted his most dangerous rival not through direct combat, but rather by waiting for the time of his enemy's incarnation, stealing his chosen vessel, and replacing it with one of the rival's powerless mortal *umagi*. Once reincarnated, the Mage's helpless new form could then be effortlessly mined for all its centuries of precious knowledge before the pitiful living husk that remained was left to wither and die in the obscurity of captive servitude.

The greatest High Mage ever to rule Eld had no intention of meeting such a fate. Long ago, before the Mage Wars, before the scorching of the world, the germ of his grand idea had formed and taken strong root. Since that moment, every day of his life had been spent in pursuit of his dream.

Ellysetta Baristani was Vadim's greatest creation, the culmination of all his long, painstaking centuries of experimentation. She was his child, born of Fey flesh but tied to pure power through Vadim's most skillful manipulation of Azrahn's darkest secrets.

She was the Tairen Soul vessel whose birth he had engineered to house the next incarnation of his soul.

Through her, he could have what no other Mage before him had ever had: the pure, limitless power and destructive force of a tairen and—best of all—the immortality of the Fey.

And Kolis had let her slip through his fingers.

Vadim's hand was trembling again, but this time from fury. He forced himself to calm. He was the High Mage, a man who mastered adversity rather than succumbing to it. He would continue with his efforts to recapture Ellysetta Baristani—she was the ideal candidate to serve as his vessel—but Vadim had always been too wise a Mage to hold all his coin in one purse.

He had succeeded with Ellysetta Baristani. He could succeed again.

The Fading Lands ~ Eastern Desert

As the Great Sun began its descent towards the western horizon, Ellysetta caught sight of a city rising from the flatness of the distant desert.

"What's that?" she asked, pointing.

"That is Lissilin, light of the east," Rain said. "Our destination for tonight."

Lissilin, which they reached before twilight cast the Rhakis into shadow, was another abandoned city of the Fey. Like Elverial, there was a haunting beauty to the place, the otherworldly grace of the immortal Fey evident in every curving archway and artistically carved stone wall. Unlike Elverial, however, there was no sense of a sleeping city waiting for its inhabitants to return. Life had left Lissilin. Its gardens were parched plots of sand, its buildings and fountains the dry, sunbaked bones of a dead city.

Ellysetta felt a deep sense of sadness as she walked through the empty, sand-blown streets. "How many Fey once lived here?" It must have been many. Lissilin was no mere village.

"Twenty thousand," Dax supplied the number.

She winced. "Where are those people now?"

They had reached the center of the city. Five thoroughfares converged on a pentagon-shaped center dominated by a large, dry fountain filled with a half a dozen stone tairen. Once, no doubt, this had been a beautiful, lush park as lovely as the cherry-tree orchard at the base of Teleon.

Rain met her gaze, his own bleak. "Gone."

"Dead?"

"Most. The rest moved to Dharsa when they realized Lissilin was fading."

Ellysetta glanced around at the dry, abandoned buildings. So much beauty lost. What a terrible, sad waste. "Of all the cities in the Fading Lands, how many are still inhabited?"

He drew a deep breath and let it back out as a heavy sigh. "A few Fey still live in Tehlas and Blade's Point, and a few live alone, but only Dharsa still thrives."

Only Dharsa. In all the vast kingdom of the Fey, only Dharsa was still populous.

Rain gestured to a beautiful rose-stone building on the left where graceful, columned arches led to a brightly tiled inner courtyard. "*Shei'tani*, you and Marissya can wait there while Dax and I hunt. That building holds a few rooms still kept up for travelers. I'll fill the fountain so you will have water to wash and drink." He turned to the tairen fountain and spun a cool, blue weave of Water magic. Moments later, clear water spouted from the mouths of the stone tairen and rapidly began to fill the fountain's large pool.

Ellysetta frowned in bewilderment. His weave had not been powerful enough to create that much water from nothing. He'd merely summoned it from beneath the sands. "I don't understand. If there's still water here, why did the city die?"

Rain didn't answer immediately. Instead, he gathered a handful of sand, spun it into a small cup, and filled it from one of the streams pouring out of the tairen mouth. He handed the cup to Ellysetta. "Taste it."

She took a tentative sip. Cool, sweet water touched her tongue. "It's just water."

"Precisely." Rain spun another cup for Marissya as Ellysetta quenched her thirst. "It's just water. But this fountain is—or was—Lissilin's Source."

Her eyes widened. She looked at the tairen fountain with dawning dismay. There was no crisp tingle of *faerilas* magic in the water pouring from those stone mouths. There was nothing but . . . water.

"It isn't lack of water that made the city die, Ellysetta. The magic of Lissilin died too."

For the first time she began to truly understand just how desperate the plight of the Fey really was. They were living in the shadow of extinction in every possible way. The death of the tairen, the decline of their numbers, even the slow eradication of their magic.

"Do you think everything could somehow be related?"

Rain took a drink of the magicless water, then poured the rest out onto the sand. "The tairen are sickening in the egg, the Fey are childless, and the magic of the Fading Lands is slowly dying. Do I think they're all related? *Aiyah.* I am certain of it. But what's causing it all is the question we have yet to answer."

Eld ~ Boura Fell

Accompanied by half a dozen servants, Vadim Maur walked down the corridor that housed the luxurious cells reserved for his most magically gifted female captives.

For many years, Elfeya v'En Celay had resided here, garbed in delicate silks and left to await his pleasure as he sought to mate his great mastery of Elden magic with her countless Fey gifts. That attempt had come to naught, except that he'd discovered truemated Fey did not breed with any but their bound mates.

That limitation was not true for unmated Fey. Though the unmated Fey females he'd captured during the Wars had been too fragile to survive more than a few decades in captivity, the males were both hardy and fertile. Over the centuries, his captive Fey and *dahl'reisen* males had successfully impregnated thousands of Celierian and Elden females, and in an effort to bring additional magic into the bloodlines, he'd even released a number of their offspring back into the Celierian populations in the magic-infused lands near the borders.

All along the borders, the unwitting descendants of Vadim Maur's centuries-old breeding program lived their lives, Celierian and Eld mortals crossbred with a mix of Fey, Elvish, and Mage bloodlines, propagating amongst themselves with the genetic drives he had manipulated into their flesh, building the pool of increasingly gifted prospective breeders, females for his *dahl'reisen* studs, males for those rare females whose genetic makeup had left them too gifted to tolerate the touch of *dahl'reisen* flesh. In his office, entire volumes of books documented the specifics of the bloodlines he had bred and crossbred over the centuries.

Three of this generation's strongest females were just entering the last quarter of their yearlong pregnancies. The fetuses in their wombs were powerfully gifted, showing signs they possessed each of the five Fey magics. And that meant it was time for Vadim to work the miracle of soul manipulation once again.

He stopped before one of several gilt-chased doors. The guards on either side hurried to unlock it for him, and with a wave of his hand the heavy door swung inward, revealing the lush wonderland inside. In what had once been an enormous cavern carved out of the rock, live trees and grasses grew along gentle hillocks bordering a stone pathway. Sun-bright Fire burned in sconces overhead that traveled the domed ceiling daily in an imitation of the Great Sun's daily trek across the heavens. A soothing breeze rustled through the trees, and in the distance, water fell gently into a clear pond.

He had discovered long ago that serenity improved the number of live births amongst his breeding females, while privation resulted in a higher level of miscarriages and stillbirths.

So he had learned to provide serenity through pleasant surroundings and a strong Mage spell that erased all memories
of his prisoners' previous lives and supplanted them with the
desire to enjoy their tiny slice of paradise, please the High
Mage above all others, and willingly mate as directed.

Vadim followed the path to the tree-shaded pool, where
he knew he would find the three women he had come for.
A young black-haired child clothed in servant's rags was
with them. A tray of food on the grass nearby explained her
presence, but he was not pleased to find her sitting beside
them, her eyes closed as one of the pregnant women sang
and ran a comb through the girl's dark hair.

A leaf crackled beneath his feet. The servant girl's eyes
flew open, and he saw a glint of familiar silver before she
scrambled to her feet. That child again. The affront to his
bloodlines. Sired by one of his own descendants—those
silver eyes made the shameful truth undeniable—but born
utterly without magic.

"What do you think you're up to, girl?" he snapped.

"Forgive me, Master Maur. They always seem happier
when they have someone to take care of. I didn't think anyone would mind." The words were submissive, those telltale
eyes downcast, but there was a tone in her voice that raised
his hackles. Just her presence raised his hackles.

"You *thought?*" His lip curled. "When I want thoughts from
you, I'll put them in your worthless skull myself." He grabbed
her chin, pinching her face between his fingers. Her silver
eyes flashed up—just for an instant, but that was long enough
for him to see the hard glitter of hatred. His nostrils flared. He
summoned power and stabbed it into her with merciless force.
She gave a choked cry and dropped to her knees. "Slaves do
not think. They serve. Silent and unseen. And don't dare to
think those eyes of yours grant you any special worth in Boura
Fell. Magic is the sole coin of this realm, and you have none.
Now get out. If I find you in here again, you'll be the next
sacrifice to the Guardians of the Well."

He waited until she was gone, then turned back to the women gathered by the pond. They had huddled together and were clutching one another, weeping in fear and confusion.

"Shia, Tailinn, Fania, come here." They didn't immediately obey, which only infuriated him more. With a muttered oath, he summoned a rush of Azrahn, only instead of stabbing it into the women as he had the girl, he spun a powerful compulsion weave. Their lovely faces became expressionless, their eyes going flat and vacant.

"Come here," he repeated, and all three women came to his side with silent, blank-eyed obedience.

He placed his hands on their naked, heavily pregnant bellies and sent his Mage senses inward to test the health and readiness of the fetuses. All three of the pregnancies were proceeding exactly as he'd planned, and all three of the unborn responded to his presence with little cracks of power that made their mothers flinch.

Vadim selected Shia, the Celierian-born woman with the long black hair and pale blue eyes who had been singing and brushing the girl's hair when he came in. Descended of the vel Serranis line and Vadim's own Mage blood, Shia was among this generation's most promising females, so sensitive to the *dahl'reisen* that Vadim had been forced to render her unconscious before releasing the stud to mate with her. Even then, Shia had nearly roused, whimpering, as the *dahl'reisen* pumped his seed into her prepared body.

The High Mage snapped his fingers and pointed, and four servants rushed forward with robes and gold silk slippers to clothe Shia. Vadim drew an empty vial and lancet from one pocket and made a tiny cut on her arm. Bright scarlet blood welled out. He filled the vial, capped it, then closed the small wound with a swift weave of Earth.

"Take her to the birthing room and prepare her."

Leaving his servants to their tasks, Vadim made his way back to his own chambers, to the small, heavily warded room secreted in the heart of his private suite. Though an enormous vault deep in Boura Fell contained enough gold, silver, and gems to buy a kingdom ten times over, this tiny room was where the true treasure of Eld lay.

Vadim released the wards and locks and opened the door.

Inside, rows of locked chests and rack upon rack of drawers and shelves were stuffed with every conceivable tool of power, objects Vadim had inherited from his predecessors, along with the enormous personal collection he'd gathered himself. Magical implements men and women of knowledge would conquer worlds to possess. Stones to call particular demons. Rune-etched collars and manacles to contain and control them. Tikis made by powerful Feraz Black Witches for the darkest intent of Mother Night herself. Drogan chalices that, when filled with the blood of an infant, became dark mirrors through which the High Mage and his distant emissaries could communicate without any other form of magic.

One small chest, protected by no fewer than twelve deadly wards, contained his bands of power. Vadim released the wards and opened the chest. Trays of magical rings and armbands gleamed up at him. He spread them out across the counter. Four trays were filled with gleaming Tairen's Eye crystals set in gold rings; eight overflowed with black *selkahr* set in platinum.

From a deep pocket in his robes, he withdrew the small vial of Shia's still-warm blood. He uncapped the vial and poured several drops of the blood into one palm. He touched his tongue to the blood, taking the taste of it into his mouth, then rubbed his hands together until a thin, rapidly drying sheen of red coated both palms.

"*Gaz mora khan,*" he whispered. From blood power. His eyes closed as runners of rich, seductive darkness sparked in his veins. The blood on his hands grew warm, heating his palms. The remnants on his tongue assumed a dark honey flavor, rapidly taking on an overpowering sweetness that made his teeth ache.

His eyes snapped open, black now and glowing with the dark red embers of Azrahn. To his Azrahn-enhanced vision, the small treasure room was a well of shadow, set afire with blazing magical lights. The Tairen's Eye crystals were near-blinding prisms of multicolored light. He splayed his blood-smeared hands over them.

"*Vi mora ulchis,*" he commanded. To blood obedience. His palms, glowing a dull, dim red, passed slowly over the crystals. A score of the crystals gleamed brighter, minute sparks leaping from them like a shower of embers bursting from a fire. He plucked them from the tray and retested the smaller group several more times until he had whittled the score of crystals down to the four that responded most strongly to his testing spell.

Using a similar process, he selected four black *selkahr* from the other trays, then chose two of his purest, most powerful deep purple amethyst rings to adorn each thumb. Finally, the High Mage opened a separate set of trays below the first and withdrew two armbands of gold chased with ancient Merellian runes.

When he finished, he reactivated the wards guarding the chests and exited the small room.

The darkest bell of night was approaching. The time for great magic was near.

CHAPTER NINE

The Fading Lands ~ Lissilin

The cry cut through Rain like a knife. He bolted upright on the pallet he'd carried up to the rooftop in Lissilin so he and Ellysetta could sleep beneath the stars. The rush of blinding grief left him breathless and trembling. Beside him, Ellysetta gave a low cry of pain and jolted awake as well, clutching the soft sheet to her chest.

"Rain . . ." Tears thickened her voice. She did not understand what it was she felt, but she was Fey enough, tairen enough, to feel the terrible sorrow in every cell of her being.

He bent his head. His eyes burned with unshed tears. Ah, gods, too late. He should have flown straight through to Fey'Bahren, but he'd let Sybharukai's reassurances of Cahlah's improving condition convince him he still had time.

He pressed his palms to his forehead and sang a short prayer of farewell. "Soar high and laugh on the wind," he whispered.

"What's happened, Rain?" The tears had spilled over and were running down Ellysetta's cheeks.

"Cahlah is dead, and one of her kits has perished in the egg." He thumbed her tears away, kissed her gently before releasing her. "I must go. I'd like you to come with me, though when we reach Fey'Bahren you may have to wait until the worst of the pride's grief has passed before they will welcome you."

"Of course I'll go," she said without hesitation.

"Beylah vo." As they dressed, he sent a probe of Spirit

downstairs and found Dax awake and worried for his mate, who had suddenly woken and begun weeping for no reason she could explain.

"Sieks'ta," Rain apologized. *"Two of the tairen are dead. Ellysetta and I must have been broadcasting our grief too strongly. Forgive us for disturbing your mate. We are flying to Fey'Bahren. You and Marissya join us there as soon as you can."*

Moments later, he and Ellysetta soared from the rooftops of Lissilin and began winging north, towards the Feyls.

Eld ~ Boura Fell

The High Mage groaned. Naked, bathed in blood, he lay prostrate on the cold stone floor and twitched while the last of the painful spasms that had racked every muscle of his body made its final angry statement.

"Master?" Booted feet shuffled close.

"Do not touch me." He issued the warning between clenched teeth. The ringing in his ears, caused by his own screams, began to fade, and in its place he heard another sound: a steady dripping, like overturned milk spilling onto a hard surface. But he knew it was not milk. The rich, metallic scent was instantly recognizable.

Blood, thick, still warm, and lots of it. The fluid of life and of recent violent death.

No wonder the servants were terrified. If Vadim had lost his prize after the ferocious, agonizing battle he had just won, his fury would be savage.

"The child?"

"Alive, master." The voice quavered. "And unharmed."

It was not him the servants feared then. Vadim closed his eyes, focused, summoned every vestige of strength. The battle this time had been worse than any he'd ever fought before, draining every hint of magic from him, every reserve of strength. He'd almost lost. Unimaginable, but there it was. Death had been so near, he'd felt its cold breath upon the back of his neck, an enveloping mist wrapping about him like a shroud.

Without the pulse of magic throbbing within, the full weight of his age fell upon him. His bones ached; his muscles felt weak and flaccid. Will alone roused him from the stone floor, forced his spine to straighten when his body wanted instead to remain bent and hunched like an old man's. He was the High Mage. He could not afford to show weakness.

He stood. Hair matted with congealed blood impeded his vision. He brushed it back with an impatient hand and inspected the results of his latest efforts.

Shia lay on the birthing table, her lovely face splattered with blood and frozen in a rictus of pain. Her belly was open, torn from sternum to pubis. Long flaps of shredded skin lay folded outward, indicating that the deadly assault had come from within her own body. In the ruins of her womb, nestled in a warm pool of blood and decimated organs, the infant Vadim had so carefully engineered lay quietly, regarding the world from pupil-less eyes that glowed like a Tairen's Eye crystal.

Triumph swelled, filling him with renewed vigor. He reached for the child, laughed as it hissed and batted at his hands with tiny fingers curved like claws. "No, no, my lad." He plucked the child from its mother's corpse. "What a fine, strong boy you are. What a fine, strong Mage you will make."

Cradling the child against his chest, Vadim walked to a connecting room. There, a dozen servants waited beside clear, thermal-heated pools. Several of them followed Vadim into the water and silently bathed the gore of the recent magic rites from the High Mage and the tiny baby he reluctantly handed to them.

When they were finished, he stepped out of the thermal pools and let the servants dry him with warmed, scented cloths and slip a thick, plush robe over his body to ease the chill these sessions always left in his bones. Those shivers helped mask the other tremors in his hand as he sat in a cushioned chair by a steaming brazier. The servants placed the swaddled babe back in his arms.

Already the magic had begun to subside in the child, and his eyes had reverted to their natural appearance, a clear pale blue rimmed with cobalt. Shia's eyes.

A surprising trace of regret touched the High Mage. Shia had been uncommonly lovely, and she had served him well. In addition to the many hours of personal pleasure she had provided him, she had birthed half a dozen gifted offspring sired by his most powerful studs.

He ran a thin finger down the baby's smooth cheek. "Your name, child, will be Tyrkomel. Mother's death."

After the Mage and his prize had left the birthing room, the *umagi* servants of Boura Fell entered to strip and cleanse it with brisk efficiency. Three women hosed down the bloody table and floors. Two men shuffled in to wrap the torn, cooling body of the dead woman in canvas and haul it outside to the waiting refuse cart.

The ragged, dark-haired girl stood beside the handles of the cart. She flinched when the canvas parted to reveal the frozen face, silky black hair, and staring pale blue eyes of the corpse within.

A soft cry—quickly stifled—choked in the girl's throat. When the two servants turned back to the birthing chamber, her slender, grimy fingers reached out, trembling slightly as they brushed Shia's lustrous hair. A rusty knife flashed. A lock of long, shining black hair came away in the girl's hand.

Clutching it to her chest, she ran. One of the servants gave an angry shout when she came out and found the refuse cart abandoned, but the girl didn't stop. She hurried down a series of dark stairs and narrow, winding corridors that were barely more than tunnels burrowed into the rock. Bare, filthy feet scrambled over age-worn rock down to the

lowest level of Boura Fell, where the most dangerous prisoners were kept and the refuse pit reached bottom.

There, in a shadowed alcove beneath the stair, she huddled in darkness, rocking and stroking the lock of hair. She
didn't make a sound—she'd learned long ago to keep
silent—but inside her mind she sang in a hoarse, sobbing
voice the words of Shia's favorite song. When she heard the
snarl and furious barks of the ferocious *darrokken* in the refuse pit fighting over the newest morsel tossed down into
their midst, the girl plugged her fingers in her ears and
raised the voice in her mind to a shout. *Not her. Not her. Not
the sweet, soft, blue eyes with the tender hands. Meat and bone.
That was all. Meat and bone.*

The girl pressed the strand of Shia's hair to her lips,
breathed in the scent, forcing herself to visualize the happy,
smiling face of only a few bells ago. There. That was her.
Shia. Sweet, kind Shia with the gentle hands who loved to
brush the girl's hair and sing pretty songs about sunlight
and soft rain and warm, fragrant winds that smelled of
flowers instead of dark magic and death. She'd even given
the girl a name and called her by it when she came . . . *Melliandra.*

The girl breathed and sang and rocked until the growling
fury of the *darrokken* faded. In the silence, her body went
still. *Umagi* did not rebel. *Umagi* only served. Their thoughts
and memories and even their souls were not their own. But
she would not share Shia—not with the High Mage who'd
slain her.

Years ago, she'd learned how to hide small thoughts from
him. Little things at first—the crust of bread she'd slipped
in her pocket, the loose button she'd palmed from one of
the pillows in his room. Over time she'd grown bolder,
learned to hide more—like how much she hated him and
wished him dead.

Now, she took the pain and the tears of Shia's death and
used them, shaped them, forging a bright, hard shell around

that small part of her mind where she hid her secrets. She gave that part of her mind a name—it no longer belonged to the worthless, powerless *umagi* called "girl." It belonged to the child Shia had held in her arms and sung to, the child Shia had named Melliandra.

Behind that bright, hard shell, Melliandra stored her memories of Shia and those too-short bells of brightness she'd found in the dark heart of Boura Fell. The High Mage would never get those memories. She'd die first.

Or he would.

Her eyes flashed open, cold and silver and filled with fierce purpose.

CHAPTER TEN

Tairen, tairen, soaring high
Undisputed king of sky
Which great god did fearless chance
To cast thy bold magnificence?
    "Tairen, Tairen" by Kimall vel'En Belawi, Tairen Soul

The Fading Lands ~ Eastern Desert

High above the world, the light of the Great Sun turned the eastern sky watery. Streamers of wispy cloud hanging over the far horizon glowed pink in the slowly lightening sky.

Wind blew through the loose shields of Fire surrounding Ellysetta, whistling in her ears as she and Rain raced across the Fading Lands. Below them, the stark colors of the desert slowly gave way to a vast, gently rolling terrain covered with tall, waving grasses. Herds of grazing animals dotted the plains, scattering in fright as Rain's tairen form swooped over them.

Beyond the wide expanse of golden plains, the smoking, snowcapped volcanoes of the Feyls rose up in impressive majesty. One tall peak dominated the rest, towering over its brethren by at least a third. Clouds encircled its snowy peak like a misty crown. Just below them, three large tairen rode the updrafts on outstretched wings.

"Is that Fey'Bahren?" Ellysetta asked.

"It is. Torasul, Fahreeta, and Steli are flying out to greet us." The three tairen spewed jets of flame and spun around to fly towards Rain and Ellysetta with alarming swiftness.

She gulped. *"Is that a good thing?"*

"You are the truemate of the Tairen Soul, none of the tairen would dare singe a single hair on your head. But Steli is . . . fierce. She may try to frighten you. She thinks she is chakai, First Blade, of the tairen."

"First Blade?"

"Fiercest of defenders. Celierians call them champions. Bel, Tajik, Rijonn, and Gil are all First Blades of the Fading Lands. Gaelen was, too, before he became dahl'reisen."

"Oh." Wonderful.

Ellysetta's fingers tightened about the pommel of the saddle as the tairen roared. The great cats were enormous, their eyes glowing, opalescent wells of active power. One of them, a pure white beauty with deep blue eyes, sped ahead of the other tairen and roared a challenge, showing a fearsome set of sharp white teeth. Rain roared back but the white tairen did not slow.

"Is the white one Steli?"

"Aiyah."

Steli's ears were laid back against her head, her razor-sharp claws unsheathed and fully extended.

"Rain . . . " Ellie grabbed hold of the saddle, and her legs

clamped tight around Rain's neck. He and Steli were on a direct collision course, and neither showed the slightest sign of fear or concern. Neither showed any sign of slowing down either.

"Trust me, Ellysetta."

Trust him. Trust him when a ferocious two-ton flying predator raced towards them at ramming speed. Ellysetta gulped, squeezed her eyes shut, and held on tight.

"Hold on." That was all the warning Ellie received before Rain banked sharply to the left.

Ellysetta bit back a scream, and her eyes flashed open just in time to see the two tairen miss a head-on collision by a mere hand's breadth. Steli passed so close, her furred tail brushed Ellysetta's leg, and the wind generated by her pumping wings sent Ellysetta's hair flying in all directions.

Rain righted himself in moments. *"Are you well, shei'tani?"*

In hands white-knuckled from fear, Ellie clutched enormous tufts of tairen fur, and her legs clenched the saddle so fiercely that she'd all but melded herself to the leather. Slowly, her roiling belly and racing heart calmed and she managed to unfreeze her muscles enough to release Rain's fur. *"For the moment."* Except for the unfortunate feeling that she was about to lose what little food she'd eaten in Lissilin.

"You did very well." Approval hummed along the threads of his Spirit weave. *"Steli will not challenge us again. You did not scream and I did not falter. She was the first to turn away."* There was satisfaction in his voice, the prideful kind evinced by men and boys when they survived a test of manhood.

She relaxed her death grip on Rain's pelt and shook her head. Steli was not the only one to believe herself First Blade of the tairen.

The other two tairen—one a gleaming gold and the other a deep, dark brown—banked in opposing circles, and Rain flew between them. He headed straight for the massive peak of Fey'Bahren, and as they neared, Ellysetta could make out the dark shadows of caves dotting the volcano's steep sides. Rain landed on the wide ledge surrounding one of the largest caves. A shaft of Air plucked her from the saddle and set her on her feet, as Rain's great black tairen form dissolved into mist. Then he was Rainier once more, tall, fierce, unearthly beautiful.

"Come, *shei'tani*. Sybharukai and the others are waiting for us."

"Are you sure it's all right? I can wait out here if necessary." A loud roar split the air, and she turned to see Steli spouting a great jet of fire. Ellysetta gulped. "Or not."

Despite everything, the corner of Rain's mouth lifted in a small smile. "You would be safe here, but Sybharukai says I should bring you." He held out a wrist. "Come, *shei'tani*, and meet our soul-kin."

He escorted her down a long, winding passage that seemed to go on forever. The passage was wide and tall enough to accommodate three fully grown tairen walking abreast, the stone dark and worn smooth by centuries of use. Numerous smaller tunnels branched off from the main passage, but they continued steadily downward. Once the cave entrance was out of sight, Rain summoned Fire to light the crystal globes that lined the pathway.

"The tairen use lights in their lair?" she asked in surprise.

He laughed softly. "*Nei*, but Feyreisen in their Fey form find it helpful. It's said Feyreisen and their families once lived together in Fey'Bahren with the tairen, but it's been long since that was true—if it ever was. Most *fellana* are too afraid of the tairen to be comfortable here."

"Was your mother afraid of the tairen?"

His smile grew sad. "*Nei. Nei*, she never was."

The passage finally opened into an enormous firelit cavern deep within the heart of Fey'Bahren. Dark, ledged walls soared ten tairen lengths high. A thick layer of hot black sand covered the cavern floor. Ellysetta could feel the heat through the soles of her boots as she and Rain entered. All around them, glowing eyes watched from the darkness of the encircling ledges. The cavern hummed with a low, mournful growling that made her want to weep.

A smoky shadow moved along the far side of the cavern, startling Ellysetta when two large glowing green eyes appeared in its midst. Then the shadow moved again, rising to pad silently across the sand. The illusory camouflage of the approaching great dark gray cat was astonishing. Even moving, it appeared more smoke than solid flesh. As the tairen approached, Ellysetta sensed a rich mix of welcome, strength, and a powerful calming stillness. Almost as if this one tairen were singlehandedly holding the grief of the others in check.

"Sybharukai." Rain touched Ellie's shoulder. *Wait here, shei'tani.* He continued forward alone to greet the matriarch of the tairen pride. His towering Fey height seemed dwarfed against the tairen, and the gentle welcoming nudge of Sybharukai's massive head pushed him back several steps. He raised his arms and embraced the enormous cat, pressing his face against the furred jaw.

When they parted, Ellysetta saw what Sybharukai's body had previously hidden from view. Another tairen lay motionless upon the dark sands of the nesting lair. Its great head was cocked to one side, jaws parted to reveal once lethal fangs and a lolling tongue. Its eyes were open, but they had turned a flat, opaque white. The cat lay curled around six large eggs, protecting them even in death. Behind the dead tairen crouched a large, dark brown tairen who was the source of the mournful growls.

Every instinct urged Ellysetta to soothe the deep hurt that caused such overwhelming sorrow. She took a step nearer, then stopped. This was a place of mourning, and she was a stranger.

"That is Cahlah," Rain said quietly as he returned to her side. "She is—was—the mother of those unhatched kits, and it is she whose passing we felt. The male behind her is her mate, Merdrahl." Deep emotion thickened his voice, and his expression had grown stony.

Unlike the tairen, Rain was no stranger, and she needed neither invitation nor introduction to offer him comfort. She reached for his hand. As her fingers clasped it, she could feel the faint tingles of warmth passing from her body to his, healing magic, which she wove instinctively. Condolence, sympathy, gentle love.

"I'm sorry, Rain. This is my fault. If you hadn't given me time with my family—if you'd flown me here straightaway—we could have arrived days ago. Maybe we could have found a way to save them." Guilt lay heavy upon her. She tried to block the emotion so Rain would not sense it, but they were touching skin to skin. He read her guilt and grief as easily as if they were his own.

He drew a shuddering breath and pulled her into his embrace. "*Nei,* I will not allow you to blame yourself. The decision was mine. You would have come if I had insisted, but I did not. Even Sybharukai thought Cahlah was improving, and this . . . thing—whatever it is—that slays the kitlings in the egg has never taken an adult tairen before now. Sybharukai says Cahlah fought it *cha, meicha, te seyani,* fang, claw, and tail; but she had already lost too much strength, and she spent the last of it battling the thing that came to claim her kit."

Ellysetta laid her hand on his chest. "I am the one the Eye of Truth sent you to find. I am the one meant to save them. If I am not to blame for Cahlah's death, then how can you be?"

Sybharukai gave a purring growl that sounded to Ellie like both a gentle remonstration and a slightly impatient command.

Rain gave a small, rueful smile. "*She who leads the tairen has no patience for guilt. What's done cannot be undone.*" He stepped back. Still holding her hand, he tugged her gently towards Sybharukai. "Come, Ellysetta, and meet Sybharu-kai, *makai* of the Fey'Bahren pride."

They stood so close to the tairen that the great cat's breath rippled through Ellysetta's hair.

"Greetings, Lady Sybharukai," Ellie murmured politely. She'd never been introduced to an animal before, but the sheer presence of this tairen was so magnificent that offer-ing a polite greeting and attaching a noble honorific to the tairen's name seemed only fitting.

A moment later, she was glad she'd been so polite. The glowing beacons of the tairen's eyes fixed on her, and a wave of pure power enveloped her. It flowed through her body like a swift wind through the branches of a tree. Comforting warmth, followed abruptly by a brisk, forceful chill that left her gasping as though she'd been stripped bare and tossed into an icy lake. Hesitation. Surprise. Then an-other dagger-sharp probing. All the while Sybharukai's eyes held hers, deep wells of knowing green, ancient and wise.

This was no animal, but a being of great power and intel-ligence.

There was a huffing sound—tairen laughter—and a low, vibrant voice filled her mind, not tairen song but words that simply appeared in her mind. In Celierian.

"We are all animals of one form or another, kitling."

Ellysetta stared at the tairen in wonder. "I never knew the tairen could speak Celierian."

"She speaks to you in your native tongue?" Rain seemed pleased. "That is a sign of great respect. The tairen can send their thoughts in any language they desire, but they con-sider words cumbersome and restrictive. Tairen song is much more beautiful."

"Yes, but this is amazing too." She couldn't take her eyes off Sybharukai. "It doesn't feel anything like the Fey mind-speech. It's as if the words are all around me, absorbed by every part of my body."

"*Aiyah*. It is not Spirit the tairen use, but some other form of communication."

"She read my mind."

"Do not be offended. The tairen do not put the same restrictions on their magic that the Fey do, and within the pride, there are no secrets."

"I'm not offended."

Sybharukai's massive dark gray head nudged Ellie. Before Ellysetta realized what was happening, Sybharukai dipped her head and licked Ellie's face. Her tongue was warm and rough, much like a house cat's.

Sybharukai sat back on her haunches. From the ledges all around the cavern came quiet sounds of movement as the other tairen stirred. A sleek tawny beauty with golden eyes dropped silently to the black sands of the nesting lair, golden wings half extended to break her descent. Behind her, a slightly larger tairen with auburn fur landed. Together they padded towards Ellysetta.

"Xisanna and her mate, Perahl," Rain murmured. "Now that Sybharukai has accepted you, the other tairen will greet you as well."

Tawny Xisanna and auburn Perahl sniffed Ellysetta experimentally as, behind them, more tairen leapt and glided down from the ledges to the cavern floor.

"Greetings, Lady Xisanna, Lord Perahl." She jumped as the two tairen, having finished sniffing her, licked her face, then moved off to let the others approach.

Alone and in pairs, more than a dozen tairen inspected her before granting her their lick of approval and welcome. Fahreeta, Torasul, and Steli returned from outside and came forward to add their greetings.

The dead tairen's mate gave a mournful cry, the sound so full of pain that tears filled Ellysetta's eyes. She made an instinctive step towards him, but Rain held her back. "*Nei, shei'tani*. The tairen and I will see to him."

Even as he spoke, Sybharukai rose to her feet and padded across the black sands to where Cahlah's body lay. The other tairen followed close on her heels.

"It is time, Ellysetta." Rain lifted her hand to his lips and pressed a kiss on her fingers. "Merdrahl agreed to wait for me, but he cannot stand to wait any longer. There are steps carved into the wall behind us. Climb to at least the fourth ledge, and do not come down until I tell you."

Worry gripped her. "Rain?"

"I will be safe, Ellysetta, as will you, but you must do as I say. Hurry, please."

The sense of urgency in his voice made her turn and run across the sands to the wide, flat steps hewn into the side of the cavern. Magic swelled as Rain summoned the Change, and when she glanced back over her shoulder, he was loping across the lair in tairen form to join the rest of the pride.

Ellysetta made her way to the second ledge high above the cavern floor. Below, several of the tairen took all but one of the eggs in their mouths and carried them to the other side of the lair. They deposited the eggs in a far corner and buried them in a heap of dark sand before returning to join the others, where they formed a ring around Merdrahl and the dead Cahlah.

All the tairen began to growl, the sound a single deep, throaty note that made the hairs on Ellie's arms stand up.

"Higher, shei'tani."

Rain's silent urging sent her scrambling up another flight of steps. As she reached the third landing, the growling reached a higher pitch. The tairen circling Merdrahl and Cahlah rose to their hind legs, and their wings began to unfurl. Opalescent tairen eyes glowed bright with magic. Merdrahl released a haunting cry and laid his body over his dead mate's motionless form. The mountain itself began to tremble as the voices of the tairen filled the lair, reverberating in the massive cavern. Several of the tairen stretched back their heads and roared. Gouts of fire escaped from their throats, and then she knew.

She scrambled up yet a fourth flight of steps. The palms of her hands scraped against the rock, but she paid no heed to the pain. A sense of urgency had gripped her, spawned by a fierce, unshakable certainty.

Fire was coming, hot and glorious. Tairen's fire to cleanse and purify. Tairen's fire to slay and transform. Tairen's fire, deep and deadly magic.

How she knew it, she could not guess, but she was certain. Her skin felt hot and full and tight, as if the fire were already inside her, fighting for release. Perspiration dewed her skin, and her breath came in ragged gasps. She stopped on the fourth ledge, unable to force herself higher. What was coming alarmed her, but now it also drew her, calling to her like a beloved friend.

Below her, the ring of tairen were all standing on their hind legs. Their wings were fully extended, the furless undersides glistening as though paved with diamond dust. Tairen song played in her mind, pure, endless notes that grew stronger and deeper, building to a crescendo, flooding her with emotions. Aching sadness, vast love, an agony of loneliness, the promise of peace. Tears spilled from her eyes. Merdrahl had lost his mate, and his suffering was unendurable. The tairen, his family, would release him.

The visceral notes of gleaming gold and silver music flashed and trembled in the air, resonance so pure and intense it assumed visual form. The music filled Ellie's ears and mind and went deeper still to invade her blood, flesh, and bones, sinking into the very fabric of her being. Deep within, her own tairen shifted with unease. Feral, frightened, it hissed a warning even as desperate yearning filled her, an aching void, a soul-deep pain. It wanted . . . needed . . . *what*?

When the song reached its apex, the tairen on the lair

floor flung back their heads and roared. With wings flung wide, fully extended and trembling, their massive chests expanded on a single, communal inhalation. In the center of the ring, Merdrahl bared his deadly fangs and screamed a final, fierce, earthshaking roar of love and sorrow, pleading and command.

Fire exploded from the throats of the surrounding tairen, enormous, unstoppable jets of consuming flame. A fiery furnace raged where Merdrahl and Cahlah had been. Ellysetta raised a hand to shield her eyes from the blinding inferno, yet she could not look away. Tairen wings pumped like bellows. Great clouds of flame and smoke billowed outward, flooding the cavern floor. Heat blasted upwards, flinging Ellysetta off her feet.

She rolled over on her hands and knees and started to rise, but a familiar cold tingling, like the bite of an ice spider, washed over her, sapping her legs of strength. The sensation grew stronger, shooting up her spine, making her every muscle tremble. Fear clutched at her throat.

"Rain . . . "

Her hesitant call went unanswered. She crawled to the edge of her perch. The cavern floor was completely submerged beneath a deep, raging ocean of fire that buffeted the ledge just below hers. No part of the tairen was visible, yet she knew they were there, at the center of the inferno, unharmed and feeding the flames. She could hear them singing, a single, sustained note resonating in her mind.

She crouched on the ledge, shivering despite the heat. Her flesh trembled as though it would dissolve off her very bones. Beneath the pure, endless aria of the tairen, she could now hear whispers. Insidious, frightening. Voices beckoning, hissing, pleading. Wordless commands that pulled at her and shot terror through her heart.

And then she heard the sound of her name, spoken as

if from some nameless monster of the dark. *Ellysssettttt-taaaaaa.*

Gasping, she flung herself back from the edge, scrambling for something, anything to hold on to. As if what called her name could reach out and grab her. She found a small boulder and clutched it with frantic strength, squeezing her eyes shut.

"*Rain!*" She screamed his name aloud, shrieking it into the fiery wind. Then again, in Spirit and along their bondthreads, like a talisman against the summoning darkness. "*Rain!*"

Across the room, the tairens' single, sustained note ended, and a gentler melody ensued, tender and sad, but with a light, hopeful chord running through it. As quickly as they had come, the whispering voices were gone, and with them the disturbing chill that had crawled across her skin like ice spiders. The tairen's roar quieted, and through her tightly shut eyelids she could see the brightness of their flames dimming until the lair was once again shrouded in shadow.

Rain found her clinging to a small boulder. Her eyes were squeezed shut, and even in the dim light he could see the pulse pounding in her throat and hear her shallow, gasping breaths.

"Ellysetta?"

The first touch of his hand made her flinch, and he frowned in concern. Her flesh felt chill to the touch. She was shivering—and clearly terrified. "It is over, *shei'tani.* There is no need to fear." Tenderly he brushed her hair back from her face and cupped her cheeks, letting the warmth from his flesh seep into hers. All he could think was that the tairen rite of passage had terrified her. She'd probably believed she would be burned to death in the flames. "*Sieks'ta.* I am sorry. I should have warned you about the Fire Song. I know how frightening the rite can seem, but I swear to you, *shei'tani,* you were never in danger."

Sariel had always feared the tairen. They had welcomed her as Rain's mate, but she had never been comfortable around them. She had rarely accompanied him to their lair. Ellysetta was a Tairen Soul, so he'd thought she would understand better, would feel at home here, as he did, but clearly he'd expected too much, too soon.

He stifled his disappointment and pressed his lips to the smooth skin of her forehead. *"Sieks'ta, beloved. Forgive me. I should have prepared you, given you time to adjust before thrusting you into the pride and expecting you to understand our ways."* He had not pushed Sariel to accept the tairen half of his soul, nor would he press Ellysetta to accept more than she could. When she was ready, the pride would be waiting.

"I'm not afraid of the tairen." Ellysetta's voice was a hoarse whisper. "I wasn't afraid of the fire either, though perhaps I should have been."

Rain pulled back to look at her. Her eyes were open, her face pale. Her fear was just beginning to subside. "Then what was it that frightened you so badly?"

"It was the darkness, the cold." Her voice shook, and she began to shiver again. "The voices, calling to me."

His brows drew together. "Ellysetta, there was no darkness or cold, only fire. There were no voices, except the tairen singing Cahlah and Merdrahl and their lost kit into the next life. We did not call to you."

"It wasn't you or the tairen. It wasn't the Shadow Man either. It was something else. Something horrible. Something evil." Her fingers clenched, digging into his shoulders. "Rain, it knew my name."

"Shh." Rain smoothed a hand over Ellysetta's wild curls and sent a concerned look to Sybharukai. Neither he nor the tairen had sensed any danger, and yet he could not doubt Ellysetta. What she believed, she believed absolutely.

What if Ellysetta, who could bring a *dahl'reisen* back into the light, could sense what even Sybharukai, wise one of the tairen, could not? Worse, what if the evil that had drained the life's essence from Cahlah and her kits had made Elly-setta its next target? A low growl rumbled in his throat. The entity that had slain Cahlah and her kits was a mysterious, invisible, untrackable foe that had triumphed over Fey and tairen alike for centuries.

Ellysetta continued to shiver in his arms, and her teeth began to chatter as fear gave way to shock. Rain gathered her in his arms, dropped smoothly to the lair floor on a slide of Air, and headed for one of the large tunnels leading away from the nesting lair.

"Where are we going?"

"You are chilled. There is an underground lake in Fey'Bahren, warmed by the mountain's volcanic heart."

"I'm all right," she protested. "I don't need a hot bath. And there's no need for you to carry me."

"You will take the bath to ease my mind. And it is my pleasure to carry you." If the formless evil attacked her again, he wanted to be close enough to hold her and sense what she sensed.

"What of Merdrahl? He's gone, isn't he?"

"*Aiyah*. He is gone. That was the purpose of our Fire Song: to free him, Cahlah, and their dead kit from this life so they could enter the next."

She glanced across the sands to the place Merdrahl had been. Rain knew the moment she recognized what remained of the two tairen and their lost kit. Despite her shivering, her spine stiffened, and amazement flooded every point of contact between them.

"Rain, put me down." She squirmed free. "Is that . . . ?" She took three steps before he caught her hand to halt her.

"*Nei*, do not touch it. It is still quite hot." He glanced at the tumble of dark, glossy crystal, radiance glimmering in its multifaceted depths. Kingdoms had been conquered for the minutest portion of what lay there in the black sands. "*Aiyah*, it is what you think." Tairen's Eye crystal, two great boulders and one smaller, darker globe of it: all that remained in this world of Merdrahl, Cahlah, and their kit.

"How is that possible? You once told me that Tairen's Eye crystal could not be made or unmade."

"I said that the Fey could not make or unmake it. Only the tairen can do so, and only by performing the rite of passage that you just witnessed. The rite requires at least twelve adult tairen to sing the Fire Song."

She touched the two crystals that hung around her neck. "These are the . . . bodies of a dead tairen?"

"They once were, but the Fire Song transforms what was and leaves in its place something quite different." He laid the back of his hand against her cheek. "And that, Ellysetta," he warned gently, "is a secret you must never tell another soul. Even the Fey do not know how Tairen's Eye crystal comes into being. It is a treasure guarded by the tairen and the Feyreisen who walk among them as brothers."

She nodded. "I will not speak of it."

They passed through the tunnel entrance, to the broad, timeworn pathway that led down deeper into the heart of Fey'Bahren. Small pebbles clattered behind them, and Ellysetta turned her head towards the source of the noise.

"The tairen are following us." She sounded surprised.

"They are curious. It has been a very long time since anyone but me has come to Fey'Bahren."

She stopped. "I am not bathing with an audience. Even if they are tairen."

Celierian modesty. Part of him hoped she would never lose it. He loved the way her cheeks turned pink when she blushed. "I will weave a screen for you, *shei'tani.*"

The tunnel opened up into another large cavern. Rain called Fire to light the sconces around the perimeter and illuminate the clear, still waters of the lake. Though not as wide as the nesting lair nor as tall, the cavern was still impressive. Scores of adult tairen could comfortably bask on the rocks surrounding the vast, glassy lake, and above, the domed ceiling arched high enough to allow even the largest tairen to fully extend his wings for drying. The walls were smooth and polished from millennia of young tairen testing their flame beneath the pride's watchful eyes. Rain himself had joined his tairen cradle friends in spewing gouts of flame into rock, learning how to control the flame and its heat, and how to breathe fire without singeing his muzzle.

Ellysetta walked to the edge of the lake and knelt to dip her hand. "It *is* warm."

"Fey'Bahren is a volcano. Its heat warms the waters of this lake." He smiled faintly. "The tairen like their comforts." He led her to a shallow section of the lake, where underwater ledges formed a perfect soaking spot. "Here, Ellysetta."

She hesitated. "I'm really much warmer now."

"Ellysetta, if you stripped naked and raced through the tunnels of Fey'Bahren, the tairen would think nothing of it."

"Yes . . . well . . ." Her cheeks flushed a brighter pink. "I don't believe I'll be putting that to the test anytime soon."

So prim. So . . . Celierian. He smiled and shook his head. Earth blazed at his fingertips, and her travel leathers became a soft linen bathing dress. "There. Now get in the water and let it warm you. And stay there until I say you may get out."

She arched a brow at his high-handedness.

"Teska." Please.

She sniffed. "Fine. I'll get in. But I'll get back out when *I* say so, not you."

Sybharukai purred and climbed to her basking ledge. *"It is good your mate lets you know who is makai."* Her dark gray ears twitched with amusement.

Rain gave the wise one a sour look. *"You will not think so when it is you she challenges."* He took a seat on a boulder beside Sybharukai and watched his mate ease into the warm waters, her eyes closing in bliss as the heat penetrated her cold skin. "Ellysetta said she sensed a presence when we sang the Fire Song for Merdrahl and Cahlah. Something cold and evil. She said it called her name. Did you feel it?"

Sybharukai's ears flicked. *"Nei. There was only the Fire Song, and then peace and sorrow when Merdrahl and Cahlah flew free of this life."* She paused, then added softly, *"Of the kitling, there was nothing."*

Rain nodded. He had not felt the unborn kit's passing either. As with all the other victims of the withering disease, it was as if his soul had leached away before he could be sung into the next life.

Rain's gut still told him the Eld were to blame, yet there was no hint of Azrahn at work, and no indication that any sort of magic had breached the protective shields of the Faering Mists.

And yet, Ellysetta had sensed evil . . . dark and cold and beckoning.

A quiet splash drew his attention. Ellysetta had completely submerged herself and was lying still beneath the surface of the lake. With her eyes closed and the long coils of her bright hair floating around her, she looked like one of the beguiling Danae water sprites who delighted in luring unwary mortals to watery graves.

"She brings song back to your heart," Sybharukai observed.

"Aiyah."

"You no longer wish for your own Fire Song."

Rain met Sybharukai's eyes. "Nei, I want to live." Until that night when he'd flown along the borders of Eld, the tairen had never discussed how he'd longed for death after Sariel's murder, but of course, all the pride had known. They had accepted his desire. Tairen mated for life. But they had always known he would not seek death until his responsibilities to the Fey and to the tairen were met.

Sybharukai purred and stretched, flexing her claws. *"Ellysetta-kitling is a better mate for you than the other."*

"She is my *shei'tani*. Sariel was *e'tani*." The tairen had never called Sariel by name. Always, she had been "your mate" or "that one." And now, apparently, "the other."

"The other was friend, but not tairen."

Rain glanced at Sybharukai in surprise. It was unusual for the *makai* to be so talkative. "*Nei*," he agreed. "Sariel was not tairen, but Ellysetta is."

The great cat's ears flicked. *"She smells so, but her song does not sing to us. We cannot choose her sorreisu kiyr or lead her through First Change until we know her song."*

"Perhaps she does not yet know how to sing. The Celierians never could have taught her."

"Tairen sing in the egg. There is no need to teach."

"But she is tairen. I saw it in her eyes. She hears my song."

"Yet you do not hear hers."

He frowned, perplexed. No, he had never heard her song. He'd seen the tairen in her eyes, he'd felt its power coiling inside her, witnessed its devastating fury, but he'd never heard it sing. "*Nei*," he said slowly. "I thought perhaps I had not heard it because our bond is not complete."

"You hear the songs of the pride."

"*Aiyah*, I hear all the pride, but we are not mates. I hear the thoughts of all the Fey, too, but until Ellysetta and I complete our bond, I can hear only the thoughts she deliberately sends to me. Perhaps her song works the same way."

"We do not hear her either. She is . . ." Sybharukai abandoned words and sang a series of notes that summoned the image of a tangled net of string with tairen kits diligently tugging at the loose ends, only to tangle the string even more.

Rain nodded. "*Aiyah*. I could not have said it better." Ellysetta was a conundrum, a fascinating mix of innocence, astonishing power, and countless secrets that taunted him with their presence while remaining stubbornly concealed.

"When you return to the Fey-lair, the tairen will fly with you

and sing pride-greetings to Shei'Kess for your mate, since she has no song of her own.

His jaw dropped open. The tairen had not entered Dharsa since before the Mage Wars. "Why would you do that? You didn't even come to ask the Eye for help saving the kits."

Sybharukai sniffed. *"Why should we have gone then? We sent you."*

He blinked, nonplussed. *They'd* sent him? Nearly a month ago, in an act of sheer desperation, he'd laid bare hands on the Eye of Truth in an attempt to wrest answers from it. The oracle had not been pleased. Now, Sybharukai implied that she'd somehow been responsible for his actions. His eyes narrowed. "Did you put the idea of confronting the Eye of Truth in my head?"

She extended her claws and began sharpening their tips against the rock. *"You are pride. You knew our need. You did what was necessary when the time was right."*

Rain gave a short laugh and shook his head. That nonanswer was answer enough. The Fey would never dream of using their magic to manipulate other Fey, but the tairen had never pretended to be so civilized. They were not tame and did not live by the laws of those who were. "And Ellysetta? Why would you sing pride-greetings for her? What are you not telling me?"

Sybharukai heaved a breath and flapped her wings. Tairen might be wild, wicked, and unpredictable, but like the Fey, they never lied. *"Ellysetta-kitling smells tairen,"* she finally said, *"but she smells of something else too."* Her eyes closed, and a low purr hummed in her throat. *"Old magic."*

He sat up straight. "What kind of old magic?"

Sybharukai's purring ceased. Her bright green eyes opened and her claws dug into the rock. *"The scent is too ancient. This tairen's pride-memory does not go back far enough to name it, but Shei'Kess will know. Shei'Kess keeps the memories of all the prides."*

More ancient than Sybharukai's pride-memory? The possibility shocked him. Sybharukai was *makai* of the Fey'Bahren pride. She herself had lived more than two thousand years, and her pride-memory stretched back to the start of the Second Age, passed on from each dying *makai* to her successor.

A loud splash interrupted him before he could ask. Steli had entered the water and was paddling beside Ellysetta's ledge, snorting sprays of water. Ellysetta gave a tiny scream of surprise that broke into laughter, and she swept her arm across the water's surface to direct a retaliatory splash back at the playful tairen.

Steli's play surprised Rain. The tairen of the Fey'Bahren pride had never offered Sariel anything but aloof disregard and tolerance, yet here was Steli treating Ellysetta like a tairen kitling. Even without hearing Ellysetta's song, Steli and the others accepted her as one of the pride.

Fahreeta leapt into the water, sending a massive splash arcing though the air. The golden tairen gave a crowing roar of victory as her wave swamped both Steli and Ellysetta, then dove beneath the surface as Steli gave chase. Ellysetta watched, laughing.

Rain turned back to Sybharukai, intending to continue their conversation, but the *makai* of the Fey'Bahren pride had risen to her feet and was padding down towards the rim of the lake. *"Enough talk, Rainier-Eras. Time for play."* With an impressive roar, Sybharukai jumped in. The rest of the pride soon followed, and within moments, the lake was filled with wet, playful tairen.

Knowing he would get no more answers today, and unwilling to be left out of the pride's fun, Rain stood up, stripped off his leathers, and dove smoothly into the warm, clear waters to join them. Merdrahl and Cahlah were gone, but their suffering was over. The Fire Song had awakened a sense of joy and renewal in them all, and he, like his tairen family, could spare time for a little happiness before resuming the battle with the darkness that threatened them all.

Celieria City ~ The Royal Palace

Lady Jiarine Montevero, lady-in-waiting to Celieria's Queen Annoura, leaned closer to the clear glass mirror and dabbed a thin layer of fresh white powder over the dark circles beneath her eyes. She hadn't been sleeping well since the disappearance of Queen Annoura's Favorite, Ser Vale—the sinfully handsome, vivid-eyed courtier Jiarine knew and served as Kolis Manza, the Elden Mage to whom she had surrendered her soul in return for wealth, power, and noble advancement.

Eleven days without sleep—worrying not so much about Master Manza's fate as her own—was beginning to show on her face, and she could not afford for that to continue. Queen Annoura of Celieria did not tolerate less than perfection amongst the Dazzles of her inner court. Ser Vale might return, and he would not be pleased if she'd lost her increasingly favored position in Annoura's inner circle due to something as foolish as lack of attention to her appearance.

Jiarine pinched her cheeks, then deftly added a blushing hint of color from a pot of pink powder. She was wearing her hair its natural dark color today. She'd just received word that the queen was feeling peevish this morning. When that was the case, her inner court knew to abandon their hair powders and choose rich, dark shades of clothing, the better to set off the queen's silvery pale beauty and improve her mood.

Muttering a curse, Jiarine kicked the hem of the pale blue gown she'd already put on, then removed this morning. "Fanette!" she called to the young lady's maid she'd sent into the next room to press her deep sapphire gown.

"Hurry up with that gown, girl! Her Majesty does not tolerate tardiness."

Turning back to the mirror, she reached down into the cups of her tightly laced corset and plumped her breasts so the rouged nipples peeped out over the lacy tops. She knew how to use her assets to the best advantage, and there were several influential lords who liked to see a hint of rose when Lady Montevero leaned their way.

If Master Manza didn't return, Jiarine had her own plans for advancement. Starting with becoming the next Lady Purcel. The old wheezer was rich as a king, and though his breath stank like a barracks privy and his lecherous hands loved to pinch and grope any young woman fool enough to walk within reach, she'd happily ride his withered old rod straight into his grave in return for access to his coffers and control of his lands. Besides, he was so old, it wouldn't be hard to arrange a timely death for him in the event frequent and enthusiastic copulation didn't do the trick. And thanks to that weave-driven night of lust two weeks ago, Purcel had already sampled Jiarine's wares and knew they were to his liking.

The bedchamber door opened. "Finally! What in the Dark Lord's name took you so—" Jiarine's voice broke off at the sight of the two unfamiliar men who stepped into the room. She grabbed the first thing within reach—a cushion—and held it to her chest. "Who are you? How dare you! Get out this instant!"

Both were dressed as nobles, but she had lived at court for the last three years and recognized neither of them. The taller of the two was a handsome, lean man with forest green eyes. The shorter one was built like a barrel-chested longshoreman from the wharf. His pale blue eyes, surrounded by stubby black lashes, swept over her with undisguised interest.

When neither man obeyed her command to leave, she raised her voice and screeched, "Fanette!"

"Silence, *umagi*." The tall one spoke, his voice a cold

commanding hiss that slapped her like a brisk, hard hand across the face.

Jiarine froze and fell silent. Every drop of blood drained from her face as the skin above her left breast turned cold as ice. Streams of glacial cold spread quickly through her body. *Oh, gods.* Something *had* happened to Vale. Her lips trembled. Her fingers clenched tight around the pillow. The question burst out before she could censor it. "Where is Ser Vale—Master Manza?"

"I said be silent," the tall Mage snapped. "You may speak only when I give you leave."

She flinched and clamped her jaw shut. She'd come to know Mages well enough to have learned that obedience, instant and unquestioning, was the best tool of survival.

"*Sulimage* Manza will not be returning. I am Primage Nour, the new holder of your leash. Now get on your knees and show me the proper respect."

The pillow fell from her hands. She dropped to her knees and bent forward, touching her forehead to the floor near his feet. Her breasts swung free, the rouged tips rubbing the carpet, but she didn't dare move to tuck them back into the confines of her corset.

The hard leather sole of the Mage's boot pressed against the back of her neck, driving her face into the carpet until she could hardly breathe. Fighting the instinctive urge to stiffen her spine and push back against the pressure, she forced her body to go limp.

The submission seemed to please her new master. After a moment, the foot on her neck lifted.

She stayed where she was, not daring to do more than take short, shallow breaths. He had not told her to move.

For nearly a chime she stayed there, prone and silent, waiting. Then, at last, the cold command: "You may rise."

She pushed herself up on her palms and rose to her feet, keeping her arms at her sides, her eyes downcast.

"Raise your eyes, *umagi*."

She lifted her lashes, fixing her gaze straight ahead as Vale had taught her four years ago, when she was an ambitious seventeen-year-old girl willfully making her Dark bargain. She'd not realized the true price, but he'd taught her. For six months, he'd led her farther into the shadows of his service, each week claiming a little more than she'd originally thought to give, coaxing her into surrendering the next bit of her soul. Slowly, methodically, he'd seduced her, broken her, subjugated her to his will. He'd trained her to obey him without question and serve him in any capacity he desired. And she'd come to do so willingly, even eagerly at times.

Now he was gone, but the invisible collar of enslavement he'd settled around her neck remained firmly clasped in place. She had a feeling its weight under Nour's hand would not be half so light as it had been under Master Manza's.

Master Nour lifted her chin and inspected her face with cold eyes. She was careful not to let her eyes meet his. Master Manza had allowed her certain liberties, but Master Nour did not seem so accommodating. From the corner of her eye, she saw the barrel-chested man staring at her exposed breasts. Master Nour didn't even glance at them.

The Primage's expression gave no hint of his thoughts, and when he concluded his inspection all he said was, "Manza always did have an eye for the pretty ones."

Master Nour turned away, and Jiarine allowed herself one deep breath. The movement made the stocky man lick his thick lips. She knew right then, he was no Mage. He could not possess the rigorous discipline Master Manza had told her was required for Magecraft yet still be so easily distracted by a pair of plump tits. An *umagi,* then, like her. She flashed him a glare and knew she'd guessed right when all he did was curl up the corner of his mouth in a leering grin.

"Manza claimed you were quite useful to him," Master Nour said, and both Jiarine and the stocky *umagi* snapped back into expressionless statues. "I hope I will find you so.

Your first task is to arrange an entrée for me into the queen's court. I will be Lord Geris Bolor, from a small estate near Sebourne's lands in the north."

Jiarine took a breath. "Master, may I speak?"

"What is it, *umagi*?"

"Great Lord Sebourne is a regular at court. Your identity will be too easily discredited." The words came in a rush. She wasn't certain how this new Mage would react to an *umagi* daring to give him advice, but if she didn't speak and his plans failed, he would blame her. She would rather take the punishment for impertinence than the punishment for failure. "A landless Ser or bastard son of a nobleman would be a better choice, less likely to be questioned by the members of the court."

"But I will not be a Ser, *umagi*. Manza went that route and it did not serve him nearly well enough. Lords have opportunities and influences mere Sers do not. Beside, though the news has not yet had time to reach the court, the real Lord Bolor has just met an untimely end, and I am his long-lost son and heir from a secret elopement. I have brought the marriage certificate and birth records and, if necessary, can produce the witnessing priest to prove it."

The current diBolor was a lord whom Jiarine had met before. He had a wife and two small children. If all that happened to him was disinheritance and reclassification in the Book of Lords as a bastard rather than a legitimate son of title, both he and his young family would be lucky. Somehow, she doubted that would be the case. Most obstacles in a Mage's path had a way of ending up dead or vanished. She dismissed the innocent man and his family's fate without a qualm. Better them than her.

"As you will, my Lord Bolor. But if I may be so bold, while you may pass for a lord of title, your *umagi* here will not." She cast a haughty glance at the stocky man. "He does not have the look of nobility about him. The wharf seems more likely."

The shorter man's brows drew together in a scowl. Master Nour just glanced back at him and then, surprisingly, laughed. "The wharf, eh? I suppose he does look a bit of the roustabout."

"I suggest you garb him as your servant. But keep him close by. The lords will assume he is your bully boy, and those fists are large enough that they might think twice before challenging your presence."

Nour's lips pursed, and he eyed her with new interest. "Perhaps you are more than just another of Manza's pretty faces after all, Jiarine."

"Thank you, my lord." Relief made her spine start to wilt. She squared her shoulders quickly. "Will there be anything else, Master Nour?"

"Yes, there will." Over his shoulder he barked, "Brodson, leave us. Close the door behind you. Have the maid send word to the queen that Lady Montevero is feeling indisposed this morning."

The click of the door latch falling into place rang like the toll of doom in the silent chamber.

The Primage took a step closer. "I think, pet, I should like you to show me how well my friend Kolis trained you to serve him."

Jiarine risked a glance at the Mage's face. Then she wished she hadn't.

For the first time since entering her room, Gethen Nour was smiling, and the sight shot terror through her heart.

Eld ~ Boura Fell

Pain enveloped Shan like a blanket. Every nerve ending burned and throbbed. Elfeya huddled on the periphery of his consciousness, singing his favorite Feyan and Elvish tunes from their long-ago life in the Fading Lands. Her voice helped keep the worst of the pain at bay as they waited for Maur to finish toying with them and let Elfeya heal him.

A sound at the door of his cell drew his attention. Elfeya stopped singing.

"*He returns?*" There was such dread in her voice. If Maur were back, they both knew the last thousand years of captivity would soon be at an end. In his current condition, there was no way Shan could survive more torture.

Voices murmured in the hall outside, too muffled for him to make out the words. The cell door swung open. Shan started to tense, then hissed as the tug of tightening muscles shifted the fragments of shattered bone in his flesh. He could not move except to tilt his head back in an attempt to see who came in.

There was another low murmur of voices; then the broad shape of the guard stepped outside. Shan caught a hazy glimpse of the newcomer—a slight figure whose face was still cloaked in shadow. The scent of food teased his nostrils, and Shan closed his eyes. Not Maur but an *umagi*, with food for the High Mage's favorite toy. The end of his torment wasn't near after all.

Soft footsteps carried the *umagi* towards the barbed *sel'dor* bars of Shan's cage. Cloth whispered against stone, followed by the scrape of metal as the *umagi* set a platter on the floor.

"I cannot move to feed myself," Shan told his visitor. "Your master enjoyed his work too well."

To his surprise, a morsel of food touched his lips. He opened his eyes, saw the thin arm stretched through the bars of the cage, holding the food to his mouth.

"Eat," a soft voice commanded. A female voice. Young. A child's voice. "Even the strongest Fey needs food."

Warm, flavorful liquid touched the tip of his tongue. Juice from the small piece of cooked meat. How long since he'd had cooked meat? Shan licked his lips. The taste was extraordinary. It occurred to him that the meat could be poisoned or drugged in some manner, but he was beyond caring. The smell of the food was making him ravenous.

He opened his mouth and took the bit of meat, forcing himself to chew slowly to savor its flavor and warmth and texture. Another piece brushed his lips before he was finished with the first, and he ate that too.

"Why do you still live?" the child whispered as he ate. "He shatters your bones, peels the flesh from your body, yet still you cling to life. Why?"

Shan just closed his eyes and kept chewing without answer. Apparently the food did not contain any drugs to loosen his tongue, because silence was all too easy.

The child held the next morsel of food away from his mouth, then sighed and gave it to him. "You are wary. I understand. They say you have been here a thousand years."

So long . . . half his years with Elfeya had been spent here, in darkness and torment. *Ah, shei'tani, sieks'ta. Our bond has been more curse than gift.*

Nei, she answered instantly. Love, deep and endless, poured across the unbreakable threads of their truemate bond, and with the love came her unshakable certainty, her pure and shining truth. Long ago she'd made her choice and bound her soul wholly and without reservation to his, and nothing—not even the living hell of their last thousand years—would make her regret it. *I would not trade even these centuries of torment if it meant one less day with you. You are all the joy I need. So long as we live, we have hope.*

"They say he's never broken you in all that time," the child said. "You must be very strong . . . and how your defiance must vex him." Dark glee curled like an invisible smile in the girl's voice. "They all fear you, you know. Even him. I can smell it on them when they set foot down here."

Despite himself, Shan's curiosity was roused. Who was this child? Why was she here?

He took a slow, deep breath and embraced the burn of

broken ribs as his lungs expanded. "What do you want?" he growled.

"Your help."

"My *help*?" He gave a soft, hoarse laugh. "Have you looked at me, girl? What help could I give in this state?"

"You will heal," she answered. "They say you always do, no matter what he does to you. What's important is you are not Marked. You can do what none of the rest of us can."

"And what's that?"

The child leaned forward, pressing her face to the *sel'dor* bars and lowering her voice to a whisper so soft he had to strain his ears to hear it.

"Kill him."

CHAPTER ELEVEN

The Fading Lands ~ Fey'Bahren

"You should have warned me."

Rain smiled. "You should have known. It was the obvious outcome."

Swimming was over, and Steli, who seemed to have adopted Ellysetta as her own kit, now held Ellysetta firmly between her forepaws and, like tairen mothers throughout the ages, was diligently licking her kitling dry. The tairen's deep blue eyes gleamed happily, though Rain thought he detected a hint of mischief mixed in with the happiness.

Ellysetta accepted the maternal attention with patience and good grace, once she recovered from her initial shock. By the time Steli finished and blew puffs of warm air to complete the drying, Ellysetta was nearly purring. She leaned against Steli's neck and stroked the tairen's soft white fur. "Thank you, Steli."

Around them, tairen lay basking on the broad, flat drying rocks that encircled the lake. The slow flap of drying wings sent warm breezes circulating through the chamber and rippled the lake's glassy surface. The familiar warm scent of tairen filled Rain's nostrils. It wasn't the clean, light fragrance of the Fey, but something deeper and more complex. Fey smelled of blossom-filled meadows and spring breezes. Tairen smelled of the earth, rich and full of life.

Steli rose to stretch and yawn before settling back down and lifting her own wings to dry. Ellysetta ran her hands through her hair and winced as her fingers snagged on a tangle.

"If you come here, I will brush it for you," Rain offered.

She glanced up, startled, then smiled when she saw a brush appear in his hand. "Magic can be convenient." She walked over to sit beside him.

"Rain?" she asked as he methodically worked the brush through her curls. "What do you think I heard during the Fire Song?"

He paused in midstroke. "I don't know, *shei'tani*. Sybharukai says you have the scent of old magic about you. Perhaps that allows you to sense what the rest of us cannot."

She turned around. "What's 'old magic'?"

He sighed. "I don't know that either. *Sieks'ta*. I should have answers, but all I have are the same questions as you. Sybharukai says the tairen will follow us to Dharsa and sing pride-greetings to the Eye of Truth in the hope it will give us more information than it has in the past. The Eye is tairen-made. Perhaps the pride can convince it to cooperate."

"If that's the case, why didn't they do the convincing last time, when you asked it for help and it sent you to me?"

There was a fierce light in her eyes. She hadn't forgotten that the Eye of Truth had hurt him. Now he realized he probably should have kept that information to himself.

"Apparently, it wasn't the right time." The tairen were like that—mysterious and unpredictable—and Sybharukai often knew much more than she let on.

"But this *is* the right time?"

"So it would seem."

Ellysetta's lips pursed, but she nodded and turned back around. He plied the brush again.

"Rain?"

"Aiyah?"

"What happens if I can't do what everyone thinks I can? What if the kitlings still perish, the Fey remain barren, and the magic continues to die in the Fading Lands?"

"I have faith in you, *shei'tani.*"

"But what if your faith is wrong?" she persisted. "What if I fail?"

"You ask that as if you expect me to revile you." He set the brush aside and moved in front of her to grip her shoulders and look her steadily in the eye. "Listen to me, Ellysetta. I vowed the night of our wedding that I would never turn from you again, and I will not—no matter what miracles you do or do not bring about, no matter what sort of magic you possess, no matter even if you never accept my bond. I am yours, utterly and completely, from now until the end of time."

"But—"

"We are both beings of great power, but we are not gods. You are not to blame for our troubles, nor will you be to blame if you cannot solve them." His thumbs traced the soft fullness of her lower lip, then brushed the creamy silk of her cheeks. "Just do the best you can, *shei'tani.* That's all anyone can ask of themselves." He lifted her hand and pressed a kiss to her palm, then another to the fragile pulse point at her wrist, and gave her a reassuring smile. "Enough of this dire talk. Come with me, and let me show you the wonders of Fey'Bahren."

The caverns of Fey'Bahren were wondrous indeed, an entire city of tunnels and chambers hollowed out beneath the volcano. The tunnels, Rain told Ellysetta, extended beyond Fey'Bahren itself to the jagged peaks of the surrounding Feyls, a reminder of the days when the tairen had not teetered on the brink of extinction.

Rain showed her the crystal-lined caverns at the mountain's deepest heart, where veins of gemstones and precious metals colored the walls with glittering mosaics, and a stunning, mist-filled chamber where the still-warm waters of the bathing lake merged with the cool silver ribbon of an underground river and plummeted down a sheer cliff face. At the base of the waterfall, another smaller lake formed and spilled over into a stream that disappeared from sight.

Ellie's favorite was a chamber Rain called the Cavern of Memory, whose entrance was guarded by a pair of exquisitely carved stone tairen with diamond claws and glittering Tairen's Eye crystal eyes. Within, every wall was covered with etched reliefs that depicted the countless past ages of tairen and Fey. The scenes, Rain told her, had been carved by artistically inclined Feyreisen over the millennia. Ellie recognized familiar Fey-tales in some of the carvings, famous battles in others, but most were of scenes that the mortal world had long ago forgotten. Ellie could have stayed in that chamber for months, years even, absorbing the amazing visual documentary of ages past without ever losing interest.

It was only as Rain escorted her out that she saw the series of reliefs retelling the fateful day when all the world had changed. She stopped in her tracks, her fingers trembling as she reached out to touch the image of a man's face carved with raw, untutored starkness in an expression of eternal anguish.

"Oh, Rain . . ." Beside that single, heart-stopping image were others, more crudely made, of a tairen blasting a battlefield of tiny soldiers, of a woman crying out as a robed man brought a blade slicing down towards her neck, of a barren, desolate wasteland empty of all but the broken skeletons of dead trees and a tiny kneeling man lifting his arms in grief to the heavens.

"I lacked the artistic skills of those who carved the walls before me," Rain said softly.

"You carved these yourself, without magic," Ellie murmured. She could feel the embedded memory of his ancient torment locked within the very stone itself, captured for all time as the images were carved. Rage and pain and grief beyond reckoning. She pulled her hand away. "You channeled your sorrow into the stone."

"Did I?" He sounded surprised. "I didn't realize. I knew only that working here, carving my own story into the stone, was the one thing that gave me some small measure of peace."

He had suffered so much . . . and now, all his suffering, all the sacrifices he had made to save the Fey, were threatened by the nameless power that was slowly eradicating the tairen. For a thousand years, he had lived in torment, fighting for sanity and for release from the mad grief that consumed him, fighting to live because the Fey needed him to survive.

Rain said he didn't hold her responsible for saving the tairen, but that did not absolve her. She had sensed something in Fey'Bahren that neither Rain nor any of the tairen had ever felt. Something evil and gloating. It wasn't the familiar malevolence of the High Mage or the nightmares that had haunted her all her life, but it was just as frightening.

She touched the carved image of Rain's face, absorbing the echoes of his torment and his desperate resolve to live when all he wanted was to die. Had she ever been so selfless? So brave?

No, she'd been frightened all her life, running from her nightmares, her enemies, her magic. She was tired of being afraid. And she was definitely through with running.

"Would you take me back to the hatching grounds? I don't know if there is anything I can do to help, but I'd like to start trying."

The tairen had all returned from the lake and were perched on the ledges of the large cavern when Ellysetta stepped out onto the nesting sands and approached the still-buried tairen eggs. Steli glided down and flapped her white wings to blow away most of the black sand covering them before leaping back to her ledge.

The five remaining mottled gray eggs were nearly as big as Ellysetta was tall, reaching up to her shoulders. She laid her hand on the snub, bluntly rounded top of one of them. The outer shell was a tough, leathery, pebbled substance, neither as hard nor as brittle as the eggs of birds. She gave a gentle, experimental squeeze and jumped as the egg twitched in seeming response.

Yanking back her hand, she turned nervously to Rain. "Can the baby tairen feel when I touch it?"

He nodded. "The tairen are sentient even in the womb, though until the eggs are actually laid on the sands, their sentience is mostly limited to emotion and sensory impressions rather than actual thoughts, much the same as what we receive from an unborn child of our own species." A shadow darkened his eyes. "Sybharukai says there are still three fertile females in this clutch. The one taken last night was male." A muscle ticked in his jaw. "I suppose we should be grateful for that."

On her ledge above him, Sybharukai growled softly. Ellie glanced up at the tairen. Fourteen pairs of eyes watched from their ledges, gleaming in the red-orange glow of the nesting lair. Fourteen. All that remained of the once-thriving prides. And if these unhatched female kits died, the pride would end with this generation.

She laid her hand on the nearest egg and concentrated, cautiously lowering her internal barriers and stretching out her senses as Marissya had taught her to do in their lessons together. *Las, Ellysetta. Find the stillness inside you. Don't try to rule your magic. Let it flow freely. Let it fill you, become you.* She closed her eyes and tried to find the tranquil silence in her mind, where the world was glimmering light. *Relax. Breathe. All living things are made of Air, Water, Fire, Earth, and Spirit. Do not seek their essence; let their essence come to you.*

Gradually, the sounds and scents of the world faded, and the shimmering darkness sprang to glowing life behind her eyes. Threads of magic—silvery Air, red Fire, green Earth, lavender Spirit, blue Water—all gleamed and shimmered, some threads radiant, others barely more than a subtle glow. The tairen were so bright they nearly blinded her. So much magic, so brilliant and untamed. Their light hummed with music: the beautiful, bold, colorful notes of tairen song, gleaming just beneath the surface, singing even when they were silent.

Beside them, Rain's colors were slightly dimmer, as if covered by a thin layer of shadow. She'd noticed that about him once before, that veil of darkness, as if the weight of all the souls he carried dimmed the brightness of his own soul.

When she turned to the eggs, the shimmering lights winked out. She could see Rain beside her, the tairen around her, but where the kitling in the egg should have been, there was only darkness and silence.

"What is it?" Rain asked.

She frowned. "I'm not sure. I think I'm doing what Marissya showed me, but I can't sense the kitlings at all. It's as if there's nothing but a blank void inside the eggs."

They are afraid. Sybharukai's bright voice flared across Ellysetta's open senses. *They know Cahlah, Merdrahl, and one of their nestmates are gone. They shield themselves just as kits hatched outside the lair did long ago to hide from hunters."* Along with the words flowed the image of a mounded nest covered with sand, baking in the sun rather than in the dark protection of a volcanic cave. A predator pawed and nosed at the sand around the nest.

Ellysetta's spine straightened. Of course the kitlings were afraid. They were babies who'd just been attacked and terrified, who'd just felt their parents die. A fresh surge of confidence filled her. Magic might still be mostly a mystery to her, but soothing frightened children was something she'd always been good at.

She knelt beside the egg and did her best to cradle it as if it were a child. So many times, she'd rocked Lillis and Lorelle, holding their small bodies close to hers and singing to them until whatever sadness or fear they suffered melted away. Remembering those times, she rocked against the egg and stroked the nubby shell as if it were a baby's soft cheek. Quietly at first, and then with growing assurance, she began to croon the melodies and lullabies she'd sung to her sisters.

At first the kitlings remained stubbornly silent, their light utterly hidden, but gradually, as she continued to sing, faint colors began to swirl in the dark centers of the eggs.

Something fluttered at the edge of her consciousness, hesitant, weak, but curious. She turned her attention towards it. Tiny, frightened, so tired. She probed gently, stretching out towards the sensation, and blinked back tears as a thready, shimmering song played weakly in her mind. She huddled closer to the egg, stroking its surface with encouragement. *"Hello, there, little kit. Can you hear me? My name is Ellysetta, and I've come to help you."*

Celieria City ~ The Royal Palace

Gethen Nour buttoned the flap of his silk trousers, straightened his jacket, and toed the trembling woman curled on the floor at his feet. "You may get dressed now, pet. I'll have Brodson send in your maid."

Lady Montevero nodded, swiping at the tears making streaks through the remnants of powder and rouge on her face.

"The maid—Fanette, did you call her? Does she have someone she loves, someone she would feel compelled to protect? A child perhaps? A mother?"

He saw Jiarine's bare shoulder tense. She knew why he asked. "A baby," she whispered.

"Excellent." It pleased him that she surrendered the information, even knowing his intentions. Brodson would follow the maid home tonight. By this time tomorrow, young Fanette would bear the first of Gethen's own six Marks. "And, pet—"

"Y-yes?"

"You will come to me tonight in Manza's rooms by the wharf. You may demonstrate any other intriguing tricks he's taught you." Gethen smiled for the second time that morning, enjoying the way her flesh, not nearly so pampered and flawless as it had been when he'd first arrived, shuddered at the prospect.

And still she answered dutifully, "Yes, Master Nour."

Perhaps Kolis hadn't been quite the softhearted weakling Nour had always considered him when it came to the training of *umagi*.

"I look forward to it. Oh, and one last thing . . ." He bent down beside her and stroked a thumb across the delicate pulse in her throat. His voice dropped to a gentle whisper. "While we are apart today, I want you to find out everything you can about any recent activity near the Garreval. Do not rouse suspicion, but don't come to me empty-handed either. I'm not a pleasant man when I'm disappointed."

The choked sob escaped before she could bite her lip to hold it back. Fresh tears spurted from her eyes. The mass of tangled dark brown ringlets bobbed as she gave a jerky nod.

"Excellent. I can see we are going to get along famously." He rose to his feet and left the room without a backward glance.

In the adjoining room, the maid Fanette, a plump little partridge with cornflower eyes and brown hair wrapped in a tidy plait, sat still as stone in a chair across from Den Brodson. Her hands were clenched so tight in her lap, her knuckles shone white. "Your mistress needs your assistance, girl."

As the maid rose to her feet, Nour reached into his pocket. When she passed by him, he grabbed her arm and blew a small cloud of *somulus* powder into her face. Her frightened blue eyes went blank. "You came in this morning to discover that Lady Jiarine has had a run-in with a rather . . . brutal . . . nobleman. You know what harm he will cause if rumor of his habits gets out. So you will tend your lady and you will keep silent, for her sake as well as your own. Now go."

The girl walked with dazed, slow steps into the adjoining bedroom.

"Come, Brodson." He waved to the butcher's son. "The day's half-gone, and we've much to do."

Eld ~ Boura Fell

Elfeya v'En Celay lay upon her *sel'dor*-laced bed, exhausted and aching and filled with self-loathing after the last several bells she'd spent healing the High Mage of Eld. Hatred was a dark emotion no *shei'dalin* should ever clutch to her breast, but over the last thousand years, it had become as much her companion as the constant acid burn of the dread Eld metal against her flesh. Gods forgive her, but she did hate. She hated with every ounce of flesh and every drop of blood in her body.

And if it were not for her *shei'tan*, Shan, chained in the lower levels of Vadim Maur's dungeon fortress, she would have done what no *shei'dalin* ever did.

She would have killed.

If not for Shan, she would have twisted her *shei'dalin* powers and used them to slay the evil Mage who came to her for healing. And she would have wept with joy as the torment of taking a life struck her dead.

Elfeya flung an arm over her face, covering her eyes as the weak, useless tears trickled from them. There was no sense in weeping. A thousand years of tears—enough to fill an ocean—had not spared her one moment of misery.

"Shei'tani." Shan's voice, so beloved, whispered across the threads of their truemate bond. Soothing, comforting, Shan's consciousness caressed her own with such vibrant richness, she could almost pretend he was there beside her, holding her, making love to her with the wild, sweet, passionate abandon they'd shared in their all too brief bells together.

She wiped the tears from her face, then laughed at the uselessness of the small vanity. He could not see her tears, but he already knew she'd shed them. *"I am here, beloved."*

"You are alone?" he asked.

"Never so long as I have you." A smile trembled on her lips, then fell away. *"He was here,"* she told him, *"but he is gone now. His health is failing."* The truth should have pleased them both, but she could feel Shan's deep concern, an echo of her own.

"He will be more dangerous now than ever. Desperate men always are."

"Aiyah. He knows he cannot delay the inevitable much longer." Time was against Vadim Maur now. He could no longer afford the skillful patience that had been the hallmark of his reign.

"At least our daughter is with the Fey now. They will protect her."

"As much as they can," she agreed.

Vadim Maur was too powerful a Mage for Elfeya to rifle through his mind without his notice, but he had come to her many times over the years for healing . . . and other things. She'd used those occasions to gain what advantage she could, testing his shields, gathering what thoughts he did not consciously guard, and slowly—very, very slowly—burrowing an imperceptible path into the secrets he held locked away in his mind.

She could not pluck thoughts freely from Maur's mind, but when he was weary and came to her for healing—as he had begun to do with increasing frequency—that tiny thread of Spirit allowed her to influence him slightly, pushing him to relax in her presence just enough that the occasional useful tidbit of information could rise to the surface of his thoughts, where she could draw it unnoticed into her mind for later review.

"You discovered what he is planning?" Shan asked.

Vadim's *umagi* spies in Celieria had been disappearing by the dozens, rendering him blind and weakening the foothold he'd established in northern Celieria. Whoever was behind those deaths, she didn't know, but the Fey owed the mysterious agent a debt of gratitude. With the loss of his *umagi*, Maur had no way to open the portals to the Well of Souls that would enable him to deliver an army for a surprise attack.

He had something up his sleeve, though. Something so important he would not even let himself think about it when he was with her.

"Nei, his mind was too full of last night's triumph. He has created a second Tairen Soul. A boy this time, with vel Serranis blood." She closed her eyes in horror. The poor, doomed child. There was no one to save him as she and Shan had saved Ellysetta.

"He must be stopped. If he Mage-claims a Tairen Soul . . . "

His voice trailed off. Twenty-five years ago, that same fear had pushed Shan and Elfeya to willingly risk death in an effort to bind their daughter's magic and smuggle her out of Eld so Maur could not enslave her soul. The devastating power of the tairen under Mage control—it was a horror so dark Elfeya could scarcely think of it without shuddering.

"Elfeya . . . beloved . . ."

Her body tensed. When her *shei'tan* said her name like that outside of mating, it never boded well.

"The girl who was here earlier—the umagi who came to feed me—she asked for my help. She wants me to kill Maur."

Her blood ran cold. *"Nei."*

"Elfeya—"

"Nei! It must be some sort of trap. Some new way to torment us. She is umagi. None of them could even think such a thing without the one who owns their souls knowing it."

"Perhaps another Mage is her master then. One who wants Maur dead."

"Even if that's true, there's no way you could kill him without being slain yourself."

She felt his soul sigh. Then he said, in a voice so soft and weary it made her throat close up, *"After all these centuries of torment, can death truly be so terrible a fate, kem'san?"*

The tears she kept telling herself she would not shed pooled in her eyes and spilled over. *"Nei, teska, do not think that way. So long as we live, there is hope. A thousand years we have suffered. A thousand more would I bear, just for what few bells he grants us together. Do you love me any less?"*

"You know I don't."

"Then promise me you will not do this."

"Elfeya . . ."

"Promise me, Shan."

For a long moment he did not answer, and then finally, in a defeated whisper, *"What choices we make, we make for us both. If you do not wish it, it will not be done."*

The Fading Lands ~ Fey'Bahren

"Your mate needs feeding," Sybharukai chided.

Ellysetta had been sitting with the eggs for several long bells. Even now, she leaned against them, her hands stroking gently over the leathery shells as she crooned little songs of encouragement and praise.

"Aiyah," he agreed, "and sleep." Though inside, the nesting lair remained dark and unchanged, outside the Great Sun had passed its zenith and was already approaching the western horizon. Most of the day was gone, and Marissya and Dax were less than eighty miles away. They would be here before nightfall.

Rain regarded Ellysetta. There was no hint of the weariness he could feel beating at her. Was she even aware of it? Her concentration was wholly focused on communicating with the five small, unborn tairen huddled in their eggs. She was weaving love around the unborn kitlings the way Fey wove the elements, only her weave wasn't Spirit. It wasn't illusion. It was genuine emotion, real love, warming and welcoming. Tenderness. Devotion. Pride. Encouragement. It shone from her like sunlight, bathing the kitlings in its warmth.

"Shei'tani." He touched her shoulder. Still singing, she turned towards him, and for a brief moment the song of warmth, love, and tenderness poured over him, soaking into his skin. His breath stalled, and his eyes half closed in pleasure.

He gave a small frown of protest as Ellysetta cut her song short.

"I'm sorry." She started to rise, and a surprised look crossed over her face as her legs—cramped for so long in their crouched position—collapsed beneath her.

He caught her, swept an arm under her legs, and lifted her off her feet, carrying her with effortless strength up the main entrance tunnel.

"Where are you taking me?" she asked as they veered right into one of the larger passageways branching off of the main tunnel.

"You are weary. You need to eat and sleep. There is a sleeping chamber above where you can rest." Globes of light flared to life as they walked, illuminating their path. This tunnel was narrower than the main tunnel but still quite wide. The walls were smooth, the floor well worn.

"But the kitlings—"

"We have time." The tunnel forked in three, one path leading below, two others leading up. They went up and to the left. "The sickness attacking the tairen comes most often in the bells between dusk and dawn."

"I don't think it's really a sickness, Rain. When I was singing to them, I tried to find signs of injury or illness, but I couldn't. I could be wrong, of course—Marissya is a far more experienced healer—but to me they all seem healthy. Tired and frightened, but healthy."

He gave her a grim look. "I feared you might say that."

"So you don't really believe it's a sickness."

"*Nei.* My instinct has always told me the Eld must surely be to blame, but I have watched far too many kitlings die in the egg—dozens of them in my arms when I tried to cut them from the shell to save them—and never once have I sensed Azrahn."

"Well, if it's not Azrahn and the Mages, do you think whatever I sensed during the Fire Song could be behind the deaths of the kitlings?"

"I don't know, *shei'tani.* I just don't know."

The passage snaked around, doubling back upon itself and continuing to rise. Above, dim light shone in from a large opening at the top of the next U-shaped curve. As they passed it, Ellie glimpsed the bright blue afternoon sky. She lifted a hand to shield her eyes, surprised that it was still light outside. She'd lost all sense of time deep within the caverns of Fey'Bahren.

She squirmed in his arms. "You should put me down. I'm certain I must be heavy."

"You are no burden." He bent his head to take her mouth in a long, sweet kiss. "Besides," he added when he lifted his head, "we are already here."

He carried her through another, slightly smaller tunnel that ended in a tall, Fey-sized wooden door. A flick of his fingers sent green Earth spinning out to lift the latch, and silvery Air blew open the door to reveal the chamber beyond. He gestured again, and Fire blossomed in sconces all about the room, adding their light to the sunlight filtering in from yet another passage leading off the main chamber.

Rain finally set Ellysetta on her feet, and she turned in slow circles to glance around the room. The chamber was obviously made for Feyreisen: spacious enough for a tairen to maneuver, yet furnished with human comforts, including a bed piled thick with furs and pillows, and large, beautifully woven rugs to soften the hard stone of the floor. Against one wall stood an elegant, carved desk and matching gilded chair.

"This is your room," she guessed.

"It used to be Johr's—the previous Tairen Soul—but it's been mine since I returned to sanity. There were other furnished rooms, but I burned them out in the early days of my madness and never made the effort to restore them." The corners of his eyes crinkled at her look of dismay. "I'm much better now."

"How can you joke about it?"

He cupped her cheek, his thumb stroking. "Because you restored my joy."

"Rain . . ." She reached for him, wanting to wrap her arms around him and hold him close, but he stepped back.

"Food first. Then rest. Then perhaps I will show you what a grateful *shei'tan* I am."

Heat curled in her belly at the sight of the silken promises in his eyes. Until Rain, she'd never realized lavender could be such a seductive shade, but now she realized she'd never see it again without thinking of breathless passion and love.

"Come," he murmured. The dark velvet of his voice slipped over her skin, making her breath quicken and her pulse speed up. "I thought we'd eat outside. The view is spectacular." He gestured for her to precede him through a broad archway.

Ellysetta walked past what appeared to be a private bathing chamber and through a smaller, unadorned cave with a large opening that led to the outside world.

She passed through the opening to the broad, wide-lipped ledge that jutted out from the side of the mountain, walking slowly to the farthest point. There, with the wind whipping around her, clouds close enough to touch, and the ground so far, far below, it was easy to believe she was once again aloft in the winds, flying over the Fading Lands. Her belly tightened with exhilaration. She closed her eyes and drew the cool, fresh air into her lungs.

"Just standing here is almost like flying."

He stepped close behind her and wrapped his arms around her waist. "*Aiyah*. You feel it too. As if you could leap from the ledge and the wind would welcome you and send you soaring."

"Yes, that's it." She opened her eyes and looked down at her feet. The toes of her boots touched the edge of the precipice, and yet she was unafraid. No hint of vertigo touched her. No sense of even the slightest fear. Only appreciation and thrill and longing.

"I miss this place," he murmured close to her ear. "I don't come back as often as I should. Mostly only when I need the simplicity of being tairen."

"Simplicity? The tairen don't seem simple to me." She thought of the mysteries of the mountain, and Sybharukai with her green eyes so full of secrets. Ellysetta had been here less than a day, but already she knew there was so much more to the tairen than she'd ever realized.

"Do they not? They eat when they are hungry, sleep when they are tired, and kill their enemy without doubt or regret when he threatens them. Do you know how calming that is?"

"To kill your enemy?"

"To have no regrets."

She turned in his arms and lifted her face to his. The shadows were back in his eyes, the memories of all those who had died in his flames. She stood up on the tips of her toes to kiss him, then bent her head to the hollow of his throat, and they stood there together, on the edge of the precipice, alone above the world as the cool winds of the high mountain swirled around them.

"I hesitate to ask what we'll be eating. I'm not particularly fond of raw herdbeast." She tilted her head at the grazing animals so far below.

His eyes crinkled, not quite a smile but close. "*Nei*, I would not think so. Though I must say, to a hungry tairen, *tavalree* on the hoof is a choice morsel."

With a casual weave of Earth, he spun a table and two chairs out from his chambers to the cliff's edge, then wove a small basket containing food, a corked vessel, and a pair of golden goblets. At her surprised look, he confessed, "I keep a small store of food stocked in one of the caves below with a protective weave to ensure freshness. I don't always want *tavalree* when I come here either."

The food was simple fare: a block of cheese, round loaves of flat, golden bread, and several of the tear-shaped *tamaris* fruits. Rain uncorked the bottle, poured a stream of crystal-clear water into the two goblets, and offered her one. A sip confirmed it was *faerilas*. "From Dharsa," he said in answer to her questioning look. He pushed a plate of food towards her. "Enough talking. Eat. Your body needs nourishment to replenish its strength."

Ellysetta reached for a round of bread, then layered slices

of cheese on top. The first bite was heavenly. The cheese was creamy and flavorful, the bread a melting delight. She hadn't realized how hungry she was, but once the food hit her tongue, ravenous appetite took over. She devoured the meal in a few quick, voracious bites, and moments later found herself staring in bewilderment at empty hands sticky with *tamaris* juice. How had that happened?

Rain laughed softly. "Hunger comes upon you quickly when you weave magic for so many bells." At her confused frown, he elucidated. "Your singing. You were weaving love and courage on the kitlings through your song. Even Sybharukai was impressed. In many ways, your weave imitated tairen song."

"I didn't realize."

"You never do, it seems, when you are weaving great power." He helped himself to the remaining portion of the food and leaned back in his chair as he took a few bites. "I've been thinking about that since we left Celieria City. The circumstances of your birth forced you to use your magic more as instinct than a controllable skill, Ellysetta. While that served you well in its time, the practice appears to have conditioned you to trust your powers only when you do not know you are weaving them."

She sat up straighter, a bit offended. "I've been weaving magic. All those bells spent with Marissya on our journey here, when she was teaching me how to heal, I wove magic—powerful magic. What would you call that?"

"Frustration." When she crossed her arms and her eyes flashed, he hurried to add, "I am not dismissing your efforts, *shei'tani*, but you've been trying to pour the force of an ocean through the mouth of a stream. And when you cannot forget how vast and potentially dangerous that ocean is, your powers either dam up or overwhelm you.

"So you think I can't control my magic because I fear it?"

"I think, *shei'tani*, you have feared what you are for so long, there's no room in your heart for trust. And until you trust yourself, you will find it difficult—if not impossible—to control your magic . . . and impossible for us to complete our bond."

"So what's your solution?"

"The same as it is for a *chadin* of the Cha Baruk. Practice. And much of it. Some things cannot be learned by any other means. As you gain confidence, your fears will diminish."

"So who will teach me this confidence?"

"I've been thinking about that, too." He sat back, plucked a Fey'cha from the straps across his chest, and began twirling the blade on his fingertips, razor-sharp steel and black hilt flipping end over end, the pinch of his fingers so perfect the knife edge never broke his skin. "Until our bond is complete, I cannot merge with your mind the way a *chatok* must to guide your learning. The *shei'dalins* will teach you to wield a *shei'dalin*'s gifts, but you are a Tairen Soul as well. There are skills you need that no *shei'dalin* can teach you."

Ellysetta watched the steel flashing in his fingers. The blade was a mere blur now.

"The mentors of the Warriors' Academy are masters of magic as well as war. They are our most skilled teachers—and all of them are mated, which will make it easier for me to allow them close to you." He caught the black Fey'cha in midspin and returned it to its sheath. "I will ask one of them to be your *chatok* and teach you the ways of Fey magic."

"You want a warrior to teach me to wield my magic."

His eyes lifted, and Ellysetta's mouth went suddenly dry. Thick black lashes framed gleaming pale purple irises that were just beginning to glow. Instantly she was reminded of his expression when he'd stood beside her in Chakai as she healed the *rasa*.

"Want? *Nei*. But it's what you need." He stared down at the table, where his thumbnail had just dug a deep groove into the finish. A muscle ticked in his jaw. Green Earth flared briefly, and the groove filled back in. "If our bond were complete, I would teach you myself, but it is not." His shoulder lifted and fell. "If there were another Tairen Soul, I would ask him, but there is not. It must be a *chatok* from the Academy. They are the only ones who can teach you what you need to know."

She leaned across the table and put her hands on his. "There is no need for you to torment yourself, Rain. You are my *shei'tan*, the man I dreamed of all my life. My heart has no room for another."

"When it comes to some things, *shei'tani*, tairen do not listen to reason."

"Do they not?" She slipped out of her chair and sat on his lap, looping her arms casually around his neck. "Perhaps they just need convincing."

She smiled as the tense brackets around his mouth eased and the glow of his eyes grew more pronounced—and much warmer.

"Perhaps you're right," he purred. "Why don't you try it and see?"

CHAPTER TWELVE

*The slopes of Fey'Bahren run dark with the blood of
enemies, fools, and prey.*

Ancient Fey Maxim

The Fading Lands ~ Fey'Bahren

Ellysetta woke with a yawning stretch, smiling at the pleasant tug of muscle and the warmth of Rain's body stretched
out beside her. She rolled against him, burying her face in
his hair and breathing deep to take his scent into her lungs.
She would never tire of waking beside him, skin-to-skin,
knowing this was where she belonged.

After their meal, they'd retired to Rain's bedchamber to
make love with breathtaking intensity before falling into
deep, exhausted, and blessedly dreamless sleep. Now Ellysetta was awake and refreshed, and rapidly discovering that
Fey males weren't the only ones to harbor insatiable desire
for their mates.

She slid a leg up over his and slipped an arm around his
waist. Her fingers traced the steely ripples of his abdomen
and moved up across his chest, and she smiled against the
soft skin of his neck as one flat male nipple hardened beneath her fingertips. "Mmm." She stroked the small nub
and nuzzled his ear. "Are you well rested, *shei'tan*?" Her
hand trailed back down his ribs to his hips to stroke a far
more interesting bit of hardening male flesh. Her smile
grew wider. "Ah, I see that you are."

She squealed with laughter as he turned in one quick

burst of motion and rolled her on her back, pinning her to the bed. "Feeling bold?" he growled. He lowered his head, and his silky black hair fell in dark veils around them, casting his face in shadow so that the glow of his eyes seemed more intense.

"You don't like it?"

White teeth flashed. "I never said that." His lips took hers in a deep, passionate kiss, not releasing her until her pulse was racing, her nails were scoring his back, and her lungs were gasping for air. "This Fey loves bold. Bold is good."

She closed her eyes as his lips tracked down her throat to her breasts. Moist heat closed around one sensitive tip while warm fingers worked their seductive magic on the other. "Very good," she groaned. Her legs wrapped around him, heels pressing against the tight curve of his buttocks, urging him upwards. Much as she loved his hands, his lips, his magic upon her, what she wanted was him, inside her where he belonged, completing her. She never felt so whole as she did when their bodies were united, their souls so close she could almost reach out and grasp those elusive, final threads of their bond.

A rumbling purr rolled across her skin, and a puff of warm, richly scented air swirled around her. *"Fine, strong mating is good. Rainier-Eras and Ellysetta-kitling will hatch many kitlings for the pride."*

The happy, purring voice—definitely not Rain's—hit Ellysetta like a bucket of frigid water. Her eyes flew open, and she found herself staring straight up into very large, very glowing, very curious blue tairen eyes.

"Ahhh!" Ellie shrieked, and shoved Rain away from her with such force he tumbled off the edge of the bed and hit the rock floor with a thud. She snatched fistfuls of furred coverlets and silky sheets and yanked them up in a desperate attempt to cover herself.

"Good sweet Lord of Light!" she exclaimed, staring at the white tairen in mortification. "What are you doing here? Have you never heard of knocking?"

Steli snorted and sat back on her haunches. A miffed growl rumbled in her chest, and her tail whipped against the chamber wall, making little flakes of rock fall to the floor. *What is "knocking"?*

Rain, naked and utterly unashamed, stood up and rubbed his bruised hindquarters. He fixed Steli with a disgruntled look. "Ellysetta-Feyreisa means Steli-*chakai* should sing greetings before entering the sleeping lair of the Feyreisen and his mate."

The tairen cocked her head. *The pride sang greetings before, in the nesting lair.*

His lips twitched. "*Aiyah*, but Ellysetta-Feyreisa was raised among the mortals . . . the two-legs who mate only in private. She needs time to become accustomed to the ways of the pride."

Steli looked at Ellysetta, who still held a death grip on the covers. The tairen's ears and tail twitched; then she snorted again. *What is "private"?*

Rain laughed. "*Private* means that Steli-*chakai* should not enter this sleeping lair unless Ellysetta-Feyreisa or Rainier-Eras says you may."

Steli's ears went back. *Steli does not like private.* She growled. *Or knocking.* Fur ruffled, clearly offended, she twisted her sinuous body and headed back out to the ledge where she must have come from. *The Fey-kin are here. They wait on Su Reisu.* She sniffed as she left.

"Steli, wait!" Ellysetta ran after the white tairen and caught up with her on the ledge outside. There was enough irritation still whirling in Steli's eyes that Ellysetta stopped short of coming within claw reach of the white tairen. "*Sieks'ta.* I'm sorry. I did not mean to hurt your feelings. I am not used to pride ways—and you surprised me. Please, *teska*, forgive me."

The supplication seemed to soothe the white tairen's injured pride. She swished her tail, then wrinkled her nose and sniffed again for good measure before saying, *"Steli forgives."*

Ellysetta flung her arms around the cat's neck. *"Beylah vo, Steli-chakai."*

"Ellysetta-kitling did not hatch in Fey'Bahren. She was not raised in the ways of the pride." Steli began to purr and gave the side of Ellysetta's face a warm, maternal lick. *"Steli will teach."* The white tairen sounded alarmingly pleased by the prospect.

Pride appeased, Steli flew down with Rain and Ellysetta to Su Reisu, the low, flat-topped plateau at the base of Fey'Bahren where Marissya and Dax were waiting. After an initial threatening growl at the truemates, the white tairen settled into a protective crouch behind Ellysetta, and other than an occasional warning rumble if the newcomers moved too close, she left the Fey to exchange greetings.

Ellysetta explained her findings to Marissya. "There are five eggs left. I tried to look for the source of their illness, as you taught me. Maybe it's my own inexperience, but other than the kitlings being tired and frightened and very weak, I couldn't find anything wrong."

"She sang love and strength on them," Rain added.

Ellysetta grimaced. "Without realizing it, of course."

Marissya started to pat her hand, then glanced at the blue-eyed tairen and changed her mind. "You just need practice, Ellysetta. It's not lack of ability, but lack of confidence that holds you back."

Ellysetta glanced over at Rain, who arched a speaking brow. "Rain said much the same thing last night. He wants me to train with the Academy's *chatok* as well as with the *shei'dalins* when we reach Dharsa."

Marissya's eyes widened. "Does he?"

"She is a Tairen Soul," Rain said. "There are skills she must learn that the *shei'dalins* cannot teach."

"The Massan will not approve."

"The Massan have no say in the training of young *feyreisen*."

Steli growled and crept closer, poking her head around Ellysetta to fix whirling blue eyes on Marissya. The edge of her mouth lifted up, baring fangs, and her nostrils flared, sniffing the air as if scenting for potential threats—or prey.

"Perhaps not, but tread lightly with them, Rain." Marissya frowned at the white tairen and edged back, reaching for Dax's hand. "They deserve your respect."

"And they have it. But that does not mean this king must seek their approval for his decisions."

"Change takes time."

"Time is a luxury I do not have." Rain's eyes flashed lavender sparks. "War is coming, and my bond with Ellysetta is not complete. I must do what I feel is necessary. I allowed Ellysetta to heal the *rasa* because I need blades to fight. Ellysetta must be trained as both a *shei'dalin* and a Tairen Soul, because both are the gifts the gods gave her. If she cannot accept the entirety of herself, what hope is there for the completion of our bond?"

Before Marissya could answer, Steli pushed her nose against Marissya's brown leathers and sniffed again. *"This one has strong pride scent for a Fey-kin."*

"Marissya?" Rain eyed the tairen in confusion. "She is of the vel Serranis line. Many *feyreisen* were born to her family in the past. Perhaps that is what you sense?"

"Perhaps." Steli growled noncommittally. She sniffed some more, nudging Marissya with her nose, then sat back on her haunches. *"This one can help Ellysetta-kitling heal our young?"*

"We believe so."

The *chakai* thumped her tail. *"Sybharukai says this one may enter the lair."*

Leaving Rain staring at her in astonishment, the fierce white tairen leapt into the sky and flew towards the wide mouth of the cave that led to the interior of Fey'Bahren.

"What is it?" Marissya asked when the tairen were gone. "What did she say?"

Rain gave her a look of sheer disbelief. "She said you may enter the nesting lair."

The *shei'dalin's* jaw dropped open. "I don't understand. I've been here before, and the tairen never let me set foot beyond Su Reisu."

"Marissya, I'm as confused as you. Steli said you bear pride-scent. Maybe while you've been teaching Ellysetta, some trace of her scent was transferred to you. Does it really matter?"

Marissya shook her head emphatically.

"Good. Then let's go. You can check the kitlings yourself and tell us definitively whether *shei'dalin* skills can heal them."

Marissya started forward, then stopped. "Wait. What about Dax?"

"He stays behind," Rain answered without hesitation. "There are eggs in the lair, and three tairen died last night. The pride would kill him before his foot touched the nesting sands."

"But he is my *shei'tan*. The tairen have always welcomed the mates of those they welcome into the pride."

"You were not welcomed into the pride, Marissya. Sybharukai merely said you could enter Fey'Bahren to help Ellysetta save the kitlings." He glanced at Dax. "I don't know how long we'll be, but you have my oath I will protect your mate as if she were my own."

"I know you will." Dax waved them off. "Go."

Rain flew Marissya and Ellysetta up to the main entrance of the lair. Together, with Rain in the lead, they walked down the winding tunnel towards the nesting sands.

Marissya's eyes were wide with wonder, peering down every tunnel and drinking in the mysteries of Fey'Bahren as they descended towards the volcano's heart.

"When we enter the nesting lair," Rain instructed, "we will all walk slowly across the sands to the eggs. Marissya, if at any time tonight the tairen seem agitated, stop whatever you're doing."

"Would the pride really kill Dax if he entered the lair?" Ellysetta asked the question on a private weave, troubled by the possibility. The tairen were intelligent and powerful beings, not mere animals. She found it difficult to reconcile the warm welcome she'd received from the pride with the mindless, wild savagery Rain seemed so certain they would exhibit.

"Survival is a tairen's strongest instinct, and this is where tairen hatch their young," he answered. *"Any intruder is considered a threat. When it comes to the safety of their young, tairen will kill anything and anyone that threatens them. Don't ever doubt that."*

They reached the bottom of the tunnel, and hard stone gave way to a thick carpet of fine, dark black sand. Inside the nesting lair, the tairen had returned to their ledges except for Sybharukai, who lay curled around the eggs, crooning songs of tairen strength and ferocity to the kitlings.

The tairen closest to the tunnel mouth growled and fluttered their wings when they saw Marissya, but a roar from Sybharukai kept them in place. Her eyes whirled bright and green in the smoky grey of her face, and she remained curled around the eggs, her tail thumping the sand.

"The Fey-kin may approach the eggs, but if she wounds the kitlings, her blood will soak the sands."

One of Marissya's hands rose to her throat; the other held Ellysetta's in a crushing grip. Sybharukai had spoken in very distinct Feyan, on the common path.

"I . . . I have no intention of harming them, wise one," Marissya assured the tairen. "I am here only to offer what help I can to the Feyreisa."

"The Fey-kin is warned." With that, Sybharukai rose up on her paws and backed up three steps to grant Ellysetta and Marissya access to the eggs. In a show of silent menace, the great cat extended the long, ivory spikes in her tail and stabbed them into the sand.

Ellysetta led the way, moving towards the center of the clutch of eggs. She laid a hand on each and crooned a quiet song of greeting. "They like when you sing to them. This is Miauren." She stroked the closest egg. "He is a fine, brave tairen. And this is Hallah, who I think will be fierce and beautiful like Steli-*chakai*. And these little ones are Letah, Sharra, and Forrahl."

"You picked fine tairen names for them," Marissya said, cautiously stepping closer.

"I didn't pick them. The kitlings told me their names when I sang to them earlier today." Ellysetta smiled at the *shei'dalin*'s surprise. "Rain tells me tairen kitlings are sentient even in their mother's womb, months before she lays the eggs in the nest. Here, come lay your hand on Hallah's shell and sing to her." She moved aside so Marissya could step in beside her. "She likes warriors' songs. Letah and Sharra prefer lullabies."

"What does Forrahl like?"

Ellie smiled fondly. "Everything. When I sing to him, he purrs so loudly his egg shakes. Watch." She turned and began to sing a Celierian hymn, and sure enough, the egg beside her began to rock happily.

"You are a wonder, Feyreisa," Marissya murmured. "I don't think it's the song he enjoys half so much as the love you're weaving on him when you sing it." Still, gamely, she crouched beside the eggs closest to her. "So you two like lullabies, do you?" Tilting her head, she began to croon the tunes Feyan mothers sang to their children when they were small.

As they sang, Marissya reached out with her magic to check the kitlings. She kept her weaves featherlight and as unobtrusive as possible without sacrificing efficacy. The care slowed her down, but her results were conclusive. Just as Ellysetta had said, there was nothing physically wrong with the kitlings. Marissya could find no infection, no imperfections, weaknesses or blockages in their vital organs, no malignancies anywhere in their bodies. They weren't

even tired anymore, thanks to the inadvertent healing Ellysetta was weaving on them as she sang.

And yet, without a doubt, they were dying.

Ellysetta hadn't been around enough death yet to recognize it, but Marissya had. She'd served too long in the healing tents during the Wars, knelt by the sides of too many
mortally wounded Fey, Elves, and men. Death was here.
She'd fought it so often, so desperately, it was as familiar to
her as the sight of Dax's beloved face. A faint, cold shadow
buried in the heart of the kitlings' warm brightness.

Marissya closed her eyes and summoned the *shei'dalin*
power that could rip truths from even the most corrupted
souls and anchor mortally wounded warriors to life while she
healed them. She closed her senses to everything around her,
condensing her awareness. Gently, carefully, she reached out
to the kitling closest to her, the one named Sharra, and on a
weave of intense Spirit, blazing golden white with the power
of her considerable *shei'dalin* magic, she sent her consciousness into the egg.

The kitling's bright light abruptly winked out, and steely
shackles clapped around Marissya's wrist, yanking her hand
from the shell of the egg. Her eyes flew open in confusion.
She blinked away her Fey vision and found Ellysetta beside
her, holding her wrist in a bruising grip. The Feyreisa's eyes
were glowing green and whirling with opalescent lights,
and her pupils had completely disappeared.

"Whatever you're doing, Marissya, stop." A vibrating
hum deepened Ellysetta's voice to a growl.

A louder, much more menacing growl sounded behind
Ellysetta. Marissya looked up and her mouth went dry.

Sybharukai's pupil-less green eyes whirled faster and
brighter than Ellysetta's, fixed on Marissya with such intensity, the *shei'dalin* couldn't move. Venom dripped from the
tairen's exposed fangs, her poisonous tail spikes were completely extended, and she was whipping that tail through the
air like a weapon.

Marissya released her magic. "I–I'm sorry." Once the first word escaped, the rest began tumbling out in a rush. "I didn't mean any harm. The kitlings aren't sick or injured, but they *are* dying. I was just trying to find out why. Rain . . . tell them." She turned to him, only to find that his eyes, too, had gone more tairen than Fey.

Her first instinct was to call Dax, but she didn't dare. If she called him, he would come for her. He would come and the tairen would kill him. Frightened, but desperately trying to keep that fear from spilling over across her truemate bond with Dax, Marissya slowly rose to her feet, careful not to make any sudden moves.

"What was that you were weaving?" Ellysetta asked, and a measure of Marissya's tension drained away when she turned and saw that the Feyreisa's eyes were slowly returning to normal.

"It was Spirit."

"That didn't feel like any Spirit I've ever woven."

"The pattern was a *shei'dalin*'s weave, Ellysetta. I was trying to merge with the kitlings, to see if I could sense what is killing them."

Ellysetta released her and gave a humorless laugh. "No offense, Marissya, but I suggest you not try to merge with any more tairen. Apparently they don't like it."

Marissya glanced back up at Sybharukai, who was still eyeing her as if she were a meal on the hoof. "So I see." She backed away from the eggs. "I'm sorry, Rain. Whatever's killing the kitlings, I don't think I'll be able to stop it."

His jaw worked and he nodded. "I'll take you back to Dax, but I'd like you to stay the night, in case what hunts the kitlings returns. Perhaps when that happens, you'll be able to sense something you can't now."

She looked around the cavern at all the tairen crouched overhead.

"The choice is yours of course," Rain added. "As you just discovered, it's not a choice without risk."

"Of course I'll stay." With a smile that projected far more confidence than she was feeling, Marissya added, "After all, how many *shei'dalins* ever get the chance to save a tairen pride?"

Despite a night of waiting and watching, the thing that had killed Cahlah and her kit did not return, and by sunrise the next morning, four great tairen were winging across the Fading Lands. Rain carried Dax and Marissya on his back, while Steli carried Ellysetta. Sybharukai had sent the mate-pair Fahreeta and Torasul along as well to join Steli in singing pride greetings to Shei'Kess.

"Do you really think the Eye will tell us any more than it already has?" Rain asked Steli as they flew. Tairen-made or not, the Eye had been perniciously silent for centuries, adamantly refusing to offer help or guidance to the Fey until Rain had forcibly wrested from it the clues that had sent him to Celieria City—and Ellysetta.

"The Eye sent you to Ellysetta-kitling. It knew you would bring her to back to the Fey-kin and to the pride. Now that she is here, Shei'Kess may have more to say."

"Well, I hope singing to the Eye earns a more pleasant response than the one it gave me." The all-consuming pain that had ripped through him when he'd laid hands on the Eye was not something he would ever forget.

Steli chuffed. *"You issued Challenge. We are not so . . ."* She sang an image of a foolish tairen kit biting the tail of a grumpy elder.

Ellysetta laughed, then tried ineffectively to hide it from Rain's narrowing tairen eyes with a cough and a rapid change of subject. *"I still don't understand why the tairen haven't visited Dharsa since the Mage Wars. I thought the tairen considered the Fey kin."*

He allowed the insult of her laughter to pass with a disdainful sniff. *"They do, but the kinship doesn't extend to any particular affection or desire to socialize."*

"Why not?"

Rather than answer her himself, Rain directed the question to the tairen themselves. "*Ellysetta wants to know why the tairen of Fey'Bahren have not visited the Fey-kin city since the Mage Wars.*"

"*Why would the tairen go there?*" Steli sounded surprised by the question. "*You were not there, and the Fey-kin are not tairen.*"

"*They have no wings or beautiful fur,*" Fahreeta added, twirling her sleek body in graceful spinning rolls across the sunlit sky to show off her well-shaped wings and the pure golden color of her pelt. "*And they break too easily if you play with them.*"

"*They smell much like prey,*" Torasul agreed, "*but are not for eating. Is confusing. Makes a cat . . .*" Words gave way to a vivid image of a tairen snarling, his fangs dripping with venom and saliva.

"*I . . . see . . .*" Ellysetta replied slowly.

Rain laughed. The sound came out as a series of amused chuffs. "*To the tairen, only the Tairen Souls are true kin. Other Fey are really only kin-by-proxy. Not prey, but not entirely part of the pride either. Wingless, fangless, furless, flightless, two-legged not-prey creatures who might, many millennia ago, have been something distantly related to tairen. In some respects, the tairen regard the Fey rather like that kitten your sisters gave Kieran.*"

Her jaw dropped. "They think of the Fey as pets?"

"More like distant relatives. More primitive, less powerful relatives."

She paused to mull that over. "Do the Fey know that? The warriors are always talking about "the tairen in them.""

"All Fey know where the line is drawn. Those who are not Tairen Souls admire the tairen, appreciate their power and beauty and magic, but they respect their fierceness as well. The Fey have a saying: "The slopes of Fey'Bahren run dark with the blood of enemies, fools, and prey." Which may have something to do with the fact that a tairen's idea of negotiation is a warning growl before he rips and roasts you with fang and flame."

"I know it must be true, but part of me finds it so hard to believe. Just look at Fahreeta." Ellysetta pointed to the sleek golden cat soaring and diving through the skies nearby. *"She seems so . . . sweet and playful, like a kitten."*

As if sensing eyes upon her, Fahreeta gave a series of purring roars and flew in dizzying circles around her mate, Torasul. The great male just eyed his cavorting mate with a long-suffering eye and kept flying. She flew too close once, and he swatted out with one large paw, catching the tip of her right wing. With a yelp, the playful golden beauty went tumbling. She broke her fall and righted herself easily, but the tumble left her fur ruffled and her green eyes shooting sparks. Torasul gave chuffing huffs of tairen laughter and blew smoke.

Fahreeta's muzzle drew back, baring a mouthful of gleaming white, razor-sharp fangs. She gave a snarl. Her tail whipped through the air like a giant lash. Large, curving claws sprang from her forepaws. She pumped her wings and, with a scream of fury, shot across the sky towards her mate.

Ellysetta gasped and clutched fistfuls of Steli's white hair, but Torasul only gave his mate an indolent look. Then, with a speed that made Ellysetta gasp again, he folded his wings and drop-rolled straight into his mate's oncoming attack. Torasul's wings spread at the last moment to stop his fall before he crashed into Fahreeta, and the two cats came together in a roar of fury, ivory fangs and curved, razor-sharp claws. Limbs tangled. Each tairen's massive jaw grabbed the other's neck in a deadly grip. Wings batted the air with ferocious speed, then folded tight. They spun together, dropping through the sky, wings and tails twining together.

"Rain!" Ellysetta cried, terrified the pair would kill each other right before her eyes. "Stop them."

Steli glanced down at the tumbling pair and sniffed. *"Juveniles."*

Just when it looked as though both Torasul and Fahreeta would crash into the earth below, the pair spread their wings and broke apart, soaring in opposite directions, then circling around. They flew upwards, gaining altitude and speed until both were flying alongside Rain and Steli once more.

Fahreeta resumed her purring and prancing through the sky, taking every occasion to rub wing and fur against her mate. Torasul rumbled happily, then returned to his stoic, unflappable calm and kept his wings pumping in steady flight.

"Oh, *aiyah*," Rain sang in tones laden with irony. "*Sweet and playful. Very like a kitten.*"

Celieria ~ Teleon

"Good morning, my sweet kitlings." Sol Baristani beamed at his young twin daughters as they skipped into the sunny breakfast room in Teleon's main tower. "Don't you both look bright as a summer sky?"

Lillis and Lorelle were both wearing cerulean blue frocks covered with white lace pinafores that tied in big bows at the back of their waists. Their mink brown hair bounced in curling ringlets around their shoulders, and circlets of beautiful, aromatic white bellflowers crowned their heads.

"Good morning, Papa!" Lillis sang. "Look what we found!" She held up a bouquet of the same flowers she and Lorelle wore in their hair. "Aren't they pretty? They bloomed last night all over the garden we planted with Ellie and Lady Marissya."

Sol made a show of inspecting the delicate white bellflowers. The blooms, each about the size of a baby's fist, nodded on the half dozen slender green stems clutched in Lillis's hand. Each deep bloom boasted six starry petals curled back from a pale pink center accented with shimmering, opalescent veins and deep pink stamens. The flowers were stunning, their aroma an entrancing mix of freshness and heady fragrance, like jasmine drenched in a cool spring rain. Laurie would have loved them.

"Those are beautiful, kitling," Sol agreed, his voice going gruff. "We'll just put them here in this glass, eh?" He poured water into an empty glass and held it out to Lillis so she could put the flowers in it. He set the makeshift vase in the center of the table. "Very pretty. Now, both of you come sit down and eat before your breakfast gets cold." As the girls danced past to take their seats, Sol's eyes widened in dismay. They'd left a crumbling trail of muddy footprints in their wake.

"Girls!" He scowled. "Did you go to the gardens to pick flowers or dance in the mud? Look at the mess you've made!"

The twins glanced back. Lillis's mouth formed an O, but Lorelle only gave a careless shrug. "It's just dirt, Papa. Kieran can clean it up in half a chime."

"Oh, can he?" Sol put his hands on his hips. "Kieran may be able to clean with just a weave of magic, but there's plenty of work for him to do around here without your making more for him. Both of you, take those shoes off at once. Lillis, get a broom and start sweeping. Lorelle, you fetch the mop. And just for your sass, you can clean the breakfast dishes this morning as well."

"Papa!"

He pointed. "Go."

The girls pouted and trudged off. Sol frowned after them, shaking his head in dismay. Laurie would be beside herself. The last several weeks of living around magic had clearly spoiled the girls into forgetting the lessons of responsibility and discipline their mother had worked so hard to instill in them. But what was Sol to do? Their lives *had* changed. Forever. Cling as he might to mortal ways, magic was going to be a daily part of his daughters' lives, and there was no getting 'round it.

"Good morning, Master Baristani," Kiel greeted as he and Kieran walked in with Lord Teleos. The two Fey and the border lord had begun breakfasting with the Baristanis each morning before heading off to continue the restoration of Teleon. Not that there was all that much to do anymore. The warriors Rain had sent to accompany Lord Teleon to Orest had worked nonstop for the last seventy-two bells to repair the bulk of the fortress. They and Lord Teleon would be departing for Orest on the morrow.

"Looks like someone's been walking in the mud this morning," Kieran said with an eye on the muddy footprints. He lifted his hands and started to spin magic, but Sol stopped him.

"No, please, Kieran. The girls made the mess. I've told them they're to clean it up. I won't have my children turn into slovenly little pamperlings just because they live amongst the Fey."

"Kieran." Kiel spoke his blade brother's name in a strange, strangled voice, and poked him in the arm. "Kieran, look." He pointed to the breakfast table.

Kieran turned—and froze.

"What is it? What's wrong?" Both Fey were staring at the bouquet of white flowers on the table, and Sol's chest squeezed tight. Were the blooms poisonous?

But Kiel was reaching for the bouquet with shaking hands, and Kieran was making no move to stop him. The Water master lifted the bouquet to his face and breathed in deeply.

Even Lord Teleos was staring. "Are those what I think they are?"

"Master Baristani," Kieran rasped, "where did those flowers come from?"

"The girls brought them in. Why?" Sol was torn between alarm and confusion. The three men were acting as if they'd seen a dead man, but clearly the flowers were not dangerous. "What's going on? Did they do something wrong?"

Kieran didn't answer. Instead, he pivoted on a heel, marched back out into the hallway, and, in a very un-Fey-like manner, shouted, "Lillis! Lorelle!"

The twins came running, mop and broom banging behind.

"What is it? What's wrong?"

Kieran pointed to the flowers in Kiel's hand and on their heads. "Where did you find these flowers?"

"Outside." Lorelle pointed through the arching stone windows to the graceful curving terraced gardens beyond. "In the gardens we helped Ellie and Lady Marissya plant."

Lillis beamed. "Aren't they pretty? There's lots and lots of them. They must have bloomed in the night."

"Fey! Ti'jensa! To the gardens! Hurry! Tell me what you see." Kieran sent the call on the common path, and outside, half a dozen warriors raced for the terraces.

Moments later the cry went up, "It blooms! The white bell blooms!" In voices that rang with excitement, they announced their discovery on the common path for all the Fey to hear, *"Amarynth, brothers! The white bell blooms in the gardens of Teleon!"*

There was a moment of shocked silence; then a shout rose up throughout the keep, a great hurrah that rattled window glass in its panes. "Amarynth blooms! *Mioralas!* Blessings on this house and all who dwell here!"

"Amarynth?" Sol's brows drew together in surprise. Many woodcarvers used the six-petaled Amarynth blossom, also called the star flower, as a motif in their carvings, but he had never seen a live bloom. "They're real?"

"They are indeed, Master Baristani, and they bloom only in the footsteps of a Fey woman bearing young."

Sol's eyes went wide. "You mean Ellysetta . . . my Ellie-girl is—"

"Nei. Not Ellysetta," Kiel said. "She and Rain are not yet fully united, and truemates do not breed outside the bond. These flowers bloom for Marissya and Dax."

Kieran had a silly, stunned grin on his face. "I'm going to be a brother. A brother, Kiel. My *mela* is with child." Tears filled his eyes.

Kiel smiled. "*Mioralas,* my friend. I couldn't be happier for you." He clapped his hand on Kieran's back. "You should be the one to tell them. Weave the news now, quickly, before our brothers shout it all the way to Dharsa."

"*Aiyah . . . aiyah,* I will . . . right now." He could hardly concentrate. He closed his eyes and pressed the bouquet of Amarynth to his face, careful not to bruise the precious blooms. Weeping, laughing, soaring with joy, he spun the weave. "*Mela . . . gepa . . . it's Kieran. . . .*"

The Fading Lands ~ Plains of Corunn

Rain, Ellysetta, and the others were halfway to Dharsa when Kieran's weave reached them. They'd just stopped to eat and stretch their legs, which was good, because Dax's legs folded beneath him when he heard his son's words.

Kieran expanded his initial private weave to include them all as he heaped love and blessings upon his stunned parents. Dax was now sitting on the ground, holding his truemate in his arms. The fierce Fey lord wore a look of such staggering joy and devotion, it made Ellysetta's throat go tight.

Amarynth bloomed in Teleon. Marissya was with child.

Fertility had returned to the Fey.

Rain dropped to his knees beside the *shei'dalin* and her mate. "*Miora felah,* Marissya. *Miora felah,* Dax. Brightest blessings of the gods upon you."

Laughing and crying at the same time, Marissya enfolded Rain in her arms. "Joy and blessings to us all, *kem'maresk, kem'Feyreisen.* And joy to the Feyreisa most of all."

"Me?" Ellysetta blinked in surprise. "But I haven't done anything."

The *shei'dalin* turned a radiant, tear-stained face in Ellysetta's direction. "Your weave," she explained. She gave a choked laugh and shook her head. "That awful, inescapable seven-bell weave you spun in Celieria." Her joyous laughter pealed out, stealing any possible sting from her words. "Ellysetta . . . little sister . . . sweet gift from the gods. You wove much more than Spirit that night—and may the gods shower ten lifetimes of blessings on you for it."

"Steli! Fahreeta, Torasul!" Rain sang the news to his pridekin, who were chasing tavalree on the plains just to see them run. *"Come celebrate and wish us joy. Marissya of the Fey bears young!"*

The three tairen joined them swiftly, and Steli bent her head to sniff both Marissya and Dax, then sang a few notes of tairen song. A soft, unevenly pitched and offbeat echo rang in Ellysetta's ears. The white tairen sat back with a satisfied look on her face.

"So that is the scent I smelled," she declared. She spoke not in tairen song but in plain Feyan, woven on Spirit so Marissya and Dax would be sure to understand. *"The Fey-kin bears one of the pride."*

Marissya and Dax both gaped. "I bear *what?*" Marissya gasped. She splayed one hand across her flat belly; the other clutched Dax like a vise.

"A Tairen Soul?" Rain threw back his head and laughed. He grabbed Ellysetta up and swung her around in circles. "*Shei'tani.* Ah, *shei'tani*, you wondrous woman. This is definitely not how I expected the gods to spin this weave, but I welcome it all the same. A child of the Fey—a Tairen Soul—thanks to you." He showered her face with kisses.

Dax started laughing. "You know what this means, of course, once word reaches Dharsa? Our women will insist the Feyreisa be fed a steady diet of keflee and pinalle until all the Fading Lands bloom white once more!"

Ellysetta's eyes went wide.

"Oh, no!" Marissya gave a laughing groan. "Gods save us all."

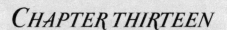

CHAPTER THIRTEEN

No moon, sun, or star ever dazzled the night
Like the radiant grace of Ellysetta the Bright.
From "The Star of Chakai," a warriors' song of
Ellysetta the Bright

The Fading Lands ~ Dharsa

The remainder of the journey to Dharsa passed rapidly. Spirit weaves carrying exuberant greetings and well wishes continued to pour across the common path. By midday, the wide, rolling grasslands of the Plains of Corunn gave way to graceful swells of densely forested earth that rose and fell like waves on the ocean, all building towards the Shining City.

Constructed entirely of white stone, its many towers capped by gleaming gold spires and domes, Dharsa rose like a jeweled diadem from the rich greenery of the forested hills. The city was built upon a ring of five outer hills, all circling a larger central peak topped by an immense, shining palace. Graceful buildings of incredible beauty and delicacy soared amid lush stands of greenery, terraced gardens, and trees laden with scented blossoms and plump, shining fruit. Water cascaded from breathtaking fountains and artfully arranged cliffs, feeding streams that wound down the hillsides before merging into the wide, shining ribbon of the River Faer. Birds of every shape and color flitted and swooped from tree to tree, filling the sky with a rainbow of dancing colors and song.

Ellysetta had never seen something so perfect, so beautiful. *"Rain . . . oh, Rain . . ."*

The black tairen turned his head, his lavender eyes glowing bright. *"Welcome to Dharsa, shei'tani. The shining heart of the Fading Lands."*

Rain dipped his wing and banked left, soaring along the perimeter of the ring of hills. Steli, Fahreeta, and Torasul followed close on his tail, and the four tairen landed in a small clearing where the Fey returning from Celieria City waited with Ellysetta's *lu'tans* and the rest of the former *rasa*.

The warriors were smiling as they had not smiled in years. A palpable aura of joy surrounded them, and they had already buffed their gleaming black leathers and polished their steel to a mirror shine in preparation for their entrance into the city. Waiting Air masters spun Ellysetta, Marissya, and Dax clear of their saddles.

Gaelen was there the moment his sister's feet touched ground. He caught her in his arms and held her tight. *"Mioralas,* little sister. Gods' blessings upon you." Still holding her tucked against his side, he offered Dax a smile and a hand, which his bond brother clasped warmly. *"Te a vo,* Dax. My heart sings for you both." He turned back to his sister, grinning proudly. "A Tairen Soul, no less. I never thought v'En Solande had it in him."

Dax was too happy to take offense. "Just wait, bond brother. When my son finds his flame, he'll teach you respect."

"Some miracles are beyond even a Tairen Soul's power." Bel smirked at Gaelen's narrow-eyed look and added, "Release your sister. There are other Fey who would wish her well."

While Dax and Marissya accepted the congratulations of the Fey, Earth masters enveloped the pair in swirling threads of power, changing their leathers to rich flowing robes in shades of green and white to celebrate the precious life growing in Marissya's womb. The hundreds of Fey surrounded her like the treasure she was, and each of the former *rasa* took a moment to kneel and touch her hand in a way they would never have allowed themselves to do only a few days earlier.

When all had offered Marissya their joy and she had spun a *shei'dalin*'s blessing on the assembly, the warriors stepped back to form ranks.

Rain took his place at Ellysetta's side. He had changed into full ceremonial dress, black leathers, purple-silk-lined black cape, his boots tooled with the scarlet and purple outlines of tairen rampant, Tairen Crown resting upon his brow. Ellysetta, in her plain brown traveling leathers, felt out of place beside the others, but when she asked Rain to weave a more appropriate gown, he smiled mysteriously and nodded towards Bel, saying, "Your *lu'tans* have prepared something for you."

Bel stood at the front of the gathered warriors. When all eyes were upon him, he bowed low and said. "It is the custom of the Fey that a *shei'dalin* who has won the bloodsworn bond of a warrior should wear his blade at all times, both for her protection and as a symbol of the honor in which she holds the warrior's bond. But three nights ago in Chakai, the Feyreisa proved yet again she was born to set tradition on its head."

The *lu'tans* laughed and shouted, "*Miora felah ti'Feyreisa!*"

Bel waited for their shouts to die down before he continued. "Three hundred seventeen Fey bound their souls to the protection of the Feyreisa after her legendary night of healing. Counting Gaelen and me, Ellysetta Feyreisa now claims three hundred nineteen bloodsworn champions. No *shei'dalin* has ever won the bonds of so many."

"Nor ever will again!" the *lu'tans* cried.

White teeth flashed in a brief grin of agreement before Bel once again raised his hands to quiet his exuberant brothers. "This posed quite a challenge, since the Feyreisa clearly could not wear so many blades, yet not to do so would dishonor the bond. We"—he turned to gesture toward

the assembled Fey—"the warriors who have bloodsworn
ourselves to her service, have devised what we hope is an
acceptable solution."

He gestured to Gaelen, Tajik, Rijonn, and Gil. The four
Fey stepped forward, holding Fey'cha belts and a set of
studded leathers in *shei'dalin* red.

"Gaelen and I have agreed that Tajik, Gil, and Rijonn
should join us to serve as your primary quintet," Bel continued. "Our blades are here, in this hip belt. The other
lu'tans threw lots to see whose blades you would wear in
your Fey'cha belts, and the rest we transformed into the
studs in your leathers. They are all here"—he gestured to
the studded leathers and the weapons belts—"every one of
your bloodsworn blades. Let a single drop of your blood fall
on any stud or blade, and you will summon the warrior
who bound himself to you."

Ellysetta accepted the gift with reverent hands. "*Beylah
vos.* I will wear these with pride."

"*Sha vel'mei, kem'falla.*" Bel bowed. "Today, however, we
thought this might be more appropriate." He nodded at Rijonn and Tajik, who raised their hands and loosed bright
weaves of Earth. The leathers disappeared and re-formed on
Ellysetta's body as an ornately embroidered gown woven
from the silvery Fey steel of her *lu'tans'* blades. Two sashes of
purple and scarlet crisscrossed her chest like Fey'cha belts,
holding dozens of sheathed bloodsworn blades, while the
Fey'cha of her primary quintet dangled at her hips alongside
the Tairen's Eye crystals of the warriors who'd died to protect her back in Celieria. Her hair they left in a thick rope of
red coils down her back, bound by a series of silver rings.

"Nicely done, my brothers," Rain approved. Steli,
Fahreeta, and Torasul purred their agreement. With the
concentration of so many Fey nearby, Ellysetta's own power
was rising. Her entire form gleamed with a golden-white
radiance that made her gown of silvery Fey steel shine like

a star. "You will dazzle them, *shei'tani*." He lifted his wrist for her hand. "Come meet your people, *Feyreisa*."

The main gate of Dharsa, flanked by a pair of crouching stone tairen, was an exquisitely carved white stone arch of immense proportions. Beyond the arch, an avenue lined by giant sentinel trees, whose intertwining branches formed a soaring, sunlight-dappled corridor, led the way into the fabled Fey city.

Thousands of immortal Fey had gathered on rooftops and the main thoroughfare. They cheered the arrival of the warriors returning from Celieria, but when they caught sight of Marissya and Dax in their robes of verdant green, a celebratory roar rose from the crowds. Celebration turned to tearful joy as more than a thousand former *rasa* returned to their city and loved ones for the first time in many long years.

Joy turned to awe as Fahreeta and Torasul stepped into view. Fahreeta roared and growled and held her shining wings high in a show of beauty and fierce majesty. She stopped occasionally to spout small jets of flame, much to the Fey's cheering delight. Torasul, stoic and deadly, padded with lethal grace at her side, lowering his head every now and again to glare at the Fey gathered along the avenue and bare a threatening fang, which made the warriors grin and bow.

Behind Fahreeta and Torasul marched Ellysetta's three hundred *lu'tan*, and as they stepped into the streets of Dharsa, their voices rose in a song of their own, called "The Star of Chakai," which several of them had composed to celebrate the *shei'dalin* who restored their souls.

Finally, it was Rain and Ellysetta's turn to enter the city.

"Are you ready, *shei'tani*?" Rain's eyes were aglow with a mix of tenderness and pride.

Though the shy Celierian in her wanted to turn and flee,

Ellysetta drew a deep breath and put her hand on his wrist. "*Aiyah*, I'm ready." Together they stepped from the sheltering avenue of trees onto the broad, white stone streets of Dharsa.

The moment she appeared, a deafening roar arose from the Fey.

"Ellysetta *Beilissa, Eiliss o Chakai*. Ellysetta the Bright, the Star of Chakai!"

The reverberant cry stole every ouce of breath from Ellysetta's lungs and startled thousands of birds into flight.

Ellysetta froze in dazed surprise. Fluttering wings filled the skies of Dharsa, and fragrant petals rained down from the blossoming orchards of the surrounding hills. From every road and rooftop garden, every path and walkway, the Shining Folk sang her name with breathtaking, boundless joy. Thousands of Fey hearts opened to her in an outpouring of love and welcome so abundant, so genuine, it stunned her to her soul.

The hand on Rain's wrist began to shake. Tears filled her eyes, turning vision to a watery blur until she could no longer see the faces of the thousands gathered to greet her. Never had she dared to dream of such a welcome.

"*Meivelei, shei'tani.*" Rain's Spirit whisper sounded oddly choked. "*Meivelei ti'Dharsa.*"

Somehow she kept walking, though her knees were quaking so hard she thought she would crumple in a puddle to the paving stones. The outpouring of love drew out her own magic, lighting her from within until she glowed bright as the star the *lu'tans* had named her.

Behind them, Ellysetta's bloodsworn quintet followed in a protective semicircle, while Steli paced at the rear as the self-appointed sixth member of the quintet. The tairen strode like the *chakai* she was, proud, stately, her eyes gleaming sapphires in the pure white of her face. Her claws, half extended, clicked on the paving stones as she walked, and she held her wings unfurled in a show of protective might.

The procession halted at the base of Dharsa's central mount, where the five lords of the Massan and their *shei'dalin* truemates stood waiting. The warriors burst into their final song: a booming, joy-filled rendition of "Ten Thousand Swords." As the Fey voices built to a soaring crescendo, Fahreeta, Torasul, and Steli reared up on their hind legs, pawing the sky, roaring, and shooting jets of searing flame upward as their great wings beat the air: tairen rampant, the symbol of the Feyreisen's power. The three held their pose as the *lu'tan* sang in perfect, stirring pitch the song's final verse: "Ten thousand swords protect you, beloved of us all."

With a final roar that shook the ground like thunder, all three tairen leapt into the air. Mighty wings beat hard and fast, gaining speed and altitude until the tairen were circling the city overhead, the first true tairen to do so in a thousand years. They filled the skies with roars and flame, then soared north and disappeared from view.

Rain lifted his arms and called out both aloud and in a Spirit weave that carried to every corner of the city, "*Mioralas,* Fey! *Mioralas, kem'ilanis!* With pride, this Fey presents Ellysetta Feyreisa, truemate of the Tairen Soul, she who shines light on shadowed souls, restores hope where none remains, and brings fertility back to the Fey." He lifted her hand and raised it high. "*Miora felah ti'Feyreisa!*"

The former *rasa* took up his cry: "*Miora felah ti'Feyreisa! Miora felah ti'Feyreisen!*"

The crowd burst into explosive cheers and applause, and thousands more Fey added their own voices to the exuberant cries.

Rain let his gaze sweep over the crowd, finding dozens of faces he knew, seeing the subtle nods that told him the message of this carefully orchestrated show had not gone unnoticed. And as his eyes met and held the gazes of the five Massan and their mates on the podium, he knew they had not misunderstood either.

If they had truly been considering Challenge, they'd just

realized they were outmatched. Ellysetta had saved the *rasa* and been accepted by the tairen and, thanks to her powerful fertility weave, had brought the promise of life back to the Fading Lands in the form of Marissya v'En Solande's unborn Tairen Soul son.

Despite the looming threat of war, the gods were clearly smiling on the Fey once more. Thanks to Ellysetta Feyreisa, the Star of Chakai.

With a faint, deliberate smile, Rain leapt into the air, his body dissolving in a swirling cloud of rainbow-shot mist. Moments later, pure black, magnificent and deadly, his tairen form wheeled overhead. He swooped low over the crowds, and Ellysetta's *lu'tans* spun a whirling jet of Air that lifted her high and deposited her smoothly onto his back as he passed overhead.

"Hold on, shei'tani."

"Rain, wait. What about the Massan? Are we not going to meet them?"

"They will join us in the palace in a few bells, before the banquet to celebrate your arrival begins. For now, let them celebrate Marissya's joy and the return of the rasa, and let us enjoy what I fear will be the last chimes we will have alone for many days. I have a feeling all of Dharsa will want to greet you personally and ask for your blessing."

Rain circled one final time over the crowds before soaring towards the palace at the top of the city's central hill to give Ellie an unimpeded view of her new home.

Wider than several Celierian city blocks, the five-sided white marble hall rose up from lush, manicured gardens. Gilded tairen rampant crouched on the rooftop at all five corners, and in their great jaws, each cat clutched a gleaming globe of Tairen's Eye crystal. A large tower capped with a golden dome rose above the center of the complex, and at its apex stood a silverstone Fey *shei'dalin* draped in rippling golden robes. Her face was upturned, her arms raised over her head, holding aloft a sixth crystal globe, larger than all the rest, that shone pure white and radiant as the sun.

"Legend says the white stone is the kiyr of Lissallukai, the tairen who breathed magic into the world," Rain told her as they circled. "The tairen at the corners of the building represent the five makai who led their prides to follow her here."

"And the shei'dalin and five warriors?" Below the shei'dalin holding Lissallukai's soul crystal, five statues of fierce Fey warriors ringed the base of the dome. They leaned out over the edges of the tower roof into the winds, silver seyani swords unsheathed and clutched in their pale stone hands. Each warrior wore finely scaled armor gilded gold and silver and covered with tabards enameled in rich shades of scarlet, silvery white, rich purple, cobalt, or verdant green.

"The five branches of Fey magic, of course, and the love that gives us hope and holds Fey warriors to the Bright Path. They guard and bless the Hall of Tairen, throne room of the Feyreisen."

On the northeast side of the dome lay a large, open courtyard sown with a green expanse of grass. They descended onto the thick grass, and Rain Changed back into the Feyreisen's ceremonial garb.

"This is beautiful," she said, looking around.

"When the prides were many, and the makais came to Dharsa to meet with the Feyreisen, this is where they would gather before entering the Hall of Tairen. Steli and the others will join us here tomorrow when they return to sing to the Eye."

The walls of the courtyard were covered with a mural of mosaic tiles that depicted various scenes: tairen soaring the blue skies above Fey'Bahren and Dharsa, hunting on the plains of Corunn, stalking through verdant forests, and swimming in aqua waters beside silver-sand beaches. The tiles shimmered with magic, and Rain showed her how to make the scenes come alive by turning her head. Ellysetta laughed in delight and turned her head from side to side to watch the tairen stalk and the trees rustle in a breeze.

He led her to the south wall of the courtyard, where a shimmering pool lay waiting under the southern eave. A silverstone maiden and warrior poured continuous streams of water from crystal urns into the pool, while on the wall, mosaic tairen crouched on either side and appeared to drink. Rain plucked a golden cup from a small niche beside the pool, held it under the stream of water, then offered it to Ellysetta.

The moment the water touched her lips, her eyes went wide. One small sip erased every hint of weariness and filled her with vibrant energy. "*Faerilas.*" She sipped again, then drained the cup, shuddering a little at the rush of refreshing power. "But much stronger than any I've tasted yet."

"The pool is fed directly from Dharsa's Source," he told her. He filled the cup for himself when she was done. "There is no more potent *faerilas* to be found in all the Fading Lands."

"What makes it so much stronger?" She watched his throat work as he swallowed and saw the glow of his skin grow brighter as the *faerilas* renewed his magic.

"No one knows," he admitted.

Her brows rose. "Well, where do Sources get their magic?"

"No one knows that either." He drained the cup and returned it to the niche. "We *do* know that Tairen's Eye crystals lie at the heart of each Source—we discovered that when we tried to repair Lissilin—but just replacing the crystals does not rejuvenate a failed Source. There must be some other factor, some great old magic now lost to the Fey."

"Sybharukai said she smelled old magic in me."

His mouth curved up at the corner. "That did not escape me." He held out a wrist. "Come. Let me show you your new home."

Ellysetta started to put her hand on his wrist, then smiled and threaded her fingers through his instead. Fey did not hold hands. It was considered unsafe in a world where a warrior needed instant, unfettered access to his magic or steel.

"We are safe enough here," she said when he raised his brows. "There aren't many Celierian customs I prefer to Feyan, but this is one of them."

He smiled, curled his fingers loosely around hers in the Celierian way, and led her into the palace.

The palace of the Fey king was a marvel, more beautiful than anything Ellysetta had seen yet in this most wondrous of all Fey cities. Golden doors, white marble stone floors, soaring cathedral-like ceilings, walls covered with bright tapestries that depicted Fey wars and legends long lost to the rest of the world. Long drapes of rich fabric framed glassless windows that opened to terraces overlooking breathtaking city vistas.

Everywhere there was magic, from the shimmering mosaics of the tairen courtyard, to the fountains of *faerilas* splashing in every courtyard within the palace walls, to the cleaning weaves that whisked away the slightest smudge of grime or dust, leaving every inch of the palace gleaming with Fey perfection.

Ellysetta was actually surprised to find that the palace had kitchens. Quite large ones, too, and filled with dozens of real, live Fey women and even Fey lords, industriously baking, chopping, and kneading a staggering array of food in preparation for tonight's feast. They all paused to greet her warmly before returning to work.

"Why don't they just . . ." She wiggled her fingers. "You know."

Rain laughed. "Certainly, there is some of that," he told her, "but a fine meal is like a song, art that is meant to be consumed by the senses. Besides, what pleasure is there to life if you never create anything with your own hands?"

Ellie raised a skeptical brow. She'd spent one too many hours laboring at the monotony of cooking, cleaning, and housework to consider it a pleasure.

"Perhaps you will change your mind after you've lived your first hundred years," Rain suggested. "Magic is just a tool, not a replacement for the experiences and accomplishments of life. Forget that, and the pursuit of magical perfection will become all that matters, and the Fey will follow the same dark path as the Eld."

After leaving the kitchens, they continued on past banquet halls, conservatories, rooms of state, the palace library, and the king's private courtyard and offices. Room after beautiful room, each a treasure in its own right.

From his well-appointed offices, Rain led her down a small corridor to the king's personal armory. There, displayed on three tall stands in a sconce-lit alcove, was the war armor of the Fey king.

Made entirely of gleaming golden-hued steel, the armor consisted of a woven chain mail, a complete set of Fey blades whose hilts were embossed with the purple tairen rampant, seal of the Fey king, and protective plate mail made of golden steel and layers of hardened and embossed black leather.

"The king's armor was made in the Time Before Memory," Rain told her. "Passed down from Feyreisen to Feyreisen since Tevan Fire Eyes, the first Tairen Soul of the Fading Lands."

"I'm surprised it has never been damaged or lost," Ellysetta said. "Fey kings have certainly fought in many terrible wars over the centuries."

"There is a repair spell forged into the steel, and a return weave that brings the king's armor back to this room if the Tairen Soul wearing it dies."

He approached the center stand, where the shining black and gold of the king's armor gleamed like shadows and sunlight. Across the black leather, tooled in gold and silver, were symbols surrounded by a varying number of circles. His fingers brushed over them without touching. "These are the name symbols of every Defender of the Fey who ever donned this armor and led the Fey into battle. The rings indicate how long each reigned. One silver ring for every hundred years, one gold ring for every millennium."

She stepped closer, peering at the symbols. No name had more than one gold ring, and very few had both gold and silver. "Where is your name?"

"It is not there." At her surprised look, he explained, "Only those who have worn the armor have their name set upon it. I never have. Johr Feyreisen died at the Garreval, only a few days before I scorched the world. The armor returned to Dharsa, and I couldn't leave the battle to retrieve it."

"You've never even tried it on since then? Just to see how it fits?"

In a voice both soft and grave, he said, "This is the war armor of the Fey king, Ellysetta. The moment a Feyreisen puts it on his body, he commits the Fading Lands to war, and he commits himself to one of only two fates: victory or death. Only then can the armor be returned to this room, and only then can the Fey cease fighting." Her horror must have shown in her eyes, because he gave her a bleak smile. "War is no game to the Fey, *shei'tani*, and surrender is no option."

Barely conscious of doing so, she gripped his arm and pulled him away from the gleaming gold-and-black armor, tugging him towards the armory door. "Then I pray your name will never be inscribed there." But they both knew it soon would be.

From the armory, Rain led Ellysetta back to the wide gallery that opened into the tairen courtyard where her palace tour had begun. Bel, Gaelen, Tajik, Gil, and Rijonn were waiting in the courtyard. They had changed from warriors' leathers to rich robes for the evening's celebrations, and were all grinning proudly and discussing the highlights of the Feyreisa's procession and her overwhelming welcome by the Fey.

Before Rain and Ellysetta could join them, Marissya and Dax entered the far end of the gallery, followed by the five Lords of the Massan and their truemates.

Rain quickly stifled his brief, instinctive surge of aggression and greeted the Massan. "*Meivelei*, Fey." Putting a hand in the small of Ellysetta's back, he ushered her forward. "With pride this Fey presents to you his *shei'tani*, Ellysetta of Celieria. Ellysetta, these are the honored Fey lords of the Massan, the council that governs the Fading Lands."

Rain clasped the forearm of the first Massan, a silvery blond Water master with eyes the same deep blue-violet as the waters off the black cliffs of the Bay of Flames. "This fine Fey is Loris v'En Mahr—Water master of the Massan—and his *shei'tani*, Nalia."

Rain smiled when genuine welcome filled Loris's eyes, then laughed when golden-haired Nalia took Ellysetta's hand and dragged her into a warm embrace as if they were sisters, long separated. Nalia had that sort of way about her. Loris might be the Water, full of secret depths and unseen currents, but Nalia was both the wind that drove him and the rock that stood firm against even his most furious waves. What Nalia wanted, Nalia got. Thank the gods what she wanted was usually best for all.

"*Meivelei*, little sister," Nalia greeted. "Welcome. Long have we truemates of the Massan prayed the gods would bring our king peace. And now you have come." Nalia pulled back to give Ellysetta a searching look. "Word of your miraculous weaves reached us days ago, as did rumors of your brightness, and I can see now none of it was exaggeration." A dazzling smile beamed across Nalia's face, and she clasped Ellysetta tight again.

After a brief hesitation and a slightly dazed glance at Rain, Ellysetta returned the hug.

"Let her breathe, *kem'alia*," Loris chided, touching his mate's arm. "She is used to *shei'dalin* restraint, not your exuberance."

Nalia laughed, unoffended, and pulled back. "*Sieks'ta*, Feyreisa. I forget myself. Long ago, when I was a child, my mother would shake her head and sigh in fear of what havoc I would wreak on the world. She always thanked the gods for sending me Loris. He smoothed the worst of my rough edges."

"She should have been named Nimshorra, the whirlwind, instead of Nimalia, the windflower," Loris said with a fond look for his mate.

Rain touched Ellysetta's elbow lightly and directed her attention to the next matepair. "And this is Nurian v'En Soma, Spirit master, and his *shei'tani*, Sianna. Nurian is a very old friend and bond kinsman. Sariel was the daughter of his cousin."

"*Las te miora a vo,* Feyreisa," Lord Nurian murmured. "Peace and joy upon you." The Spirit master and his mate were as dark as Loris and Nalia were fair. Lord Nurian bowed, the folds of his robes swirling gracefully about him, while his *shei'tani,* Sianna, smiled warmly enough but kept her hands clasped firmly at her waist. She was not half so effervescent as Nalia.

"*Beylah vo,*" Ellysetta murmured. "I'm honored to meet you both."

Rain introduced the next couple. "Ellysetta, may it please you, this is Air master Eimar v'En Arran and his truemate, Jisera."

Eimar's sun-bright locks were threaded with tiny crystal bells that sang with every shift of his head, but his eyes were clear and cold as a winter sky. Rain wasn't completely certain what welcome Ellysetta would receive from him, until

Eimar's tiny, dark *shei'tani* offered a shy smile and told Elly-setta, "My brother, Lothan, is among those whose souls you restored. His return brings my heart much joy."

At that, Eimar bowed his head, crystal bells tinkling, and said, "*Meivelei*, Feyreisa, *te sallan'meilissis a vo.*"

Earth master Yulan v'En Belos and his *shei'tani*, Mahri, greeted Ellysetta with a noncommittal reserve similar to that of Nurian and his mate. Last, they came to the Fire master Tenn v'En Eilan, a Fey with whom Rain had butted heads on numerous occasions.

"Tenn is the leader of the Massan," he told her. "His brother Johr was the Feyreisen when I found my wings. Tenn's *shei'tani*, Venarra, is the keeper of the Hall of Scrolls." Tenn, who was constantly comparing Rain to his dead Feyreisen brother, was the source of much of Rain's tension with the Massan. And Rain knew he hadn't managed to hide that tension when Ellysetta's fingers flinched on his wrist.

"Lord v'En Eilan." Ellysetta inclined her head and fought to remain open-minded towards the leader of the Massan, but it was difficult when Rain's emotions were flaring against her fingertips despite his efforts to keep them caged.

The Fire master's robes shimmered like flames leaping in a hearth. His hair, brown and cropped to shoulder-length, held glints of gold and red, and his eyes were dark cinna-mon shot with sparks of gold. His fire-kissed gaze made her belly clench tight, but she couldn't tell how much of that instinctive reaction was her own and how much was a re-flection of the emotions emanating from Rain.

She turned her gaze quickly to Tenn's truemate, a black-haired, black-eyed beauty who seemed only slightly more welcoming. "Lady v'En Eilan."

"I understand you have quite an interest in Fey legends and poetry, Feyreisa," Venarra said. The *shei'dalin*'s dark eyes pierced Ellysetta. A foreign consciousness brushed across Ellysetta's senses, probing lightly. Ellysetta narrowed her eyes and slammed her mental shields shut so hard and fast the *shei'dalin* flinched.

"I do indeed." Ellysetta held the other woman's gaze steadily. Rain shifted so close his arm rubbed against hers. "I've devoured everything I could find about the Fey since I was a child. Little did I realize I was learning about my own heritage."

Venarra inclined her head. "Rain has suggested I show you the Hall of Scrolls. It will be my honor to do so tomorrow, after the tairen sing to the Eye."

With their introductions to the Feyreisa over, the Massan turned to greet Bel, Tajik, and the rest of Ellysetta's blood-sworn quintet. Ellysetta watched them closely, waiting to see how they would welcome Gaelen. She didn't realize how tightly her nerves were wound until the brush of Rain's hand over hers nearly made her jump out of her skin.

"Las, shei'tani," he whispered on a private weave. *"You look fierce as a mother tairen guarding her kits. Gaelen does not need your protection."*

Only then did she realize her fingers were knotted in fists and her jaw was clenched so tightly her back teeth ached. For herself, she accepted the suspicion of the Massan, but not for Gaelen. *"He has suffered enough. Can they not just welcome him?"*

"He knew he would find more suspicion than welcome when he returned to the Fading Lands. This is the path he chose to walk."

All five of the Massan wore expressions of impenetrable stone, and their truemates had begun to glow with gathering power. Even smiling, friendly Nalia looked formidable.

Marissya stepped between her brother and the Massan. "You need not Truthspeak Gaelen. I did so the day the Feyreisa restored his soul, and the Mists let him pass without challenge."

Ellysetta could feel her own magic rising. The memory

of what had happened to her in the Mists was still painfully fresh in her mind. If these *shei'dalins* dared attempt to Truthspeak Gaelen against his will . . . well, Marissya wouldn't be the only one stepping to Gaelen's defense.

Rain moved forward, open palms lifted in a gesture of peace. "Marissya is right. There will be no Truthspeaking here tonight. Ellysetta Feyreisa has come to Dharsa. Marissya *Shei'dalin* bears Tairen Soul young." The faint glitter in the lavender gaze that swept across the faces of the Massan turned his next calm, smiling words to warning. "If there must be Challenge, let it come tomorrow. Tonight is a night for joy."

After a brief silence, Tenn bowed his head. "Of course, Feyreisen." He held out a wrist to his *shei'tani* and gestured for Rain and Ellysetta to lead the way.

The celebration that ensued throughout Dharsa lasted long into the night. The entire city lit up after sunset as Fire spells turned Dharsa's fountains and waterfalls into cascading rainbows of light, and garden paths shimmered with dancing fairy flies. Intoxicating fragrance filled the air, turning each breath into a perfumed delight. And everywhere, Fey voices rose in joy as the Shining Folk danced and sang.

In the palace, the Massan and their mates joined Marissya, Dax, Rain, and Ellysetta at the head table for a grand feast extravagant even by Fey measure. When the meal was over, Ellysetta's *lu'tans* took the floor, daggers in hand, to perform the fierce warriors' blade dance called the Cha Baruk, the Dance of Knives. Thousands of razor-sharp Fey'cha flew from shining hands, flashing like arcs of silver lightning across the circles of dancing, weaving warriors until, with a final fierce shout, the Fey'cha flashed back to their sheaths, and the warriors' struck a final, triumphant pose. The crowd erupted into cheers and applause. As the *lu'tans* made their way back to their seats, a gentler music began to play. Rain held out his wrist to Ellysetta and they made their way to the dance floor to lead hundreds of mates in the beautiful, courtly steps of the Felah Baruk, the Dance of Life, better known to the mortal world as the Fey Dance of Joy.

And all through the night, until the celebrations finally came to an end at the break of dawn, a never-ending stream of Fey approached Ellysetta, not just to ask for her blessing but also to offer their thanks for the return of the sons, brothers, and beloved warriors so nearly lost to shadow.

CHAPTER FOURTEEN

The Fading Lands ~ Dharsa

Ellysetta and Rain were awakened at midmorning by a large white paw poking through the open arches of their bedroom suite. The paw batted at the edges of their bed, nearly dumping them both to the floor. *"Steli is knocking, Ellysetta-kitling. Come. Come. Time to sing pride greetings to Shei'Kess."*

Rain swore and threw a pillow at the great cat, but Ellysetta only laughed. "Thank you for knocking, Steli-*chakai*."

The paw withdrew, and mischeivous, chuffing tairen laughter wafted in. Air whooshed, and a dull thud rattled the chandelier as the tairen jumped up onto the palace roof. Moments later, a trio of loud roars broke the sleeping city's silence.

Rain swore again and put a hand to his head. "She thinks she's being funny."

Ellysetta snickered. "She *is* being funny. If you hadn't drunk so much pinalle last night, you'd think so too." Much to Ellie's mortification, Marissya and Dax had let slip the truth of the dreadful keflee-and-pinalle-induced Spirit weave she'd spun on Celieria's royal court, and some wicked Fey (Ellie's coin was on Gaelen) had promptly produced numerous cases of the blue Celierian wine. Though Ellysetta had adamantly refused to imbibe, Rain had drunk countless toasts to the health and fertility of his mated friends and was now paying the price. He deserved his pounding head for trying to get her drunk and lusty, but when he groaned again she took pity on him and spun a small healing weave.

By the time they finished dressing and made their way to the tairen courtyard, a small crowd had gathered, including Marissya, Dax, and Ellysetta's new quintet. Rain was less pleased to see the Massan among them as well.

Steli wasn't pleased either. The white tairen leapt down from the golden roof into the grassy courtyard, forcing the Massan and other Fey to step back. She bared her fangs and growled in tairen song: *"Pride-song is for pride only, Rainier-Eras. These Fey-kin are not welcome."*

"The tairen say you must wait here," Rain told the other Fey.

As Rain, Ellysetta, and Steli passed through the archway that led to the enormous, carved doors of the Hall of Tairen, Marissya turned to her truemate. Her eyes were filled with wonder. "I heard them, Dax. I heard their tairen song. Or rather, our child did, and I through him." She clutched Dax's arm, her fingers digging deep. "Dax, beloved, it's the most beautiful thing I've ever heard. As if the stars themselves were singing."

Fahreeta, who had started to follow Steli, now stopped and turned back to pad towards Marissya and Dax. *"The kitling's song is strong. He is powerful tairen. Grows well to hear our song so soon."* The golden cat lowered her head to nudge

Marissya's belly gently with her nose. *"Pride-greetings, kitling. Sing Fahreeta your pride-name."*

The response was a gathering of power, a strange, electric feeling deep in Marissya's womb that tingled and pushed against her from the inside out. Tiny, frenetic little flutters danced across her belly like fairy-flies playing in the evening grass. And then . . . small as a sigh, but very distinct, the bright notes of the baby's song formed a single shining word: *"Keralas."*

Marissya clutched Dax's hand to her belly. "His name is Keralas, *shei'tan*. Our child's tairen name is Keralas."

"A good name. Very strong. The tairen Keralas who lived before was mighty hunter. Fierce defender of his pride." Fahreeta's whirling eyes bathed Marissya in a warm green glow. *"You give the kitling a Fey-kin name, little mother, and by that name he will be known. Only to the pride will he be Keralas."*

"I understand," she agreed solemnly. "His father and I will choose for him a Fey name of strength and valor, a name that will do his pride-name honor."

Fahreeta purred her approval. *"You understand pride-law well for one without wings."*

Marissya smiled. "I come from the vel Serranis line. My family bred many Feyreisen in the generations that came before mine."

The golden cat nodded sagely. *"Explains much. Prey scent not so strong on you."*

Steli glanced back. *"You may come, mother-kin. Keralas-kitling should hear our song to the Eye."* Marissya accepted the invitation with alacrity, but when Dax offered her his wrist and they both began to follow, Steli growled low in her throat. *"The Fey-kin may not come. Pride-song is for pride ears only. The mother-kin may come, but no others."*

Marissya stopped and shook her head. "I will not go without Dax. He *is* my pride—and our child's as well. He is my *shei'tan*. If you want our child to hear your song, both Dax and I must come."

Fahreeta chuffed. Steli considered silently, then growled assent. *"The mother-kin's mate may come, but he may never speak of what he sees or hears. What songs we sing to the Eye are for pride only."*

The Hall of Tairen was easily the most spectacular palace chamber she'd seen yet. Ellysetta gazed around in goggle-eyed amazement. Within the massive room, a domed ceiling soared above the wide hall, flanked on both sides by intricately carved marble columns. On a raised dais at the end of the hall, the golden Tairen Throne rose in gleaming splendor, its back a pair of fully extended wings gleaming with platinum, scimitar-shaped midspan claws. The armrests were snarling tairen's heads with bright, rainbow-swirled Tairen's Eye crystals for eyes.

But it was the object in the center of the room that captured Ellysetta's attention and held it.

Shei'Kess. The Eye of Truth.

Perfectly spherical, the Eye was an enormous globe of Tairen's Eye crystal—even larger than the still-smoldering crystals left after Cahlah and Merdrahl's Fire Song. A man-high stand fashioned from three golden tairen held the Eye aloft on the backs of their outstretched wings.

This was the oracle that could see the past, the present, and the future. The oracle that had sent Rain to find her.

The oracle that had hurt him when he'd asked it for help.

She knew Rain and the tairen were hoping the Eye would reveal how Ellysetta was supposed to save the kitlings, but she didn't trust the thing. If it was so willing to help, why wouldn't it have done so before? And what sort of power hurt those who came to it for aid? Not an honorable one, it seemed to her.

Besides—and here her belly curled into tight, painful knots—if the Eye could see into the past and the future, what would it see about her? She hadn't forgotten what those voices in the Faering Mists had said to her. *Mage claimed! Dark soul! ENEMY!*

"Ellysetta?"

She bit her lip and glanced up into Rain's too-understanding eyes. "I'm afraid, Rain," she whispered. "Afraid of what it might show . . . about the future . . . and about me." Another voice from another nightmare hissed in her mind. *You'll kill them, girl. You'll kill them all. It's what you were born for.*

"*Las.*" Rain brushed his lips across hers. "Fear is for the hunted, not for the hunter. Trust that I will protect you. And trust in your own strength. You are a tairen of the Fey'Bahren pride. The Mage cannot take what you refuse to give him. And even if the Eye does show something unpleasant, remember that visions of the future are only possibilities, not destiny. Only the past is certain. All else can yet be changed." He held her gaze until she lifted her chin and nodded.

The tairen had approached the Eye without any of Ellysetta's hesitation or trepidation and were sitting in a loose circle around it, each facing one of the three gleaming tairen statues holding Shei'Kess aloft. The cats dwarfed both the Eye and the tairen statues.

"Join us, tairen-kin," Steli invited. *"Six sing pride-song better than three."*

"But I don't sing tairen song," Marissya said.

"Keralas will sing."

"What about me?" Ellysetta asked.

Steli purred, her tail swishing. *"Sing whatever song rises in your throat, kitling. You are tairen-kin. The Eye will hear you."*

Rain Changed and the three of them went to stand between the tairen. Steli began to croon, her voice a growling vibrato purr that reverberated through the room. Fahreeta and Torasul joined in, as did Rain, who stood between Steli and Torasul. Their eyes began to glow and whirl. The notes of their song were bright and full, swirling in the air around them and shimmering like sparkling multicolored jewels. Flanked by Fahreeta and Torasul, Marissya closed her eyes and swayed as the vibrant tones of tairen song swept over and through her.

At first, Ellysetta remained silent as the tairen sang. She did not know the pride-song, but each note was like a powerful bell pealing deep inside her. The pattern of the sounds resonated in her heart, her soul, setting off tiny avalanches of emotion. Longing. Joy. Belonging. Pride. As the notes swirled around and through her, she could almost feel the brisk rush of wet air against her face as she soared through the clouds, the rhythmic pull of powerful muscles as her wings bore her aloft on a swirling updraft of warm air, the burn of fire on her tongue, the visceral thrill of being tairen, master of the sky, fearless and free.

The scent of Fey'Bahren filled her nostrils, rich, earthy, magical. With pride-song ringing in her ears, she could discern particular scents within the whole, like bright threads shining in a darker weave, each so distinct and vivid the scent became a picture: calm, majestic Sybharu-kai, fierce Steli, wise warrior Corus, playful, pretty Fahreeta.

The Eye began to gleam with inner radiance, turning the opaque globe into a glowing orb of deepest red. Small rainbows sparked and swirled within the Eye's crystalline center. Slowly, gradually, the darkness lightened. The cloudy depths of the Eye became a window to a time when the Fading Lands were green and lush and rich with life. Water ran in abundant rivers through forests and flowering meadows and snaked across a wide, grassy plain that led to a towering range of volcanic mountains. Smoke and clouds wreathed the majestic peaks, and soaring high above, too numerous to count, tairen filled the air. Their roars rang like thunder claps, and fire shot from their muzzles like flashes of lightning in a distant cloudbank.

"So many," Rain breathed on Spirit as his voice continued

to sing. *"There were never so many in all my lifetime. Nor my father's. Nor his father's before him."*

Fey'Bahren wasn't the only lair in the Feyls. Other tairen could be seen emerging from caves in peaks both near and far, leaping into the sky to join their pride-mates, swooping low to hunt the scattering herds grazing on the plains below.

"Do you think the Eye is showing us the time when it was a tairen?" Ellysetta asked.

"I do not know, shei'tani. The Eye has been in Dharsa since before the dawn of the First Age."

In the forests below, tiny figures crept along the banks of a stream. A dozen, clad in cloaks, tunics, and leggings that blended well with the surrounding woods. Hunters. Half had quivers strapped to their backs, arrows notched and bowstrings drawn. The other half glowed with silvery luminescence and clutched curving steel in their hands. Slowly, quietly, they crept forward. Ahead, their prey, a small herd of pronghorns, was grazing and drinking by the riverbank.

The vision swooped close with abrupt swiftness. A tairen-shaped shadow darkened the ground. The pronghorns lifted their heads in fear, caught sight of the predator overhead, then sprang from the riverbank and bounded into the thick brush of the forest. The hunters looked up, and Ellysetta caught a glimpse of pointed ears in silken hair, and faces of stunning beauty, some laughing, others shaking fists in mock anger. Elves and Fey, hunting together, clearly friends, and there were at least two women in the group, one Elf, one Fey, both armed with bow and blades. The leader gestured, and the hunters raced after their prey, disappearing beneath the forest canopy.

When the pride-song ended, and the images faded. The Eye dimmed, but the rainbow lights continued to sparkle in its depths. It was almost as if the tairen song had awakened the oracle and roused a once-living being's ancient memories.

Ellysetta's hand went to the large Tairen's Eye crystal on her wrist, the *sorreisu kiyr* of Rajahl vel'En Daris, Rain's father. She remembered the faint tingling harmonic in the stone when she'd first put it on, and the way Bel's crystal reacted similarly. And she remembered those steaming, glittering crystals lying in the dark nesting sands of Fey'Bahren: all that remained of the tairen Cahlah and her mate.

Perhaps the pride-song *had* awakened an ancient's memories: the memories of the once-living tairen whose body had been transformed by the Fire Song into the great Tairen's Eye crystal now called the Eye of Truth.

After a brief lull of silence, Steli started singing a new verse. Not pride-song, but a greeting of a different sort. A greeting and a plea, from creatures Ellysetta had thought possessed no humility. The others' voices dropped back to sing harmonies and croon melodic echoes of Steli's words.

"The tairen of Fey'Bahren sing pride-greetings for the unborn kitling Keralas and for Ellysetta-Feyreisa, the one you commanded Rainier-Eras to bring. She has come, as you desired. Her song is silent, but Sybharukai, makai of the Fey'Bahren pride, offers you our pride-song in its stead. Know that Ellysetta-Feyreisa is a tairen of the Fey'Bahren pride. Help her, as you would help those with whom you once flew. Teach her as once you taught the pride. Guide her to hunt the enemy we cannot see so that she may save our kitlings dying in the egg. Share what knowledge you possess, so our pride may live and grow strong once more and our song will not fall silent in this world."

This time however, the Eye did not answer. It chose, instead, to remain silent and dark.

"Sing to it, kitling," Steli urged. *"It listens. It will hear. Sing to it. Ask for the knowledge you seek."*

Ellysetta glanced around the circle of tairen and Fey. Marissya nodded encouragingly. Rain and the tairen merely watched her intently, no expression on their faces, waiting.

The song she sang was Fey, selected not so much by conscious thought as by instinct. The notes spilled from her lips, the words bubbling up like water from a spring. It was the song of Fellana the Bright, the tairen who had fallen in love with a Fey king and surrendered her wings and a portion of her soul to the Elden Mages to be with him.

As the chorus built to its crescendo, the Eye began to shimmer. The whirling rainbows in its center started spinning faster, their light becoming a pale blur and spreading until it seemed the interior of the Eye was clouded with mist. Ellysetta lifted her voice, hitting the refrain on a crystalline note that shimmered in the air like starlight, white and pure.

As the last note died away, the misty center of Shei'Kess began to clear, and a light flared in the crystal's untouched depths.

The light pierced Ellysetta, sinking deep into her soul. She gasped at the searing energy of it. So much power . . . so ancient . . . so ruthless. The Eye's magic held her in an iron grip while it tore through her memories and ripped open the locked places where she hid her most horrifying nightmares and desperate fears.

The Eye filled with images of war and devastation. The Fading Lands in smoldering ruin. The white beauty of Dharsa scorched and ravaged, its golden spires melted, its soaring towers fallen and crumbled, a wasteland of ashes and shattered beauty.

Atop the blackened hilltop, where the Hall of Tairen stood, the soaring white walls had been seared black, the golden spires transformed to great, threatening spikes of *sel'dor* that stabbed the sky like spearheads. The water of the Source ran red, a thick, scarlet river pouring down the mountainside like blood gushing from a mortal wound. All along the mount, beside gardens turned into grim orchards of impaled and rotting corpses, the High Mage's legions gathered, a grim, malignant shadow on the land.

Inside the palace, beside a dark and twisted mockery of

what had been the Tairen Throne, stood the figure from Ellysetta's dreams: herself, clad in dark red armor the color of blood. A goddess of destruction, beautiful and fell, whose hand poured poison upon the earth, whose kiss blew death on all who dared oppose her.

Her face was death white, hair flame red, and her eyes were twin bottomless black pits sparkling with red lights. She wore a full complement of Fey blades made of *sel'dor* instead of shining steel. Rain's Tairen Crown rested upon her brow, but its six gleaming globes of Tairen's Eye crystal had been turned to black *selkahr* glinting with malevolent flashes of scarlet.

Before her stood a dark congregation cheering her name, but this time they were not Eld and their corrupt allies. This time they were faces she recognized.

Gaelen. Bel. Tajik. Gil. Rijonn. Each and every one of the *lu'tans* who'd bloodsworn themselves to her service. Their faces pale as corpse flesh, their eyes black, soulless chasms.

Ellysetta's hands rose to her face, fingers curved into claws. The horror left her breathless. She'd restored their souls. She'd meant to save them. And they, who'd sworn to serve and protect her in this life and the next, had fulfilled their oaths.

When the Feyreisa they had proclaimed to be their Light fell into darkness, they had followed.

The dark Ellysetta looked up, her hideous gaze pinning the real Ellysetta where she stood. A cruel, mocking smile curved her lips.

Fury, hot and searing, burst in Ellysetta's chest. The tairen rose with shocking swiftness, wild with rage. Power, vast and deadly, rose with it. *They hurt us!* the tairen howled. *We will scorch their souls!*

"Ellysetta!" Marissya gasped.

"*Shei'tani, nei!*" Rain cried.

The doors to the Hall of Tairen burst open. Ellysetta's quintet raced in, swords and magic blazing. The lords of the Massan followed swift on their heels, five-fold weaves spinning with vibrant power.

All of them stopped in their tracks, stunned at the sight that met their horrified eyes. Ellysetta crouched before the Eye of Truth, her mouth pulled back in a snarl of fury, her fingers curved into claws. Above and behind her loomed a great, shadowy black tairen formed entirely of swirling, ember-kissed Azrahn.

CHAPTER FIFTEEN

A sword in the sheath is safe, but that's not what Fey steel was made for.
Tevan Fire Eyes,
    first Feyreisen of the Fading Lands

The Fading Lands ~ Dharsa

"You knew what she was, knew what taint lay upon her, yet still you brought her." Tenn paced the Hall of Tairen. The soles of his deep red leather boots slapped the marble tiles in an agitated rhythm.

"What would you have done? Left her there, among the mortals, for the Eld to take at their whim?" Rain glared at the leader of the Massan. He'd given them the truth, about Ellysetta and the Marks she bore, about the High Mage's interest in her. There hadn't been much point in hiding it after Gaelen leapt forward crying, "Quickly, Fey! Five-fold weaves around her before the Mage traces that Azrahn back to her!" Apparently, their quick action succeeded. Ellysetta—who had been escorted back to Rain's suite by her quintet—said she hadn't received a third Mark, but damage of a different sort was unavoidable.

"She wove Azrahn!" Yulan, the Earth master, accused. "It is a banishing offense."

Rain's spine went straight as *seyani* steel, and magic surged in an instinctive rush, ready to fly in defense of his mate. "Only an intentional use of the forbidden magic is cause for banishment, and Ellysetta wove it by accident. *Aiyah*, she weilds Azrahn. All of us do to some extent—just as all of us weave Spirit—but she does not yet control her power. Her tairen perceived what she saw in the Eye as a threat and tried to defend herself against it."

"She is Mage-claimed!" Tenn snarled. "She is a threat to the safety of the Fey."

"She is my truemate! The first truemate to a Tairen Soul the world has ever seen."

"Even more cause for grave concern!"

Rain's face went blank as stone. "What is that supposed to mean?" His voice was soft as silk, but the last word ended on a faint, throaty growl.

The leader of the Massan continued to pace, either not hearing the telltale rumble of sound, or not recognizing it for what it was: a tairen's hunting purr. "A Mage-claimed, Azrahn-wielding female of questionable parentage and incredible power appears out of nowhere—and she just happens to truemate the only Tairen Soul still living after the Mage Wars?"

Rain leaned forward. "I do not like what you imply, v'En Eilan. Do you truly believe the Eld could have found a way to create a woman who appears Fey in all ways, truemates a Tairen Soul, and houses a tairen in her own soul?"

"It's no less incredible than the idea that a Fey lord would keep his *shei'tani* outside the Fading Lands, unprotected and away from her kin, for a thousand years after the Mage Wars."

"There's a possibility her parents may not have been from the Fading Lands," Rain said.

"Impossible!" Yulan v'En Belos snorted.

"So we have always believed," Rain agreed, "and so it has always been. Yet less than two weeks after I found Ellysetta, Adrial vel Arquinas truemated a mortal-born woman. Her father bears both Fey and High Elvish blood in his ancestry, but his matebond was a purely mortal one. He didn't even know his daughter possessed magic until her soul called Adrial's." He glanced around the room, seeing Yulan's sudden consternation echoed in the expressions of others. "We must at least consider the possibility that something we've never seen before is happening along the borders. So much magic was released there in the Mage Wars. Who knows what the effects of that might be? Ellysetta's adoptive mother spoke of mortal children born with magic."

"Yet another cause for concern," Tenn interrupted. "We all know what sort of creatures the remnant magic has spawned: lyrant, shadow snakes, blood vines, and bone wraiths. Fell, evil creatures all. *Nei*, what Eld magic touches, it corrupts. That has always been true, never more so than now. You all saw the same vision I did." He cast a steely glance around the room, meeting each Fey lord's eyes in turn. "Those *rasa* you allowed to bloodswear themselves to her will become her personal army, as foul and corrupt as she will be."

"When it comes to the future, the Eye shows only possibilities, and you know it," Rain snapped. "Do not dare suggest that what you saw is certainty."

"Neither is it an impossibility," Tenn bit back. "The Eye does not lie."

"For all our sakes, we'd best pray to the gods that she is not the Elden Mages' creature," Loris, the Water master, interrupted. "And if she is, we're better served finding a way to free her of their taint rather than wasting time condemning her for it."

"The only way the Fey have ever destroyed Eld evil is to burn it out of existence," Tenn snapped.

Rain's tense muscles drew even tighter, and his body dropped into a slight crouch, like a cat preparing to spring.

"Harm Ellysetta, v'En Eilan, and no place on earth will shelter you from my wrath."

A loud growl from overhead made all the Fey look up. Steli crouched on the wide ledge rimming the domed Hall of Tairen, her pupil-less eyes bright with whirling blue radiance. White wings unfolded and flapped, sending powerful downdrafts gusting into the main portion of the hall. The Massan clutched at whirling robes and stepped aside as the white tairen touched down in their midst.

"This pride does not welcome Ellysetta-kitling. Steli-chakai growls mother-warning." The great cat lowered her massive white head and bared her fangs. A low, loud, warning growl rumbled from her chest and throat, making the bells in Eimar v'En Arran's hair chime.

With a warning scream, Fahreeta leapt down to join her, Torasul close behind. The pair of them flanked the Massan, growling and hissing and herding the Fey leaders back towards the center of the room. All five Fey lords put their hands on their blades, though not one of them dared pull steel on the tairen. *"Warning, Fey-kin. Steli-chakai growls mother-warning. Fahreeta and Torasul growl pride-warning."*

"Ellysetta-kitling is Fey'Bahren pride." The white head thrust forward, and she bared her fangs at each of the Massan. *"Be warned, Fey-kin. Rainier-Eras claims mate rights, but Steli-chakai claims mother rights. Steli-chakai is fiercest of the Fey'Bahren pride."*

Tenn shot Rain a furious glare. "What are they saying, Feyreisen?" The Massan could not hear the tairen's song. All they heard were rumbling growls, hisses, and muted roars.

"They say Ellysetta is part of their pride, but you are not." The answer did not come from Rain, but from Marissya, who had returned from tending Ellysetta and now stood beside Dax in the doorway, her hands clutched over her still-flat belly. "Steli, the white tairen, is the First Blade of the Fey'Bahren pride. She advises you to treat Ellysetta—

whom she has adopted as her own kitling—with caution and respect. The others, Fahreeta and Torasul, suggest the same." She let a long, commanding look settle over the Massan. "I suggest you heed them."

Loris spread his palms in a calming gesture. "*Las*, my friends. We all know Tenn. He occasionally falls prey to the hotheaded tendencies that afflict so many Fire masters, but he would never suggest harm to another Fey's mate. Would you, Tenn?"

He settled an unblinking violet-blue gaze on the leader of the Massan until the glaring Fire master muttered, "*Nei*, of course not," then stalked to the far side of the room.

"There. You see?" Loris turned back to his fellow Massan. "It doesn't matter where she came from or even what blood runs in her veins. She is Rain's *shei'tani*, which means we have no choice but to free her—or at least shield her—from whatever Eld taint lies upon her so that she and Rain can complete their bond."

"What if the taint on her corrupts the bond—and Rain through it?" Yulan interjected.

"Then we are doomed," Tenn said.

"Don't be ridiculous." Eimar's hair chimes sang as he glanced around to frown at Tenn. "I've never heard of any Mage powerful enough to corrupt a completed *shei'tanitsa* bond."

"I've never heard of a Mage-claimed woman completing the bond either," Yulan retorted.

"Shei'Kess sent me to find Ellysetta," Rain reminded Yulan sharply. "I will not believe its purpose was to cement the destruction of the Fey. *Nei*. There is no doubt in my mind that she holds the power to save us. Our task must be to help her find it."

Tenn sighed and rubbed his face wearily. "You may not wish to hear it, Rain, but you need to consider the possibility that perhaps your *shei'tani* has already done all she was meant to do." His expression grew sympathetic. "The

Amarynth blooms for Marissya, and the pride has said her child is a Tairen Soul. You told us last night it was Ellysetta's weave that was responsible. Could *that* not be the role Ellysetta was destined to fulfill?"

A chill worked down Rain's spine. That possibility had never occurred to him, not even when the Mists had Challenged Ellysetta and him so fiercely. "She is a Tairen Soul," he countered. "The first female Tairen Soul in recorded history—and the first *shei'dalin* ever to be able to heal the souls of Fey warriors other than her own *shei'tan*."

"And as the Eye just made abundantly clear, that last power could be deadly to us all. If she falls and her *lu'tans* follow her into shadow, we are all lost."

The idea of Ellysetta lost to the darkness made Rain's soul shudder in denial. That could not happen—*would* not happen so long as he drew breath. "You look at her, Tenn, and you see danger. When I look at her, I see hope. For me, for the tairen, and for the Fey."

"She is your truemate," Tenn said. "Of course that is what you see."

"Your loyalty to your mate does you honor," Yulan added, "but no one here can deny that our concerns are valid. The future shown by the Eye may be only a possibility, but it proves the Feyreisa is a potential threat to the safety of the Fading Lands."

"All great gifts of the gods come with a price," Rain countered. "Why should you think the first truemate of a Tairen Soul would be any different?"

Loris stepped towards Rain, the folds of his blue robes swirling around him. "I stand with Rain." His dark blue eyes caught and held them all, and his voice, though calm, brooked no defiance. "Regardless of what threat the Feyreisa may pose to us in the future, she is a *shei'dalin*, our king's truemate, and a Tairen Soul of the Fey'Bahren pride in her own right. I will accept and defend her. The only other choice leads down the Dark Path. No matter what risk or sacrifice may be required, that is a road I will not travel."

"I stand with Rain also," Marissya said. "No matter what the High Mage may have done to her, no matter what he may intend, Ellysetta is as bright a soul as I've ever known."

"Rain, Loris, and Marissya are right," Eimar agreed. "As a *shei'dalin* of the Fey, the Feyreisa deserves all the protection and aid we can offer her."

The four of them standing in agreement was enough to earn Tenn's and Yulan's grudging silence, and the matter was decided. Shortly thereafter, Rain sang his farewells to the tairen, took his leave of the Massan, and returned to his suite to comfort his *shei'tani.*

"They must hate me now." Ellysetta sat curled up in Rain's lap in a broad chair by the open archway in their suite, her eyes still red from the storm of tears she'd shed against his neck.

"*Nei,* they do not hate you." Rain stroked his hand down her back, tracing the delicate ridges of her spine. "They are concerned, of course, but sooner or later we would have had to tell them the truth. Tairen do not keep secrets from their pride." He pressed his face into her hair, breathing the sweet aroma of her bright curls. "They have even all agreed that you should be trained both by the *shei'dalins* and by the *chatok* of the Academy. So you see? The Eye's vision caused no irreparable harm."

"Rain . . ." She pulled away and gave him a chiding look. "I know it was not so easy."

Much as he wanted to, he would not lie nor dance the blade's edge of truth, not even to set her mind at ease. "*Nei,* it was not. What futures the Eye shows are not certain, but they are possible. Several of the Massan are afraid what they saw may come to pass."

"So what do we do now?"

"We do exactly as we planned: save the tairen, complete our bond, and defend Celieria against the Eld." He gave a little huff of rueful laughter. It sounded so easy, but he knew they were facing the most difficult challenges of their lives. "Tomorrow, Venarra will take you to the Hall of Scrolls while I make arrangements for your magic training and meet with the Massan and the warriors to begin preparations for the defense of Celieria. There is much to do, and little time to do it if I'm to march warriors and weapons to Orest by month's end."

Ellysetta laid her head in the hollow of Rain's throat and stared out through the billowing veils framing the open balcony. Last night she'd floated on a euphoric cloud of joy, thinking she'd finally come home to the place she belonged, and that the Feytale life she'd always dreamed of was finally at hand.

Today, the Eye had brought her crashing back down to earth and shown her in no uncertain terms that the nightmares she'd lived with all her life were far from over.

The Fading Lands ~ Dharsa

The moment she met Venarra v'En Eilan at the palace entry hall the next morning, every last fear and doubt stirred by Shei'Kess rose up again.

Either Venarra had seen Ellysetta's Azrahn weave and the vision in the Eye or Tenn had told her what happened. Either way, when the woman's black eyes fell upon her, Ellie was instantly reminded of the cold, relentless *shei'dalins* in the Mists. The sensation intensified as they walked in silence through the morning mist that wreathed Dharsa's central hill. The city was still sleeping, and the world was shrouded in white silence. With each step, Ellie half expected to find herself back in the avenue of trees with the wall of *shei'dalins* and their grim-eyed warriors standing in wait.

Instead, halfway down the hillside, they left the palace grounds and turned down a white stone road. Ellie's soft-soled, embroidered half boots whispered along the stone. A few chimes later, the mist began to clear, and they came to an enormous beautiful, columned structure built at the foot of a lacy, multitiered waterfall.

"This, Feyreisa," Venarra said, breaking her silence, "is the Hall of Scrolls, repository of all Fey knowledge since the dawn of the First Age."

Ellysetta tilted her head back, speechless with awe. The building appeared to grow right out of the hillside, and the sheer size of it was intimidating. She followed Venarra through the massive, towering columns into an exquisitely tiled entrance gallery, where a Fey woman in a sumptuous blue-green gown was waiting by the entrance.

"Feyreisa, this is Tealah vol Jianas, my assistant here in the Hall of Scrolls. If you ever need anything when you visit the hall, just call for either of us and we will come."

"*Meivelei*, Feyreisa." Tealah had a shy smile, warm blue-green eyes, and skeins of shining black hair hanging in waves down to her waist. "Nalia said you were bright as a star. I can see she was not exaggerating." Tealah bowed and waved a hand at the doorway behind her. "*Teska*, enter and be welcome."

Beyond the large, arching doors a massive and multilevel atrium opened up, stealing the breath from Ellie's lungs with its sheer magnificence. The glassed ceiling soared so high and so long, a tairen could easily take wing within its confines. Light filtered down, bright and plentiful, illuminating case after case containing piles of neatly stacked books and scrolls. Ringing the perimeter of the hall, five balustraded levels opened to the center of the atrium, whose floor was a neatly ordered field of tall bookcases and reading desks.

"How many books and scrolls are there?" Ellysetta asked.

Compared to this wonderland of Fey history, Celieria's extensively stocked National Library was a meager collection.

"There are close to four million documents in the main hall. And there are five storage levels below this one, each containing at least three times the number of texts you see here."

"It would take a lifetime to read everything." The amount of knowledge waiting to be discovered was both staggering and exhilarating.

"Several lifetimes," Venarra corrected. "Even among the Fey, I can't think of a single keeper who ever managed it."

Ellysetta's heart sank. "But how will I ever have any hope of finding the information I need to save the tairen? Just reading the titles of the books on this one level will take me months."

"Come. I will show you." With a wave of one elegant, tapered hand, Venarra led Ellysetta down the curving staircase to the center of the hall, where an oval frame containing what appeared to be a clear sheet of silver-tinted glass was mounted on a pedestal.

"Mirror," Venarra said, and colors began to shift and swirl across the glass. A moment later, a beautiful, disembodied Fey face appeared in the glass. A Fey man's face, silvery pale and glowing, with blazing emerald eyes and hair the color of polished fireoak. The long strands of his fiery hair flowed around his face like billowing clouds of flame and smoke.

"This is the Mirror of Inquiry. Ask it to find a particular text or information about a particular subject, and if it exists in the hall, the Mirror will locate it."

"Why does it wear someone's face?"

"All the Mirrors do. No doubt the makers thought it would be easier to ask questions of a person than a blank sheet of glass." Her tone became brisk. "Which scrolls would you like to see first?"

"Perhaps you could recommend a good place to start."

Venarra hesitated as if surprised that Ellysetta had asked her for guidance, then said, "The kitlings are dying. Healing seems the obvious place to begin."

"I would agree, but neither Marissya nor I could sense any sort of physical ailment in the kitlings. They are healthy, yet they are dying."

"There are types of ailments that do not manifest themselves as obvious physical abnormalities. Even the best healer might easily overlook them."

"Then let's start there." Ellysetta offered a smile that went unreturned.

Venarra turned back to the shimmering oval glass. "Mirror, find all records in the hall regarding illnesses that cannot be detected by a healing weave, and bring them here to an available reading table."

The Mirror, which had been waiting patiently without a hint of expression on the face within, now shimmered with renewed life. The blazing emerald eyes of the disembodied visage slowly shut. The flame-kissed hair blew back as if on a sudden gust of wind, then began to billow gently again. When the Mirror's eyes reopened, they were filled with myriad sparkling green lights.

Ellysetta stepped back in surprise as the sparks streamed out, escaping the glass to swirl above the Mirror like a swarm of tiny fairy-flies before shooting off in every direction, leaving trails of shimmering green light in their wakes.

She spun around, trying to follow the paths of as many as she could. Dozens shot up to race around the upper levels of the atrium, performing a series of aerial acrobatics before zooming with guided precision towards specific scrolls and books inside the numerous bookcases. Each book and scroll the lights landed upon blazed with a sudden, electric green glow.

Venarra stepped out of the circle and walked towards the

closest table. She'd taken only a few steps when the green lights came zipping back and splashed down in tiny bursts of bright color. First on the table, then on the floor beside the table, the explosions of color coalesced into rapidly growing piles of scrolls and books, all glowing with a green aura.

"There are so many."

"My request was very general," Venarra explained. "Once you decide which topics seem the most promising, you can use the Mirror to narrow the search."

The *shei'dalin* reached for one of the scrolls at the top of the first stack just as Ellysetta reached for one nearby. Their hands brushed. Venarra jerked back as if she'd been burned—or, rather, as if Ellysetta's Mage Marks were a contagion that could be spread by simple contact.

"*Sieks'ta.*" Venarra clasped her hand tightly at her side. Ellysetta could see her fighting to cover her emotions, to hide her revulsion behind a mask of studied politeness. "As I was saying . . ." She cleared her throat. "You needn't worry about putting the documents back. When you leave, the Mirror will automatically return everything to its proper place."

"Venarra . . ."

The *shei'dalin* continued as if Ellie hadn't spoken. "The hall is warded to prevent any of the original texts from leaving the grounds, so if you find a document you want to take with you, ask the Mirror to make a copy."

"Venarra . . ." She started to reach out to the other woman, then caught herself as the *shei'dalin* flinched away. "Please. Don't shut me out. Talk to me. I need your help."

"There's nothing to say. If you don't have any other questions, I'll leave you to your reading."

Ellysetta persisted. "I know that what happened with the Eye was very upsetting. I understand how you must feel." She could put herself in Venarra's shoes all too easily. She'd felt exactly the same when Gaelen first revealed the truth of her

Mage Marks. "Even Rain fled from me in revulsion when he first learned the truth. He loathes the Eld—almost more than he now loves me—and when he learned I was Mage Marked, he was ready to choose death rather than risk the safety of the Fey by bringing me back to the Fading Lands."

Venarra's black eyes, shuttered and suspicious, fixed on Ellysetta. "Why are you telling me this?"

"Because you need to know. In truth, part of me is relieved the Eye revealed what it did. As Rain and Steli have told me, the tairen do not keep secrets from their pride. Rain could have left me in Celieria after learning about my Mage Marks. He wanted to at first. He feared what the Mages would do if they successfully completed their claiming—he still fears it, as do I—but the tairen stopped him. They believe I *am* the one who can save them—the only one who can."

Venarra looked down at her own tightly clasped hands. "That may be, Feyreisa—and I do pray it is so—but I saw the vision in the Eye. I saw the future it foretold. I saw the heads on the pikes behind your throne." Venarra's voice began to shake. Not with fear, Ellysetta realized, but with an almost tairen fierceness. "My *shei'tan*'s was among them." Her eyes flashed up. The black irises had turned to fiery gold suns, and the piles of books and scrolls on the desk began to quake and rattle. "I'll call for your death myself before I let you harm him."

Ellysetta's mouth went dry.

The stack of documents toppled and scrolls clattered to the floor.

The sound seemed to snap Venarra out of the fury that had gripped her. She spun away, putting distance between them, and bent over as if in pain.

Ellysetta knelt and, with shaking hands, began to pick up the scattered scrolls.

A moment later, Venarra knelt beside her to help. Her

emotions were once more locked tightly away, her face an impenetrable mask of aloof calm, and she was careful not to let her hands brush Ellie's again.

When they were finished, they stood in tense silence on opposite sides of the reading desk. The physical distance was but a fraction of the great, invisible gulf that truly lay between them.

"Venarra, I—"

"*Teska*, Feyreisa. Forgive my outburst." Venarra kept her head high. "I realize you are not to blame for the circumstances set upon you. As a *shei'dalin*, I am not without compassion, but I cannot pretend a warm welcome for the woman who may well become the destroyer of the one I love most." She took a breath. "I realize the tairen commanded Rain to bring you, even knowing the taint you bear, because they believe you are the only one who can save them. Tenn fears that you've already done all you were meant to do, but your *shei'tan* refuses to even consider the possibility. Let's hope for all our sakes that Rain and the tairen are right, and that you find the solution before the other prophecy of the Eye comes true."

Ellysetta bit her lip. How could she blame the woman for wanting so desperately to protect her *shei'tan*? She would have reacted just as fiercely if someone were threatening Rain. Still, that didn't make the wound of Venarra's distrust hurt any less.

"Well," Ellystta said, turning to the enormous stack of books and scrolls, "I suppose I should get started right away then." She glanced back at Venarra. "Is there anything else I should know before you go?"

After a brief, tense silence, the *shei'dalin* said, "*Nei*. If you have any other questions, consult the Mirror, or ask it to locate Tealah or myself."

Once Venarra was gone, Ellysetta stood there, fighting off the tears that threatened to fall. She told herself Venarra's reaction wasn't any different from what she'd faced all her life. Countless times as a child, she'd faced the suspicion and outright hostility of neighbors after one of her seizures. Railing against it had never changed anything before, and it wasn't going to change anything now.

She took a deep, restorative breath and turned around in a slow circle. She was standing in the Fey Hall of Scrolls, probably the most ancient collection of documents in existence, surrounded by millennia of history and legends and ancient secrets lost to the world.

Just being here was the fulfillment of one of her most cherished dreams, and she was not going to let anything cast a pall over it. She was going to dive into the stacks of books and scrolls and discover all the wonders held within their pages, and she was going to find some way of saving the tairen.

Ellysetta flipped the catch on the scroll case and unraveled the first handspan of parchment. There was no telling how old the scroll was. Fey magic had kept it in perfect condition. She drank in the elegant, artistic Fey calligraphy, her mind instantly processing the familiar script of Feyan words and sentences: *On the Identification and Treatment of Illnesses of the Spirit, Observations of the shei'dalin Carenna vol Espera.*

While Ellysetta immersed herself in the knowledge of the Fey, Rain immersed himself in military planning. He stood before the great map wall that showed a detailed tairen's-eye view of the Fading Lands, Celieria and their surrounding neighbors: Elvia, Eld, the Pale, and Danael. Behind him, the five lords of the Massan were seated at a broad table, watching as tiny figures moved across the map with each gesture of Rain's hand.

"One thousand of our brothers are already on their way to Celieria's northern march." He waved, and tiny Spirit Fey armies dispersed across the southern banks of the flowing Heras River. "They will train the mortals and help them prepare for the coming conflict, but I intend to put another six thousand blades on the march within the next three months."

"Six thousand?" Tenn interrupted. "Why should we send so many? Do they not have armies of their own?"

"They do, but it's been too long since they have known real war. Except for the occasional Eld raid, many of their soldiers have let their blades grow dull with disuse."

Yulan grunted. "Perhaps that is the gods' way of putting an end to them, then."

Rain bit back a retort. As one of the Fey who, up until three weeks ago, had shared Yulan's opinion of Celieria, Rain could hardly condemn the Earth master's views; but he no longer agreed with them. The Fey were few. Celierians were many, but they could not stand against the Eld without Fey help. And as Ellysetta had once pointed out, if the Mages conquered Celieria, all the mortals would find themselves Mage-claimed conscripts in the army of Eld.

"Celieria has always been only a stepping-stone to the Eld," Rain said instead. "We all know their ultimate destination."

"Let them come," Yulan scoffed. "The Mists will devour them."

"Will they?" That Rain did not let pass unchallenged. "For how long? How much Mage Fire will the Mists withstand before failing? And if the Mists fall, what then? Celierians outnumber us two hundred to one. Can we afford to let the Mages claim so many? They may be only mortals, but even ants can bring down a lion if they attack in large enough numbers."

Rain saw consternation cross their faces, as if the thought had not occurred to them. "We have to assume the Eld will come. We have to assume the Mists will fail. We have to plan for that and take steps to protect ourselves in every way possible."

He turned back to the map. "I've already spoken with

Eren Thoress at Blade's Point. I will fly there later this week to light another two of the forges." All Fey steel was made at Blade's Point in the great forges that could be ignited only by tairen flame. There were six forges in all, and he hoped he would not need all of them working day and night, as they had during the Mage Wars. "I promised Teleos I would come to Orest by month's end, to bring him a thousand more blades to defend the Veil and enough swords and armor to outfit his own warriors. Our best defense is to help the Celierians defend themselves."

He turned back to the map and continued marching Spirit weapons and troops to key strategic positions throughout the Fading Lands and Celieria's northern border, but when he was finished, his main concern became easily discernible.

"As you can see, our defenses are thin. We'll need the Elves." He turned back to the Massan. "Hawksheart's ambassador in Celieria extended an invitation for me and Ellysetta to visit Deep Woods. I was going to send Marissya and Dax in my stead, but with the child, we cannot risk her safety outside the Mists."

His gaze fell upon Loris. Of all the Massan, the Water master was the one Rain had always trusted most after Marissya. He wasn't a hothead like Tenn, or a stubborn rock like Yulan. He was . . . adaptable . . . yet steady and relentless, like the element he mastered. A perfect ambassador.

"Loris, how long has it been since you and Nalia last dined with the Elves?"

The corner of the Water master's mouth curved up. "Too long, my king. My mate and I would enjoy a chance to dine again with our southern cousins."

"Good." Much as he hated losing Loris's support on the council, there was no other Fey better suited to negotiate the terms of an alliance. "Meet with me after we're through here."

Tenn leaned forward. "Until the Elvish troops set foot on

Fading Lands soil, we'll need every one of those six thousand blades you're planning to send to Celieria for ourselves."

Rain frowned. "But I need those six thousand on the borders, if we're to give Celieria any hope of holding back even a tenth of the army that attacked during the Mage Wars."

"Again, you've just proved my point. We should be worried about Fey lives, not Celierian." Tenn crossed his arms. "You've already committed one thousand to the borders, another thousand to Orest, and the five hundred in Teleon. Two thousand more perhaps we could spare, but no more than that or we might as well tear down the Mists ourselves and welcome the Eld within."

Rain regarded the map with a frown. Two thousand was too few, but Tenn had a point. Until the Elves arrived, he could not afford to send more without weakening the Fading Lands' own defenses. He needed more warriors. Or a way to make the ones he had more effective.

Sequestered in the Hall of Scrolls, Ellysetta pored over book after book, scroll after scroll, until the stack of texts she'd read began to outnumber the dwindling piles she hadn't. She lost all track of time, until a pair of booted feet entered her field of vision and she looked up to find Rain standing beside her, his lavender eyes filled with amusement and affection and a hint of scolding.

"I was beginning to worry you'd gotten lost in the city, but now I see you've never moved from this spot."

"I've been reading."

"So I see."

"You told me about the Hall of Scrolls, but you never mentioned how big it was. There are millions of scrolls and books here." Her Fey-lore–hungry mind still boggled at the thought. Histories lost to the world, tales and legends no living man had ever heard. Who knew what she might yet find? "Millions!"

Rain's mouth curved up at the corner. "*Aiyah, shei'tani*, but you needn't read them all in one sitting." He put a hand beneath her arm, helping her to her feet. "Come. It's late. Have you eaten?" His gaze drifted to an untouched plate on the neighboring desk.

"Tealah, Venarra's assistant, brought me something, but I wasn't hungry."

His expression turned stern. "Here all day, with no food to sustain you?"

"I could eat something now," she offered to appease him.

"I imagine so. Night has fallen."

Only then did Ellysetta realized that the daylight streaming in from the glass roof above had been supplanted by the bright glow of myriad orbs now shining overhead like stars plucked from the sky. When had that happened? Who cared?

"I found some interesting possibilities."

"You can tell me all about it—over dinner."

"I can't leave now! I've still got all the rest of those books left to read." She pointed to the stacks she hadn't yet touched. "Venarra told me the books will all be returned to their places if I leave, and I don't want to lose count of which ones I've already read."

"She didn't tell you how to set aside the books you want for your next visit?"

"I can do that?"

His lips compressed. "Of course. Here." He walked to the blue circle around the mirror and said, "Mirror, set aside the books Ellysetta Feyreisa requested but has not yet read. Put them back on the table when she returns."

The face in the Mirror murmured in a low voice, "*Doreh shabeila de.*" So shall it be. The stacks of texts Ellysetta had already read disappeared in a flurry of green sparks that shot out in all directions.

"There," Rain said. "The others will be awaiting you when you come back. Now, come with me to the palace and we'll find you some food."

Outside, the sky was dark, the stars abundant and bright, and the Mother and Daughter were waxing cresents riding low on the western horizon. The scent of honeyblossoms and jasmine perfumed the air as Rain and Ellysetta climbed back up the mount towards the gleaming white-and-gold brilliance of the palace. Fairy-flies danced in the shadows of the surrounding gardens.

"How did your meeting with the Massan go?" she asked as they walked.

He shrugged. "As well as could be expected. Tenn and Yulan think I am a fool for risking Fey lives in defense of Celieria. They think I should leave Celieria to its fate and concentrate our efforts and strength on protecting our own. How can I blame them? I felt the same until you reminded me that Celieria's fate is but a preview of our own."

"But you are Defender of the Fey. Command of the Fey army is yours. They cannot interfere with your decisions, can they?"

"*Nei*, but they can cause distractions and delays I cannot afford. The Eld will move quickly to establish a foothold in Celieria, and they won't be gentle about it. You've seen how well the Mages turn doubt and fear to their advantage. If our warriors go into battle with even the smallest doubt in their minds, the Mages will use it against them. We must be united. It is our only hope of victory."

"Surely the Massan know that."

"They know, and I am counting on their honor to keep our differences private. Tenn thinks I am acting rashly, but so far he does not distrust me enough to risk open Challenge."

She glanced at him, alarmed. "Would he do that? Challenge you?"

They turned down a dimly lit path bordered by scented hedges and rows of blooming flowers. Glimmering fairy-flies darted and whirled from flower to flower, leaving trails of sparkling light in their wake.

"A thousand years ago, no member of the Massan would even have considered it. The Tairen Soul was king, and the Massan only offered guidance and counsel. But this Massan has spent the last thousand years directing our defenses in my stead. It does not sit well with some of them that Rain the mad Feyreisen may actually expect to rule." He gave a brief huff of humorless laughter. "And I criticized Dorian for letting his council usurp his power."

"What will you do?"

"What I must. See to the defense of the Fading Lands as the gods have tasked me to do. The Massan will not like my methods, but I have neither the time nor the temperament to lead by consensus." A muscle jumped in his jaw, and he admitted in a low voice, "I have asked Gaelen to teach the Fey his *dahl'reisen* skills."

"You—" She broke off, already envisioning the heated scene that would erupt when the Massan learned what he had done. If there was anything those Fey lords would consider more of an affront than a Mage-claimed *shei'tani*, it would be the idea of a former *dahl'reisen*—a Fey who'd surrendered his honor—acting as mentor to the warriors who had stood fast against the call of the Dark Path when he had not. "You don't look very happy about the idea."

His mouth twisted. "I confess, I am not." He dragged a hand through his hair, a gesture of distraction that showed more plainly than words how unsettled he was. "Like most Fey, I do not embrace change easily, *shei'tani*. In part because stability and routine were what I clung to as I fought my way back to sanity, but also because rules and discipline make life . . . less dangerous. The Fey live by a strict code of honor, because honor is what binds us together and shields us from the lure of the Dark Path. It is a good way—and a just way—because it keeps us a force of good in the world."

"Do you truly think that even without that code the Fey could ever become truly evil?"

The dimly lit walk cast flickering shadows across his face, revealing his bleak expression. "Every *chadin* who passes through the Warriors' Gate at the Academy learns the cautionary tales of once-great Fey warriors who abandoned their honor and fell from the Light, just as the Eld have done. Those Fey, who once walked the streets of Dharsa as heroes of the Fading Lands, became *dahl'reisen* and eventually *mharog*, monstrous, corrupt creatures of evil who have extinguished every glimmer of goodness in their souls."

"But *dahl'reisen* aren't all evil," she pointed out. "Some simply chose life over *sheisan'dahlein*. Is that so bad?"

"Every journey starts with the first step, and the first step down the Dark Path is choosing self over sacrifice." He turned to her, his eyes shadowed. "Our strict code of honor is what allows Fey warriors to trust themselves and the blades at their backs—and that can mean the difference between life and death, victory and defeat. Especially when the enemy is the Eld, and doubt is a weapon they use to claim and destroy souls."

"If you still feel so strongly about it, then why do you want Gaelen to teach the Fey?"

"Because I have no other choice. The Fey are dying. Our numbers are too few . . . and will grow fewer still once the Eld unleash their armies. If Gaelen can teach a Fey to last even a few chimes longer in battle, that could well mean the difference between victory and defeat."

They came to a small, exquisitely carved bridge that crossed one of the gently burbling streams winding through the palace's hillside gardens. Rain's steps slowed as they crossed the bridge, and he paused to look down at the lights of the city below.

"I keep telling myself that perhaps the gods set Gaelen in

your path and gave you the power to restore his soul for this very reason. That perhaps he chose self over sacrifice because this—his presence here, now, with us—was the pattern the gods spun into his weave all along." He gave a humorless laugh. "I'm not sure I believe it. The Fey in me will probably always think he should have chosen *sheisan'dahlein*. But no matter what I think of his choices or his honor, the one thing I cannot deny is that Gaelen has spent most of the last thousand years defending Celieria against Eld incursions. There's no one more capable of teaching this generation of Fey warriors how to fight the Eld and win."

Ellysetta could feel how torn he was. "Well, at least you'll have Marissya on your side to help smooth things over with the Massan."

"She probably could—she has a way with them—but she has already stepped down from her service in council."

"What?" Her jaw dropped. "But why?"

"Because of the child. Don't look so outraged, *shei'tani*. She will continue to serve the Fey . . . just not as our *Shei'dalin*. Until her child is born, she will walk the Fading Lands to sow Amarynth and hold back the desert. Venarra has agreed to serve as the *Shei'dalin* in Marissya's stead and continue the training you began with Marissya."

"Oh." Ellysetta bit her lip.

"This does not please you." His brows drew together and his eyes sparked with lavender fire. "Venarra was discourteous?"

"No, of course not." Good gods, the last thing she needed was to cause further ill feeling between Rain and the Massan. "She wasn't rude. . . ." Fury and rudeness were not the same. "It's just that . . . well, Rain, you know how hard it is for me to trust *shei'dalins*. It took me weeks to warm up to Marissya. Now I have to start all over again? With a woman who thinks the High Mage is going to take over my mind and use me to destroy the Fading Lands at any moment?"

His brief flare of temper subsided. "Ah, well . . ." He gave her hand a reassuring squeeze and they resumed walking. "Give yourself and Venarra time to get to know each other, *shei'tani*. The Eye deliberately sowed discord among us. I do not know why. At the moment, all the Massan are wary, but once they come to know you, they will love you as I do."

Would they? Ellie wasn't so sure. She'd spent a lifetime as an outcast—and no matter how hard she'd tried, she had never managed to win most people over. And for all Rain's talk about sacrificing self for the good of the many and choosing death rather than risking corruption, he didn't seem to see the parallels between herself and the *dahl'reisen*.

The *dahl'reisen* scar was a visible mark of the former Fey warrior's slow slide towards corruption. How were the Mage Marks she bore any less condemning, even if they were impossible to see except in the presence of Azrahn? If *sheisan'dahlein* was the only honorable choice for *dahl'reisen*, then what did that say about her?

Ellysetta looked up at the stars shining over the palace and followed Rain slowly up the hill.

Celieria City ~ Royal Palace

Half a continent away, the flames of a thousand candles gleamed like stars from the chandeliers overhead, and the sparkle of ten thousand jewels glittered from the resplendent raiment of the courtiers gathered in the gilded ballroom of Celieria's Royal Palace.

A voice called out in ringing tones, "Lord Geris Bolor," and the members of the court watched with interest as the broad-shouldered and handsome newcomer to the court made his entrance to bow before their royal majesties, King Dorian and Queen Annoura of Celieria. Despite the titillating scandal of the prior Lord diBolor's disinheritance, the royals welcomed the new Lord Bolor warmly enough. Moments later, one of Queen Annoura's own favorites, Lady Jiarine Montevero, was escorting the new lord about the ballroom and introducing him to the nobles gathered there.

Nour's gaze scanned the ballroom, then stopped abruptly. His spine stiffened and his shields instinctively locked into place. "And who, my dear, is that lovely young lady there in the rose and the gentleman in bronze beside her?"

Jiarine followed his gaze and arched a brow. "You have a good eye, my lord. That is Great Lord Barrial and his daughter Talisa diSebourne. One of the Fey who accompanied the Tairen Soul claimed she was his truemate."

"But she's married to Sebourne's heir?"

"Yes, that's why she has such a tragic, melancholy air about her. The king upheld Lord diSebourne's marriage claim, and the Fey who tried to claim her left with the rest of his countrymen two weeks ago. She's been quite distraught ever since." Jiarine heaved an exaggerated sigh, and then her red lips curled.

Nour's eyes flickered with faint irritation. "You may understand the court, my dear, but you have much to learn about the Fey." He directed his attention back to the very beautiful and indeed quite melancholy Lady diSebourne and let his gaze sweep across the section of ballroom surrounding her, counting the faint telltale glow of Fey invisibility weaves. A full quintet, to guard the precious *shei'tani*, plus another two off to one side. The unfortunate suitor, no doubt, with a friend to keep him from doing something rash like starting a war.

The corner of his lip curled up. The possibilities of that situation bore careful consideration. For now, however, he had other work to do.

"Where is this Great Lord Darramon you were telling me about?"

"Over there, just approaching Queen Annoura." Jiarine nodded her head in the direction of Celieria's beautiful queen. "As I told you, his wife is very ill, and from what Fanette was able to pry out of his servants, the Fey have offered to heal her. He's preparing a caravan to take her to the Garreval. Fanette tells me they're scheduled to leave tomorrow."

"Then we must move quickly."

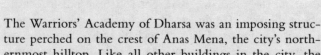

CHAPTER SIXTEEN

We are the steel no enemy can shatter.
We are the magic no Dark power can defeat.
We are the rock upon which evil breaks like waves.
We are Fey, warriors of honor, champions of Light.

Fey Warriors' Creed

The Warriors' Academy of Dharsa was an imposing structure perched on the crest of Anas Mena, the city's northernmost hilltop. Like all other buildings in the city, the Academy was built of gleaming white stone, but the golden spires on its roof were great *seyani* blades stabbing up into the sky, and all along the rooftop, silverstone Fey warriors crouched in battle stance, arms extended, curved *meicha* gripped in silverstone fists.

At the front of the building, the Warriors' Gate leading into the compound was a broad, barrel-arched corridor with a series of four inner gates that symbolized the four-hundred-year journey undertaken by every boy who grew to become a lethal, disciplined Fey warrior within these walls.

The first gate was *Shalin*, the boy, carved from fresh-scented fruitwood that portrayed dozens of scenes from the first hundred years of a Fey youth's warrior's training. The second was *Cha*, the blade. Forged of shining steel, its gleaming surface was etched with the symbols of the advanced sword moves taught to Fey warriors during their second hundred years. The third gate, *Faer*, which meant "magic," was woven entirely of hundredfold weaves of power, symbolizing the mastery of magic that was the focus of the third century of a Fey's training.

And finally, *Chakai*, the champion, a carved silverstone gate as thick as a Fey was tall and spiked with hundreds of sharp steel Fey'cha blades. Across its weighty, unyielding surface, impossible to move except through magic, the Warriors' Creed was written in blazing five-fold weaves.

Gaelen, Bel, Tajik, Rijonn, and Gil stood beside Rain on the stone-paved road leading up to the gate. All of them stared up at the looming entrance, flanked on each side by two massive silverstone Fey warriors who looked down as if in grim warning upon all who entered.

"You are certain you want to do this?"

Rain glanced at Gaelen. That had to be at least the fourth time the former *dahl'reisen* had asked the question since breakfast two bells ago. Though Gaelen looked as cocky as ever, his oft-repeated question revealed just how thin that facade of self-assurance truly was.

"I am certain," Rain answered, as he had each of the previous three times. "Are you?"

The former *dahl'reisen* arched one black brow. "Of course. Why wouldn't I be?" He gave a dismissive snort. "There are none within who could give me cause for concern, even on their best days."

"Good," Rain said. "Because I'm sure there will be more than a few eager to try. You broke your honor. They will not let you off gently." He turned to lead the way through the Warriors' Gate. Tajik, Rijonn, and Gil followed on his heels.

Gaelen hesitated just long enough to earn a knowing look from Bel.

"You are Fey once more," Bel said with quiet reassurance. "Give them time to remember that, treat them with the respect your blade brothers deserve, and they will welcome you."

Gaelen adjusted his weapons belts and set his jaw. "Let them keep their welcome—and their disapproval. If they allow pride to prevent them from learning what skills I have to teach, they deserve their fate."

"True," Bel agreed. "Cloaking one self in blind pride is as foolish as donning glass armor for war. I'm glad you recognize it for the danger it is."

Gaelen gave vel Jelani a sour look. "You are as subtle as a *rultshart* in rut."

Bel responded to the insult with a grin. "Humility isn't a poison draft," he said. "It wouldn't kill you to try a sip."

"Where's the fun in that?"

"Just think of the joy on your sister's face when she sees you leading the warriors of the Fey into battle like the hero you once were." With a speaking lift of his brow, Bel turned and jogged after Rain, Tajik, Gil, and Rijonn.

Gaelen stood there, gaping after him. Without a backward glance, Bel thrust a hand behind his back, spun a fly out of Spirit, and sent it buzzing straight into Gaelen's mouth.

Vel Jelani was most definitely a master of Spirit. The bug felt entirely too real, right down to the wild flutter of its wings and unpleasant taste. Gaelen spat instinctively before he had the sense to unravel Bel's weave. His eyes narrowed as soft laughter trailed back to his ears. "You will regret that, vel Jelani." Setting his jaw, he loped after the Spirit master through the long, arching tunnel of the Warriors' Gate.

Rain, Tajik, Rijonn, and Gil emerged from the Warriors' Gate and crossed the small first courtyard where, in days before the Wars, when the Fey had flourished, young recruits would gather at the beginning of each season to be evaluated and assigned a *chatok* who would guide them through their Cha Baruk. Six steps led from the courtyard to the arched doorway that opened to the Walk of Honor, a long, continuous corridor that bordered the Academy's large, central training field. There, inside the walk, statues of famous warriors and *chatoks* lined the gleaming marble corridor, while polished Fey steel and the *sorreisu kiyr* of long-dead heroes hung on the walls.

Rain walked past the statues, feeling the weight of their inanimate stares, and unpleasant worms of doubt uncurled anew in his belly. He'd walked this corridor more times than he could count, activating the Spirit weaves that recounted the triumphs and sacrifices attributed to each of the great Fey until he could repeat each tale from memory.

Honor had been no mere word to the Fey enshrined here. They'd considered it an immutable truth, clear and uncompromising. They'd died for it, selflessly, leading by example. What was he doing, bringing a *dahl'reisen* to join their honored company?

Bel and Gaelen caught up just as he passed through the door leading to the training yard. Rain turned his head to meet Gaelen's eyes, expecting to see his doubt reflected in the former *dahl'reisen*'s gaze. Instead, he found shock and something even more surprising . . . humility.

"It welcomed me," Gaelen whispered. "As I passed through it, the Warriors' Gate said, 'Greetings, Gaelen vel Serranis, warrior of the Fey, Champion of Light,' just as it did when I completed my Cha Baruk. Just as if I'd never trodden the Shadowed Path."

Bel clapped a hand on Gaelen's shoulder and smiled, and Rain closed his eyes in relief. The tension that had been gathering in his shoulders and belly flowed out like waters released from a dam. The Mists had welcomed Gaelen. Now, the Warriors' Gate had welcomed Gaelen. It was as if all the great magic of the Fading Lands were trying to reassure Rain that Gaelen's honor truly *had* been restored, that the shadows of his past had been wiped away as if they'd never been.

He took a deep breath and strode through the door onto the Academy's training ground.

Open to the sky above, the yard was a vast expanse of bare ground surrounded by covered, colonnaded walkways. From one corner to another, the warriors had gathered. Thousands of them. Ellysetta's *lu'tans* and every unmated warrior in Dharsa—even a few dozen of the mated ones.

All eyes turned towards Rain as he and Ellysetta's quintet entered and made their way to the end of the field, where a gallery of gilded chairs sat under a rounded marble roof.

Long ago, when Feyreisen had been numerous, the Defender of the Fey and his Tairen Soul brethren would visit the Academy each month and sit in those chairs to observe the training of the Fey warriors who would fight at their sides. Today, as they had been for the last thousand years, the chairs were occupied by the venerable *chatok*, the mentors, of the Academy. They stood as Rain approached.

"Welcome, Feyreisen." Jaren v'En Harad, the oldest of the *chatok* and Lord of the Academy, bowed and waved one arm towards the large, central chair carved with tairens' heads that had an unimpeded view of the field.

Rain hesitated for the briefest moment before moving forward to stand before it.

The grounds were silent, all eyes upon him.

"You have heard by now that the Mages have returned. Celieria needs our aid." His eyes roved over the gathered warriors, seeing the knowledge reflected back in their grim, stony faces.

"Evil has risen in Eld once more. It casts its shadow over our neighbor. Celieria cannot survive without our help, and so we must give it. Because, as the words written on the *Bor Chakai* remind us each time we pass through the Warriors' Gate, fighting is what Fey were born to do."

He looked around at the faces of the Fey, most of whom had fought in the last Mage Wars, and saw the same memory, the same realization on many of them. They knew exactly what he was asking of them, exactly what grim evil they would face if the Mages had grown strong again, but they knew that facing such evil was the task the gods had set upon them.

"But we have grown too few, my brothers. We will not long last against an Eld army even a quarter of the size we faced in the Mage Wars. That is the reason I gathered you here today." Rain crossed his arms and widened his stance, instinctively bracing for the storm about to erupt around him. "I'm certain you've all heard how the Feyreisa restored a *dahl'reisen*'s soul—and not just any *dahl'reisen*, but the Dark Lord, Gaelen vel Serranis, himself." All eyes went to the tall, icy-eyed warrior standing to Rain's left. "He has spent most of the last thousand years fighting Eld on the borders. I asked him here to teach those of you who are willing to learn from him."

"You want us to accept . . . *him* . . . as our *chatok*?" Outraged exclamations sprang from the lips of the gathered Fey.

"I do," Rain said. "Bel, Tajik, show them why."

The two warriors exchanged a brief glance, then shimmered into invisibility.

"An invisibility weave," scoffed Tael vel Eilan, one of Tenn's youngest cousins. "Any Spirit master here could do as much."

"Could he?" Rain arched a brow. "Let's put that to the test." He cast a cool gaze over the assembly. "Which among you claim a master's level in Spirit?" Thousands of hands rose. "Excellent. Then among you, you should have no trouble discovering where my two friends went." He waited, but the warriors lowered their hands and glanced around in confusion, clearly unable to discern where Tajik and Bel had gone. "You cannot find them? But invisibility is a simple weave. Any Spirit master should easily be able to detect them."

He let a full chime pass, giving the warriors ample time to find their prey, then pinned Tael with a challenging glance. "It seems this Spirit weave is not so simple after all. Perhaps you can tell me where my friends are? *Nei?* Shall I show you? Very well. My brothers, reveal yourselves."

As quickly as they had shimmered into invisibility, the two warriors reappeared. Tajik was standing behind one of the Spirit masters, Fey'cha held at his neck.

Bel was at Tael's side, holding the younger Fey's steel in his hands.

The young warrior clutched the empty space where his Fey'cha harnesses and *meicha* belts should have been. "How . . . ?"

Bel thrust Tael's weapons belts back into his hands. "Arrogance is no substitute for experience, Fey. You might consider that perhaps—just perhaps—a Fey who survived most of the last thousand years battling Eld along the Celierian border might have a thing or two he could teach you about magic—and survival."

Leaving the young warrior flushed red and fumbling to don his stripped weapons, Bel returned to stand at Gaelen's side.

The former *dahl'reisen* cast Bel a sidelong glance and a faint smirk. "I'm touched, vel Jelani. I had no idea how much you cared."

Bel grimaced and rolled his eyes, which made Gaelen laugh softly.

Rain raised his voice to address the gathered warriors. "That Spirit weave was a technique Gaelen taught these warriors in less than a day. Can you imagine how such a skill might serve you on the battlefield?"

The *lu'tan* were nodding, but many of the gathered Fey still looked skeptical, and several outright hostile.

"Fancy weaves don't change the fact that he walked the Shadowed Path," one of the Fey called out. "His presence besmirches the honor of all *chatok* who have taught within these walls."

"Changed times call for changed attitudes," Rain replied. "War is coming. Our ancient enemy has risen again, and grown strong while we have grown weak. I will not turn away a Fey who was once counted among our swiftest and surest blades." Rain let his gaze travel the length and breadth of the training ground. "What punishment the gods passed upon him for his crimes has been paid, and he has been given new life so that he may serve the Fading Lands once more. The guardians of the Mists judged him worthy—even the Warriors' Gate welcomed him as a blade brother and a champion of the Light. Will you do any less?"

He waited for his words to sink in, then said, "In a moment, the warriors' gong will ring." As was the custom for any training day in the Academy, each of the Academy's *chatok* would strike a blow to call the *chadin* to order. "Those who refuse to learn from one who was once *dahl'reisen* may leave before Gaelen strikes his blow"—he turned to regard the gathered mentors of the Academy—"as may any *chatok* who refuses to accept him into their honored company. I will not hold you in any less esteem for your decision. I know this is a difficult thing I ask, and I know it will be troubling to many. If you choose to remain, that choice will serve as your sworn and binding oath that you will give Gaelen vel Serranis the respect any other *chatok* commands."

He saw numerous warriors and half a dozen *chatok* shift in their places and knew they were among the first few who would walk for the door after the first strike of the gong.

"Before you decide, my brothers, consider this. We are few. The enemy is many. Loris v'En Mahr will soon be traveling to Elvia to meet with the Elf king, Galad Hawksheart.

It is my hope the ancient alliance between our peoples can be renewed and Loris can convince the Elves to join us in this fight; but no matter what comes of his mission, the Eld will strike, and the Fey must be ready to stand against them.

"And before you decide, consider this also." Rain's hands went to the circlet of silver sword blades twined by golden vines and Amarynth leaves perched on his brow, the non-ceremonial sign of his kingship. "I ask nothing of you that I do not first ask of myself." Lifting the crown from his head, he placed it gently on the gilded tairen's chair, then stepped down into the training field beside his brother Fey.

Jaren v'En Harad approached the warriors' gong and struck the first blow.

Of those who had gathered on the field, only six thousand remained when Gaelen struck the final blow to the gong. A fourth of those were Ellysetta's *lu'tans* and the other *rasa* whose souls she had restored. Not the overwhelming numbers Rain had hoped for, but more than he'd truly believed would stay.

Half the *chatok* had departed as well. In a quiet ceremony of disapproval, each had waited for his time to ring the warriors' gong, then made a point of exiting in proud silence rather than striking a blow.

When it was over, Jaren nodded at the gathered Fey. "This is a good beginning. I had not expected so many to stay."

"Nor I, but it's still not nearly enough," Rain said. "And I've cost you half your most skilled *chatok*."

"You but winnowed out those who have made their pride a funeral shroud." Jaren met Rain's eyes. "Our world has changed, Feyreisen. I have watched great Fey cities die, seen our forests fade back into desert, and listened to my *shei'tani* weep for the children her womb will not bear. It seems to me when the ways of the past lead only to death, then change is the only hope for life."

"What if that change leads only to more death?" Rain asked.

Jaren smiled sadly. "Great change always does. That's why it's so hard to embrace. But we are not a people born to hide from danger." He put a hand on Rain's arm. "Lead with courage, my king. Make them remember what it is to be Fey."

The *chatok's* smile became a bold slash of white teeth, and his face lit with a fierce, proud light. In an instant, Jaren was transformed from a man weighted with weary sadness to a proud, deadly warrior of the Fey, fearless and fierce. "*'We are the steel no enemy can shatter. We are the magic no Dark power can defeat. We are the rock upon which evil breaks like waves.'* Keep reminding our brothers of that—make them believe it—and the Eld could outnumber us two hundred to one and still not defeat us."

Ellysetta's stomach curled in nervous knots as she approached the Hall of Truth and Healing, the serenely beautiful building on Dharsa's central mount where the *shei'dalins* gathered to work their magic and perfect their craft.

The air of the hall was filled with the soothing sounds of splashing fountains, and lush blossoms, hanging plants, and potted greenery turned each room into a paradise of peace and beauty. Scores of *shei'dalins*—their devastating beauty unveiled, their unbound hair spilling down slender backs— laughed and smiled from every corner, chaise, and chair.

Tiny, dark Jisera v'En Arran, Eimar's mate, crossed the room, hands outstretched, to greet her warmly. "Feyreisa, welcome to the Hall of Truth and Healing. Venarra is expecting you."

She led Ellysetta through a series of connected rooms, and as they walked, Jisera whispered on a quiet weave of Spirit, *"I can feel your unease, little sister."*

Ellysetta gave her a startled look, but didn't try to deny the truth.

The *shei'dalin's* earnest expression was filled with compassion and understanding. *"I know Venarra can seem cold, but that is only because she feels things so strongly she must discipline her emotions like a warrior. When you get to know her better, you will see her heart is fierce but full of love."*

They had reached a small sitting room filled with cushioned chairs. Jisera escorted Ellysetta inside, gave her an encouraging smile, and departed. Ellie fought the urge to cling as she watched Jisera's departing figure.

A sound behind made her turn.

Venarra stood in an arched doorway. She was clad in red silk from neck to toe, which set off her dark eyes, dark hair, and pale skin to perfection. Ellysetta was glad for the silvery drape Rain had spun from her *lu'tans'* steel, and the five blades of her quintet hanging at her hips over the violet velvet gown she wore beneath. The steel gave her a measure of confidence, just as Bel's dagger had back in Celieria when she'd faced Queen Annoura and the nobles of the Celierian court.

After several moments of silence, Venarra said, "Walk with me." She led the way through a second, spiral-columned archway to a small, private garden. Abundant flowers and blossoming trees filled the air with perfume. Birds and butterflies flitted from branch and bloom. *Faerilas* burbled from wall fountains shaped like tairens' heads.

"As the *Shei'dalin*, it is my duty to see that you are properly trained in the *shei'dalin* arts. I had thought—given the words that passed between us yesterday—that you might prefer to have someone other than me instruct you, but Marissya tells me your power overwhelms even her." She glanced at Ellysetta. "Marissya is our most gifted *shei'dalin*, but I am stronger at seeing past the strength of a weaver's threads to the actual pattern of a weave. She believes I am the one best suited to train you and teach you the discipline you need to hold your power in check."

Venarra bent her head and paused to pluck a spray of honeyblossom. A tinge of rose touched her pale cheeks. "Her faith may be misplaced. As you saw yesterday, I am not always as disciplined as I should be."

Ellysetta wished she were less able to put herself in other people's shoes. The cold anger she wanted to hug close was already melting in the face of Venarra's slight blush and shamed admission. "You were afraid for your truemate."

"I still am. I don't trust what is inside you. Some Mage-claimed are innocent—I know that—but it doesn't stop the horrors they wreak in their master's name."

Ellysetta bit her lip. "I know."

Venarra looked up. "I think perhaps Jisera would be the better *shei'dalin* to conduct your training. You restored her brother's soul. Like Rain, she sees only the good in you, while I cannot look past the potential for evil. I cannot pretend otherwise, and you will not be able to open yourself to me as you must."

Before Ellysetta could answer, the sound of running feet grew near. "Venarra!" A trio of *shei'dalins* burst into the garden. "*Shei'dalin*, come quickly!"

Venarra sprang towards them. "What is it? What's happened?"

Ellysetta ran close on their heels, following the four of them as they hurried to one of the healing rooms near the front of the hall. A warrior stood shaking by the door, his hands and chest streaked with blood, his face ashen.

"She fell," he wept. "She stumbled at the top of the century stairs. I didn't know until it was too late."

A Fey woman—her skin entirely drained of its Fey luminescence—lay motionless on the healing table. Her hair was matted with blood, her neck and limbs twisted. Jisera and several *shei'dalins* were already with her, their hands splayed and glowing, but when Jisera looked up at Venarra her eyes were grim.

At the look, the warrior began to weep. "*Nei*. Please . . . *nei*."

Venarra caught his face in her hands and forced him to look at her. "*Las*," she said. The word tolled like a bell, and the warrior instantly calmed. "I will not let her die."

What followed was a healing like none Ellysetta had ever seen. Venarra leaned over the broken Fey woman and power gathered in her. The black eyes turned to molten amber, glowing like suns, and the fierce control that made her seem so cold fell away, revealing a face of such intense, overpowering love that Ellysetta wanted to weep. Venarra lit up bright as a Lightmaiden of Adelis, a golden-white aura swirling around her. She put her hands on the dying woman's chest and sent that brightness into the limp body. Her eyes closed. "Stay, beloved," she said, and her voice was a song, a prayer, an order, a plea, a command so strong even Ellysetta felt its compelling power. "Stay for your *e'tan*."

Two bells later, the Fey woman who had been teetering on the cusp of death walked out wrapped in the protective strength of her mate's arms, and Venarra, exhausted and drained, slumped against the healing table. The other *shei'dalins* passed by her, touching her arm and sharing a bit of their own strength with her until the *Shei'dalin*'s pale skin began to glow with faint luminescence once more.

"What just happened?" Ellysetta asked. "What did you do?"

Venarra glanced up wearily, but Jisera answered for her. "She held Carina's soul to the Light until the rest of us could heal her body." Jisera laid a hand on Venarra's shoulder and sent a soft pulse of golden light into the *Shei'dalin*. "She was too far gone for the rest of us to reach. Without you, my friend, she and Daran would both be dead."

When Jisera and the others were gone, Ellysetta asked, "Can Jisera teach me to do what you just did?" She remembered her mother, remembered trying desperately to hold her to life even as Lauriana slipped farther and farther away. If she could have spun Venarra's weave then, perhaps Mama would still be alive.

"Eventually," Venarra said. Already, she'd shaken off the

soft edge of weariness, and her cool reserve had slipped back into place. "Assuming you learn to control your magic well enough."

"Can she teach me to do it as well as you?"

Venarra raised a brow. "Why do you ask?"

Instead of answering, Ellysetta said, "Marissya thinks you are the one who should teach me, correct? That you are the one most able to help me control my weaves?"

"*Aiyah*," the *Shei'dalin* agreed slowly.

"Then if you are willing, I would like you to teach me."

"Why?"

"Because when the war comes, I want to be the best *shei'dalin* I can be. If I can save even one life the way you just did, that matters more than any amount of personal distrust between us."

Venarra eyed her consideringly. "I am a harsh instructor. I expect perfection from my students."

Ellysetta squared her shoulders. "I will work until I give you that perfection."

A long silence stretched between them, and then Venarra nodded. "Very well. Come sit here beside me and give me your hands." Venarra patted a spot on the table beside her. "The first lesson you must learn is how to open your mind to mine, and then I will show you how to anchor yourself so you don't get lost in your healing."

Celieria City

Gethen Nour stood over the body of the cook Lord Darramon had hired to accompany his traveling party west to the Garreval. "Come here, *umagi*," he commanded, and Den Brodson stepped forward. Nour seized his skull and held him tight as the memories of the dead cook poured from Gethen's mind into Brodson's.

When he was done, Brodson stood there, dazed and swaying. Powerful magic swirled in the Primage's hands, and Brodson's face began to shift like a lump of potter's clay. The partially flattened nose was reshaped, the lips grew thinner, the jaw less square. Brodson's brown hair grew long and straight and paled to yellow-blond. His stocky body shrank to wiry leanness. When Nour's weave was complete, nothing remained of Den except his pale blue eyes staring out from the dead cook's face. The cook's eyes had been a different shade, but there was no help for that. Though the Elden transformation magic could change every other aspect of a person's appearance, the eyes always stayed the same.

"Here." Nour handed Brodson an amber amulet. "Wear this. It will give you some protection against Fey mind weaves and allow me to hear your thoughts and observations so that I am kept apprised of your progress. Any other form of communication would be too risky. And here." Nour pressed his index finger hard against Brodson's left temple and murmured a Feraz witchspell that left the *umagi* trembling. "If you do run into the Fey, whisper the command I just gave you. It will wipe out your own memories for three bells, and leave only the cook's."

Brodson nodded, lifting his new hands to his newly formed face.

"Quickly," Nour snapped. "Put on his clothes and get back to the caravan."

Den stripped the body, shivering at the bloodless wound that split the skin of the dead man's chest. The Mage's black blade had plunged into the cook's heart, and not one drop of blood had spilled. The crystal in the pommel of Nour's wavy black dagger was now shimmering with red lights.

A bell later, clad in the dead man's clothes, Den was in the back of the cook wagon, secreting the bag of *chemar* stones Master Nour had given him in the small trunk that held the cook's personal belongings.

When he stepped back, a loud screech and a scratch on his ankle made him curse. "Jaffing hells!" he yelped, and turned with a scowl to discover that he had stepped on the tail of a nursing mother cat, who was curled up in a nest of cloth with a litter of kittens. A memory floated to the surface of Den's mind: the cat was the cook's mouser, Florrie.

Den's eyes narrowed when Florrie hissed and took another swipe at his ankle. The kittens, as if sensing their mother's distress, began mewing. Loudly. Den bent down, intending to grab the nest box and toss the cat and her kittens out the back of the wagon, when memories of his own flashed: his sister cooing like a daft looby over every fuzzy, big-eyed kitten she ever came across. He hesitated, struck by an idea.

If Ellie Baristani's sisters were anything like his own, what better lure to bring them close than a litter of kittens?

"But you," he warned, jabbing a finger at Florrie. "Scratch me again, and I'll put you in a sack and drop you in the nearest river."

Den crawled out of the wagon and circled 'round to climb up to the driver's box, waving at the members of Darramon's party who called greetings to him. Not one of them seemed to realize he was not the cook, and twenty chimes later, reins in hand, Den was driving along the cobbled roads, following Lord Darramon's caravan as it headed west out of Celieria City.

The Fading Lands ~ Dharsa

The next weeks passed in a blur. Gaelen and the other *chatok* spent the first five days evaluating the skills of every warrior, pressing them beyond the challenges of *Ro Faer* and *Ro Chakai*. The tests continued day and night, as each warrior demonstrated his sword mastery, his power and skill in each branch of magic, even his knowledge of military strategy and tactics. The strongest Fey in each field of expertise became the *chadins* Gaelen taught personally.

Gaelen's tests were often brutal. Some of the physical

combat maneuvers and swordplay resulted in broken bones and bloody wounds, particularly in the first few days of training on a new move. The warriors checked their red Fey'cha in the Academy's weapons room before assembling in the training ground each day, but apart from that they fought with bare blades, and plenty of them.

"Do you think the Eld fight with sticks?" Gaelen snapped when anyone complained. "Be grateful there are no sel'dor arrows in the Fading Lands. I'd shoot you full of them, then demand you fight with the barbs in your flesh, just so you wouldn't be caught unprepared in a real fight."

When their efforts did not meet his exacting standards, he would grab the offending warriors by their tunics, thrust his face right into theirs, and snarl, "Why do you think there's no banishment for blood spilled on Academy grounds? Fight like you mean it, Fey. Fight like your life depends on it, because when you face the Eld in battle, I assure you, it will."

More than one Fey gave back as good as—and occasionally better than—they got, and Gaelen spent as much time on his back, bruised and bloody, as he did on his feet ordering the Fey to prove their mettle. He took the battering without complaint, allowing the *shei'dalins* to heal him only when his wounds were so grievous they impeded his ability to fight.

"It is no less than I expected, and much less than I deserve," he told Ellysetta quietly after the *shei'dalins* healed four broken ribs, a shattered collarbone, and a sword thrust that had gone completely through the muscles of his thigh. "I walked the Shadowed Path. I betrayed my honor and my oath as a warrior of the Fey. Let them punish me for my shame. As long as they keep learning so they can better protect you and Marissya, I can bear what price they would have me pay."

Gil, Tajik, Rijonn, and Bel assisted him in those first

training lessons, and despite their initial misgivings, the Academy's *chatok* observed with an interest that soon developed into active participation. Before the end of the second week, the *chatok* had mastered Gaelen's invisibility weaves and several of his other techniques, and began assisting in training the others.

Much to the disgruntlement of the Massan, Eimar v'En Arran joined the warriors training at the Academy and turned himself over to Gaelen's tutelage.

"If another Mage War is indeed on our doorstep," the Air master said with calm pragmatism, "all Fey may be called to defend the Fading Lands. I am not too proud to learn what I can to ensure the safety of my mate . . . even if that means learning from a *chatok* who once walked the Shadowed Path."

Eimar's participation encouraged more of the Fey to join as well. Rain's meetings with the Massan became tense, curt skirmishes, and Gaelen's grueling training classes at the Academy filled to capacity. Soon, they even spilled over into the Academy's surrounding fields and buildings to accommodate the increasing number of *chadins* who came to learn the new skills their brothers had shown them. Even Tenn's cousin Tael showed up to learn Gaelen's magic Spirit weave.

As Rain and the warriors prepared for war, Marissya and Dax walked the hills of Dharsa to sow Amarynth and weave blessings of fertility on the Fey. Ellysetta concentrated on her magic studies and continued searching the Hall of Scrolls for information that might help her save the tairen kitlings. Most nights she and Rain would fly back to Fey'Bahren, so she could sing love and healing on the kits and begin to learn the ways of the pride.

Despite her rocky start with the Massan, Ellysetta began to make friends among the men and women of the Fey. Hardly a day went by without half a dozen couples coming to her for a fertility weave, and at least a score of beaming

Fey maidens and former *rasa* had asked her to bless their *e'tanitsa* union. Though war was on the horizon, hope was blooming in Dharsa as quickly and abundantly as the tracts of Amarynth dotting the hillsides.

Ellysetta began to make significant progress with her magic. Though she still couldn't summon the trust necessary to throw open her mind to Venarra, she did manage enough of a connection to let the *shei'dalin* correct imperfections in her weaves and guide her in the summoning and control of her magic. Ellysetta's resulting weaves were reliable enough that Venarra had begun to allow her to heal the wounded *chadin* under her supervision.

Trust was much easier when practicing warriors' weaves with Jaren v'En Harad, whose affection for Rain Ellysetta could sense every time he took her hands to lead her through her next lesson. In truth, she owed much of her increasing discipline and control to his kind but strict guidance. The most difficult thing he required of her was spinning the weaves exactly as he showed her—without the golden glow of her *shei'dalin*'s love coloring the threads— because he feared that allowing *shei'dalin*'s love in her weaves might leave her open to the same empathic death other *shei'dalins* suffered when they spun killing weaves. Determined not to disappoint Rain's mentor, Ellysetta struggled tirelessly to eliminate the golden tint from her warriors' weaves while still infusing it in her healing patterns.

After each morning's magic lessons, she returned to the Hall of Scrolls to continue combing through the texts, looking for any clues that would help her solve the mystery of what was killing the tairen. The texts from her initial search hadn't turned up anything useful, so she began searching for everything related to the tairen, past sicknesses or mysterious deaths among the prides, and even demon lore, hoping something would lead her in the right direction.

Ellysetta learned how to ask the Mirror to lead her to a

particular book, and began exploring even the tightly packed lower levels. The tomblike silence of the hall began to make her restless, so she had the Mirror make copies of the texts and began packing a bag of documents each day and carrying them to the Academy. She read while she watched her *lu'tans* and the other willing Fey master the skills Gaelen had to teach them.

At first some of the Fey worried that the violence of Gaelen's training methods would torment her empathic senses. But surprisingly, though the soul pain of the *rasa* had driven her nearly to madness with the ceaseless need to ease their suffering, the bruises, blood, and even broken bones of the warriors on the training field didn't cause the smallest twinge. Even the rare handful of times one of the Fey suffered a truly life-threatening injury, her alarm sprang more from concern for the warrior's life than empathic distress.

Until the day Rain suffered a serious wound.

One of the warriors sparring near Rain rushed in for an attack, stumbled, and sent his *seyani* plunging into Rain's unprotected back. The sight of a Fey blade protruding from Rain's chest, glistening scarlet with his blood, brought Ellysetta out of her chair, power crackling so furiously that her hair rose up in a fiery nimbus around her head. She was across the field, at his side, in an instant, not even aware of the warning growl rumbling from her throat or the blaze in her eyes that sent the warriors stumbling back in alarm.

Forgetting all the lessons of control and moderation Venarra and Jaren had taught her, Ellysetta healed Rain with an instinctive, searing blast of power. As was typical with her magical outbursts, she healed him so swiftly and so well that when he came up off the ground, his eyes were blazing bright as stars, and his own power was rising as quick and hot as his blood. He carted her off the field to the nearest room with a door—an armory, as it happened—and they proceeded to rattle every shield and scrap of armor off the shelves. When they returned, Rain was smiling, the *lu'tans* and even the other warriors were grinning, and Ellysetta's cheeks stayed red as apples the rest of the day.

After that, the *lu'tans* began boasting of her tairen fierceness and calling her Ellysetta-*makai* instead of Feyreisa.

A few of the other Fey women, drawn by the admiring stories of Ellysetta-*makai*'s courage and strength, began to pay afternoon visits to the training grounds too, but none of them could stay more than a few bells before the constant thud of flesh on flesh and the occasional sprays of scarlet blood sent them fleeing for more peaceful venues.

"I don't know how you can stand it," Tealah told Ellysetta after her fifth valiant attempt to sit with Ellysetta at the training grounds. Venarra's assistant had turned out to be a friendly woman, curious, bright, and much more willing than the hall's keeper to accept Ellysetta as a sister instead of a potentially dangerous interloper in need of constant watching. "If I don't keep my barriers at full strength, I feel each blow as if it were striking my own flesh. Don't you?"

Ellysetta shook her head. "I feel the serious injuries—the worst of them I sense like a stabbing pain in my chest or my belly—but the rest"—she shrugged—"*nei*. I'm aware of the pain, but I don't . . . *feel* it. Does that make sense?"

"*Aiyah*, of course. That's what my barriers do for me, though mine are clearly nowhere near as strong as yours, and apparently you don't need to constantly reinforce them like the rest of us do." Tealah uncorked the flask of *faerilas* she'd brought with her and took a sip. After her third visit to the Academy, she'd begun bringing a bottle of water from the Source, using it to restore the magical energies she expended maintaining her shields so she could stay more than a bell or two at a time.

Ellysetta crossed her arms over her knees. "If being here on the training ground is so difficult for Fey women, how do you manage to serve in the healing tents during war?"

"Only the *shei'dalins* serve in war—well, except the Mage

Wars. But those were such desperate days. Any Fey beyond the first blush of childhood served in some capacity."

"But I thought all Fey women were *shei'dalins*."

Tealah laughed. "No doubt that's because the only Fey woman Celierians have known in a thousand years is Marissya. *Nei*, many of us—most of us, these days, in fact—aren't *shei'dalins*. Or at least not *shei'dalin* enough to matter. We're all empaths, of course, and all healers—some stronger than others—but only the strongest of us can Truthspeak. That's what *shei'dalin* means: speaker of truth. With that gift comes the ability to withstand considerably more pain than other empaths can bear."

"But you're a *shei'dalin*?" She'd seen Tealah a number of times in the Hall of Truth and Healing.

Tealah nodded. "A minor one, though. Not nearly as strong as Venarra or Marissya."

"That explains why you can stay here, near the training ground, longer than the others who came."

"That," she agreed, then shook her *faerilas* flask, "and this. Nalia, Venarra, and Marissya could stay much longer than I—and without rejuvenation—but I doubt any of them could come and sit all day, day after day, as you do." She cocked her head to one side, her teal blue eyes considering. "There's even a sense of energy about you when you're here that you don't have when you're in the Hall of Scrolls or even in the Hall of Truth and Healing."

"Is there?"

"Mmm. You shine brighter here, and not because your shields are stronger. It's almost as if some part of you thrives on the violence."

Ellysetta drew back in horror. "You think I *enjoy* seeing them hurt one another?"

Tealah clapped a hand over her cheeks. "I'm sorry. That came out wrong. Of course, I don't mean you take pleasure in their pain. No *shei'dalin*, no matter how strong, would ever do so. I only meant . . ." Her voice trailed off. She

shook her head and bit her lip. "Do not listen to my bab-
blings. I am a fool. I don't know what I was thinking. Of
course you shine brighter here. Your truemate is here. It
must be his presence that affects you."

Despite Tealah's belated reassurances, her comment about
Ellysetta seeming to thrive on the violence of the warriors
echoed in Ellysetta's mind throughout the rest of the day.
Later that night, after she and Rain had retired to their
rooms, she posed the question to him.

"What does it mean, Rain, that I can watch you and all
the warriors batter yourselves senseless and not feel horrified?"

They had bathed in the Feyreisen's enormous silverstone
tub—which involved more laughter, splashing, and love
play than cleaning—and were now lying naked amid the
softly billowing silken sheers hanging about their bed, nib-
bling on a bowl of succulent redberries and enjoying the
cool jasmine- and honeyblossom-scented breeze blowing in
through the balcony arches. The remains of their private
repast lay discarded on a nearby table, beside an uncorked
bottle of blue Celierian pinalle on ice and a steaming pot of
keflee, which Rain had once again been trying unsuccess-
fully to convince Ellysetta to share with him—for the benefit of all those Fey couples hoping for the blessings of
fertility, of course.

Freshly washed and freshly healed by Ellysetta's warm
hands, Rain drizzled a trail of sticky redberry juice up the
soft, flat plane of her belly from her navel to the tip of one
small, round breast, then followed the trail with lips and
tongue until she shuddered with a mix of pleasure and irritation.

"*Parei.* I mean it." She grabbed his hands. "I'm worried,
Rain. You've all said I'm a *shei'dalin*. Shouldn't I be . . . oh,
I don't know . . . weeping and wailing over the warriors'
pain when they injure themselves?"

"Weeping? And *wailing*?" Rain's brows shot up. "Poor Marissya, is that what you think she does?"

Ellysetta gave him a shove. "You know very well that's not what I meant. Be serious." She dragged a sheet over her body. "I'm truly worried. Tealah said something about my thriving on the violence of the training battles, and I haven't been able to stop thinking about it. What if she's right? And what if that's some sign of the Mage's power growing stronger?"

The teasing humor on Rain's face faded in an instant. "*Nei*," he said flatly. "It's true you are more at ease within the walls of the Academy than any other *shei'dalin*, but that has nothing to do with the Mage's power. You are a Tairen Soul, Ellysetta. And tairen are fierce, not frightened . . . predators, not prey. Challenge is play to us."

"Yes, but—"

"Ask any warrior out there on the training field if he is enjoying himself. Hard and painful as the training may be, every one of them will tell you *aiyah*. We all feel the same rush of energy—of power and magic and life—when we match blades with one another. It is the tairen rising. The tairen rises in you, too, *kem'reisa*. That is what you feel, not the Mage."

She frowned at him. "What if you're wrong and I'm not really a Tairen Soul? What if the High Mage only manipulated my soul to make me seem like one so you would bring me back to the Fading Lands—and *that's* the real reason the tairen can't hear my song? What if I really am what Gaelen first thought and the Massan now fear: a creature the High Mage of Eld created to destroy the Fading Lands from the inside out?"

"You're forgetting one very important fact, Ellysetta. Your soul called out to mine." He caught her hands in his. "You are my truemate. No matter what part of you the High Mage may have manipulated, *shei'tanitsa* is a bond of infinite love and unconditional trust. That is a power the

Mages could never understand—and certainly never create with their corrupt magic."

Sincerity, unwavering and absolute, flowed from his fingertips to hers. She could not doubt him. The problem was, she had little *but* doubts about herself. "I'm afraid of what I am, Rain. I always have been. Even here, I'm still different, still the odd one, the dangerous one. The one people look at with suspicion. You can say they don't, but I know they do. Venarra, Tenn, some of the others. I hear it in their stray thoughts, sense it in their emotions."

"Perhaps they fear because you do," he suggested. "You live among powerful empaths now, not mortals. They can sense your self-doubt."

"So how do I stop being afraid?"

He sighed and enfolded her in his arms. "When we discover that, *shei'tani*, I think we will have discovered the key to completing our bond."

CHAPTER SEVENTEEN

The Fading Lands ~ Dharsa

By month's end, the number of warriors training at the Academy had increased to sixteen thousand. The Spirit masters among them could weave invisibility without a trace and extend the weave to mask a full quintet from detection. Certain of those Fey had also discovered the near-unlimited potential true invisibility offered to the practical jokers amongst them. They and their traps for the unwary popped in and out of sight with gleeful abandon until Gaelen threatened to skewer the next idiot who annoyed him. (That didn't stop their pranks; the culprits just became more selective of their victims.)

Spirit masters weren't the only ones to benefit from Gaelen's experience. The Earth masters had learned a little trick that, while not effective for long, could block an oncoming rush of *sel'dor* missiles or blade strikes. All the warriors could fire the Fey'cha in their chest straps half a chime faster than before, and Gaelen promised that with additional practice, their speed would increase even more.

All told, Gaelen's training was a resounding success. And though Loris had sent word from Elvia that an emergency in South Elvia had prevented him from even meeting with the Elf King yet, Rain was pleased with the month's progress. The warriors were ready and spirits were high.

Ellysetta wished she could say the same for herself. Each passing day brought Rain's departure nearer, but she was no closer to discovering what was killing the tairen.

"What in the name of all the gods made me believe *I* could find answers that have eluded Fey who've been searching for a thousand years?" she groused to Rain after reading what seemed the millionth scroll. They were sitting on the chairs overlooking the Academy's training grounds, the remains of their midday meal sitting nearby. "I don't even know what I'm trying to find. For all I know, the answer could have stared me in the face a hundred times and I'm just too blind to see it."

She slumped in her chair in dispirited frustration. "I haven't found any answers. I haven't found my tairen song, and I don't even know how to complete our bond." She covered her face in her hands. "Maybe Tenn and Venarra are right. Maybe I *have* already done all I was meant to do."

Rain's hands closed around hers in a firm grip. Emotion flooded her senses: trust, belief, reassurance, all riding on a rumbling undercurrent of irritation. "Venarra should never have shared that with you. All it did was make you doubt yourself even more than you already do." His lips thinned. "*Sieks'ta, shei'tani.* I have been too preoccupied to look after you as I should. I have not even been courting you properly since we reached Dharsa."

Ellie sighed and leaned against him. "You've been busy. We both have." She had a growing collection of courtship gifts tucked away in glass cases in their room, but once their training had begun, the only real time they'd spent alone was when they flew to and from Fey'Bahren to tend the kits, or the few bells of restless sleep they snatched each night.

"A Fey should never be so busy he cannot see to his mate." He rose and pulled her to her feet. "Come with me."

"Where are we going?"

"Somewhere I should have taken you weeks ago." Rain tracked down Gaelen and informed him that the Feyreisen and the Feyreisa would be leaving Dharsa for a few days.

Gaelen eyed the pair of them, smirked, and said, "About time, Feyreisen."

Rain's response was to shoot back a string of Feyan words Ellysetta had never heard before, but several of the warriors nearby laughed and cheered their king so robustly she was certain whatever he'd said didn't bear repeating amongst the women. Gaelen whirled on the *chadins* and barked with such ferocity they snapped back to instant, stone-faced order. Leaving the Fey to Gaelen's gleefully merciless instruction, Rain cleared a spot to Change, and a few chimes later, he and Ellysetta were winging west, away from Dharsa.

Celieria ~ Teleon

"Lord Darramon has arrived."

Leaning against the stone wall of Teleon's highest guard tower, Kieran sent the message arrowing into the Mists to the warriors and *shei'dalins* waiting in the war castles of

Chatok and Chakai. To the west, a caravan of carriages, wagons, and mounted riders crossed the hilltop and started down the sloping grade.

"We come." The voice of the returning weave was distorted by the energy of the Mists.

"He took his time, considering he's here to have his wife cured of a deadly illness," Kiel murmured. "I was beginning to think he wouldn't show."

"Those mounts are mortal-bred, not *ba'houda*." Kieran counted three dozen outriders and two more wagons carrying servants and provisions. "I doubt they've been on the road less than three weeks."

"Shall we head down to meet them?"

Kieran straightened up from the wall. *"Aiyah*, but let's stay clear of the Stones grid." Lillis and Lorelle were playing Stones with the quintet assigned to guard them today—and soundly beating them, by all accounts Kieran had been receiving throughout the morning. *"Ravel."* He spun a quick Spirit weave to the leader of the quintet currently watching over the twins. *"Lord Darramon has arrived. Kiel and I are going down to greet them. Keep the girls out of sight."*

Though the twins understood how vital it was that they remain within the Spirit-weave-concealed confines of Teleon, lately they'd been showing signs of boredom, which translated into a proportionally increased propensity for wandering. Only yesterday, Kieran had found them playing Princess in the Tower in the lower-level guard towers, and he'd barely caught them before they climbed down the knotted bedsheet they'd thrown over the ramparts. Had he arrived even a few chimes later, they'd have landed on unprotected land and been visible to any passersby.

"Understood." Ravel's weave sounded harried, as if the twins had been running him ragged.

Kieran swallowed a quick grin. They probably had. Lillis and Lorelle had energy to spare.

"Fey, ti'bor," he sent on the common path, calling the other warriors to join him at the outpost's front gate. He and Kiel ran along the main road that zigzagged down the mountainside to the outpost, cutting corners by making use of several stairways and a few quick Air slides. Behind them, four dozen warriors followed their lead. They stepped through Teleon's Spirit weave and into the mortal-built outpost at the bottom of the mountains before the first of Lord Darramon's outriders reached the main gate.

With a salute to the guardsmen manning the gate towers, the Fey passed beneath the raised portcullis and gathered on opposite sides of the open gates to await the approaching caravan. Each warrior kept nimble fingers within easy reach of his red Fey'cha blades.

"Your uncle would come in quite handy right about now," Kiel remarked silently. *"A quick weave of Azrahn and we'd know if there was any killing to be done."*

Kieran shot him a sour look. *"Not funny, Kiel."* He re-garded the approaching party. *"Fey have survived for millennia without weaving the forbidden magic. And so will we. Just keep a steady hand and a sharp eye."*

The first dozen riders to reach the outpost were coated in travel dust and clearly saddle-worn, but Kieran couldn't detect anything suspicious about them. He exchanged brief introductions with the lead rider, a Captain Waters, who had a steady, no-nonsense gaze that any Fey could appreciate.

"The caravan will not enter until I give the all-clear, Ser vel Solande," Captain Waters said. His horse whinnied and pranced nervously in Kieran's and Kiel's presence, sensing the latent predator in the two Fey. "I'm sure you under-stand. These are unsettled times."

"Of course," Kieran answered easily. "Make your in-spection. The stable master's boys will tend your horses when you're done." He pointed through the gate to the stable on the right side. "Our barracks are full, but you may make camp along the south wall after we inspect your party and their belongings."

With a nod and a tip of his brimmed hat, Captain Waters spurred his nervous mount forward, past Kieran and Kiel. Once within the walls, the Celierian captain's eyes scanned the interior of the fortress in quick, assessing sweeps.

Kieran watched the man from the corner of his eye, wondering if he was checking for traps or looking for weaknesses in the fort's defenses. Despite the prohibition against reading Celierian minds, he sent a quick Spirit weave brushing against the captain's consciousness. Outright burrowing in a mortal's mind for information was a breach of the Fey-Celierian alliance, but skimming the thoughts of a potential enemy to ensure the protection of Fey women was not. The captain's mind was guarded, but devoid of suspicious thoughts.

A few chimes later, Captain Waters rode back through the front gate and signaled to the waiting caravan. Drivers clucked and slapped the reins, and the carriages and wagons resumed their forward motion.

While the wagons and servants' carriage peeled off towards the open field along the south wall, Lord Darramon's carriage drove straight to the outpost's gate. Its lacquered sides were coated in thick layers of dust, the shiny yellow-painted wheels chipped and cracked along the edges from weeks of travel over rutted, unpaved roads and rough terrain. At Kiel's signal, the coachman drew the horses to a halt.

The carriage door swung open even before Kiel came within reach. Lord Darramon leaned out, his hair mussed, his face pale and strained and pinched around the mouth. "Are they here, the *shei'dalins*?"

"They come, my lord."

"Tell them to hurry. My wife has lost consciousness. I think she may be dying."

Within chimes of their arrival, Lady Darramon was lying on the freshly laundered sheets of the garrison commander's own bed, and shortly after that a small knot of scarlet-clad, heavily veiled *shei'dalins* entered the room in the company of a dozen stone-faced Fey warriors who bristled with steel and leashed menace as they stationed themselves in protective positions throughout the room.

The *shei'dalins* examined Lady Darramon, then informed her husband that—while the malignancy was indeed draining her life—her current distress rose from a different source.

"Pregnant?" Lord Darramon stared at the five veiled *shei'dalins* in shock. "My wife is pregnant? B-but how? She's been so ill I haven't . . . we haven't . . ." His voice trailed off. Shock shifted to suspicion, then hardened to certainty. "That night. That thrice-damned night at the palace, when the Tairen Soul spun his weave." His voice choked off in sudden silence as his jaw snapped shut. Then, between gritted teeth, he demanded, "What effect will this have on my wife's healing? You'll still be able to help her, won't you?"

"There is some risk," one of the *shei'dalins* said. "We'll need to go more slowly to avoid harming the child, but no matter what precautions we take, our weaves will be powerful and we will be spinning them in the baby's earliest days of life. Our magic will imprint on the child."

Darramon's spine stiffened. "Imprint how? Will the child be deformed?" He was an old-school lord, born and raised in a harsh part of Celieria, where even now the common fate of children born with physical deformities was to be abandoned on a hillside, left to the animals and the elements. Winding, they called it. As if the winds plucked the child from the earth and carried it off to some happier clime. Romantic tripe meant to soothe the aching hearts of mothers who had their newborns ripped from their arms. Basha would never allow it. She'd tear the manor down with her own frail hands before allowing anyone to wind her child away. Even if the thing were a damned two-headed monster.

"*Nei.*" Another of the *shei'dalins* spoke, her veils fluttering gently. There was something ineffably calming about her voice. Despite himself, Lord Darramon felt the edge of his temper and his nerves begin to settle. "We are healers," the *shei'dalin* continued, "not Mages. Our weaves carry no possibility of harm. What my sister means is that if we expose the child to such strong magic at such an early stage in her development, some remnant of our abilities will take root. She will most likely manifest her own magical traits once she is born."

"She? The child is a girl?" Lord Darramon's facial muscles went lax, and his voice cracked on the last word. "Basha always wanted a girl. Our six are all boys—men now." A girl. A little daughter with Basha's big blue eyes, a daughter to pamper and love, who would wrap him as firmly around her tiny finger as her mother had wrapped him around her heart. It was the secret dream he'd always harbored but never voiced aloud.

He caught himself before the fantasy took too strong a hold on his heart. His jaw grew firm again. "You didn't answer my question. Will you still be able to heal my wife even though she's pregnant? I won't risk Basha—not even for a daughter."

"*Las*, Lord Darramon." The first *shei'dalin* spoke again. "We are five, and our weaves are strong. We will heal your wife of the malignancy that drains her life, if that remains your wish."

"But be warned, my lord," a third *shei'dalin* said. "Your child will be born with magic. How strong a gift we cannot say, but her life in your world will be difficult."

Darramon took a deep breath. He was no youngling to mistake the seriousness of their warning, and he knew better than many a lord exactly what difficulties might lie ahead. His lands lay along the Eld border, with Cann Barrial's holding to his east, Griffet Polwyr's and Teleon's to his west. The dark Verlaine Forest, home to lyrant and all

manner of other fell creatures, shadowed his southern
flank.

His estates had been among the hardest hit in all Celieria
during the Mage Wars. The bones and ashes of Drogans,
Feraz witches, Elves, Danae, Eld, and Fey rotted beneath
the black soil of Darramon, and to this day, there remained
many a bleak place where naught but the unholy thrived.
For centuries, Darramon's villages had produced hearth
witches and hedge wizards by the dozen, and even now, his
villagers winded scores of peasant children each year—some
because they were born with hideous deformities, but most
because they manifested dangerous magical gifts.

Ta, he knew what the *shei'dalins'* warning meant. He
knew exactly. And he had only one possible response.

Lord Darramon stroked the frail hand cradled so gently
in his own, and gave the *shei'dalins* his answer. "Save my
wife and our child."

The Fading Lands ~ Dharsa

Rain and Ellysetta flew west and north, following the River
Faer that flowed from Dharsa to the Bay of Flame, stopping
twice to rest, eat, and refresh themselves in the magic-infused
waters of the river. Unlike the eastern half of the Fading
Lands, the west was still heavily forested. The smoking,
snowcapped peaks of the Feyls dominated the northern horizon, and to the west, the rolling hills Rain called the
Vanyas followed the western coast of the Fading Lands,
which they reached late that afternoon. Beyond lay the
endless blue of the Lysande Ocean, and from inside the
Fading Lands, the western Mists appeared no more than a
gleaming shimmer that turned sparkling waves and blue
skies into radiant, opalescent vistas.

The northern tip of the Vanyas ended on a curving spit
of land capped by a walled city built of gray stone. Across a
wide channel that fed an enormous bay, the mighty Feyls

came to an abrupt end at the ocean's edge. Waterfalls plummeted down sheer black cliffs and tumbled into the crashing waves below.

"*The fortress is Blade's Point, the northernmost city of the Fey, and the source of all Fey steel,*" Rain said as they flew closer. "*And that is the Bay of Flame, where legend says the great tairen Lissallukai first sang magic into the world.*"

A small group of fifty Fey clad in shimmering robes greeted them when they landed. They were led by a Fey lord who introduced himself as Eren v'En Thoress, lord keeper of Blade's Point.

"*Meivelei ti'Cha'Rik*, Ellysetta Feyreisa," the Fey lord greeted her. "Welcome to Blade's Point." And to Rain, he bowed and said softly, "*Meiruvelei*, Rain. My heart is glad to see you here again. Too long has it been since your last visit."

"Too long has it been since I wished to hear what the night might have to say," Rain replied.

"Well, you are here again now. That is what matters." With a warm smile for Ellysetta, Eren said, "Come, Feyreisa, meet my *shei'tani* and the Fey who keep Blade's Point."

After Eren made the introductions, one of the Fey women led the way to a private room where Rain and Ellysetta could refresh themselves. Fresh silver and twilight blue robes that smelled of honeyblossoms and spring rain had been laid out on a velvet chaise, and a bath scented with rose petals had been drawn in an open-air marble tub that overlooked the city's sheltered harbor and the Bay of Flame.

"They were expecting us?" Ellysetta asked as she and Rain bathed and dressed in the clothes laid out for them.

"I sent word ahead." He had set aside his steel, retaining only a single black Fey'cha, which he sheathed and tucked into the pewter gray silk band cinched at his waist. Ellysetta followed his lead, leaving behind all her bloodsworn blades except the ones belonging to her quintet.

Outside, the Fey who had greeted them earlier had prepared a meal for Rain and Ellysetta. In addition to the robed lords and ladies of the Fey, twenty warriors in black leather and steel joined them. Conversation was pleasant for all that it revolved around the Fading Lands' preparations for war and the armaments the master smiths here had been making for Celieria.

After the meal, all the Blade's Point Fey requested Ellysetta's blessing, which to her great relief she spun without any unruly or embarrassing flares of power.

"I think I owe Venarra an apology," she murmured to Rain afterwards as they walked through the quiet, well-tended gardens of the fort. "I've been thinking uncharitable thoughts about her, but that was the first time my magic has ever come so easily when I called it and still done only what I meant it to do."

A stone stair led up to the ramparts overlooking the Lysande Ocean. Rain stepped aside to let Ellysetta precede him. "I think sometimes, even among *shei'dalins*, *chadins* learn more from hard challenge than they do from kind instruction," he said as he followed her up. "Marissya is a much stronger empath than Venarra, and although she is an excellent teacher, she sometimes has difficulty separating herself from the emotions of those she instructs. Venarra does not. In that regard, she reminds me of Gaelen. She is a hard taskmistress, but her weaves are always impeccably precise."

"Oh, yes," Ellysetta agreed with an eye roll. "Venarra is very precise."

Rain laughed softly. How many times as a young *chadin* had he bemoaned his own *chatok* in just such a voice? "Even though you may not appreciate it at the moment, precision is what you want in a *chatok*. It makes learning more straightforward and instills the discipline necessary to master great power."

At the top of the stair, Rain gave her hand a tug. "Come.

I want to check the city's defenses, and we have only a little more than a bell to do it."

"What's the rush?"

"You will see." Her sulky scowl made him want to laugh. Ellysetta did not like secrets. At least, not those kept by others.

The crenellated ramparts ran along the hilltop, the stone surface wide enough for defenders to stand four deep and still leave plenty of room for maneuvering men and weaponry and for evacuating the wounded. Every two tairen lengths, the outer wall curved out to form large semicircular platforms for the bowcannon and catapults.

"There's something very important I need to ask of you," Rain said as they circled the city. "As you know, our army marches to Orest in three days, and I must go with them to secure the Veil. I'm going to appoint you my proxy on the council while I'm gone."

"You're going to—" Her voice choked off and she stared at him, aghast. "Rain, have you lost your mind? Two months ago I was a woodcarver's daughter who'd never even seen the inside of a palace. Now you want to appoint me to a council that leads a nation?"

"I know it is a great deal to ask, and if I had any other choice, I would not add this burden to the ones you already bear. I need someone I trust to lead in my absence and ensure my will is carried out."

"But—"

"The Massan are all honorable Fey," he continued quickly, "but they are not comfortable with the changes I've introduced. That's why I need you to stay here and be sure my commands are carried out. Tenn and Yulan may think to . . . reinterpret my orders. And with Venarra taking Marissya's place as the *Shei'dalin*, Nuri will not oppose them. Loris won't be back for another two weeks at least, and the others will silence Eimar's objections if you are not there to prevent it."

Her eyebrows shot up to her hairline. "And you think they'll listen to *me*? Half of them are waiting for me to turn into the Hand of Shadow and usher in the end of the world!"

He grimaced. He'd known this would be her reaction, but he had no choice. "If it's any consolation, I'm not just throwing you to the thistlewolves. Bel has agreed to stay behind in Dharsa to guide and advise you. There is no Fey I trust more."

"Oh, well. That will do the trick then." She spun away, her skirts twitching furiously as she stalked a short distance down the battlements.

"Ellysetta. *Shei'tani*." He went to her side and caught her arms, holding her when she would have turned away again. "I need you to do this. Listen to me," he ordered, giving her a shake when he saw that stubborn jaw of hers clench.

She glared at him in angry silence, then focused her gaze on a point in the distance.

He ground his back teeth together. Really, much as he loved her, there was no woman alive who could infuriate him more. "There is another reason I want you to serve as my proxy. You need to understand how the Massan governs and learn how to work with its members. Because if I don't return, you will be the next Tairen Soul."

Her gaze whipped back to his, horror etched upon her face. "Good sweet Lord of Light. That's what this is really about." She gave a disbelieving laugh. "You're preparing me for your death."

She tried to wrench her arms out of his grasp but he would not allow it. "Stop. *Parei!* Flames scorch it, Ellysetta! We do not choose what tests the gods set before us. We only decide how we will endure them!"

"Well, I'm not going to stand here while you tell me what to do after you die fighting the Eld in Celieria. There's no need for this discussion because you *will* be coming back."

"There is nothing I want more, *shei'tani*. But if I do not, you must rule. At least until Marissya's child is old enough to claim the throne for himself."

"But our bond—"

"—is not complete. You will survive my death." He held her tight as she struggled against him. "Listen to me. Listen!" He gave her a brisk shake, and she grew still. "The Massan will not make your rule easy. They are used to command and will try to convince you to do as they want. Do not allow it. Tenn and Yulan delude themselves that if we leave the Eld in peace, the Eld will not attack us—or that we can hide behind the Mists and somehow live in peace with an enemy whose sole desire is to extinguish Light from the world and enslave souls for the glory of Seledorn. You cannot let yourself be swayed by their arguments—and they will be good arguments, full of reasonable concerns. But they will be wrong. You and I both know the Fey will not long live free if the Eld are left to spread their evil unchecked."

"And why ever would they listen to me?"

"They will listen to you, Ellysetta, because you will be the Defender of the Fey."

She yanked her hands free of his grip and crossed her arms. "I'm no warrior, Rain. And I'm no real Tairen Soul, either. I've found neither my song nor my wings."

"Sybharukai has accepted you into the pride. You are tairen enough. As for being a warrior, don't forget I've seen you in battle. You slaughtered two Primages and sent Eld soldiers fleeing like mice—and that you did with no wings and no training."

"There's a lot more to being a leader than just being good at killing people."

His spine went stiff, then he gave a humorless laugh. "No one knows that better than I, Ellysetta."

Remorse flickered in her eyes. "I wasn't talking about you."

"Perhaps you didn't mean to, but truth is truth. I know my shortcomings all too well."

She ran a hand through her hair in frustration. "You're a good king, Rain. You have the best interests of the Fading Lands at heart, and you're willing to make the hard decisions, not just the easy ones everyone agrees with. That's what leadership is."

"Up until the last month, I haven't been making any sort of decisions. I've been letting Marissya and the Massan rule in my name. It's only because of you that I've finally begun to be the king I should have been all along." He drew a breath and squared his shoulders. "*Teska*, I need you to do this for me, Ellysetta. Promise you will serve as my proxy while I'm away—and that you'll lead the Fey if I don't come back."

Her arms crossed again and she scowled down at her feet. "Fine. I promise."

"*Beylah vo.*" He wanted to say more, but he was coming to know his *shei'tani* well enough to realize that rock-stubborn clench of her jaw meant she was no longer listening. Anything he said now would just be wasted words. He glanced up at the sky. The sun was well past its zenith, the afternoon more than half-gone. "It's getting late. Let's finish the inspection."

He offered Ellysetta his wrist, but she only gave him a dark look and stalked away without him. He sighed and followed. She was not pleased with him or the plans he'd been making for her, and he couldn't blame her. He was asking too much of her, and he knew it. But what choice did he have?

They continued their walk of the perimeter, stopping occasionally to check defensive positions and greet the handful of Fey warriors manning the battlements. Though her eyes still flashed with temper, Ellysetta was a woman of her word. She clenched her jaw, listened to Rain and the Fey as they discussed the city's armaments and defenses, and asked pertinent, probing questions that proved she was paying attention and trying to absorb and process the information.

By the time they circled back around to the northern wall overlooking the city's sheltered harbor, the Great Sun was a scant two bells from setting, and Eren was waiting for them at the top of the stairs.

"All is ready, Feyreisen," he said when they drew near. "But you haven't much time."

"What is ready?" Ellysetta's brows drew together in suspicion.

"The surprise I promised you, *shei'tani*. The real reason we came." They returned to the fortress only long enough to change back into their leathers before Rain led Ellysetta to Blade's Point's sheltered port, where a sleek, low-slung boat carved of gleaming golden wood bobbed in the harbor, secured to the stone pier by thick woven docking ropes.

"You're taking me sailing?" She stared at the boat in disbelief. "You bring me here, tell me you're preparing me for your death, and you think I want to go *sailing*? Have you lost your senses?" She planted her fists on her hips, her eyes snapping with outrage.

"Las." He held up his hands in truce. "Not just sailing. This is the Bay of Flame, and the Great Sun will set within the next two bells. I thought you might like to partake of its magic."

Ellysetta remembered the legends of the Bay of Flame. According to ancient Fey myth, Lissallukai, the first tairen ever to cast a wing shadow over the Fading Lands, had breathed her fire upon the waters of the bay at sunset and spun magic into the world. Young Fey boys came here on their Soul Quest to swim in the waters of the bay at sunset and dream beneath the light of the fairy-flies to find their soul's true magic.

"This is another thing you think I need to do so I can take your place as Defender of the Fey, isn't it?"

He sighed. "I simply thought that since you've never had a Soul Quest, you might want to give this a try. There *is* magic here. Perhaps even enough to help you find your song or learn to trust yourself. Perhaps even enough to show you the path to completing our bond."

The patience in his voice made Ellysetta feel petty. Rain was the one going to war. She was the one staying safely behind in the Fading Lands, risking nothing.

Nothing except the possibility of spending the rest of her life without him. She bit her lip and looked away, blinking against a sudden rush of tears. That possibility didn't bear thinking about.

"*Sieks'ta.* I'm being childish. It's just that . . ." Her chin trembled. Her throat grew so tight she couldn't speak, and the tears she was fighting spilled over. She swiped at them with the backs of her hands. "I don't want to lose you, Rain."

His arms enfolded her, drawing her against his warm strength. "That is an impossibility, *shei'tani.* I am yours forever."

She turned, burrowing against him, pressing her face to the hollow of his throat. "You know what I mean." She spoke against his skin, feeling the pulse in his throat against her lips, the taste of him mingling with the salty wetness of her tears.

"I know." He stroked her hair and held her. "If I could, I would stay by your side and never leave you. But that's not a choice I can make. I must be a Feyreisen worthy of my crown. Only then will I be worthy of your bond."

"You're worthy now," she protested.

"*Nei,* I am not. You've always believed me better than I truly am, but now it's time for me to become that honorable Fey I see in your eyes." He tilted her chin up and thumbed away her tears, smiling with such gentleness she nearly started crying again. "*Las, kem'san.* Come share the magic of the bay with me. I've never known anyone yet who hasn't found a measure of peace after swimming the waters at sunset."

She drew in a ragged breath and nodded, drying her eyes with her palms. He would be leaving in a matter of days. There was no guarantee he'd ever return. She wasn't going to waste the time left to them on tears and accusations.

She gave him her hand to help her into the slender craft. Once she was seated, he pushed off from the dock, then took his own seat near the stern and spun a weave of Air to fill the sail and send them skimming across the bay towards the black sand beaches on the distant northern shores. The small, Elvish-made craft was swift and sleek, cutting through the waves and swells with ease.

The Bay of Flame was large, more a small gulf than a bay, and even with the Air-spun winds driving them, the sail from Blade's Point to the northern shores was going to take almost a bell. Needing to be close to Rain, she carefully made her way to the back of the craft to sit between his feet and rest her head on his thigh as he manned the tiller. "Do you know any Elvish sailing songs?"

"A few."

"Will you sing them for me?"

He smiled and stroked her hair. "If you wish." A moment later, his deep baritone joined the sounds of the wind and waves. She closed her eyes and let the melancholy ancient Elvish melody wash over her like the fine spray blowing up from the swells.

When the boat touched shore on the black sand beach at the base of the Feyls, the Great Sun was nearing the horizon, and already the waters of the Bay were glimmering with gold and orange lights. Rain lifted Ellysetta out and carried her to shore, setting her down in the soft black sand.

"We have about twenty chimes before sunset," he estimated. His hands went to the buckles of his leather Fey'cha straps and sword harnesses.

"Do you really think we'll find any answers here?"

"How can it hurt to try?" Deftly slipping the strips of leather free of their binding, he shed his steel with a quick shrug. He shed his tunic next and tossed it casually on the sand before sitting down to remove his boots and leather trousers. He jumped to his feet, completely and magnificently naked, and arched one speaking black brow.

Ellysetta cast a nervous glance towards the towers and ramparts of Blade's Point across the long miles of bay. Fey sight was far keener than mortal, and though more than sixty miles of bay stretched between this shore and those towers, she still half expected to see Fey eyes gleaming at her from the silhouettes of the distant turrets. "Are you certain we're alone?"

"You mean apart from the legion of Fey that followed us from Dharsa?"

"Ha-ha." With an exaggerated sigh, she stripped off her own leathers and arched a brow back at him, refusing to be cowed, though she was quite certain she wasn't glowing Fey silver but rosy red. Her chin tilted up.

His brows rose. "*Tema storris,*" he acknowledged with grave approval. "Very brave."

Ellysetta made a face, tossed her leathers and steel in the boat, and dove into the waves. She surfaced immediately, shrieking and trembling from head to toe. "It's freezing!"

He laughed. "Of course. What did you expect? The currents that feed these waters come from the Pale, the ice desert that lies north of the Feyls. If you hadn't been in such a hurry, I would have told you most boys who come here on their Soul Quest wait to take the plunge until the Great Sun touches the horizon." His lips curved. "That way they spend less time freezing in the water."

"Oh!" She swiped her arm across the waves, sending an icy spray showering towards Rain, but he spun a quick weave of red Fire to evaporate the spray before it touched him. She clasped her arms over her chest, shivering and glaring at him. "It will serve you right if I catch my death of cold."

Rain smothered his laugh and tried to look penitent. "Ah, *nei*, do not say such things." He stepped into the waves and waded to her side, unflinching as the icy water lapped around him. "You are Fey. The cold cannot harm you. You need not even feel it, unless that is your wish. Here, I will warm you." His eyes glowed, and red light gathered around his right hand. He touched one finger to the water, and brilliant fiery red weaves spun out. The water around them rose quickly to the temperature of a warm bath. "Better, *kem'san*?"

"Much." Her teeth stopped chattering. She let her knees fold and sank beneath the now-steaming waves to warm her head and shoulders. They swam together in the circle of water kept warm by Rain's magic and watched the Great Sun descend slowly in the western sky until its lower edge almost touched the horizon. "So if the Fey don't feel the cold," she asked as they waited for the sun to set, "then what was that Fey tale you were telling me about boys on their Soul Quest freezing in the water? Or were you just taunting to get a rise out of me?"

"I? Taunt you? *Nei*, I am too sweet a *shei'tan* for that." When she narrowed her eyes, he laughed again and stopped teasing. "I said Fey don't *need* to feel the cold. Even those who do not weave Fire can spin a simple Spirit weave to block the chill. But the Soul Quest is meant to be a journey without magic. Those who swim here for their Quest do not weave even for their own comfort."

She frowned, cast a regretful look at the steamy water, and said, "Then you should stop weaving. Quickly, before the sun touches the water. We came here for answers. I wouldn't want to ruin our chance of finding them by breaking the rules."

"As you wish, *shei'tani*," he said. His Fire weave went out and the water's pleasant warmth quickly faded.

When her teeth began to chatter, Rain wrapped his arms around her and shared the heat of his body to ward away the cold. Together, they floated in the salty bay, Rain's face pressed against hers, as they watched the Great Sun sink towards the horizon.

The moment the huge, glowing orange ball of the Great Sun touched the horizon, the waters of the bay lit up as if they'd caught fire. Across the vast expanse, dolphins and whales broke the surface of the waves to watch the sun's descent and dance on the fiery waves.

"It truly is magic," Ellysetta whispered as tingling warmth and breathtaking wonder washed over her.

"*Aiyah.* Every night, so long as the Fading Lands still live, this is Lissallukai's great and lasting gift to this world: a moment of pure magic to celebrate the greatest magic of all."

Enchanted, Ellysetta turned to Rain, her body bobbing and sliding against him in the rhythmic rock of the waves. "What greatest magic?"

"Life, Ellysetta." His hands slid up to cup her face and carry her lips to his. "And love."

Her arms wound about his neck, holding him close. All the world around them burned with the cooling fire of the setting sun, while between Rain and Ellysetta the now familiar flame of passion ignited.

"*Aiyah,*" she murmured against his lips. "The greatest magic."

CHAPTER EIGHTEEN

There was a time so long ago
When warriors side by side,
We fought the Dark with sword and bow
With strength and burning pride.

Now ghosts remain in Shadow's scorn
Imprisoned not by will
Soon in time the child is born
And stolen to the hills

From the poem "Shei'tanitsa Reign"
by Lady Flarien diChanis

In the dimming twilight after the Great Sun had disappeared below the horizon, Rain and Ellysetta swam back to the shore where their boat was moored. He dug two long lengths of absorbent cloth from a basket in the boat and handed one to her.

She wrapped the cloth around herself. The air was much warmer than the bay had been, and her shivering quickly faded. "What now?"

"Now we make our bower so we may sleep beneath the light of the fairy-flies and dream of our soul's true purpose. Look." He pointed to the forests nearby. "They are waking." Sure enough, in the dark forests at the volcano's base, tiny lights were flickering.

He led the way into the forest. His bare Fey skin glowed faintly silver in the darkness and made him easy to follow as he picked his way down a narrow pronghorn trail through the dense brush and soaring trees.

"Here." The trail opened to a small glen at the base of the nearest volcano. "This will do." The glen was little more than a bare space in the forest where the rock lay too close beneath the fern-covered ground for trees to grow. A waterfall streaming down the side of the volcano had formed a small pool at one side of the glen. "Come, *shei'tani*." Rain unwrapped the cloth from about his waist and snapped it out to its full length, lowering it over a dense bed of ferns. "Time for sleeping." One black brow arched, and his lavender eyes began to glow. "Or other things."

Smiling, she went to him and offered no protest as he tugged free the end of her wrap and let the cloth slip from her naked, gleaming body. Her hair spilled down her back and over her shoulders, framing her small, round breasts with vivid licks of flame and curling down her back to brush the swell of slender hips.

Sunset on the Bay of Flame was indeed great and powerful magic. Without a doubt, something had changed in her tonight as she'd swum in the flame-kissed waters set afire by the setting sun. For the first time she stood naked before him and was not the least bit ashamed. Instead, her veins hummed with nascent womanly power.

She reached up to cup his face in her hands. "Do you love me, Rain?"

"More than I knew it was possible to love. All the stars will fall from the heavens before I ever stop."

His truth was pure and absolute. So unswerving there was no hint of doubt in him. She took a deep breath, dazzled by his utter devotion to her.

He had told her he must go to war to become a king worthy of his crown and a Fey worthy of his truemate's bond, but the truth was, he was already so much more than she deserved.

She ran her hands over the sleek, rounded muscles of his arms, adoring his faint trembling when she touched him, the crackles of magic that leapt to her touch as if every part of him yearned to become a part of her. Such a fine, beautiful Fey. Her Fey. Her love, her heart, her soul's truemate. So strong, so brave. Everything she never had been.

Everything *she* must become to be worthy of *him*.

Not a frightened girl, clinging to him for reassurance and protection, but a brave woman, strong and self-assured in her own right. A Tairen Soul. His equal.

All around them, the dark of the forest began to glow with shimmering lights as fairy-flies by the dozens awoke and took wing from whatever small nest had sheltered them through the day. The small, glowing creatures danced like stars in the shadowed forest. The waterfall splashed softly into its pool, and in the distance the muffled roar of the surf filled the air with the tang of the sea. Ellysetta stepped back, her bare foot finding the soft expanse of the cloth he'd laid down for them. Her knee bent and she sank lightly to the bower he'd prepared, pulling him with her, but when he would have covered her body with his own, her hands pushed against his shoulders, urging him to his back.

"*Nei, shei'tan.* Let me." She'd taken the lead in their lovemaking before, but only when her tairen had roused and its passions overrode the shy Celierian that remained so much a part of her. This time, she was neither wild nor shy, neither tairen nor mortal. This time, she was simply Ellysetta, mate of Rain, a woman taking the final step from girlhood.

"Do you know how much I love you?" It stunned her how much that love had grown in so short a while. And she had grown, too, from the breathlessly infatuated girl who'd loved Fey tales, to the grief-stricken realist who'd seen her mate leave and her mother die, to the raging tairen in the Mists who'd reached out in desperate fear and trust for her mate, to the young Feyreisa determined to master both *shei'dalin* and warrior magic and find the answers to save her new kingdom. Each step of the journey, she'd taken because of him. For him. Nourishing her increasing strength with the deepening love she bore him.

Her hands slid down his body, marveling at the smooth warmth of his skin. Pale as silver mist, sleek as satin. She loved the feel of him beneath her hands, the strength and power coiled within such devastating beauty. She laughed softly as she discovered his ticklish feet and the way his thighs quivered when she smoothed her hands over the long ropes of muscle and bent her head to take tiny bites across his flesh.

"*Fellana* . . ." he growled, hands reaching for her.

"*Nei*, Rain," she admonished, evading his grasp. "This time is mine." His sex was already full and thick, pulsing with the heavy beat of his heart. She stroked him, filling her palm with the hard heat, brushing her lips across the velvety softness of his skin, then dancing away to lave kisses on the flat, ribbed muscles of his abdomen.

He groaned and shifted, his hips bucking up against her in instinctive demand. "You tease."

She purred and touched her tongue to the round indent of his navel. "I but prolong the pleasure." The sweet fragrance of his skin—anchored with the darker scents of tairen—made her muscles tighten. Arousal became a heavy ache, a ripple of clenching inner muscles, a slow burn of flesh.

His nostrils flared at the betraying scent of dark honey, and his eyes, which were already glowing, blazed with sudden fire.

"You want me," he whispered.

"More than you know." She bent to his chest, nipped at the taut buds of his nipples, followed with savoring licks, tasting him, drawing him into her mouth.

A low, vibrating growl purred in his throat and chest, the seductive hum of his tairen's need. "Then come, *kem'fellana*, *kem'tani*, and take what you desire."

The low purr sent heat flashing through her veins. Her breasts grew tight, the nipples hardening to aching points. She sat back, straddling his thighs, and flexed her spine, hissing as his hands rose to cup her breasts and his thumbs flicked over their sensitive tips. *Gods.* All it took was one touch of his hand on her, and the harmonic pleasure intensified so rapidly it was all she could do to hold back her first shuddering orgasm. She didn't want that yet. This was her time, her seduction, her night to tease and torment until his control hung in shreds and he begged her to take him. This was her time to claim him, as he had so often and exquisitely claimed her.

Gasping, she arched away from his dangerous hands. "Do you think weaves spun for loving would keep the fairy-flies from working their dream magic?" Her fingers trailed along his chest, and she shared her essence with him the way he'd taught her back in Celieria.

He shuddered and gave a laughing groan. "I'm willing to risk it."

With a slow smile, she bent her head to his chest and wriggled her way down his body, trailing kisses and teasing sparks of magic in her wake. She caressed his flat belly, his lean hips. Her fingernails scraped lightly across his skin, and she reveled in every tiny shiver and catch of his breath and the brightening glow of his half-lidded eyes as he watched her near the length of straining flesh that throbbed in anticipation of her touch.

Smiling up into his eyes, bold with feminine power, she bent her head and took him into her mouth. His eyes closed on a groan and his jaw thrust up in the air as his head tilted back and he abandoned himself to her. The heat, the salty-sweet taste of his skin, the rich, heady scent of male Fey arousal bathed her senses.

His hands came up, lavender Spirit glowing brightly around them, but she waved them away. *"Nei, shei'tan. This weave is mine to spin."*

Always before, he had been the one to weave the magic over her, his Spirit spun with such vivid perfection and devastating power, she'd not been able to separate reality from illusion.

Now, it was her turn.

She called upon her power, summoning it as Jaren and Venarra had spent the last weeks teaching her. The magic came to her call, a heady rush of pure power. She pictured the images and sensations she desired, spinning the intricate pattern of the weaves. Spirit was her strongest branch of magic—it always had been.

When the weaves were as full and rich as she could make them, she let the magic spill forth in great shining flows. It fell over him like a veil, wrapping him tight in the enchantment of illusion so finely spun, even he could not tell where reality became magic.

Rain gasped as his blood ignited, becoming liquid flame, searing him from the inside out. Heat filled him, gathering in his loins and swelling his flesh near to bursting as her sweet mouth devoured him with relentless ardor and her magic overwhelmed his senses. Every muscle in his body clenched and strained as he fought to hold himself in check.

The wild coils of her hair feathered across his burning skin, stroking him in a rhythm that matched the devastating ebb and flow of her mouth. His lungs filled with her warm scent, his hands with the hot satin of her flesh. She was everywhere, commanding his body, whispering in his mind, torturing him with teasing touches and long, slow licks of velvet heat, pouring out upon him such boundless, unfettered passionate love as he'd never known before, never dared dream of. All the while, her mouth drove him to madness until he shuddered and cried her name on a sob. "Ellysetta!"

He spun a Spirit weave of his own, merging it with hers, urging her to give him the union he wanted. She slowly—ah, blessed gods, so slowly—released him and sat up, straddling his thighs. His hands clutched her hips, fingers digging into the soft curves, dragging her closer.

Ellysetta shivered as Rain's need beat at her. Her body was on fire. Every delicious, incendiary touch and stroke she'd bestowed upon him had come back to her tenfold through the press of his naked, burning flesh against hers.

A trilling melody filled the air. The fairy-flies, sensing the Fey in their midst, had come to investigate. They swooped and soared in dizzying aerial displays. Trailing sparkling showers of dust from their jeweled wings, they spun and danced in the air above Rain and Ellysetta. Strangely, their presence did not seem an intrusion, but just a natural part of the sweet, wild enchantment of the moment.

Ellysetta closed her eyes, letting the wordless crooning tunes of the fairy-flies wash over her. Fey vision came without call, and the glen became a jeweled wonderland, velvety darkness shining bright with iridescent magic and showers of tiny sparkling lights falling like crystals in the wake of the fairy-flies. Beneath her, Rain was a blazing maelstrom of power, dazzling, brighter than she'd ever seen. The dark web that usually veiled him had all but disappeared before the radiant blaze of his essence. And she . . . she was as golden-white as the Great Sun.

"Now, beloved," he begged. "*Teska*, come to me now."

"*Aiyah*," she agreed. "Now." She guided him to the entrance of her body. The moment the blunt tip of his sex touched her, his hips surged up in one powerful stroke. Her eyes squeezed shut and she bit back a ragged cry as pleasure ripped through her. Her inner muscles clenched around him, holding him tight and drawing him deep.

She began to move, slowly at first, then with increasing speed as each rise and fall of her hips brought her closer to the brink of orgasm. She could feel every thread of their partially completed bond, pulsing in rhythm. She could hear the tairen roaring inside her—and in him—the sounds wild and fierce and passionate.

"Rain . . ."

His hands gripped her, urging her faster, faster, until her vision began to whirl. Her eyes flew open, her gaze locking with his. His skin was shining bright as the moon, his eyes twin purple stars, his soul a gleaming beacon that had called to her long before she'd ever met him. She bent to take his mouth in a kiss, lips meeting, tangling, breaths mingling.

"*Ve sha kem'san*," she whispered against his mouth. "*Ke vo san.*" And with one last thrust of her hips, she pushed them both over the brink. Their voices cried out in a single, inextricably woven thread, and sparkling lights showered down upon them from the fairy-flies dancing overhead.

Ellysetta dreamed of darkness, warm and comforting like a thick blanket tucked 'round a sleeping child. She dreamed of voices singing, both tairen and Fey. The songs were different, yet somehow all familiar, comforting, crooning to her in dulcet multilayered tones. The voices sang of courage and strength, of love and joy, of welcome and of hope. She wanted to sing back, but the notes and words would not come.

She shifted, limbs pushing and fluttering against the confines of the warm darkness. The songs became a sweet lullaby. Hush, little kitling . . . patience. *A whispered warning, sung in silence.* "Las, ajiana. Shh. Be silent. Be still. Do not let him hear you."

The darkness changed, growing colder. Flutters for freedom became tremors of distress. Sickly sweetness filled her nostrils, making her dizzy and ill. Cold hands dragged her back from the warmth of the voices. She cried out in fear. Anguished wails mingled with roars of fury and blistering sorrow.

The multi-ply song grew thinner as the tairen songs faded and fell silent, leaving only Feyan voices, male and female. An unmistakable thread of fear and concern ran through their melody now. A low, cold voice spun a new thread into the mix, this one an icy, sibilant whisper that struck terror into her heart. She curled up in a tight ball, trembling helplessly, and the warm Feyan voice sang urgently in her ears, gentle but commanding: "Be silent . . . be still."

And she was.

The Feyan song became discordant, the notes broken, weeping. "Sieks'ta. Forgive us, kem'kaidina. Forgive us."

Lights shone in the darkness, brilliant, spherical, surrounding her like a ball spun of rainbows. Warm and bright, almost as beautiful as the vibrant colors of tairen song. She stared up at the lights, transfixed by their beauty and unafraid, not understanding when the sphere contracted, shrinking, closing in upon her. The lights filled her vision and drew tight around her.

The world went dark again. Dark and silent and kissed by an icy chill.

When light returned, it came from two round silver coins that shone like twin full moons in a night sky. The light grew brighter, and the moons became a pair of cold silver eyes, gleaming in a pallid, cadaverous face. Triumphant laughter turned her blood to ice as clawed hands lifted a tiny newborn high.

The scene changed. She was in a dark, black-walled cave dimly lit by weak torches on the its walls. Two shadowy figures, a man and a woman, stood inside a barbed cage, locked in an embrace. The man was manacled and chained to the wall. She couldn't see their faces, but their skin had a dim silver glow. At first Ellysetta thought she was looking at herself and Rain, captured by their enemies, but then, as if sensing her presence, the man lifted his head.

His eyes blazed with fearsome savagery, filling her vision completely.

Pupil-less. Radiant prisms of opalescent green that whirled with powerful magic.

Tairen's eyes.

Slowly they began to change, turning from green to gold, and the scene shifted once more. The man's face became the proud, regal head of the tairen Cahlah. The dark cave where the man and woman had been became Fey'Bahren's nesting lair. Cahlah lay on the black sands, curled around a tairen egg, filling the tunnels of Fey'Bahren with her keening wails. She gnawed and clawed at the leathery shell until at last it broke open and spilled out the limp body within.

But the motionless form that tumbled forth wasn't a kitling.
It was Ellysetta, naked and lifeless, her eyes gone milky white.

Ellysetta woke with her pulse racing and her lungs starved for air, as if she truly had been sealed in that tairen's egg, slowly dying.

She sat up and pressed a hand against her hammering heart, willing herself to calm. The forest was still night-dark around her. The fairy-flies swooped and chittered with anxious energy, darting in and out of the nearby trees and whirling in dizzying circles.

Something was wrong.

Beside her, Rain lay still sleeping, one arm flung over his head, his hair a sprawl of dark strands, silky, straight and black as night. He frowned in his sleep. She leaned over to shake him awake.

"Rain . . . *shei'tan* . . . wake up. Something's wrong." The oppressive feeling nearly overwhelmed her.

His eyes snapped open, and he sat up so quickly, she sat back on her heels. His hands went to his chest, instinctively seeking the Fey'cha normally strapped there. When he saw her, a little of his tension dissipated. He caught her by the arm, dragged her behind him, and threw shields of five-fold magic around them. He sniffed the air, trying to scent the source of their unease.

"The danger isn't here," he murmured. "It's somewhere else."

Then came the summons, Sybharukai's rich, commanding tones sung on the winds. *"Rainier-Eras, you and your mate must come."*

They flew as fast as Rain's magic and wings could carry them, pausing only to collect Marissya before continuing on to Fey'Bahren. Marissya was a far more experienced healer than Ellysetta, and Ellie wasn't willing to risk the kitlings' safety by trying to heal them on her own. When they reached the nesting lair, they found the entire pride ringed around the remaining five eggs, alternately crooning and growling fiercely.

Rain steered Ellysetta and Marissya clear of the dangerous, twitching tails of the female tairen. The venomous spikes were fully extended, pale and shining in the dim firelit glow of the lair. His own tairen's anger was rising rapidly.

He peeled away the ever-present barriers that shielded his Fey mind and flung his consciousness outward. No hint of the source of the danger came back to him. There was only the desperate fear of the kitlings, struggling in their eggs against . . . nothing.

Then a cold finger of dread trailed up his spine.

Fear, but not his own and not the kits'. "Ellysetta."

She was shivering despite the thickness of her leathers and the heat of the nesting sands. "Can't you feel it?"

"Feel what?"

"The cold . . . I hear voices, whispering."

"I feel nothing." He took her hands. Her skin had gone ice-cold. He glanced at Marissya, who shook her head.

"It's the same as when the tairen sang the Fire Song." Ellysetta saw the concern on both their faces and realized neither of them could sense the evil presence. Why was she the only one who did?

"I'm going to see if I can tell where it's coming from." She pulled her hand from Rain's and resolutely approached the tairen eggs. As she drew near, a cold chill ran up her spine, making her flesh pebble. Her knees quivered with sudden weakness. She reached out to the nearest egg to steady herself.

The moment her hand made contact with the leathery shell, the tairen kitling within lurched towards her. The egg rocked, and a frightened cry mewed in her mind. The kitling's consciousness reached for her as a tiny babe reaches for its mother, blindly grasping, instinctively seeking the security and warmth of her presence. Tears filled her eyes. She wanted to tear away the outer walls of the egg and gather the frightened tairen infant in her arms. This was a baby, just like any Fey or Celierian baby, small and vulnerable and innocent. And some dark, horrible hand of death stalked it as if it were prey to be captured and consumed.

She touched the other eggs, receiving the same frightened, lurching response from each of the unborn kits. Worse, each time she lifted a hand from one egg so she could reach out to another, she could hear the little kitling cry out in fear, could feel its desperate, too-weak attempt to cling to her.

"Oh, Rain, they're so frightened."

In two long strides, he was at her side. "Tell me what I can do to help."

"Touch them. Talk to them. Let them know they aren't alone. Sing to them."

He began to murmur, hesitantly at first, but the hesitance quickly faded as Rain, too, sensed the kitlings' frantic fear. The murmur became a purring croon and then a deep baritone song, strong and comforting. Marissya's voice joined his, and the tairen moved closer, lowering their great heads and adding the breathtaking gold and silver beauty of tairen song to the mix.

Ellysetta opened her senses, trying to find the source of the attack. She could feel the whispering chill dancing at the periphery of her senses, everywhere and nowhere all at once. Dark, cold, its voice was a hissing iciness that battered against the melodious warmth of the songs sung by Rain and the tairen. The thing's presence was so strong she could almost see it, but every time she tried to focus on it, the attacker faded like mist, insubstantial and elusive. Present, but always just beyond her reach, taunting her.

"Marissya, try healing the kitlings again. Maybe whatever it is goes dormant except when it attacks."

The *shei'dalin* stepped forward. Green Earth and lavender

Spirit, both shining with golden hues, looped and swirled in glistening flows above her palms as she gathered and shaped her power, then released it upon the nearest egg.

Her brow furrowed as she sent the magic into the egg-bound kitling. "I still can't find any sign of physical illness, Ellysetta, but I can feel them dying. It's almost as if something's draining their lives away." She looked up, her face wan, deep blue eyes filled with concern. "I can try to hold them to life, to give you time to find and stop what's killing them."

"Do it." Ellysetta moved from egg to egg, singing, soothing. She spun the healing weaves just as Venarra had taught her, but she had no more success than Marissya. Frustration coiled inside her. The infant tairen were sobbing, their little bodies shivering in fear despite the welcoming tairen song that flowed around them. Each time she laid hands on one egg, soothing the infant within, another would cry out. And each time she turned to comfort that one, a third would start to whimper. Almost as if . . . as if . . .

"Bright Lord save them," Ellysetta breathed, horror washing over her in an icy wave. "They're being hunted."

As soon as she said it, she knew she was right. Except the kitlings' hunter—whatever it was—wasn't making an outright attack. It was testing the kitlings' defenses, weakening them like a pack of thistlewolves driving a herd of sheep to exhaustion before moving in for the kill.

Rain stopped singing. His spine straightened. His face hardened to a mask of etched stone. "Mage?"

"I don't think so. It doesn't feel familiar."

"Ellysetta. Rain." They both turned at the sound of Marissya's voice. The *shei'dalin's* face was pale, her mouth pulled back in a grimace of pain. "Something's wrong." Suddenly, she gave a cry and stumbled back away from the eggs, falling to her knees in the black sands. She hunched over, curling up into a ball, her arms wrapped around her waist.

"Marissya!" Ellysetta rushed to the *shei'dalin*'s side and dropped down beside her in the sand.

Fear stripped Ellie's mind of all Venarra's careful instructions about how to choose the threads and weave them in specific, controlled patterns. Instead, pure, desperate instinct took over as she reached for Marissya. *Dear gods, help me. Let me heal her.* The magic roared up in response, potent and vast. It poured into Marissya without caution or restraint, connecting the two of them with powerful, unchecked flows.

In that instant of unfettered connection, Ellysetta sensed a familiar, frightening consciousness, a distant, dark awareness that turned with sudden interest in her direction.

The skin over her heart went suddenly and icily cold. Horror coated her mouth with a bitter metallic tang. *Oh, gods. Oh, gods, no.*

Power inside her shifted with a swift, hard lunge, eager and fierce and furious. Magic fountained in a shocking response. It filled her in an instant, then billowed out in a blinding cloud before she could slam her shields tight.

The force flung her backwards, sprawling against Rain's legs.

"Ellysetta!" He grasped her arms and helped her right herself. "What is it? What just happened?

Before she could answer, the tairen screamed.

"Oh, no!" Ellysetta whirled back to the nest of tairen eggs, gathering her magic to fight, but the moment she peeled back her barriers, she knew she was already too late.

The enemy was gone, but he had not left in defeat.

Just moments ago, five tairen kitlings had shivered in their eggs. Now only four did so.

"No . . . oh, no . . ." Ellysetta ran to the motionless egg that belonged to Forrahl, the sweet little tairen whose egg rocked with joy when she sang to him. "Gods, please, *teska*. Don't do this." Summoning her power with desperate hope, she laid her hands upon the egg and spun the brightest healing weave she could summon.

This time, she sensed nothing. No whispering voices. No familiar evil. Just a dead, empty silence where before a precious kitling's voice had sung.

Eld ~ Boura Fell

Vadim Maur clutched the edges of the birthing table in a fierce grip as his servants carried the child to the cleansing pool. His hands and legs were trembling so hard he didn't dare release the table for fear of falling.

For the second time, Ellysetta Baristani had caught him by surprise. He'd sensed her presence mere instants before she'd sensed his, and if not for that brief advantage, her furious blast of power might have scorched him as it had once before. As it was, she'd sapped the strength from his limbs and forced him to flee to avoid serious injury.

She'd forced him to *flee*. Him. The High Mage of Eld.

The mere thought was an abomination.

The only consolation from tonight's near-disaster was the prize now held in his servants' arms. He turned his head to watch his *umagi* bathe the newborn infant. The child was another boy. Despite Ellysetta Baristani's interference and his abrupt departure from the Well, the binding had gone smoothly, without the violent battle he'd fought for Tyrkomel. Unfortunately, Vadim was also not nearly as certain of his success this time. The baby's eyes had not swirled with radiance as Tyrkomel's had when he emerged from his mother's womb.

Of course, this child had not torn his mother apart during his birth either. Fania was unconscious but unharmed. That was a victory of sorts. Even if the boy was not the fierce triumph Shia's son was, Fania would live to breed again.

"Bring him to me," he barked, and a servant hurried over to hold out the baby for his inspection.

At least the infant appeared Fey rather than mortal. His eyes were a clear, vibrant green with slightly elongated pupils, and though scarcely a quarter bell had passed since his birth, his skin had already assumed the pearlescent paleness of the Fey. He did not cry and flail about, nor object to the servants' careful yet brisk handling of him. Instead, he lay quietly, his bright eyes scanning the room with seeming intent.

Vadim bent closer. Deep within the pupils of the child's green eyes, Vadim glimpsed the shimmer of latent magic. He lifted one hand and summoned a small ball of Mage Fire. The child grew still, and his eyes focused on the concentrated glow of blue-white magic. Now the shimmer in the child's eyes grew more pronounced, magic rising in response to the presence of Mage Fire.

Satisfied, Vadim dissolved the glowing ball. Such a swift and unmistakable response bespoke substantial power. This child was gifted, considerably so. Fania had done well.

"He shall be called Coros." The name meant potential, not a certainty but a possibility. "Take him to the nursery and lay him beside Tyrkomel."

As the servants carried the child away, sudden weariness fell upon the High Mage like hundredweights. He sagged and only kept from falling by grabbing hold of the nearest servant.

Vadim fought back a wave of dizziness and nausea. He thought he'd escaped the searing lash of Ellysetta Baristani's magic, but apparently he hadn't evaded it all.

The servant helped him to a cushioned chaise in the next room and began to tend him, washing the blood from his hands. He allowed their assistance without protest. Only his own *umagi*, the ones he owned utterly, were allowed to enter this room and tend him when he was at his most vulnerable. There was no thought in their minds, no desire in their souls, that he had not put there himself.

They would plunge a knife into their own hearts if he commanded it.

"Fetch Elfeya," he ordered. He didn't have the strength to climb the stairs, and he couldn't risk being seen in such a weakened condition. "Bring her to me. Quickly. And make certain no one sees you."

The Fading Lands ~ Fey'Bahren

Ellysetta sat slumped against the lifeless, silent shell, stunned by searing grief. Night after night, for weeks now, she'd flown to the lair to sing to the kitlings. She knew every note and measure of each infant tairen's song, knew the happy patter of each small heart and the little sounds the kitlings made when they sensed her approach. They'd loved her, trusted her.

And she'd failed them.

Worse, she'd endangered Marissya.

She raised hollow, stricken eyes to Rain. "He was here. When I tried to heal Marissya, he was here."

Rain froze. "The High Mage? You sensed him here in the lair?" Five-fold weaves sprang up instantly around them, humming with raw power.

"You don't need those. He's already gone again." Her voice thickened. Tears were gathering as shock gave way to devastation.

Rain's shields stayed put. He dropped to his knees beside Ellysetta and grasped her upper arms. "Talk to me, *shei'tani*." Fear rode just below his surface fierceness. "Is the High Mage the one killing the kitlings?"

"I don't know. If he is, he's somehow masking his presence. I didn't sense him at all until I touched Marissya." She bit her lip. "I think he might have—" Her throat clamped tight, as if all her body were fighting to keep from giving the terrible words voice. She forced herself to speak. "I think he might have used me as some sort of conduit to attack her."

She braced herself for pain, half expecting Rain to pull back in horror.

Instead, after one brief, shocked moment, he enfolded her in his arms. "Not possible, *shei'tani*. Even if he could use your Mage Marks to attack another Fey, Marissya is truemated. The bond secures her soul from any possibility of corruption. No Mage can ever harm her except through direct physical assault."

"Maybe that's what he was doing, then. Maybe he somehow twisted my magic—"

"*Las.* You're letting fear torment you." He brushed her hair back and held her gaze with unwavering reassurance. "You bear two Marks, Ellysetta. Gaelen has already assured us two Marks do not give the Mage enough power to control you against your will."

She wanted to believe him. She wanted it so badly her belly ached. "But he was here. If he wasn't attacking Marissya, then what was he—" Her voice broke off. She remembered Marissya doubling over, her arms wrapped around her still-flat belly. "The baby. Marissya's baby isn't protected by a truemate bond."

She and Rain stared at each other, paralyzed by horror until Marissya uttered a soft groan that sent them both racing to her side. Blue eyes fluttered open, and her brow creased in confusion when she saw the two of them hovering over her. "Rain? Ellysetta?"

"How are you feeling, *kem'mareska*? Can you sit?" Rain put a hand behind her back and helped her up.

"Of course. I'm fine. Why wouldn't I be?"

"You collapsed. Don't you remember?"

"I—" The *shei'dalin* put a hand to her head.

"Marissya," Ellysetta interrupted. She understood that Rain was trying to find a gentle way to pose the question, but some things a mother deserved to know immediately, without coddling. "Marissya, check your baby."

Fear drained the light from Marissya's skin, leaving her pale and shaken. "My baby?"

Ellysetta grabbed her hands and laid them flat on her belly. "*Teska!* Check him now. Is he healthy? Look closely." Her heart rose up in her throat and stayed there, pounding like a blacksmith's hammer, as the *shei'dalin* spun the weave and directed it inside her own body. "Well? Is he unharmed?"

Tears sparkled on Marissya's lashes, catching the glow of the firelight. "He's fine." Her mouth curved into a trembling smile. "*Beylah sallan*, he is healthy and well." She gave a soft sob of relief, then fought to regain her composure. "What is this all about?"

After a brief prayer of thanks, Rain helped the *shei'dalin* to her feet. "Ellysetta sensed the High Mage when she healed you. She feared he might have used her as some sort of conduit to attack you while you were trying to heal the kitlings."

"The High Mage." The *shei'dalin's* eyes widened. "But that's not possible. Dax and I are bonded truemates. The High Mage couldn't access my soul no matter how he might try. No Mage can."

"*Aiyah*, but as she reminded me, your child is not truemated."

Marissya's arms curved around her belly in an instinctive gesture of maternal protection. "But . . . the High Mage can't just Mark whomever he chooses. There has to be a connection."

"I bear two Mage Marks," Ellysetta reminded her grimly. "I may have been the unwitting connection." She glanced away from the horror in Marissya's eyes. "Gaelen should check the child for Mage Marks when we return to Dharsa."

"*Nei*, he cannot." Rain held up a silencing hand when

she started to object. "We're in the Fading Lands now, Elly-setta. What leeway I granted him in Celieria, I cannot grant him here. Weaving Azrahn, even to check for Mage Marks, is a banishing offense."

Before she could argue, Sybharukai moved closer, her green eyes whirling. *"The pride must sing the Fire Song."*

Ellysetta glanced around. She'd been so caught up in her worry over Marissya and the High Mage, she'd blocked out the fierce grief of the pride. All around them, the gathered tairen were almost wild with distress over the loss of yet another kitling.

"Should I take Marissya out of the lair?" Rain asked.

Sybharukai's ears twitched. *"She may stay. Her kitling should hear our song. But Ellysetta-kitling and the mother-kin should take shelter on the upper ledges, as before."*

"I will fly them." Rain summoned the Change as Syb-harukai bent to take Forrahl's egg from the nest and carry it off to a safe distance. Fahreeta and Torasul used their paws to sweep a thick protective layer of black sand over the remaining eggs.

"What is it?" Marissya asked. "What's going on?"

"Another kitling was lost," Ellysetta told her. "The pride is going to sing the Fire Song. It's similar to what the Fey do when they return a fallen warrior's body to the elements." Rain lay on the sand so the two women could climb into place. "Get on Rain's back. We need to fly to safety before they start."

"Which kitling perished?" Marissya asked as Rain leapt into the air towards one of the upper ledges.

Ellysetta's fingers squeezed the leather pommel. "For-rahl. The sweet little one who loved to sing."

Marissya's arms tightened on Ellysetta's waist. "I'm so sorry. I know how much you loved him."

Shei'dalin compassion and sympathy swirled around Elly-setta in shining waves, but it didn't soothe her. She had loved Forrahl. She'd loved him as if he were her own. But in the end, that hadn't mattered. She'd still failed him. Whatever she was supposed to do—whatever gift she supposedly had that made her the only person who could save the tairen—she hadn't discovered it yet.

Rain deposited the two of them on an upper ledge seven levels above the sandy lair floor. From this distance the tairen looked so much smaller . . . and so few. The pride—all the tairen left in the world—consisted of those fourteen great cats and the four remaining eggs that held the only hope left for the survival of their kind.

Ellysetta watched them in growing agitation as Rain glided down to join the pride in the ring around poor Forrahl's dead egg. What was she missing? What was she failing to understand?

Now, like Rain, she couldn't help thinking that somehow the High Mage must be involved. She'd sensed him, and if Rain was right about the Eld never doing anything without purpose, then he'd been there for a reason. He hadn't been trying to Mark her again.

So what had he been doing?

Down below, the tairen had begun to sing. Ellysetta closed her eyes as the vibrant song resonated within her. She could hear each tairen's unique song as a thread in the tightly woven pattern, Sybharukai, Rain, Steli, even the small voices of the surviving egg-bound kits.

As the song swelled, Marissya reached out to clutch her hand, and reverent joy flooded into her. "It's so beautiful . . ." Marissya breathed. "When this child is born, and I can no longer hear the glory of tairen song, I will mourn the loss."

The Fire Song reached its crescendo. Flame burst from tairen throats. Heat exploded upwards in a blast.

And then, just as before, Ellysetta felt the finger of ice scrape down her spine, heard the whisper of voices calling her name.

The hand in hers gave a sudden squeeze . . . but this time not from joy or awe.

"Ellysetta." Marissya's voice trembled. The ocean of flames below had lit the nesting lair bright as day. Marissya's eyes were wide and frightened. Her free hand splayed across her belly, while the hand clutching Ellysetta's squeezed tight. She was shivering.

"You feel it, too." Relief warred with horror. "Can you hear them as well? The voices? The whispering?"

Marissya's head jerked in wild agreement. "They're saying 'Keralas.'" Tears filled her eyes. "He's afraid. He's so afraid."

Terrified that the evil haunting the nesting lair might claim yet another victim, Ellysetta dropped to her knees before Marissya, and without hesitation flung open every one of her senses and sent her consciousness plunging into the *shei'dalin*. She found the baby, barely more than a tiny candle burning within his mother's brilliant light. He was whimpering, terrified, just as the kitlings had been.

Gathering all the warmth and love in her soul, she sang to him, just as she'd sung to the baby tairen. Love and warmth poured out of her, into him, soothing, calming. Gradually his whimpers fell silent, and then Ellysetta heard a small, tremulous echo, so soft it was barely audible. Shock made her pull back.

Marissya's child, still barely formed in her womb, was singing. His voice was sweet and soft, his notes barely more than dim flickers of color, but he was singing tairen song.

Just like the unhatched kitlings did when she sang to them.

A wave of ice washed over her.

The floodgates opened in her mind. Memories tumbled out in a stunning rush. Her childhood nightmares of wings and fire and fang . . . Sybharukai's pleasure as she sniffed Marissya's scent and announced, *"The Fey-kin bears one of the pride."* . . . the image of Ellysetta's dead body rolling from the tairen egg, and Cahlah mourning her lost kit . . . the two shadowy Fey, chained and imprisoned . . . the triumphant cold silver eyes of the High

Mage as he lifted a newborn high . . . the Mage's sneering voice that horrible day in the cathedral when he'd declared, *I'm the father of your soul, girl. I created it, and now I've come to claim it.*

And, lastly, Gaelen saying, *The Well of Souls . . . the Eld have long used Azrahn and selkhar crystals to summon demons from the Well . . .*

The Well of Souls. The Underworld.

Home to the souls of the dead who hadn't yet earned passage to the next life.

Womb to the souls of the unborn.

Good sweet Lord of Light.

"Ellysetta!" Marissya cried out as Ellysetta ran for the ledge and leapt off.

Air came without effort, the weaves spinning exactly as Jaren had instructed to cushion her descent. The Fire Song was over and the flames had already dissipated. She landed on her feet beside the eggs. Another weave of Air blew the hot sands away so she could touch the cooler leathery shells beneath. One by one she went to each egg and found the kitling inside shivering and whimpering in fear; one by one she sang to them until they calmed and she received their response.

Each kitling had felt the cold. Each had heard the whispering dark voices calling its name.

"What is it, Ellysetta?" Rain stood beside her. The tairen, growling in agitation, had gathered around as well.

She looked at them all in a daze. "I know why I sensed the High Mage. I know why the kitlings are dying." She moistened trembling lips, stunned by the enormity of the puzzle she'd finally pieced together. "You were right, Rain. It is the High Mage. It's been him all along. He's behind everything."

CHAPTER NINETEEN

The Fading Lands ~ Dharsa

"The High Mage is using the Well of Souls to steal the souls of unborn tairen." Rain announced the news without preamble to the carefully selected group of Fey he'd gathered in the King's Courtyard behind the Hall of Tairen.

Dax sat on a stone bench, his arm wrapped protectively around Marissya. Ellysetta's quintet stood near the small fountain, and Steli, who had flown back with them from Fey'Bahren, squeezed into the corner, crouched on the flattened remains of a small flower garden, her blue eyes whirling with scarcely contained menace. A privacy weave glowed around the courtyard.

"Stealing their souls?" Tajik repeated. "For what reason?"

"To tie them to the souls of unborn children," Ellysetta said in a low voice, "so he can create his own Tairen Souls."

The gathered Fey exchanged shocked glances.

"But . . . that's not possible," Gil protested. "Even if he could tie the two souls together, he'd need Fey children who are masters of all five Fey magics—and for that he'd need Fey matepairs. No half-breed child has ever been born a master of one magic, let alone five."

"He has matepairs," Ellysetta said. "At least, he must have when I was born."

"When you were—" Tajik's voice broke off and his face went blank. "You're one of them. One of the Tairen Souls he bred."

"Yes." It was just as well Rain was standing several paces

away. If he were within reach, she'd be squeezing his hand so tight she'd break all his fingers. "Rain took me to the Bay of Flame. We swam in the waters at sunset and we dreamed . . ." She drew a quick breath, near tears as she remembered the shadowy Fey mates clutching each other in desperation. "I dreamed of my birth . . . and of my parents. My Fey parents as well as the tairen whose kitling's soul was stolen and tied to mine." Cahlah and Merdrahl had been the kit's parents. Forrahl had been its—*her*—brother. "Here, see for yourself." She summoned Spirit and spun the entirety of her dream.

When she finished, Marissya was weeping, Steli was growling pride-warnings, and the warriors stood in frozen silence.

"They must have been captured during the Wars," Bel said. "How else would the High Mage get his hands on a Fey woman?"

Marissya covered her mouth. "Dear gods, and they've been prisoners all this time?" The horror stamped on her face made each of the warriors' expressions turn to stone.

Ellysetta turned to Rain. "Do you recognize them?"

Rain shook his head. "*Nei*. There were several Tairen Souls who had green eyes, but I don't recall any of them disappearing with his mate."

"Perhaps the male wasn't a Tairen Soul when he was captured," Gaelen suggested. "If the Feyreisa is right, and the High Mage is stealing the souls of unborn tairen in order to create his own Tairen Soul, perhaps she wasn't the first."

Steli growled low in her throat and ripped at the flower bed with her front claws. *"Many kitlings have died,"* she sang to Rain and Ellysetta. *"Many times many."*

"Does it matter who they are?" Marissya cried. "We've got to save them."

Rain's expression went grim. "Marissya, how can we do that when we're barely staving off our own extinction as it is?"

"We can't just leave them there!"

"What choice do we have?" His eyes were bleak. "We don't have any idea where they are—or even if they're still alive—and we certainly don't have the strength to invade Eld to find them."

"*Shei'tani*, Rain is right." Dax took his truemate's hand.

"We can't even stop the Mage from killing the kitlings." Rain spat. He ran a hand through his hair and began to pace. "If Ellysetta is right, we have to figure out how to stop that first, or anything else we may do is meaningless. The only power the Eld truly fear is the might of the tairen. Can you imagine what they'd do if they could control that power for themselves?"

Ellysetta knew. She'd seen it in vivid, horrifying, blood-filled color in her nightmares. "The world would fall."

The warriors met one anothers' gazes with grim understanding. No mortal army would be able to stand against Eld armies led by Mage-claimed tairen. And if the Mages destroyed the Fey, no magical race would have the strength to defeat them either.

"It may already be too late," Tajik said. "If he's been stealing the souls of tairen since the Mage Wars, there's no telling how many Tairen Souls he's already created."

Gaelen gave a skeptical grunt. "If he had many, we'd have seen them already, vel Sibboreh."

"Would we?" Gil challenged. "Could be he's just biding his time and building his army."

"Or waiting for his Tairen Souls to find their wings," Rain suggested. "Ellysetta was a mere babe when she was smuggled out of Eld, and her power has yet to fully manifest itself."

"So how do we stop him?" Ellysetta interjected. "We can't do anything about the Tairen Souls he may have already created, but we have to find a way to keep him from making more."

"If he's stealing souls from the Well, then we must cut off

his access to it—or find a way to separate the kitlings from the Well of Souls," Gaelen said. "Azrahn is the only way."

"*Nei!*" Gil, Tajik, Rain, and Dax roared as one.

"Azrahn is the enemy's tool, not ours," Tajik said.

"What we're talking about here is the manipulation and theft of souls," Gaelen snapped back. "What tool should we use to combat *soul* theft if not the *soul* magic?" He threw up his hands and stalked a short distance away. "Bright Lord save me from pompous fools."

"Pompous!" Tajik snarled. "Is it pompous to live with honor?"

"What honor is there in the destruction of everything we hold dear? I'd rather live as a reviled outcast and keep my people safe than die a noble corpse along with everyone I love."

"And that's precisely the thinking that led you down the Shadowed Path to begin with! Honor is the anchor that holds us to the Light."

"Oh, *aiyah,* an anchor indeed," Gaelen snapped. "But what happens when you're thrown overboard, still chained to that great scorching anchor? You flaming drown, that's what— along with every other brother chained to it with you."

"*Dahl'reisen rultshart!*" Tajik's red hair all but caught fire. He lunged for Gaelen, whose eyes flashed to blue ice just before he lunged too.

"Enough!" Rain stepped between the two of them, his arms outstretched, palms flat against the chests of the two snarling warriors. "Scorch you both! Save your fury for the Eld." He glared at Gaelen. "Azrahn is the forbidden magic. You accepted that when you returned to the Fading Lands. You will either live by our laws or be banished once more. Is that clear?"

Gaelen's eyes narrowed. "It's clear."

"*Kabei.*" Rain shoved him away and turned to Tajik. "Dull the edge of that blade, vel Sibboreh. The Mage Wars would have happened with or without Gaelen, and your sister would still be dead. Do not forget: His own sister was the first to die."

A muscle jumped in Tajik's jaw. With a sullen nod, he turned away and stalked to a corner of the courtyard.

After a brief silence to let tempers settle, Marissya said, "Separating the kitlings from the Well wouldn't work in any case. If you sever that connection before they're born, you'd sever their souls from their bodies. They'd die."

Ellysetta's brows drew together. "Then isn't birth the obvious answer?" She glanced at Rain. "The Mage hasn't ever attacked tairen once they've hatched, has he?"

"Not in this manner," he acknowledged, "but this clutch was laid only three months past. It's far too soon for hatching. Tairen spend twelve months in the womb and eight months on the sands. No kitling with less than six months in the egg has ever survived."

"Can't a *shei'dalin*'s healing weave speed things up?" She turned to Marissya. "It's only a matter of a few months. Surely, if the most powerful healers can regrow severed limbs or hold a dying person to life, they ought to be able to accelerate the gestation of an unborn child."

Marissya shook her head. "It's not that easy, Ellysetta. Not even the most powerful *shei'dalin* can pull an infant's soul from the Well before its time, no matter how mature the child's body may be. As long as a soul lives more in the Well than the world, we can do nothing."

Ellysetta rubbed her tired eyes. "We should consult the scrolls again. Now that we know what we're looking for, perhaps we can find clues we've overlooked before. Marissya, can you call the *shei'dalins* to help us? We need as much assistance as we can get to search."

"Of course. I'll ask Venarra to summon them first thing in the morning."

Ellysetta glanced up. The eastern sky was already light. "That should be about now," she said with a wan smile.

"You and Marissya need to sleep first," Rain said. "We've

waited for centuries to find the answer to this problem; we can wait a few more bells." He turned to the fierce white tairen. "Steli-*chakai* should lair in the Hall of Tairen."

"*Agreed. Steli will sing to Shei'Kess,*" the tairen growled. "*Perhaps the Eye will reveal what secrets it still keeps.*"

"I won't hold my breath," Rain muttered. In a louder voice, he said, "*Beylah vo*, Steli-*chakai*." Rain tore down the privacy weaves, and Steli leapt into the air, leaving the Fey to head for their own chambers.

Rain escorted Ellysetta back to their palace suite and spun shades against the brightening dawn so she could sleep for a few bells. As he slid beneath the cool silk of the bedsheets next to the warmth of her slender body, she turned and snuggled against him.

"Rain?"

"Mmm?" He nuzzled the soft spirals of her hair and breathed in her sweet scent.

"Do you think the Fey who bore me could still be alive in Eld?"

His body went still. "For their sakes, I hope not, *shei'tani*."

Her palm lay over his chest, the fingers stroking lightly across his skin. "Do you think they could have been captured during the Mage Wars?"

Her caught her hand and pressed a kiss in her palm. "I doubt it. Eld don't treat their prisoners kindly. A thousand years of torment would be too much for anyone to bear."

"You did," she whispered.

"Only because the tairen would not let me die." He drew a breath. "*Nei*, I'm sure the ones who bore you could not have been long in Mage hands."

He stroked her hair, half of him wishing now that he had not taken her to the Bay of Flames. "I'm sorry, *shei'tani*. I had hoped the Bay of Flames would bring you peace, not more worries. I wanted our last days before I left for Orest to be a joy." A time of memories that would last in the event war broke out before he could return. "I meant to take you to my *shellabah*, as I promised you in Celieria I would."

She tilted her head back, her eyes shining in the dim light filtering past his shade weaves. "But our bond isn't complete yet. You said you would take me to your *shellabah* on the first night of our union. Let's wait until then. So I'll have something to look forward to when you come back to me."

His lips found the soft skin of her neck, and he nuzzled the warm pulse point there, loving her scent, her taste, the feel of her satiny skin against his mouth. "*Bas'ka*," he agreed. "We will wait until then. It shall be my last courtship gift to you."

"I will be very cross if you disappoint me." Her arms slid around his neck, and she pressed her body to his. "Tell me you love me."

"I love you." He dragged his mouth down her neck and across her shoulder. His hands spanned her slender waist and slid up her ribs to cup her small breasts. "More than I have words to express."

She caught his face and bent to take his lips with hers. "Then love me, Rain, for what time we have left."

The silky bed linens whispered against her skin as he bore her down among the soft cushions and coverlets. His skin gleamed lustrous silver and his eyes glowed with warmth and passion. "I will love you much longer than that, *kem'reisa*."

Despite the *shei'dalins'* best efforts over the next few days, their searching turned up no clues to long-lost weaves that might speed a child's birth from the Well of Souls, and the day of Rain's departure for Orest dawned without any sign of victory in the battle to save the kitlings.

As the warriors leaving the Fading Lands prepared for their departure, Rain walked alone to the king's armory.

There, in the silence of the chamber broken only by the

melodic splashing of *faerilas* pouring into a private bathing pool, Rain undressed and set aside his leathers and steel and even his gleaming rainbow-lit Soul Quest crystal and the carved Tairen's Eye signet ring he'd worn since becoming Defender of the Fey.

Naked, he walked to the edge of the bathing pool and went down on one knee, his arms extended, palms up, as he softly sang the words of the ancient prayer all warriors invoked before battle. When he rose, he plunged into the falling stream of *faerilas* and gasped. This fountain—like all those in the palace—was fed directly from Dharsa's Source. The water was icy cold and rich with potent magic. It froze and seared him and set his magic afire inside his flesh.

He stood beneath its flow until his body shone with the purified force of his considerable power, and then stepped out of the pool and dried himself with a swift weave of Air. Six steps brought him to the altar niche, where thirteen fresh, unlit candles in various shades of earth and sky had been laid out in a pattern of divine power. He passed his hand over the candles, loosing a faint weave of Fire as he spoke the name of each god or goddess. One by one, the wicks burst into pale yellow-orange flame, and a heady mélange of fragrances filled the air.

Rain knelt before the altar and sang the invocation of the Feyreisen. "Light of world, shine your grace upon this Fey. Grant me the wisdom to guide my brothers in battle, the strength to drive back the enemy, and, if it is your will, the courage to die bravely and with honor. Light be victorious."

Last, he sent up silent a plea of his own, *If I fall, let my life be the sacrifice that frees Ellysetta from the Mages. If I fall, help her to lead our people with strength and wisdom so the Fading Lands may thrive once more.* And the hardest wish for any Fey who wanted his *shei'tani* bound to him and him alone . . . "If I fall . . . let her live to find love and joy with another."

The candles flickered, and with one final word of prayer and thanks, he blew them out and waved the aromatic smoke from the extinguished wicks over his face and bare skin, closing his eyes and filling his lungs with the warm fragrance.

He'd performed a similar ritual in his youth, before he'd marched out to war. Then, the smoke and *faerilas* had filled him with a sense of peace and purpose. He'd been so young back then, so unaware of the true horrors war could bring.

Now he knew better. Now he knew how damning even victory could be.

He approached the alcove that held the armor of the king, then stopped. The moment he donned the golden steel, the Fading Lands would be at war and there would be no turning back until the Eld surrendered or the light of the Fey was extinguished.

He could almost hear Johr's voice, full of hard edges and fierce challenge: *You think you have the right, Fey? Are you certain?*

He recalled the day Johr had donned the armor. He'd summoned all the Tairen Souls of the Fading Lands into this room to bear witness. There were twenty of them then, ranging in age from Rain's own youthful two hundred years to Johr's almost sixteen hundred. Rain had stood in the same spot he was now, his body trembling with a mix of excitement, dread, and anticipation. Gaelen vel Serranis had just wreaked his dark vengeance upon the Eld, and the world had gone mad.

He and his brothers had watched Johr strip away his leathers and steel. They'd sung with him the songs of prayer and purification as he'd cleansed himself in the waters of the Source and lit the sacred candles as Rain had just done. Magic—Johr's own great tairen power—had swirled around him, draping his nakedness in great, blinding swaths of light as he stepped resolutely toward the alcove where the king's armor awaited.

"You think being king is about power?" Johr had asked them. He'd stood so tall, his shoulders broad, his face carved from stone. His eyes had whirled tairen-bright, pupil-less, their normal brown transformed to glowing amber that burned like molten steel. "Power is nothing. Kingship is about choices. Hard, bloody, damnable choices. One day, any one of you may be the Feyreisen. When the time comes for you to make those decisions, will you be wise enough to make the right one?" His searing eyes had scorched them. "Think long and hard, my brother-kin. We are creatures born for killing, but war is a poison draft. No matter why you drink it, the cup holds death—and not just for your enemies. So be sure—be soul-scorching sure of two things before you take the smallest sip: first, that you have no better alternative, and second . . ."

His voice had trailed off. He lowered his head as though the effort to keep himself standing tall was too great.

"And second?" asked one of the younger Tairen Souls, a Fey barely older than Rain.

Johr drew a breath. Slowly, he lifted his head and drew his shoulders back, square and strong once more. "And second, be sure that once you tilt the cup, you are Fey enough to drain it though its poison rots your flesh, lays waste your lands, and leaves everyone you love writhing in bitter anguish."

His power had blazed, and the armor in the alcove had dissolved, re-forming on the king's body, fitted to him as though the steel had been forged to his form. He'd stood there for one last, silent moment, a shining Fey prince clad in black, scarlet, and gold, his eyes as bleak and grim as Rain had ever seen them. "To war, my brothers." Johr lowered the battle helm upon his head. "To victory or death."

"To victory or death!" they'd cried.

And so the Mage Wars had begun.

Now, standing alone in the king's armory on the brink of

a second Mage War, Rain found Johr's ringed name symbol on one of the black leather plates. "If you can hear me, Johr Feyreisen," he murmured, rubbing a thumb across the sigil of the previous Fey king, "guide me now as you did when I first found my wings."

When Rain emerged from the king's armory and stepped into the Hall of Tairen, Bel and Gaelen were waiting. Bel glanced at Rain's plain black leathers and silvery steel, but all he said was, "The warriors have gathered."

Gaelen's ice blue eyes narrowed. "You still believe this can end in any way but one?"

Rain adjusted his *meicha* belts. "*Nei*, I am not so big a fool."

"Then why this?" Gaelen's hands spread to indicate Rain's old leathers.

"War is coming—I know that is as inevitable as it was a thousand years ago—but the moment the Eld see the Feyreisen's golden war steel on the ramparts of Orest, the first battle will begin. Let us position our men, secure our allies, and plan our defenses before throwing down the gauntlet." When Gaelen continued to look askance, he sighed. "If all I do is buy time for Ellysetta to save the tairen, that will be enough."

"Enough for what?"

Bel answered for him. "Hope."

All of Dharsa came out to see the warriors off, and tears mingled with the voices raised in exultant song. Though Rain wore no golden steel, no one in Dharsa believed the departing Fey would return before open war began. And most still remembered how few had returned the last time the Fey strode off to war.

Garbed in flowing purple silks and flanked by Bel, Gaelen, and Steli, Ellysetta stood on a garland-draped platform and watched the column of Fey warriors march past, Rain at the lead. She sang with the other Fey, her voice rising pure and sweet, and on a private weave of Spirit, she called, *"Be safe, kem'san. Come back to me."*

Just before he rounded the corner and marched out of view, he turned toward her. *"I will see you soon, shei'tani."*

Then he was gone. She remained standing on the platform, watching until the last Fey disappeared down the avenue of sentinel trees in Rain's wake.

When the street was empty and the city had fallen silent, she turned to Marissya and the *shei'dalins* standing nearby. "Well, *kem'fallas*, let's get back to work."

Rain and the Fey ran flat-out across the Plains of Corunn and the Eastern Desert, but once past the abandoned city of Sohta, the rocky rise and fall of the mountainous terrain slowed their land-eating run to a jog. At dawn of the fourth day, they reached the Faering Mists and the pass of Revan Oreth where the volcanic Feyls merged with the Rhakis mountains.

Though the Mists offered no resistance to Fey departing the Fading Lands, Revan Oreth was little more than a treacherous goat path winding through a canyon of razor-sharp rocks and crumbling cliffs. The Fey took each footstep with special care.

The pass opened into the turbulent heart of Kiyera's Veil, a gauntlet of mighty, three-hundred-foot waterfalls plunging down from opposing sides of the mountains. Magic teemed in the billowing mist and furious deluge, a powerful magic that flowed from Crystal Lake, the great mountain-born Source cradled at the intersection of the Rhakis, the Feyls, and the Mandolay ranges. Those waters, which then went on to feed the Heras River, burned Mage flesh the way *sel'dor* burned the Fey.

Rain and the Fey plunged into the cascades without

hesitation. Though the pounding weight drenched them and nearly drove them to their knees, they slogged through the hammering gauntlet of the Veil.

Their reward, when they finally emerged on the other side, was to step into the closest thing the mortal world had to paradise.

Billowing clouds of spray rose up from the clash of falls, and grottoes of fern and moss clung to the steep mountainside, thriving in the cool moisture. Rivulets of condensed mist became small ribbons of water that spilled constantly down the craggy, moss-and-fern-carpeted cliffsides in a delicate web of secondary falls. Rainbows shimmered in every beam of light.

There, at the foot of the majestic torrent of waterfalls and nestled in the wide upper valley carved out of the mountains, Orest, the City of Mists, rose from the rainbows like a sprawling cathedral of black pearl, alabaster, and jade. Girded by steep, impenetrable battlements, the city's beautiful heart flourished in the sweet breath of the Veil, blooming with mossy tree-and-fern-filled gardens amidst graceful colonnaded walks and domed, glistening pearl gray buildings and bridges that spanned the headwaters of the Heras.

Armored guards clad in the gold, white, and crimson tabards of House Teleos stood at attention on every corner, bridge, and tower wall, guarding Orest like the treasure she was. Before Rain had even stepped outside the misty cloud of spray from the Veil, he was surrounded by a hundred soldiers—all jabbing the business end of their spears his way.

As score after score of drenched Fey warriors emerged from the deluge of the Veil, Orest's guardsmen found themselves backing up, but before the Fey outnumbered them, a shout brought reinforcements running. Overhead, rising from the rocks and crevices of the sheer cliffs, archers took careful aim at the Fey newcomers.

Rain, unoffended by the Celierians' fierce defense, held out his hands in the universally recognized gesture of peace. "Inform Lord Teleos the Tairen Soul has arrived."

"You should have sent word," Teleos chided as he ushered Rain, Tajik, Rijonn, and Gil into a warm, dry conservatory whose glassed walls and ceilings provided an unimpeded view of the Veil and the verdant splendor of Upper Orest. "If I'd known you were coming through the Veil, my men would have given you a much more gracious greeting."

"The greeting was as gracious as a stranger should expect," Rain said mildly. "My compliments to your men for their swift action. Considering that none have passed through the Veil for a thousand years, I half expected your men to have let down their guard."

"They are well trained for mortals," Tajik agreed. "They bring you pride."

"Beylah vo." Dev nodded his thanks. "The Veil may be quiet, but the greatest threat to the mortal world lives but an arrow's flight across the Heras. And we guard the only bridge from here to the Pereline Ocean." He walked towards the east-facing side of the room, where they could look out over the city.

At the base of Orest's great wall, the mountains dropped away again, and the Heras River plunged down a second broad waterfall called Maiden's Gate before winding eastward across the continent, a wide, dark ribbon that traveled well over a thousand miles to the sea. In all that distance, not a single stone nor strand of ferry rope bridged the wide, dark waters that separated Eld and Celieria. All that had existed were destroyed during the Mage Wars and never rebuilt.

"I think you'll find the bridges of Orest less valued by the Eld than once they were," Rain remarked. "The Well of Souls is all the bridge they now need."

He ran a critical eye over the admittedly imposing

defenses of the middle and lower city. Middle Orest—called Maiden's Gate after the falls it flanked—stair-stepped down the steep cliffs of the river's southern bank in a series of well-fortified terraces. The bottom terrace of Maiden's Gate opened to the wide, walled city of Lower Orest. Like the fortress battlements of the upper city, thick walls of pearlescent gray stone ringed the lower city and loomed four tairen lengths high over the wide, dark waters of the mighty Heras. Steel-shuttered portals for bowcannon and archers dotted the solid walls, and the steel-enforced frames of heavy catapults crouched on broad platforms every tairen length along the crenellated battlements. Behind the massive outer wall, a secondary wall loomed higher, its ramparts studded with slender towers where war wizards conjured their spells during battle.

"When the Eld come," he advised, "don't rely on the lessons of the past to guide you. Their attack may come from anywhere, with little or no warning. Possibly even from within the city itself." He didn't have to explain. Lord Teleos had been in Celieria City when the Eld launched their attack at the Grand Cathedral of Light.

"The Fey who accompanied me from Teleon have already taken that into account," Dev replied. "They've already evaluated the city's defenses and spun protection weaves over everything. If the Eld open a portal anywhere in Orest, we'll know about it."

"Kabei." He'd already received the same report from his men, but Orest belonged to Devron Teleos. He eyed the shining Fey steel Dev wore and saw the familiar name-marks on the pommels. "Shanis would be proud to have you wear his blades, Dev." He clapped a hand on his friend's shoulder. "Now we'll teach you how to use them. I know I promised you safe escort to the Academy in Dharsa, but circumstances being what they are, I've instead brought the Academy to you. Tajik, Rijonn, and Gil will train you and your men in the basic forms of the Cha Baruk. How many Orestians wield magic?"

"Quite a few."

"Gather them. Any adult or child over the age of sixteen who is willing to learn is welcome. If the Eld attack as boldly as I fear they might, Orest will need every advantage." Rain looked out over the verdant, mist-and-rainbow-wreathed city, wondering where and when the first attack would come.

CHAPTER TWENTY

The Fading Lands ~ Dharsa

Nothing.

Nothing, nothing, and again nothing.

Ellysetta shoved the pile of useless scrolls away from her in frustration. Since Rain's departure a week ago, all the *shei'dalins* and healers in Dharsa had continued searching for a way to accelerate the kitlings' hatching. The search had expanded from the Hall of Scrolls to every private library and collection of healing texts they could lay hands upon. Even the women in Tehlas and Blade's Point had joined the search, but still they found nothing.

Steli had ferried Ellie and Marissya between Fey'Bahren and Dharsa every day to spin on the kits each new healing weave the *shei'dalins* had discovered, hoping it would bring them closer to hatching. But although the kitlings' bodies were much stronger and larger than they had been when they'd begun, the shining lights that were the marrow of their souls were still as fragile and thin as they had been the night Forrahl died.

Ellysetta was at her wits' end. According to every document

they'd scoured in their extensive search, what Ellysetta needed—what the kitlings needed—couldn't be done.

She scowled and pushed her chair away from the table. Irritation aroused her magic. Tiny sparks of escaping power danced around her like fairy-flies as she stood up and paced between the tables where the other *shei'dalins* were still diligently poring over text after text. She thrust her fingers through her hair, yanking at the tangled curls.

What did the authors of all these scrolls know anyway? According to them, restoring a *dahl'reisen*'s soul couldn't be done either—yet she'd managed it. She could find a way to help the kitlings survive, too.

Somewhere, someone or something must have the answers that would tell her how to do it. After all, she was the reason the Eye of Truth had sent Rain to Celieria. She was the one the Eye had said could save the tairen and the Fey.

Ellysetta stopped in her tracks.

She whirled around and ran up the stairs of the hall. Ignoring the startled calls of the *shei'dalins*, she rushed out into the fresh, bright beauty of Dharsa and raced up the fragrant footpaths towards the palace at the top of the hill.

There was one source Ellysetta hadn't consulted yet. Once source that held answers even the Hall of Scrolls did not.

Shei'Kess. The Eye of Truth.

Celieria ~ Teleon

Den Brodson hummed the melody of his favorite Celierian drinking song—a bawdy little ditty about roosters and cats—as he tucked a blanket under his arm, grabbed a lunch pail in one fist and picked up a large cloth-covered basket in the other. Humming turned to cheerful whistling as he set off across the grassy plain south of the Teleon outpost. The guards on the tower walls returned his wave as he walked by.

Since arriving at the outpost, Den had assumed his most affable demeanor in order to befriend the guards stationed around the small fort. A ready smile, quick wit, and willingness to lend an ear or offer a free pint had already made him a welcome guest among the common soldiers. He'd used those friendships to explore the nooks and crannies of the outpost and secret two dozen *chemar* in well-concealed locations: buried in the corners of the bailey, tucked into a slit in a mattress in the soldiers' barracks, dropped into the corners of the guard towers.

Den was careful not to rouse suspicion as he'd roamed, but he made note of all entrances and exits and the location and counts of all guards, mortal and Fey. He also tracked the comings and goings of the five Fey *shei'dalins* and let the amber crystal tied around his neck carry his observations back to Master Nour in Celieria City.

The only task he hadn't yet completed was discovering the whereabouts of Ellie Baristani's young sisters.

The pressure was mounting. Lady Darramon's unexpected pregnancy had forced the *shei'dalins'* healing to go more slowly than anticipated, but the great lady was already looking far stronger and more robust than the walking corpse she had been when they'd arrived. Den expected to receive word any day that the Darramon party would be departing Teleon.

He knew the twins couldn't be far away. The two Fey who had greeted Darramon's party when they arrived were the same ones Den remembered guarding Ellie and her sisters so closely back in Celieria City.

The brown-haired Fey Den remembered with particular clarity. He was the same warrior who'd laughed at Den and called him "little sausage" the day Rain Tairen Soul stole Den's betrothed . . . the same warrior who'd later held a knife to Den's throat and growled, "Little sausage, I have lost all patience with you."

Yes, Den remembered that Fey. And when the attack came, Den hoped to be there to see the insufferable, sneering *porgil*'s throat slit by a *sel'dor* blade.

Unfortunately, his numerous attempts to follow the pair had ended in failure. One moment they'd be walking around the bailey, and the next they'd turn a corner and literally disappear. No matter how often he tried to follow them—or even head in the direction where they'd disappeared—Den always found himself back in some other area of the fortress, shaking his head to clear it and wondering where'd he'd been going.

There was most definitely some sort of illusion and redirection weave spun around the rear of the fortress, and the magic was too powerful for him to get past.

Thwarted in his direct approach, he'd decided that rather than trying to find the twins, he'd encourage them to find him. Every day for the last three days, after feeding Darramon's men and cleaning up the cook wagon, he'd packed the kittens and their mother in a basket, gathered a blanket, and walked around the southwest side of the outpost to let the kittens play in the sunshine while their mother hunted field mice in the grass.

Each day, he placed his blanket just that much closer to the back of the fortress.

No nibbles yet, but he'd fished enough in Great Bay to know how to bait a hook and be patient.

"Psst. Lillis. He's there again." Lorelle clung to the upper branches of a cherry blossom tree and waved her sister up. "Here, come look." She handed down the small brass spyglass Kieran had made for them so they could play Pirates and Damsels. (Lorelle was *always* the pirate.)

Lillis wedged herself in the cradle of several smooth gray branches and raised the spyglass to her eye, turning the end to bring the world in focus. "Oooooh . . . there they are!

Six, Lorelle! He's got six of them. Oooh . . . I want the little black one. She has the cutest white socks."

Lorelle frowned down at her sister. "How will you know which one you want until you've had a chance to hold them? Maybe the one you think you want will like me better than you."

Lillis looked up. "How could we hold them? We're not supposed to go out where anyone can see us. Especially not when strangers are here."

"He's not a stranger," Lorelle countered. Honestly, Lillis could be such a noodle-spine. "He's been here all week, and all the guards wave at him when he walks by. Besides, if he were a bad man, Kieran and Kiel would already have stabbed him dead or made his insides catch fire or sucked all the water and air out of his body."

Lately, Lorelle had been interrogating Kiel and Kieran about all the ways they could kill enemies with magic. Though Lillis squealed and got all prissy, Lorelle pressed for ever more gruesome and inventive ways of killing bad people. One day, she promised herself, she'd meet the Mage who'd hurt Ellie and killed their mama, and Lorelle would find a way to kill him—and the more he suffered, the better she would like it!

Her sister's face puckered with concern. "Kieran will be mad."

"He can't be mad if he doesn't know, ninnywit. We can sneak out, play with the kittens, and sneak back before he even knows we're gone."

Lillis continued to look doubtful.

Lorelle stuck her nose in the air. "Well, *I'm* going. And when my kitten ends up liking me more than yours likes you, it will be your own fault for picking one out just by its color." She clambered down the tree and dropped to the ground, giving her skirts a good shake to free them of bark. She took a dozen determined steps by herself before a pleased smile curved her lips.

Lillis was running to catch up with her.

The Fading Lands ~ Dharsa

The Hall of Tairen was empty. Bel and Gaelen were at the
Academy, Steli was hunting, and Eimar had convinced his
fellow Massan to accompany him to the Academy to observe the new skills he and the other Fey had acquired under Gaelen's tutelage.

Ellysetta's slippers made no sound as she crossed the marble tiles and approached the great, dark sphere of Tairen's
Eye crystal held aloft on the back of golden tairen wings.

She hadn't entered this room since that first day, when
the Eye had shown her such horrible things and roused
both her tairen and the dangerous dark magic of Azrahn.

Her skin prickled as she drew near. The Eye was powerful
magic and she could feel the throbbing pulse of its energy
whispering across her skin and raising the hairs on the back
of her neck. Shadows swirled slowly in the Eye's dark
depths. Glimpses of bright rainbows darted among swirls of
deepest red.

"Who were you?" Her whisper sounded like a shout in
the stone silence of the chamber. "You lived once. You
must have had a name."

The Eye gave no answer, but then, she hadn't really expected one.

She drew a deep breath and summoned her courage. She
knew better than to touch the oracle. Rain had laid hands
upon the Eye, and it had not responded kindly. The tairen
had sung to it, and the Eye hadn't liked that either.

She would try something simpler, something less aggres-
sive. Something she could control.

A Spirit weave.

She closed her eyes to concentrate and calm her nerves,
then called the lavender magic whose bright glow reminded
her of Rain's eyes when his passions rose. It came easily,

flowing into her with a steady effortlessness that would have made her *chatok* proud.

She gathered the magic and spun it into a subtle, spider-silk-thin weave, imbuing each thread with a sense of urgent need and respect and an echo of the terrible desperation, fear, and grievous loss she'd felt when Forrahl died. She didn't know if the Eye could still feel emotion, but she hoped the weave would convince it of her sincerity. When the pattern was complete, and the threads as filled with power and emotion as she could make them, she cast the shining net over the crystal globe and used it as the conduit for her Spirit voice.

"It's me . . . Ellysetta."

All right, that seemed a silly thing to say. The Eye of Truth was the most powerful oracle in the world. It already knew everything there was to know about her, including events that hadn't happened yet. Surely it knew who she was without her introducing herself. She swallowed the lump in her throat and tried again.

"You told Rain I was the one who could save the tairen and the Fey. You sent him to find me and bring me back. Now I am here, but the tairen are still dying. I don't know how to do what you foretold I would."

Magic energy swirled and gathered. Not her own. She refused to open her eyes, afraid of what she would see, but against the backs of her lids Fey vision was already blooming in the darkness. She saw her web, a net of fine lavender threads, wrapped around a sphere of radiant stars that began to whirl and brighten.

"Teska, please, tell me what to do. They are your kin, too. How can I save them?" Thinking perhaps the Eye would be more likely to give her the answer she needed if she asked more specifically, she added, *"If I free the tairen kitlings from the egg, will they be safe from the power that hunts them?"*

The starry lights of the sphere flashed in unison. She rocked back on her heels from the surge of energy.

Within that flash of light pulsed a single word, spoken
not in a voice, not in a song, but vibrating through every
cell of her body with absolute and incontrovertible certainty:

Aiyah.

She gulped. Shei'Kess had spoken. *To her.* In a voice-
without-sound that was as powerful and all-encompassing
as Church of Light priests claimed the Bright Lord's divine
voice to be. *Good sweet Lord of Light.* Her lashes fluttered, as
if her eyes were trying to open against her will. She kept
them squeezed shut, afraid of what she might see in the
Eye.

Corralling her wayward thoughts, she tried to concentrate. The Eye was tairen-made. The Fey claimed that
meant it could not lie, but that did not mean the Eye would
always tell the whole truth either. All she'd asked was if
hatching from the egg would free the kitlings from their
hunter. She'd not asked if they would still die.

*"Is there also a way to free the kitlings from the Well of Souls so
they can hatch, survive, and remain healthy after only three months
in the egg?"* There. That seemed specific enough.

The Eye pulsed again, and that voice-without-sound
answered a second time.

Aiyah.

Her heart slammed against her ribs. She moistened her
lips. *"How?"*

The vibrations of energy grew stronger, battering her
senses. The starry lights spun so rapidly they became solid
streaks of blazing light whirling in a dazzling ball. Her
breathing grew labored, coming in shallow pants as if she
were running too fast to catch her breath. *"How?"* she asked
again. *"Teska, tell me."*

She struggled to hold her weave, spinning more need,
more urgency into the threads. *"You sent Rain to find me. If
you know how I can save the tairen, please, tell me before the High
Mage of Eld steals another kitling's soul. Tell me how to stop it."*

The voice-without-sound did not speak, but the light of the Eye took up a pulsing beat, flaring again and again, pounding in a relentless rhythm. Her eyes began to burn. Her lashes fluttered, and the tiny muscles in her eyelids jumped and fought to open. Was she supposed to watch? Was that what the Eye was trying to tell her—that it could only show her the answer?

Very well. *"Show me."*

Her eyes flew open.

Celieria ~ Teleon

"Hello."

Den Brodson clamped down on a surge of savage triumph and forced a genial smile to his face as he turned to face Lillis and Lorelle Baristani. "Why, hello. Where did you come from?"

The twins glanced at each other. "From home," one said, while the other ignored his question and bluntly asked, "Can we pet your kittens?"

He forced a paternal laugh. "Like kittens, do you? Well, I've never met a little girl yet who didn't. Of course you may pet them. Here, they like to play with these." He'd woven little spheres from strips of pliant wood, installing a *chemar* fixed with two small bells into the hollow center of each. The twins rolled the little balls towards the kittens, laughing as they batted and chased the chiming balls. "Do you live around here? I've been at the outpost all week—I'm the cook with Lord Darramon's party—and I'm sure I would have remembered if I'd seen two such beautiful young ladies."

"We are cousins of Lord Teleos." They lied with such perfect innocence, Den would have believed them if he hadn't already known the truth.

"Ah, Great Lord Teleos. A good man." As the girls picked up the jingle balls and began rolling them to the kittens, he reached for the pouch of white stones at his side, calculating exactly where to toss the *chemar* so he could grab the girls and haul them into the Well before they had a chance to cry for help.

The metallic snick of a hundred blades froze him in place, and magic burst around him in a flash of hair-raising energy. Invisibility weaves dissolved and he found himself surrounded by what looked like an entire Fey army. Their blades were drawn, their faces cold stone masks, their eyes like burning death.

Den gulped. His heart rose up in his throat. Every ounce of blood rushed to his face, then drained away, leaving him trembling and soaked with clammy sweat. With swift desperation, he muttered the spell word Master Nour had given him for just such an occasion.

An instant later, the memories of Den Brodson were gone, locked deep away where they could not be retrieved until the spell wore off, and the man who remembered nothing beyond being Lord Darramon's frightened cook was falling over himself to offer his apologies. "Forgive me, sers. I meant no harm. The children came to pet the kittens. I saw no harm in allowing it."

The girls rose to their feet, each clutching a tiny, squirming kitten and one of the woven jingle balls. One of the girls looked stricken, the other sullen. The stricken one turned eyes big as saucers upon a brown-haired, blue-eyed Fey. "We just wanted to pet the kittens, Kieran."

"You promised we could have another kitten, since we had to leave Love behind," the sullen girl added. She tilted her chin up. "We came so we could tell you which ones we wanted."

"*You* promised you would not leave the safety of Teleon. If you do not honor your word, why should I honor mine?" The blue-eyed Fey, who appeared to be the leader of the group despite the deceptively youthful look of his face, pinned the girls with such a hard, cold look that the stricken one burst into tears.

"The young ladies would like a kitten?" the cook asked quickly. "Please, take them. Whichever ones you like. Consider it my gift. I'll even throw in these little jingling balls for the kittens to play with. They do love them so." He offered up a handful of the little woven balls.

"There!" the bold child proclaimed. "You see? He doesn't mind."

The blue-eyed Fey gritted his teeth and said, "Put. The kittens. Down. And go with Kiel this instant. This instant!" he snapped when the foolish, headstrong girl opened her mouth again.

The child glared, but set the kitten down. It began mewing and rubbing against her ankle. "You see? It wants to come with me."

"Please, Kieran?" the sweet child begged. "Please, please? We'll be good forever, I promise. You won't even have to watch us. Please, can't we keep them?" She cuddled the fluffy black-and-white kitten to her cheek, her big, wet eyes filled with such longing, any man with half a heart would find it difficult to refuse her. "Please?"

The blue-eyed Fey, Kieran, exchanged a brief look with another Fey who had long blond hair. When he turned back, Kieran fixed the cook with a piercing gaze that made the man's brain buzz woozily. A moment later, the cook was blinking and holding his head, and the Fey was weaving greenish magic over one of the toy balls, disassembling it and crushing the white stone inside to dust.

"What was this?" The Fey held out the white dust that remained.

The cook bit his lip. "Just a pretty stone, ser. It makes the bells ring better when the ball rolls." He held out the pouch of stones and poured several more into his palm. "Here, you see?" The Fey picked up one of the white rocks and examined it closely. "Pretty as moonstone, but not half so dear. If the children play Stones, I'm happy to let them have these, too."

"Oooh, Lillis and I love Stones." The bold child peered over the Fey's arm.

The Fey named Kieran snapped to attention and scowled at the child. "You have a cat and a toy for it—be grateful for that. Now get back to Teleon. You are in serious trouble."

The bold child snatched up her kitten and one of the jingle bells and beamed. "Thank you, Kieran! You won't be sorry!"

He pointed. "Go."

With a grin for her sister, she went.

When the girls were gone, the Fey nodded to his companions. Their swords slid back into their sheaths. Kieran bowed to the cook. "Good day to you, Goodman. Thank you for your generosity. The girls will not bother you again."

"Oh, 'tweren't no bother, ser," the cook assured him. "And here, do take these." He put the remaining jingle balls inside the pouch with the rest of the stones. "They're bound to lose the ones they have. And there's enough of the stones in here for a game."

"*Beylah vo.* Your generosity does you credit."

"You're more than welcome. The children are welcome to come play with the other kittens whenever they—" He gulped. With a shimmer of magic, the Fey had simply . . . disappeared.

Leaving Lord Darramon's bewildered cook turning in confused circles, Kieran raced after Kiel and the girls. As soon as they crossed the threshold of the Spirit weave, he dropped his invisibility weave and stormed towards the girls.

They were cuddling their new kittens happily, but their pleased expressions faded when he drew close. They had never seen him angry, and at the moment, he was as furious as he'd ever been in his life. Anything could have happened to them. Anything!

"Get upstairs to the manor. Your father is going to hear about this."

Now they looked worried. As well they should.

Though Kieran had never in his life laid a harsh hand on any female, the mortal idea of a swift, hard paddling was sounding more appealing by the moment! He marched the girls up the long, winding roads of Teleon and into the manor house.

Sol met them at the front entrance, his face creased with worry. "What is it? What's happened?"

"The girls decided this was a good day to take a walk in the fields beside the outpost."

Sol's brows climbed up to his hairline. "They . . . *what*?"

The girls tumbled over each other to explain about the kittens and wanting to pick the right ones and how everything had turned out for the best. Sol's expression grew grimmer with each word. Before the children even finished their explanation, he snapped, "Be silent! Go into the parlor and sit. Do not dare to speak another word!"

Chastened and fearful in a way they never were with Kieran and Kiel, the twins burst into tears, shuffled past their father, and ran into the parlor.

When Kieran and Kiel would have followed, Sol held up a hand. "I'm going to ask you to remain out here. I need a few chimes in private with my daughters." He closed the parlor door.

Standing outside in the hallway, Kieran and Kiel both heard the blistering lecture Sol delivered to his reckless daughters. They heard the scrape of chairs, Lillis's and Lorelle's remorseful weeping, then four loud smacks followed by even louder weeping.

A moment later the parlor door opened, and Sol stepped aside to let Kieran and Kiel enter.

Despite his earlier desire to spank the girls himself, Kieran felt his heart almost break at the sight of Lillis's tearstained face. *Nei*, he could never have done it. Not even for their own good.

Lorelle's eyes were tear-bright, but her small jaw was set and her arms crossed. When she saw Kiel, she blinked and spun quickly to give him her back.

Kieran sighed, his anger gone. There was no need to chastise them further. He knelt by Lillis's side, pulled her to his chest, and let her cry until all her tears were gone. Kiel just stood silent behind Lorelle until her spine bent enough for her to turn and lean against him.

When at last they were both quiet and calm, he asked. "How did you get outside the weave without being seen? I am not angry at you. But I do need to know which Fey were not watching as they should."

"It wasn't their fault." Lillis sniffed. "We didn't let them see us."

Kieran frowned. "What do you mean?"

"We made them not see us," Lorelle said.

Kiel's eyes widened and he shared an astonished look with Kieran. "You . . . you made yourselves invisible? Like Kieran and I do?"

"No, not like that. It's more like we made everyone look somewhere else," Lorelle said. "Besides, you and Kieran are never really invisible. You go all purple and glowy, but we still see you."

Kieran rocked back on his heels. "You see our Spirit weaves." Mortals could not see magic. Maybe a hint of great magic, but nothing so simple as an invisibility weave. Not unless they possessed considerable magic of their own.

"Mama made us promise never to tell." Lillis looked up at him earnestly.

Sol grabbed for the back of a nearby chair as his knees started to give out. "You . . . your mama knew you could see magic?"

Lillis nodded. "We saw hers once, and she made us swear we would never tell anyone—not even you or Ellie."

Sol's wooden pipe fell from his shaking hands and cracked in two on the stone floor. "Your mama . . . had magic?" Sol's voice trailed off weakly.

"She made a fire stop in the kitchen when we were five." Lorelle bent down to pick up the broken pipe and handed the pieces to her father.

"She glowed shiny red when she did it," Lillis added.

"She was so afraid when we asked her about it." Lorelle shook her head. "She even cried."

"So we knew we had to pretend we were just like everyone else, just like Ellie and Mama did." Lillis gave Kieran a hopeful look. "Can we can stop pretending now? We're tired of it."

"You mean *you're* tired of it." Lorelle sniffed. "You're not as good at it as me."

"Oh, yes, I am," Lillis shot back. "Nobody ever guessed about me, not even Love when I was holding her."

"Girls," Kieran interrupted. They both wiped the scowls off their faces and looked up at him, a pair of sweet innocents. He felt the tug of love and affection, as he always did when the twins turned their big, soulful eyes upon him, only this time, for the first time, he felt something else too. The tiniest thread of . . . influence. A faint ephemeral weave of illusory compulsion, coming from *them*. "Why don't you both stop pretending right now. About everything. Would you do that for me?"

Lillis and Lorelle turned to their father. "Can we, Papa?"

The woodcarver nodded mutely.

Kiel stepped closer, his blue eyes filled with unveiled interest. "What is it you've been hiding, little Fey'cha?"

Ellysetta's sisters shared a final look, then shrugged and said in unison, "This." The illusion of unprepossessing mortality dropped from them like a discarded candle shade, and while the children didn't suddenly blaze like the Great Sun, they did very noticeably . . . glow.

Kieran caught his breath in shock and wonder. Their skin was softly luminescent, almost Fey in appearance. And cupped in the hollow of her palm, each twin held a small, leaping, twirling sphere of magic: Red Fire and green Earth in Lorelle's hand, white Air and blue Water in Lillis's.

The Fading Lands ~ Dharsa

Gaelen caught the downward sweep of his opponent's *seyani* longsword between his two *meicha* in a lightning-fast move, locking the curved blades tip-to-hilt. One swift twist of the blades, and his opponent's blade whipped out of his hands and fell to the ground.

"Tairen's Bite," he growled to the disarmed man. "You know the move, and you know how to protect against it, but you're still too slow." He sheathed his scimitars and bent to scoop up the other man's sword. "Practice, Char. Have one of the Earth masters fly sparring-swifts for you. When you can strike down a dozen all at once without a single feather laid upon you, you'll know you're improving."

The Fey, flushed after an exhausting several bells of training, nodded and bowed to Gaelen as *chadins* always bowed to their *chatok* at the end of a lesson.

Gaelen bowed back, then pivoted on his heel.

And scowled when, across the field, a warrior's legs suddenly shot out from under him and the Fey went sprawling backwards into the dirt, swearing. Fey laughter pealed out, and a Spirit master popped out of thin air. Gaelen muttered and rolled his eyes. He was going to regret teaching that weave to certain Fey.

Just this morning, he'd squelched the contest some of the Spirit masters were holding to see how many *chatok* blades they could pinch without being discovered. Fortunately none of them had pinched his. *Or had they?* he thought with a frown when an odd flicker of awareness prickled his nerves. He quickly checked his steel to make sure it was all there and all real, then let out a short, relieved breath. It was.

A flutter of color from the corner of his eye made him turn, and then he realized what had set his senses tingling. Ellysetta was waiting on the observation dais at the edge of the field. He jogged towards her, dodging tumbling bodies and slashing swords as he wended his way to the observation dais. As he drew closer, his tingling senses turned into full-blown alarm.

She was pale and drawn. *"Vel Jelani."* He sent the curt call instantly, one *lu'tan* to another, and leapt up onto the dais to kneel at her side. *"Kem'falla,* you are not well?"

"I'm fine. I . . ." Her gaze flickered to a point over Gaelen's right shoulder. Bel was sprinting across the field. She stood abruptly. "I'm sorry. Never mind. Please forget I came." She spun away and hurried back towards the Academy doors.

Concerned, but solicitous, Gaelen waved Bel off and followed. "Ellysetta." He caught up with her just inside the hallway. "What is it? Clearly, something has you upset. Here." He opened the door to one of the training rooms where young *chadins* learned tumbling and hand-to-hand combat. "Whatever you have to say to me, you can say in private."

She bit her lip and stared at the open door, her body poised for flight. *"Nei,* really, I should go. This was a mistake."

He caught her arm before she could turn away. *"Kem'falla."*

She froze.

He snatched his hand back as if the feel of her skin burned him. He rarely touched any Fey woman. He'd spent too many years living as an outcast whose touch could caused empathic women excruciating pain. Even though that was no longer the case, he'd not laid a hand so carelessly on a Fey woman in over fifteen hundred years. These last several weeks had made him forget himself.

"*Sieks'ta*. Forgive me. If you wish to leave, of course you may go. I will not try to stop you. Just remember that I am your *lu'tan*. If there is anything you need—if there is anything at all that is troubling you—you have only to tell me and I will do everything in my power to put your mind at ease."

She hesitated again. "Gaelen . . . I . . ."

The hesitation seemed to invite persuasion. He accepted with alacrity. "If it was important enough for you to come here, it must be important enough to discuss. Tell me what's wrong."

She shook her head. "It was wrong of me to come. This is my problem to solve." She clasped her hands together and began to pace. "I was being selfish even to think of it. Look at you. You have a chance for a new life. A good life. Your honor has been restored. The Fey are beginning to accept you. You have a chance to look after Marissya and watch her son grow to manhood . . . to live the life that could have been yours if the Mage Wars had never happened. I can't ask you to put all that at risk."

Then, of course, he knew. How could he not? He'd been waiting for it since the day she'd revealed what was killing the kitlings in the egg.

"You want me to teach you to weave Azrahn."

She stopped pacing and met his eyes, her expression one of dismay and regret. "Yes."

The tairen's roar and whoosh of wings made Bel look up into the sky. His brows drew together in puzzlement at the sight of Steli flying away from Dharsa bearing Ellysetta and a warrior who looked like Gaelen on her back.

He started to turn his attention back to his training when the sight of Tealah waving at him from the observation dais stopped him. "Carry on, Fey," he commanded, and jogged over to see what she wanted.

The *shei'dalin's* face was pinched with worry. "Is Ellysetta here? Is she all right?"

"She just left. Why?" he asked. "What's happened?"

"Sareika vol Arquinas saw her running out of the Hall of Tairen, looking as if she'd seen a ghost. And she says Shei'Kess was glowing . . . the way it does after a prophecy."

Bel glanced up at the rapidly disappearing shape of Steli in the sky, and he began to run.

In the training room that Ellysetta and Gaelen had vacated, the perfectly executed patterns of Gaelen's invisibility weave dissolved, revealing the stunned face of Tael vel Eilan.

He'd followed Gaelen off the training yard, determined to be the Spirit master who won the greatest prize of the day—a blade from *Chatok* vel Serranis's own sheath. Only, instead of prized steel, Tael clutched a belly that threatened to hurl its contents at any moment.

The Feyreisa had asked Gaelen to teach her to weave the forbidden magic.

CHAPTER TWENTY-ONE

Celieria ~ Teleon

"How could I not have known?" Sol Baristani paced the parlor's stone floor. The girls had gone outside to play with their new kittens under the watchful eye of Ravel's quintet. "They are my children. How could I not have known?"

"They are both very adept at hiding their magic," Kiel

suggested. "Perhaps they learned to do it from observing the Feyreisa."

Sol shook his head. He'd never felt so dazed . . . so . . . lost. As if the foundation of his world had been suddenly upturned and he was tumbling helplessly, with no idea which way was up or down. "And Laurie—if they're right, she had magic too."

"I confess we are as surprised as you, Master Baristani," Kieran said, "though perhaps we should not be. The Feyreisa is such a marvel, it seems only natural that your family would have its own share of unexpected secrets."

"Secrets, yes, but . . . magic . . ." He shook his head. "They're my daughters—and not adopted, as Ellie was. They're my own flesh and bone. Celierian—and mortal— just like their mother and me."

"Your wife was from the north, from an area where vast amounts of very powerful magic were released during the Mage Wars. Such a great concentration of magic would not dissipate without leaving its mark—as your wife reminded us many times. Hearth witches, hedge wizards, and many far more unpleasant mutations are common in those parts."

"Yes, but—"

"We knew your wife had a fierce aversion to magic, but to have spent her whole life hiding her own magic . . . Did she never mention anything about it?"

"No. Of course not. Lillis and Lorelle must be mistaken. They were only children. Who's to say that what they remember really happened?"

"They managed to hide their own magic all their lives," Kiel reminded him. "And they did it without the magical barriers the Feyreisa had holding back her powers. Disbelieve them if it eases your fears, Master Baristani, but Kieran and I cannot. Your wife must have possessed considerable magic to have passed on so strong a gift."

"I . . ." Sol looked from one Fey to another, his heart still struggling to reject the truth while his mind began fitting together the clues he'd seen but never recognized all his life. They slid into place like the perfectly carved pieces of a wooden puzzle box. "Laurie's young sister, Bess, was winded as a child in Dolan. When she was two years old, she set the neighbors' house on fire with magic, and her parents had no choice but to take her to the woods and abandon her. Laurie never forgave her parents for that—nor ever forgot the terrible price of magic."

Kieran's expression went grim. "Lady Darramon is nearly healed. The *shei'dalins* will be returning to the Fading Lands tomorrow. I urge you to go with them. Your daughters' gifts make them a treasure many will covet—and not just the Mages."

"Even if they could live safely here," Kiel added gently to forestall any objections, "they should be trained in the use and control of their gifts. As your wife's young sister proved, wild magic can be a danger. Your daughters are already both very strong, and if their magic rises the same way it does in the Fey, they have yet to come into their full power."

Sol had denied the truth about Ellie for so long, not wanting to see it. Not wanting to accept it. He could not continue to blind himself about Lillis and Lorelle.

Nor would he continue to risk their safety—not even to honor the last wishes of his dead wife.

"*Kabei*," Kieran said when Sol nodded in defeated acquiescence. "You and the girls should pack what essentials you wish to take with you. We'll leave as soon as the *shei'dalins* finish tomorrow. The Fey will bring the rest of your belongings later." He paused, then reached out to lay a hand on Sol's arm. "You are making the right decision, Master Baristani."

Sol met his gaze. "I pray to the gods you're right."

The Fading Lands ~ Plains of Corunn

Belliard vel Jelani ran faster than he ever had. He all but flew across the rolling, grass-covered landscape. Footfalls were but brief instants of impact launching him in long airborne leaps. Air powered his steps, and the Fey skin that never broke a sweat was beaded with perspiration.

Ellysetta was heading for Fey'Bahren with Gaelen, learning to weave Azrahn. He'd reached her on a private weave, and though she didn't want to admit it at first, she'd eventually confessed the truth. She'd confronted the Eye, and it had told her that only Azrahn could save the kitlings. And Gaelen—that infuriating, rock-headed, rules-defying *rultshart!*—had agreed to teach her how to spin it!

"Are you mad?" he'd railed at her. *"Do you know what will happen if you're caught? You'll be banished! Rain will have to leave the Fading Lands with you or die from bond madness! Elly-setta, you cannot do this. Nei! It's insanity!"*

She'd cut off his weaves and refused to answer him since. Gaelen had too.

Bel contemplated calling Rain. He wanted to. As the First General of the Fading Lands, he was duty-bound to do so. But Bel was also Ellysetta's *lu'tan*, and no matter how loyal he was to Rain, his bloodsworn bond came before all others.

And, frankly, Bel was terrified of what Rain would do if he learned Gaelen was teaching Ellysetta to weave the forbidden magic.

Blood would be spilled. Gaelen's, most likely, and lots of it. Rain might even kill him, which would cast Rain down the Shadowed Path, and then where would that leave Elly-setta and the Fey?

Nei, Bel couldn't tell Rain. What he *would* do, however, was go to Fey'Bahren himself and put a stop to their insanity. Once he'd beaten Gaelen senseless and curbed Ellysetta's foolishness, *then* Bel would call Rain to come chastise his truemate and impress upon her the insupportable madness of what she'd been trying to do.

The Fading Lands ~ in the Forests Northeast of Dharsa

"Vel Jelani is heading for Fey'Bahren, but he's running too fast for our warriors to keep up. I've told our force to fall back."

Sitting on the stump of a fallen tree while he and his companions took a brief respite from their run, Tenn stared at the signet ring he'd worn as leader of the Massan for the last thousand years. A mortal might have felt satisfaction to learn that his enemy was finally making the mistake he'd been waiting for, but Tenn felt only a growing sense of doom that had begun the moment Tael, shaking and pale and clearly distraught, had come to see him.

There was no way what was coming could end well.

Not for anyone.

"Am I doing the right thing?"

Leather swished softly. Venarra came up behind him and bent over him. "You saw the vision in the Eye. You know what is at stake."

Aiyah, he had, though now he wished he hadn't looked. "I know . . . I know, but—"

"You did not initiate this weave, *shei'tan*. Do not blame yourself for its consequences. I warned her what would happen if she chose the wrong path."

Tenn frowned. He couldn't shake the sense of wrongness . . . a roiling sickness in the pit of his belly. "I keep thinking there must be another way. Vel Serranis I could never trust . . . but Belliard's honor has always been above reproach." He stood and pulled Venarra into his arms, hoping her touch would bring him a measure of peace. "I still cannot believe he would condone such evil."

"Perhaps he has not," she soothed. "Perhaps he hopes to stop them."

Tenn rested his chin on Venarra's head. He hoped Bel *was* trying to stop them—and some part of him also hoped Bel succeeded. "Do you think there's any possibility she and the Eye could be right about Azrahn being the only way to save the tairen?"

Venarra tilted her head back. *"Shei'tan."* She cupped his face in her hands. "It doesn't matter. Azrahn is the forbidden magic, tool of the Corrupter. It must never be woven, no matter the purpose. But even if that were not true," she added, "you heard what vel Serranis said. The High Mage can claim more of her soul each time she weaves Azrahn. We cannot afford to let that happen."

Tenn nodded and stared bleakly into the heavily wooded forest. Fifty Fey loyal to the Massan were following Belliard to Fey'Bahren. When they got there, they would bind vel Serranis, Belliard, and the Feyreisa until the Massan and the *Shei'dalin* arrived to Truthspeak them. If Ellysetta had indeed woven the forbidden magic, they would banish her from the Fading Lands.

What choice did they have? They'd all seen the same dread vision in Shei'Kess the day after Ellysetta's arrival in Dharsa, seen how the High Mage and the Dark God he served would use her to wipe Light from the world. So long as Ellysetta Baristani remained in the Fading Lands, she was a danger to the Fey. She'd already built a private army of bloodsworn *lu'tans*, had convinced even honorable Fey to accept the tutelage of the world's most infamous *dahl'reisen*, and now she was planning to weave the forbidden magic.

All of her actions seemed perfectly reasonable, perfectly well-intentioned, yet bit by bit, she was chipping away at the foundations of honor and sacrifice that had made the Fading Lands strong and kept the Fey holding fast to the Light. Bit by bit, she was corrupting the very people she was supposed to save—even Tael, who'd been heartbroken by his discovery.

She must be stopped. Now, before she brought the Fading Lands to ruin.

He stood up and gestured to Yulan and Nurian. Eimar was not with them. He'd become too enamored of Gaelen vel Serranis and the Feyreisa to be trusted. "We've rested long enough. If we hope to reach Fey'Bahren by morning, we need to keep going."

The Fading Lands ~ Fey'Bahren

Gaelen walked the perimeter of the Su Reisu plateav and spun a shimmering dome of five-fold magic around himself and Ellysetta.

"Why do you need those weaves if you're going to teach me using only Spirit?" Ellysetta asked.

"The silence will help you to stay focused." He tied off the last threads of his weave. "Besides, if at any time I sense you summoning Azrahn in truth, I'm hoping my five-fold weaves will keep the High Mage from Marking you, as they did the first day you met the Eye."

On the way to Fey'Bahren—even before Bel's outraged call—they'd both agreed neither would actually weave the forbidden magic during the training. Instead, Gaelen would use Spirit to show her how to summon and spin the Azrahn weaves, and she would spin Spirit back to show she understood. The solution not only protected her from receiving another Mage Mark while she learned to spin the weaves the Eye had shown her, it also shielded Gaelen from the Massan's wrath in the event they discovered what she and Gaelen were up to.

She wanted to know the weaves, to know that she could spin them, before she revealed her plans to Rain. They would decide what to do next together, because she was through making decisions for him. Especially such dangerous ones as this.

"No protection in the world will be enough when you spin the weaves for real," Gaelen reminded her again. "You bear the High Mage's Marks. You'll be weaving Azrahn long enough for him to sense it and gain access to your soul. He'll Mark you again. There's no avoiding it. You do realize that."

She nodded grimly. She knew. The Eye had shown her what would happen. "This is the kitlings' only chance. The healing weaves aren't enough."

His ice blue eyes met hers for one piercing moment; then he nodded. "*Bas'ka*, then have a seat and open your mind to me. My Spirit weaves need to feel as close to the reality of summoning and weaving Azrahn as possible, which means I need control of your thoughts and senses."

Drawing a deep breath, Ellysetta sat down on the hard, rocky surface of Su Reisu and tore down the strong barriers that encircled her mind. "I am ready. Show me the weaves."

Gaelen sat before her, legs crossed, his hands covering hers in skin-to-skin contact. Spirit gathered and swirled around him in lavender flows. The weave enveloped her, and with a silent whoosh, Gaelen's magic sank into her skin, and his consciousness joined her own in a way she'd never trusted the *shei'dalins* enough to allow.

"*Azrahn exists in us all,*" he whispered in her mind. "*It is the soul magic, the Unmaker, the source and the destruction of all life's essence. It is a power far greater than the Fey allow themselves to wield. It is not, as the Fey believe, inherently evil, but it is beyond a doubt the most dangerous magic there is.*"

"*I understand,*" she assured him.

"*Then let us begin.*"

Celieria ~ Orest

Rain stood on the battlements of Upper Orest, looking northward across the falls of Maiden's Gate and the Heras River into Eld. A grayish haze hung over the dark-forested land of his enemies. The cooler months of fall always covered Eld in rain and mist, but the sight still made him uneasy. The last time he'd seen Eld, it had been shrouded in a similar gray haze, only weather hadn't been to blame. The fires of Koderas—the great *sel'dor* forge of the Eld—had belched smoke into the air day and night as the Eld war machine churned out weapons and armor for its soldiers and allies.

He sniffed the air. The breeze carried no hint of smoke, but he still couldn't shake the sense of unease. His tairen instincts were roused. He could feel its claws unsheathing inside him, digging deep in preparation for attack.

"Ellysetta . . ." He spun her name on a thread of Spirit. They'd spoken last night, but he needed to hear her voice again.

When she didn't answer, he frowned and called her on their bond threads, but she still didn't respond. Growing concerned, Rain sent a private weave to Bel. *"Bel? I cannot reach Ellysetta."*

There was a silence. Then, *"Ellysetta's in Fey'Bahren, Rain."*

Hope flickered in Rain's breast. *"She has found a way to save the kits?"*

There was another silence, longer this time. *"She thinks she has."*

Rain closed his eyes in relief. It was the best news he'd heard in days. *"Thank the gods. What is it? Some long-forgotten healing weave? How did she find it?"* Bel's third long silence made Rain frown. *"Bel?"* he prodded.

The Fading Lands ~ The Feyls

Rain raced across the peaks of the Feyls like a dark comet streaking against the twilight sky. He flew parallel to the northern section of the Faering Mists, careful to avoid dipping even a wing tip into the radiant cloud of magic.

The Mists had challenged him again when he'd flown through over the Veil, but this time he'd been in no mood to stand for their torment. After a brief, unpleasant few chimes, he'd answered the challenge the way any aggravated tairen would: with a blast of tairen fire. The spirits in the Mists had gone silent then. Perhaps because they'd realized that if they'd tried to stop him, he would have scorched them out of existence. Whether a single Tairen Soul could destroy the Faering Mists was not at all certain, but if they'd continued to stand in his way, he would have found out.

Screaming ropes of Spirit shot out ahead of him, calling to Ellysetta on their private path. When she did not answer, he nearly set the threads of their bond afire with his furious shout. *Ellysetta! By the gods, you will answer me now!*

At last, she did, and her voice sounded hesitant. Startled. *Rain, beloved, what is it?*

Fire exploded from his muzzle. *You are weaving Azrahn? You would do that to us? To me?*

Shock rippled across their bond. And guilt. *How did you kn—* Her voice broke off. *Bel.*

He didn't bother to confirm it. *You will stop this madness immediately! I'm coming to Fey'Bahren. If Gaelen is still there when I arrive, I will kill him.*

Rain! Wait! It's not what you think. I'm not weaving Azrahn. I wouldn't do that to you. I learned my lesson at Chakai. What choices we make, we make together, shei'tan. Please, you've got to believe me. I'm only—

Whatever else she had to say was lost when he cut the connection of their bond threads. He powered the energy of his Rage into his flight, and he raced across the sky faster than he ever had before.

It was full night when he reached Fey'Bahren, and the campfire on Su Reisu shone like a beacon in the night, illuminating the slender figure of Ellysetta and the tall, dark warrior in her company.

Vel Serranis.

Rain's wings tucked in tight. He put on a last, powerful burst of speed and shot towards the ground like a meteor.

Ellysetta must have sensed both his presence and his intent, because she leapt in front of vel Serranis and flung her arms out protectively. "Rain, wait!"

He didn't slow a bit. He simply Changed. The rainbow mist of his magic swept over Ellysetta and Gaelen like a hard wind and gathered together into his Fey body behind them. He hit the ground in a tucked roll and came up in attack stance, teeth bared and snarling.

"Rain!" Ellysetta cried again. "It's not what you think!"

He shoved her back with a puff of Air and bound her in place with a five-fold weave. To Gaelen, he growled, "Defend yourself," just before his fist shot out, plowing into the underside of Gaelen's jaw. Vel Serranis went flying. Rain leapt on him and began pummeling.

The fight didn't last long. Rain had not spent those weeks of training under Gaelen's tutelage without learning a great deal about how the other Fey fought and how best to defeat him. And Gaelen, cocky *rultshart* though he was, knew he had it coming. When vel Serranis was groaning and breathless and his pretty face was sufficiently bruised and bloodied, Rain shoved him aside, got to his feet, and released Ellysetta from his weave.

"We weren't weaving Azrahn, Rain," Ellysetta protested. "We only used Spirit. I wouldn't make a choice so grave without you."

"I know." He wiped a trickle of blood from the corner of his mouth with the back of one hand. "I realized the truth not long after we spoke. You asked me to believe you. Once I shook off the worst of my Rage, I realized you were right. I did need to believe you, to trust that you would never intentionally bring us to harm. Then I realized what Bel believed had to be wrong. That there had to be some other explanation."

Her jaw dropped. "Then why . . . ?" She gestured to Gaelen, who had rolled into a sitting position and was massaging his dislocated jaw.

"Because he deserved it." Rain nudged Gaelen's thigh

with the toe of his boot. "You need to accept the laws of this pride, vel Serranis. You may be her *lu'tan*, but I am her mate. Endanger her again—even by her command—and you will answer to me."

Gaelen held his gaze for a long moment, then laughed, spat a mouthful of blood, and nodded. "Accepted."

"*Kabei.*" Rain turned his complete attention back to Ellysetta. "And now, *shei'tani*, you can explain to me just *what in the jaffing fires of the Seven Hells you were thinking?*"

She flinched at the bottled fury that turned each word into a whip of flame, but she stood her ground. "I know how to save the tairen, Rain, but I have to weave Azrahn to do it."

CHAPTER TWENTY-TWO

Tairen heart and tairen soul will face the night as one.
The strength of two in tairen love can never be undone.
Light up the sky with tairen flame, and hear the tairen
*   song.*
It sings of hope and life to come where tairen souls
*   belong.*

    From "Tairen Song," a ballad by Merik vel Sejan,
                                        Tairen Soul

The Fading Lands ~ Fey'Bahren

Rain wrapped his arms around Ellysetta, holding her even as her arms extended to the nearest tairen egg. He wanted to snatch her back, out of the path of danger. What was he thinking even to consider this? She was his *shei'tani*, his truemate, the one being he must protect at all cost—even if that cost was the life of every tairen and Fey who still walked the earth.

"Ellysetta . . ." *Forgive me, Sybharukai.* "What if the Eye was wrong? You aren't a trained seer. You could easily have misunderstood its message."

"I didn't misunderstand."

He shook his head, afraid for her, desperate to stop her. "*Nei*, I've changed my mind. This is too dangerous." He brought her hand to his lips and pressed a kiss into her palm. "No Fey would ever ask such a sacrifice of you."

She laid her free hand over his. "But the Fey haven't asked it of me, Rain. The gods have." She feathered her fingers across his skin. "*For every great gift, shei'tan, there is a great price.*"

"This price is too great."

She forced a wobbly smile. "One more Mark isn't so much to save the world." When his eyes continued to bore into her, burning with despair, her smile faded into somberness. "I have to try. And you have to let me. If I don't do this, the tairen will die. Marissya's child will die. And so will all the Fey. If I don't do this . . . if I don't stop the High Mage now . . . it will be too late for all of us."

"Ellysetta—"

"These are not just tairen, Rain. These are the brothers and sisters of the tairen tied to my soul. They are . . . my family." She drew him close and pressed her lips to his throat. She was acting far braver and more certain than she felt, and she wanted him to know that. "*Sieks'ta*, I am bullying you, and I should not. This choice is one we must make together. I won't make it for us. I've done enough of that already. *Ku'shalah aiyah to nei, shei'tan.* Bid me yes or no. And know that if your choice is *nei*, I will accept it and walk away."

"And the world of the Fey will die."

"*Aiyah.*"

He closed his eyes and bent his head, touching his forehead

to hers. "I am afraid," he whispered. "Afraid with a fear I would never feel for myself."

Tears gathered in her eyes. She blinked them back. "I know."

His lips slanted over hers in a fierce, passionate kiss. His breath, his essence, poured into her, while his arms wrapped her tight and held her close. *"Ver reisa ku'chae. Kem surah, shei'tani."*

"Ke vo san, shei'tan."

He drew back briefly, then returned for several more kisses before he nodded and stepped away. *"Aiyah.* Though it's like stabbing a *lute'cha* into my own heart, my answer is *aiyah.* Do what you must. But just this once, beloved. Just this once to save the ones we love."

"Just this once," she agreed. She knew how difficult it was for him to let her proceed. She could feel the fear, the desperate need to protect her battering his will. If the tairen's plight were any less dire, he would have refused and let the gods and the Eld determine which kitling lived or died.

Sybharukai approached, her paws silent on the sands, her sleek body regal and purposeful. *"Be brave, Ellysetta-makai."* The shimmering music of the *makai's* voice sounded in every cell of Ellie's body, pure and beautiful, ancient and wise. *"Your mate offers you his strength, and I offer you the strength of the pride. You do not face this evil alone."* Sybharukai bent her head and opened her mouth. Tairen's Eye crystals dropped to the sands, several dozen of them, large and gleaming with bright rainbow lights in a matrix of deepest ruby. *"You have not found your song, but these are crystals carved from the kiyranis of my most powerful ancestors. Use them. Let their magic supplement and focus your own."*

Ellysetta gathered the stones, and Rain spun them into a golden necklace that he set around her throat. The *kiyr* were powerful indeed. The moment they touched her skin, their energy amplified hers. Her body tingled, and the heavy, curling mass of her hair crackled with energy.

She turned and approached the eggs. Her heart was pounding like a wild drum in her chest, and her throat felt tight and dry, as if all moisture in her body had been sucked away. *Please, gods, if you listen to me at all, listen to me now. Please let this work. Please help me save them. Don't let me fail.*

The weaves the Eye had revealed weren't all that different from some of the more advanced healing weaves the *shei'dalins* had shown her this week as they'd sought ways to save the tairen. But where healing was fragrant and warm, Azrahn had a sickly sweet odor and froze the blood in her veins. Even the illusion of it during practice had made her feel ill, which just went to show what a master of Spirit Gaelen was and how intimately he'd come to know the effects of weaving Azrahn.

She now knew, thanks to Gaelen's detailed instruction, exactly where to find the source of Azrahn within herself, how to summon it, how to feed the power into the patterns the Eye of Truth had shown her.

This time, however, the Azrahn she spun would be real, not illusion.

She drew a breath and steadied her nerves before taking the last, resolute steps towards the waiting eggs. Time to do what she'd come for.

She nodded to Rain. He raised his hands and spun a five-fold protection weave around her. It was a fool's hope—she already knew she would not survive this night without another Mark—but he had insisted on weaving what protection he could.

"Sing to them, please, Sybharukai."

Instantly, the vibrant beauty of the great *makai*'s song filled the cavern, swirling around the eggs in flashes of gold and silver. Within their shells, the hatchlings began to croon along with their grandmother's melody. The rest of the pride and Rain joined in, filling the air with magic.

In the deliberate calm of her mind, Ellysetta anchored herself as Venarra had taught her, forming the small partition in her mind, securing the heart of her essence within: the safety valve that would cut her off from her weaves before she lost herself in her healing.

Then she began to weave.

She summoned the elements first, spinning the threads into the patterns the *shei'dalins* had taught her to encourage the growth of flesh and bone. The kitlings wiggled and stretched in their eggs and chortled with little chuffs of laughter, as if the warm weaves tickled them.

Into the warm, healing weave, Ellysetta added the first cool thread of Azrahn.

The kitlings' songs and laughter turned to whimpers of distress. The tiny bodies that had wriggled against the confines of their shells now shrank and shivered in fear.

"Nei, little kits," she crooned, adding her voice to the songs of the pride. *"It's me, sweetlings. Ellysetta. Don't be afraid."*

But even as she coaxed them, she felt the flutter of something dark and dangerous. Something roused by her thread of Azrahn.

Frightened, she started to pull back, but the whimpers of the kitlings made her stop. She was their only hope. She could not abandon them. And these were the patterns the Eye had shown her she must weave.

Gritting her teeth, she spun another thread of Azrahn and added it to the mix, then another and another, weaving the chilly, rippling threads of red-tinged darkness into the shining mix of healing magic.

Eld ~ Boura Fell

In the chambers of the Mage Council, the High Mage and Eld's most powerful Primages were meeting to discuss the final preparations for war. Vadim Maur stood before the map of Eloran's largest continent, where their first targets had already been decided.

"The troops are ready, Most High." Primage Sib Vargus bowed to his superior. "Give the word and they will enter the Well."

Vadim Maur opened his mouth to utter the command, but before he could speak, a wholly unexpected, wholly familiar tingle of powerful magic swept over him. He grabbed the edges of the map table to keep himself steady and closed his eyes in a shudder of delight.

Ellysetta Baristani was weaving Azrahn. Sweet, powerful, glorious Azrahn.

It sang across his veins, resonating with incredible vitality and power. Even here, half a world away, he could feel the enormous wellspring of her potential. Her mastery of the great power was sublime—such fine weaves. Such innate comprehension and prodigal talent.

His for the claiming.

He struck, swift and hard, lashing out across the connection of her existing two Marks with a brutal whip of power and a triumphant salutation. *"Hello, girl."*

The Fading Lands ~ Fey'Bahren

Even knowing it was coming—even expecting the pain and despair of it—Ellysetta still screamed and fell to her knees when the High Mage's power stabbed deep into her breast and pierced her heart. Ice gripped her in a paralyzing embrace. Her vision went black, and in the darkness she saw the twin bloody moons of glowing ember eyes, heard the familiar taunting voice of her enemy. *"Hello, girl."*

There was no point in fighting. She'd spun the forbidden magic, knowing it would open her soul to him. Just as it had that day in Celieria's cathedral.

This time, she let the power wash over her and accepted the Mage's gloating triumph without resistance. She let it stab her, freeze her, bind her.

Then she crawled back to her feet and continued to weave.

The Mage's consciousness flickered with surprise. He was linked to her through his three Marks and the power she was wielding. He knew she was still weaving. *What are you doing, girl?* She felt the cold, probing fingers reaching into her soul, prying at her mind in an effort to read her intentions, looking for some clue that would tell him where she was and what she was up to. She clenched her teeth and tried to block him out, all the while continuing to spin the forbidden magic.

Her whole body was shivering now, her mouth filled with gagging sweetness. A third shadowy Mark had joined the first two on her left breast, and the dark trio throbbed in time with her pulse, like knives of ice thrust into her heart, vibrating with every rhythmic beat.

Rain, in tairen form, continued to sing to the kits. He didn't try to connect to her through the threads of their truemate bond. She'd made him swear he wouldn't do that while she wove the dark magic, afraid the Mage would be able to use her as a tool to Mark him. But she could still sense his fear and horror. He sang strength and reassurance to the kits, but for himself and her he had none. His tairen claws dug deep into the sand, and his tail whipped against the rock walls of the cavern in helpless distress.

Ellysetta forced herself to block out his emotions and the cries of the kits so she could concentrate on her weaves. There was no room for mistakes or wild, instinctive, uncontrollable magic. As Gaelen had impressed upon her again and again during their bells of practice, Azrahn was too dangerous a magic to allow even the tiniest lapse of control.

She drew upon the discipline Venarra and Jaren had drilled into her, keeping her mind focused and her weaves steady and strong, using the power of the Tairen's Eye crystals around her neck and waist and wrist to amplify and concentrate her magic.

She went from egg to egg, spinning Azrahn, carefully weaving the threads down the invisible, spider-silk-thin connections that tied the egg-bound kitlings to the Well of Souls. She used those threads as the conduit through which she fed her Azrahn-enhanced healing weaves.

The High Mage sensed what she was doing. His glacial anger washed over her. *Foolish girl. You are tampering with powers you do not understand.*

Eld ~ Boura Fell

Vadim Maur shoved back from the map table. She dared? The *umagi* he had created—the creature whose extraordinary powers he had engineered for his own greatness—dared use those gifts to challenge her master?

The room was silent and icy. The Primages were staring at him, expressionless and watchful. His brows plummeted, and the temperature in the room fell further.

If that troublesome little *petchka* thought she could best the High Mage of Eld, she had a harsh lesson to learn.

"Order your commanders to assemble their troops. If I'm not back within four bells, send the armies into the Well."

He turned and stalked out of the room and down the corridor to his personal chambers.

"Master Maur!" The *umagi* who tended his personal affairs leapt to his feet when Vadim stormed in.

"Fetch Tailinn," he snapped, referring to the third near-term pregnant woman awaiting her child's gift from the Well. "No, wait, fetch her and the other three who are closest to term. I want them all in the birthing chamber in half a bell!" Each word cracked with ice.

The servant bowed and scraped and nearly fell over himself rushing for the door. "Of course, great one. Immediately."

Ellysetta Baristani thought she would rob him of his Tairen Souls? She would regret her impudence. Purple robes swirled as Vadim stormed into his office and headed for the chamber where he kept his most precious implements of power, including the two remaining needles that held Ellysetta Baristani's blood.

The Fading Lands ~ Fey'Bahren

Ellysetta lost track of time. Enveloped in a cocoon of swirling magic, she sent wave after wave of healing and strength down the silk-thin threads of Azrahn into the Well of Souls, feeding that power to the kitlings' souls.

Their initial, whimpering fear had faded when they'd realized Ellysetta's magic was not the dark evil that hunted and hurt them. As she'd continued to spin and sing to them, they'd begun to sing back.

Slowly, almost imperceptibly, the kitlings' faint voices grew stronger.

Sybharukai crooned encouragement. Steli purred and nudged Ellysetta's body with her head. *"Your magic is working, kitling."*

Eld ~ Boura Fell

The four pregnant woman were strapped, unconscious, to the birthing tables. Vadim had not planned to attempt soul-binding Tailinn's child until the Mother went new again and his powers reached their next peak, but he could not afford to wait. Nor had he ever attempted to bind more than one soul in a night, but he'd be damned before he'd let Ellysetta Baristani rob him of the great prizes he'd spent months preparing to harvest.

Vadim snapped his fingers, and one of the servants offered him a crystal goblet. He lifted the cup and drained it dry. The dark red potion carried the metallic tang of blood from Tailinn and the other women, mixed with a heavy dose of several magical herbs, and powdered *selkhar* crystal.

When the tingle of the potent blood magic spread through his system, he raised his beringed hands and began the invocation of his most useful and grudging servant. "Choutarre, Soul Taker, in the name of Seledorn, Prince of Shadows, I summon thee. Choutarre, Soul Taker, in the name of Seledorn, Lord of Demons, I bind thee. Choutarre, Soul Taker, in the name of Seledorn, God of Darkness, I command thee to serve as hand of my power and executor of my will."

An icy breeze swirled through the chamber, blowing back Vadim's hair and the folds of his purple velvet robes. A voice like bones grating on stone hissed, *How shall I serve thee?*

Vadim shaped his command in flows of dark, ineluctable power. "Bring me the souls I seek."

The Fading Lands ~ Fey'Bahren

The kitlings fell silent.

Concerned, Ellysetta summoned Fey vision to examine the eggs. Concern spiked to alarm. The shining light of the kitlings, so bright just moments before, had gone out. The eggs appeared empty, with naught but a blank void inside each shell, just as they had the first time she'd come and again the night Forrahl had died.

Then she heard the whispers, the voices.

"Oh, no. Not now. *Teska, sallan,* don't let this happen." Desperately, she sent a bolus of power down her weaves, hoping she could hurry the healing.

The tairen began to growl. Sybharukai's tail spikes extended in unspoken menace.

He's coming for the kits. Rain's Spirit voice was heavy with certainty.

"*Aiyah.*" Fear made her concentration wobble as something cold and dark brushed against her weaves. The tairen kitlings began to whimper anew. She shivered, and her knees went weak. She clutched the nearest egg to keep herself upright. "But it's not him. It's the other thing . . . whatever he's using to steal their souls. A demon of some kind, or a soul doing his bidding. I don't know."

She flinched as the thing brushed against her weaves again. The sensation was too vivid, too reminiscent of the horrifying nightmares she'd suffered all her life. Like rats sliding past her ankles or ice spiders crawling up her spine. Her tairen began to growl and claw at its bindings.

«Ellysetta, come away. Do not endanger yourself any further.»

"I can't leave the kitlings to die." Whatever it was, the thing had negated the power of her healing weaves. Worse, she could feel it draining the kitlings' strength, ruining the hard-won progress of the last bells. "I've got to do this, Rain. There is no one else who can. This is why the Eye sent you to find me."

«Was this part of what the Eye said you must do?»

She bit her lip. There'd been nothing in the Eye's vision beyond the weaves she'd already spun. Now she must fight without any idea of what pattern to weave. "*Nei*, but it makes no difference. If I don't stop this attack, the kitlings will die. I will have let the Mage Mark me for nothing."

Familiar power swelled, and the sparkling mist of the Change billowed around Rain's tairen form. Even before it cleared, Rain the Fey was striding across the sands of the lair to her side, his eyes glowing bright, his face pale and strained.

"*Nei, shei'tani.*" He dissolved the five-fold weave around her and grabbed her shoulders. Intense emotions barraged her senses. "Listen to me. Mage or demon, this thing never takes more than one kitling when it comes. That's how it has always been. Let it have that life; then, when it is gone, you can resume the healing the Eye showed you."

He was terrified beyond reason, else he would never consider the sacrifice of an innocent an acceptable price for victory. And that fear told her more than words ever could how deeply and desperately he loved her.

"Rain." She caught his face in her hands. "I can't. You know I can't. If these were our children, would you stand by and watch one of them die so you could be assured of saving the others? Or would you move the very heavens and the earth to try to save them all?"

He brushed that argument aside with a growl. "I would face a thousand deaths to save them. But you're not asking me to risk my own life. You're asking me to risk yours."

"Yes, I am." She pressed her lips to his, kissing him, loving him. "You say you must become worthy of my bond. But if I let even one of these babies die without a fight, how will *I* ever become worthy of *yours*?"

"Do you think I care about our bond more than your life?" he countered. "I will gladly die if it means you may live."

She clutched him to her, threading her fingers through his hair, holding him as if the sheer strength of her embrace could complete the merging of their souls. "And do you truly think there's any hope for me if I lose you?" Gently, she pulled back to meet his gaze. "Without you, I will choose *sheisan'dahlein* just to be sure the prophecy of the Eye can never come true. I've already asked Steli to see to it."

"*Shei'tani . . .*" His expression crumpled.

"I must do this, Rain. Tairen do not abandon their kits. Tairen defend the pride."

Tears shimmered in his eyes. He closed them and touched his forehead to hers in defeat. *"Aiyah."*

That one word of acquiescence, wrenched by love from a heart drowning in fear, made her love him more than she ever had. She smoothed her thumbs across the warm silk of his skin. "If love were power enough, *shei'tan*, our truemate bond would be complete a thousand times over." Her lips curved in a trembling smile. "You bring pride to this Fey."

His arms closed tight around her, and his mouth claimed hers in a final, passionate kiss. *"Ver reisa ku'chae, Ellysetta. Kem surah."* When at last he let her go, he stepped back a pace, and grim determination settled over his features. "But if this must be done, *shei'tani*, we will do it together." He removed the Soul Quest crystal from around his neck and settled it in place around hers. "You will use my strength and everything I can give you."

"Rain, *nei*. If the High Mage can use me to Mark you—"

He pressed a finger to her lips. "Then it will be no more than you accepted as the price to save the tairen. If you can live with three Marks, I can surely live with one."

"Rain . . ."

"If these were our children, would you want me to stand by and do nothing while you risked your life to save them?"

She had no more defense against that argument than he had.

He turned to the pride's *makai*. "Sybharukai, if anything happens to Ellysetta, promise you will not let me fly." His lids narrowed over eyes gone abruptly savage. "And if this Mage succeeds in stealing the young, promise you will scorch Eld to a barren wasteland."

The gray tairen growled her assent. *"It will be done, Rainier-Eras."*

Eld ~ Boura Fell

Shan leaned his head back against the *sel'dor*-lined rock wall of his prison, welcoming the familiar searing burn. Over the years, the pain had become almost a comfort. His eyes closed. Weariness and despair crowded his heart. Hope was a thing long lost.

"He has Marked her, shei'tani. She is weaving Azrahn and he Marked her again."

In the darkness behind his lids, he summoned the image of his beloved, the sweet fire of her hair, the shining brightness of her golden eyes, so that when her answer came it was as if she were here with him, standing before him, the only light left in his world.

"She spins the forbidden magic on purpose? The Fey would never allow it."

"She tries to save the tairen. The Mage is stealing their souls." That much he'd gleaned from the link that had tied part of Shan's soul to Ellysetta's since before her birth. *"She fights him now."*

"She cannot defeat him alone."

"I know."

"We must help her."

"Maur is there in the Well. He will sense our presence, just as he did when we came to her aid before." Shan's bones were barely knitted from the price he'd paid for that effort, and Elfeya's nightmares over what the Mage had done to her still woke both of them in a cold sweat each night.

"We still must help her."

Shan hung his head, resting his chin on his chest. He had expected no other answer. *"I know."*

"Then show me her weaves, shei'tan, and be my bridge to her soul."

The Fading Lands ~ Fey'Bahren

Ellysetta gathered the strength of Rain and the tairen and fed their power into her weaves along with more power of her own. For a moment, the healing threads lit up like ropes of sunlight. For a moment, the darkness retreated. But then, just as quickly, the light was leached away.

The kitlings cried out in desperate fear, singing the bright word of her name like a talisman and a prayer. Their trust stabbed her heart as their frightened minds reached out to her the way a fearful child's fingers clutched at his mother's skirts.

With a sob, she sent another blast of power down her weaves, brightness to hold off the dark, but just as before, after a brief flaring moment of hope, shadow consumed the light.

The weaves the Eye had shown her were not powerful enough. She tried to strengthen them with song, pouring love into every word. She spun every healing weave she knew. And still nothing worked. Her Azrahn-enhanced weaves might have been enough to save the kits before the Mage loosed his soul-stealer upon them, but now the battle had changed. She wasn't just trying to draw the kits from the Well, she was fighting to keep something from pulling them back in.

The kitlings were dying. Connected as she was with her weaves, she could feel them slipping away, not just one or two but all of them. Their bodies were perfectly healthy, yet slowly, their sweet voices and the brightness of their souls were fading.

You are a shei'dalin. *Hold them to the Light.*

The thought blossomed in her mind, filled with urgent conviction. She needed to spin a *shei'dalin's* healing weave, the kind Venarra had used to hold that dying woman's soul to life. Venarra hadn't taught her the patterns yet, but her mind must have instinctively recorded them, because the knowledge was there, as if she'd spun those weaves a thousand times.

Adelis, Bright One, Lord of Light, please, teska, *help me. Guide me. Do not let me fail.* The gods had answered her prayers in the past, working their miracles through her instinctive, untutored magic. She prayed they would help her again now.

She forced herself to block out the pitiful cries of the baby tairen and surrendered to the crooning, powerful song of the tairen. It flowed over and through her, carrying away her fear and doubt. Her hands unclenched. Her muscles relaxed. Her breathing became deep and even. She was a well of calm, and into that well her consciousness dove deep.

The source of her power lay far within her, shining

bright as the sun, more white than gold, dazzling with the strength of her *shei'dalin*'s love. She absorbed the power into her consciousness until every thought blazed with magical resonance. Then, when she could hold no more, she sent her spirit, the living essence of her soul, out of her own body and into the small bodies of the tairen kitlings, just as the *shei'dalins* sent themselves into the body of another when they needed to perform great healing.

Follow your weaves into the Well.

As if guided by the invisible hands of the gods, she found the humming threads of her healing weaves inside the kits and followed them, leaving the gleaming radiance of the world and descending into the dark realm of souls.

Light was extinguished. The abrupt darkness alarmed her. Had she fallen for one of the Mage's traps?

She reached instinctively for Rain across the threads of their bond. *"Rain . . ."*

"I am here, beloved." His voice returned, a deep baritone, steady and reassuring. He was there with her in the darkness, just as he'd been with her in the blinding gray-white of the Mists. He would always be there with her.

The brief moment of doubt and fear passed, and her confidence surged anew. As long as Rain was with her, she was strong.

She traced the threads of her weave as a miner lost in the impenetrable blackness of a cave might follow a rope to guide himself back to the surface, only she followed to go deeper into the mine. Finally, after a seemingly endless plunge into dark, light reappeared. First came soft glimmers of red, then dim, faint glows of a brighter hue that, as she drew nearer, became small orbs of rainbow-hued light, flickering uncertainly. The kitlings.

And with them, the enemy she'd come to fight.

A nearly invisible, shifting darkness that merged into the surrounding black of the Well. Nothing as substantial as smoke, but rather an oily void that moved as if it were alive.

From it flowed countless tiny threads, like black spider silk, attached to the kitlings' souls, sucking at them like so many leeches, draining away their brightness.

She lashed at the dark threads, tearing them away from the unwilling hosts.

"Get away from them! Leave them alone."

The threads reared back, writhing blindly. A handful of them latched onto her. She ripped them away, only to find a dozen more reaching out to replace them. Everywhere they touched, her brightness dimmed, as if the hungry mouths were draining her soul too.

"Ellysetta!" Rain cried. A surge of power raced through her, filling her with the bright, powerful, blazing light of his love.

The black thing shrank back, its silken threads releasing her as if burned.

Yes. Yes, that's it, ajiana. *No darkness, no matter how deep, holds dominion over Light. Shine your Light, Ellysetta. Weave your love.*

The voice spoke with quiet certainty, reaffirming her strength. She could do this. She had the power. The gods had chosen her to do it.

She drew upon her magic, upon Rain's fiercely shining brightness, upon the strength of the tairen concentrated in the crystals she held and the song that swirled around her. It still wasn't enough. Too much of her own strength was tethered to that safety anchor she'd prepared, and the magic she needed to weave now demanded everything she had to give.

She released her anchor, gathering that magic into herself as well, summoning every bit of power from every source she could find. She spun it into threads, glowing, golden-white *shei'dalin's* love, burning bright as the Great Sun, and with it shadowy Azrahn, dark as the ember of a dead star. The new pattern both fed strength into the kits and began to shear away those feeding mouths from the Well.

As each dark strand withered and fell away, the kitlings' light shone brighter.

She kept feeding power into her weave, drawing upon Rain, the tairen, and the seemingly limitless source of confidence and love she'd found so unexpectedly here in the Well. Her Azrahn and *shei'dalin's* love were so tightly interwoven, the threads became a single melded rope. Light and dark strobed in rhythm like blood flowing through the life-giving arteries of a god. The light was stronger than the dark. Its radiant glow brightened the shadows, each pulse more brilliant than the last, until no hint of red-tinged black nor even sickly gray shone in the incandescent threads of her weave.

She spun that life, that love, and that fierce strength into the kits' souls, pouring it out upon them as the Source of Dharsa poured its waters upon the fountains and streams of the city, giving them everything, holding back nothing for herself.

The kitlings' voices grew louder, surer. The timid, hesitant glimmers of their song became shining stars of gold and silver light, a river of sparkling brightness that illuminated the Well as it spiraled upwards.

"*Go, dearlings,*" Ellysetta urged. "*Go.*" She gave them each a gentle nudge with sun-bright hands. The shining orbs that were the kitlings' souls shifted, spreading, stretching out small limbs and wings to become small, dazzling glows of tairen-shaped light. They soared upwards, following the river of song out of the Well.

Vadim Maur roared as he felt the bright souls of the tairen escaping from Choutarre's grip. Bitter rage and reckless fury warred inside him. He plunged the exorcism needle filled with Ellysetta's blood into his own vein and whispered the release spell. The searing rush of her powerful blood mingled with his own. His senses and his connection to her sharpened.

For the second time that night, he struck.

Ellysetta shrieked as the Mage's dark power drove a new blade of ice into her heart.

Her light shattered, and the Well was plunged into darkness.

Dimly she heard Rain calling her name, but the sound was muffled and so far away. Weariness enveloped her. She was so tired, her strength depleted. She'd given everything she had to the kitlings, keeping precious little for herself, and the fourth Mark that now bloomed on her breast had drained what Light yet remained.

In the darkness and silence, she could hear the voices, the whispers, calling her name as they had at the peak of the Fire Song. The urge to let go was nearly overpowering. She was so tired, and somehow the voices didn't seem so frightening anymore. Now, they seemed only welcoming.

"Ellysetta!" Rain's voice boomed in the silence of the Well. The threads of their bond blazed with sudden incandescence as the vast, immeasurable force of his power sizzled down them, as strong and vibrant as *faerilas* from Dharsa's Source, shocking her back to alertness.

Rain, her mate. Rain, her love.

Rain, who was weaving black Azrahn in a desperate bid to free her from the Well.

A sudden surge of dark power exploded in the Well. The High Mage, who had baited his trap and waited, now struck in earnest. His magic plunged like a dagger into Rain's weave.

"No!" she screamed in horror. *"Shei'tan!"*

The next thing Ellysetta knew, she was lying on the hot sands of the nesting lair, staring up into the savage blaze of lavender eyes. Rain snatched her up, hauling her into his arms, holding her so tight she could scarcely breathe.

"*Beylah sallan. Beylah sallan.*" His voice cracked. "I thought I'd lost you, *shei'tani.*"

Terrified on his behalf, she pushed against him and tore open his tunic with a sharp weave of Earth, baring the smooth paleness of his chest. She summoned a flicker of Azrahn, then promptly extinguished it after a brief gasp of disbelief. Rain's chest was luminous and Fey pale, without the slightest smudge of a Mage Mark upon it.

"I don't understand." Her shaking fingers trembled against his flesh. "You wove Azrahn. I saw him strike you. I felt it. Yet you are unmarked."

Rain clasped her hand to his breast and gave a sound that was half laugh, half sob. "How could he lay claim to a soul that already belongs utterly to you? There is nothing I would not give, no part of me I would not sacrifice, no law I would not break if it meant keeping you from harm. *Kem'reisa sha ver.* My soul is yours. Do with it what you will."

She felt her own soul unfurl like a flower blossoming in the sun as a brilliant new bond thread spun from her deepest being to his. Glorious and golden-white, a thread of purest *shei'dalin*'s love, a bond of truth and trust she knew would never be broken. She flung her arms around his neck, pulling him close. She wept as her lips found his, claiming his mouth as she had claimed his heart and soul.

Behind them, around them, the pride began to hum, and a rich, bright melody of tairen song flowed out into the nesting lair.

Ellysetta and Rain turned. The four eggs were rocking, tears appearing in the hardened leathery hides as razor-sharp claws poked through. Tiny muzzles, filled with egg teeth, poked through the holes, gnawing at the edges to make them larger.

Four damp, fuzzy little heads poked through, glowing, jewel-toned eyes whirling star-bright. The leathery eggs stretched and shredded. Wriggling and squirming, the kitlings clawed their way to freedom, until all four small bodies tumbled out and lay panting on the sands, mewing, trembling with exhaustion. Their damp wings fluttered.

Sybharukai bent her head to lick each of the kitlings dry, purring deep in her throat. The kitlings closed their eyes in bliss and tilted up their small heads, bodies quivering with their happy, answering purrs.

"Oh, Rain." Ellysetta held him tight, her eyes filled with happy tears.

"You did it, *shei'tani*."

She shook her head. "*Nei. We* did it, *shei'tan*. You and I."

CHAPTER TWENTY-THREE

I san, sheisan, te Liss!
For love, honor, and Light!

Fey Battle Cry

Eld ~ Boura Fell

Vadim Maur knew from his *umagis'* wide eyes and frightened silence that this trip to the Well and his reckless, overreaching attempt to deliver three Mage Marks in one night had cost him dearly. He knew it even before enough sensation returned to his body that he could feel how his legs had turned to rubber beneath him. The bony hands clutching the sides of the birthing table had turned bloodless white, the tissue beneath his yellowed nails had gone a dark, bruised purple.

"Help me to a chair." His words sounded garbled, and his tongue felt thick in his mouth.

Two of the *umagi* rushed forward to put their shoulders beneath his arms, carrying his weight as his feet half shuffled, half dragged across the floor to a chaise in an adjoining room.

Not a single tairen's soul had been claimed. Every one of them was lost. Set free by Ellysetta Baristani's use of the great magic he had bestowed upon her. The very magic that he'd intended to claim for himself, to make himself a living god—powerful beyond measure, invincible.

Immortal.

He closed his eyes with effort and sucked in a rattling breath. Bloody froth bubbled up from his lungs when he exhaled.

"Bring Elfeya to me now. Put her mate in the observation room."

The Fading Lands ~ Fey'Bahren

Ellysetta nestled in Rain's arms as together they watched the kitlings' first few bells of life. All four were healthy, their eyes bright, their songs strong, their little bodies already covered with soft, downy fur.

"Little" was a relative word, of course. Each kitling was the size of a small pony, and their wings extended to easily three manlengths across, but next to the full-grown adults of the pride, they appeared tiny. They sang as they purred, and Ellysetta recognized each one by its song. Hallah was a pure black beauty with iridescent green eyes. Sharra and Letah looked like small versions of their mother, Cahlah, with cinnamon brown fur and golden eyes. The lone little male, Miauren, was as gray as his granddam, with black tips on his ears and tail.

The kitlings were born with mouths full of teeth and bellies full of hunger, and when Steli returned with a fresh *tavalree* carcass, Ellysetta turned her face away from the exuberant carnivorous ferocity with which they attacked their first meal.

Rain laughed softly at her squeamishness. "Come, *shei'tani*. Let's leave the kitlings to their meal. I will take you back to Dharsa; then I must return to Orest."

She nodded, joy turning to melancholy. She knew without Rain's saying so, that he would collect the king's armor from Dharsa. The next time he returned—if he returned— the Fading Lands would be at war.

Steli growled and paced after them. Her blue eyes whirled. *"Fey-kin gather on Su Reisu. Growl pride-warnings, Rainier-Eras. They are not welcome with kits in the lair."*

"Bel must have arrived. I will tell him and Gaelen to leave."

The sky was still dark over the Fading Lands, and to Rain and Ellysetta's surprise, at least twenty warriors stood in the firelight on Su Reisu where they had left Gaelen. But Gaelen and another warrior, who could only be Bel, were kneeling on the plateau in the center of a ring of warriors, imprisoned by dense, radiant, multifold weaves.

"Stay here," Rain said. "I will go down."

Ellysetta clutched his hand in a tight grip. *"Nei*, they didn't come here for you." Both Bel and Gaelen were imprisoned. That could mean only one thing. "They came for me. They must have realized what I was intending to do."

"We will go together, *shei'tani*." When she would have objected, Rain pressed a silencing finger to her lips. "We made this choice together. We'll face the consequences together."

She stepped back so he could summon the Change, and together they flew down to Su Reisu to face the gathered Fey warriors.

He recognized a few of the Fey: A handful of them were those who'd made a great point of walking out that first day at the Academy, before Gaelen rang the gong. Unbending warriors, clinging to the shining, spotless ideal of perfect honor, as if only that could ever be worthy of their regard.

He couldn't blame them for their views. The idea of perfect honor was a beautiful dream, one Rain himself had fixed in his heart for years. And it was a worthy goal—as long as the pursuit of it did not become a slavish devotion empty of all compassion and willingness to accept change.

"What is your business here, Fey?" he asked. Bel and Gaelen were both speaking and gesturing at him, but neither voice nor Spirit could penetrate the twenty-five-fold weaves wrapped so tightly around them. His magic pooled within him, ready for summoning at the first hint of aggression. "By what authority do you imprison the First General of the Fading Lands and a *chatok* of the Academy?"

One of the Fey stepped forward. His eyes were bright and hard, his face an expressionless mask. "By the authority of the *Shei'dalin* and the Massan," he said.

Rain sensed the explosion of power only a split second before another thirty Fey shed their invisibility weaves. Two dense, twenty-five-fold weaves sprang up around him and Ellysetta.

Eld ~ Boura Fell

Bound in *sel'dor* manacles and collar and pinned to the wall by thick *sel'dor* chains, Elfeya hid her savage joy as she beheld the rotting wreck of the High Mage. His face was the decaying skull of a corpse. Livid flesh drooped in waxy folds beneath his sunken eyes and around his nose and mouth. His eyes were silver coins floating in pools of scarlet blood, and his once-thick mane of white hair had gone thin and sparse, sickly tufts clinging to the thin, mottled, parchment-like skin that covered his skull.

"I will not heal you," she told him with cold defiance. "If that is why you summoned me, you have wasted what little time in this life you have left."

He laughed, and it turned into a cough that sprayed bloody sputum like a red mist. "Such brave words. You grow much bolder than you should." He waved, and the wall beside her became transparent. Inside a well-lit chamber, Shan was strapped by dozens of barbed *sel'dor* bands to a table made of the same foul, black metal. His eyes were blindfolded, his mouth gagged.

The sight of him made her quail as fear and desperate love seized her in equal measures. She wanted to plead for his release, but she and Shan had already agreed they would not. She tossed her head and forced herself to speak as though her heart were not being ripped from her chest. "What else can you do to us that you have not already done? He will not survive more torture. If you kill him, you only set me free. Either way, I am through prolonging your foul life. No matter what you do, I will not heal you."

"Oh, I won't kill him. Not for a long, long time." He bent and spoke into a tube connected to the adjoining room. "Disembowel him."

Elfeya closed her eyes as one of the guards in Shan's room lifted a razor-sharp hook and approached Shan's vulnerable belly. She felt the instant the hook sank into his skin as if it sank into her own, felt the burn of his intestines tearing as the guard drew them out of his body. She didn't speak to Shan. She didn't dare, terrified that if she heard his voice, she would not be strong, as they'd agreed she must be. She felt every moment of his suffering and bit her lip until her mouth filled with blood.

"That's enough, I think. Time for healing." Maur spoke into the tube again.

Despite herself, Elfeya opened her eyes and turned her head in time to see a woman with vacant eyes being escorted into Shan's room. When the guard led her to Shan's body and put her hands over his torn belly, a green glow lit the air around the woman's hands. Shan's body arched and his throat strained as a muffled scream rattled out of him.

"She isn't nearly as skilled as you, I'm afraid, and her mind is gone, as you can see, but the poor thing can't stop healing. You've been getting . . . recalcitrant . . . so I had her brought from one of my other palaces. Alas, she causes as much pain as the wound she's healing, but she's quite adept at keeping her patients alive. Indefinitely."

Elfeya began to weep. Thrice more, the guards ripped Shan's belly open. Thrice more the poor, mindless husk of a *shei'dalin* healed him with her instinctive weaves. All the while, both Elfeya and Shan felt every burning moment, and they both knew it could—and would—go on and on and on. The pain grew so terrible, Shan lost consciousness.

"*Parei!* Stop!" In desperation, she dropped to her knees before the High Mage and seized his hands. "*Teska*, I beg you. I will heal you. Remove these bonds, stop Shan's torture, and I will heal you."

The High Mage nodded to the guard. "Remove the manacles on her wrists." To Elfeya, he hissed, "You will heal me now. If your results please me, I will halt his torture."

Weeping, she spun the weaves, feeling the acid burn of *sel'dor* as she channeled as much power as she could into the rotting shell of Vadim Maur's body. When she could do no more, her hands fell away. Her head drooped in defeat. "Please."

He commanded one of the *umagi* to bring him a mirror. His face was still disfigured, the flesh mottled and drooping like melted wax, but most of his strength had returned. He stood, grabbed a fistful of Elfeya's hair, and hauled her to her knees.

"Did you think you could interfere as you did tonight and I would not know it?" he hissed. "Did you think I could not feel you feeding her the weaves, showing her how to spin her power?" He shook her like a child. "You and your beloved Lord Death will pay for what you have cost me. You will pay dearly . . . and for a very long time." He flung her against the wall. Her head cracked against the stone, making stars flash before her eyes.

He pinned the guards with his scarlet-filled silver gaze. "Take the male back to his cell. You may begin with him again tomorrow."

"And her?"

Vadim Maur glanced down at Elfeya, the edge of his disfigured mouth curling. "Make her scream. Make her beg for death. But do not give it to her. I want her alive the day I claim her daughter's body and soul."

The Fading Lands ~ Fey'Bahren

Dawn turned the eastern sky over the Fading Lands to pale pink. Rain sat in the center of his magical cage, his body relaxed, his mind calm. He'd Raged the first few bells of his imprisonment, but no longer. Now, his tairen lay coiled within him, a silent hunter, not mindlessly wild but lethally patient, waiting for the first chance to spring. Isolated by the dense weaves of their cages, he and Ellysetta could not call for help, and could not even speak to each other except through their bond threads.

Their Fey guards stood up and turned to the west, Fey'cha in hand. A moment later, they sheathed their blades and waved to the approaching party. Tenn, Yulan, and Nurian crested the Su Reisu plateau, their *shei'dalin* mates close behind.

The six of them approached their imprisoned king and his mate. Tenn nodded to the guards, and the dome of magic around Ellysetta dissolved, leaving five-fold weaves of Spirit surrounding her so she could not call to the tairen for aid, while gleaming circlets bound her arms to her chest so she could not spin any other magic in her defense.

Tenn stepped forward. His expression was as stony as any Fey battle mask she'd ever seen. "Ellysetta of Celieria, you stand accused of weaving the forbidden magic. Will you admit your crime willingly, or must you be Truthspoken?"

Her eyes narrowed. "Release Rain. You imprison your king. In Celieria, Tenn v'En Eilan, you would be branded a traitor and sentenced to death by torture."

"We are not in Celieria," the Fire master said softly, "and our actions are not treason. We"—he gestured to include Yulan, Nurian, and Venarra—"are here to stop Rain's madness and keep him from destroying the Fading Lands."

"Madness?" she spat. "Everything he's done, he's done to save the Fading Lands! How can you betray him this way?"

"You dare suggest *we* betray *him*?" Tenn's eyes burned with red-gold flames, and his voice dropped to a low note that vibrated with fury. "He has broken every Fey law that does not suit his whim and made a mockery of the honor that serves as the cornerstone of our existence! He brings a *dahl'reisen* through the Mists and installs him as an honored *chatok* in the hallowed halls of Dharsa's Warriors' Academy. He grants a Mage-Marked woman entrance to the Fading Lands . . . stands idly by while she enchants hundreds of our finest and noblest warriors into bloodswearing themselves to her service . . . then makes her his queen even though the Eye of Truth reveals her for the foul, Azrahn-wielding corruptor she is!"

Tenn drew himself up to his full height, righteous fury swirling around him in swaths of fiery red magic. "He has betrayed us in every way possible! *Because he brought* you *into the Fading Lands!*"

"He brought me because the Eye told him I would save the tairen," she cried. "And I have! Four kitlings were born in Fey'Bahren tonight—*because Rain and I saved them.*"

Consternation flashed across Tenn's face. For a moment—just a moment—she saw doubt flicker in his gold-sparked eyes.

Yulan stepped forward, his brows drawn together in an accusing scowl. "How did you save them, Celierian? With Azrahn? Did our king knowingly allow you to weave the forbidden magic?"

"Everything Rain has done, he has done to save the Fading Lands!" she cried. "He is your king, and he would die to save his people!"

"Then he should have done so a thousand years ago!" spat Nurian, Sariel's cousin. "He is as much an abomination as you! A madman who inherited a throne he did not deserve because he did not die with his mate, as a bonded Fey should. Everything about his rise to power is as corrupt as his existence and his rule. I reject him as the rightful king of the Fey."

Ellysetta stared at him, aghast. "You hate him because Sariel died and he did not. Dear gods, all this time, he has held you in his heart, and you have wished him dead."

"Enough of this." Tenn held up his hand. "We owe you no explanation. We have come for answers, and you will give them to us, willingly or by Truthspeaking. You, Ellysetta of Celieria, stand accused of weaving the forbidden magic Azreisenahn, known as Azrahn. Do you confess to having freely and deliberately woven this magic?"

She glared at them and clamped her lips shut. *They accuse me of weaving Azrahn,* she told Rain. *They say you are a madman, unfit to rule.*

To her surprise, he laughed. *Well, you did weave Azrahn, and I am on occasion more than a little mad.*

She jerked her head around to glare at him. *You think this is funny?*

His teeth flashed in a grin more savage than humorous. *Nei, shei'tani. The fun is only about to begin. Look.* He pointed skyward.

She looked up into the sky overhead, where Steli's white form shone like a pearl in the early morning light. Her wings were spread, and as she swooped down to get a closer look at the gathering on Su Reisu, her eyes blazed like blue stars. She gave a roar that made every Fey on the plateau jump and stare upward in fear. Steli gave another fearsome roar, a call to arms, and scorched the sky with an enormous jet of flame. *"Tairen! Defend the pride!"*

Within a few chimes, the sky was filled with tairen, all of them roaring loud enough to shake down the mountainside. They dove for Su Reisu, flames searing the air, and the Fey scattered like mice. The tairen herded them together with flames and swooping attacks.

When the Fey were back on the plateau, ringed by a full dozen fierce, furious tairen, Steli-*chakai*, her fangs dripping venom, leaned her great head down and growled deep in her throat. In a pure, perfectly comprehensible Feyan, she commanded, *"Release our pride-kin from your magic, or die where you stand."*

Tenn, Yulan, even Venarra, all looked taken aback. And in an almost laughable display, they turned beseeching eyes to Ellysetta. "They would not dare . . ." Tenn said. "We are Fey. My brother was king!"

"Rain and I are tairen," Ellysetta replied coldly, "and he *is* king. I suggest you do as Steli-*chakai* commands. Quickly, before you rouse her protective instincts even further. There are four hungry kitlings in the lair tonight, and the pride considers all intruders a threat better left dead."

Glowering, Tenn nodded at the Fey, and the weaves around Rain, Bel, and Gaelen dissolved. The three warriors were at Ellysetta's side in an instant, shoving her back behind them, sandwiching her between their tall, protective bodies and the rumbling chests of Steli, Fahreeta, and Torasul.

"Shall we scorch the wingless ones?" Steli sang in tairen song. Tairen did not play politics. To them, an enemy was a creature to be shredded and scorched.

Steli's offer tempted Rain, but after a brief consideration, he turned it down. *"Nei. They are Fey, my kin whether I like it or not. Reason may be enough."*

The white cat growled. *"Reason? The wingless ones have already reasoned themselves stronger than you, or they would not have issued Challenge. Show them fangs, not belly, Rainier-Eras, and keep your claws sharp. Even Sybharukai knows a bite on the neck will remind the unruly to show respect. Show the wingless ones who is makai of this pride.*"

"*Steli-chakai is as wise as she is fierce.*" He fixed his eyes on the Massan. "Explain your presence here, Tenn v'En Eilan. Explain to me why fifty warriors of the Fey, three of the Massan, and three *shei'dalins* have come to the foot of Fey'Bahren to imprison their king and accuse the Tairen Soul's mate of weaving the forbidden magic."

"Do you deny our accusations?" Tenn retorted instead. "Your mate has already woven Azrahn once, and we had very good reason to believe she was bringing Gaelen vel Serranis here with the deliberate intent of weaving it again."

Rain's jaw worked. "How long did it take you to run here from Dharsa?"

The question took Tenn aback. "Eighteen bells. What has that got to do with—"

"Eighteen bells. Eighteen bells ago, you set out for Fey'Bahren because you believed my mate was planning to weave a magic that could corrupt her soul and endanger the Fading Lands." His lips drew back in a snarl. "And yet not once in all that time did I receive a single word of warning from you or any of your fellow Massan that my mate was endangering herself. Why is that, Tenn?"

The Fire master clenched his jaw and did not answer.

Yulan leapt to his friend's defense. "We are not the ones who have done wrong!"

"Are you not?" Sparks began to fly around Rain as magic and fury bubbled up inside him. "Every warrior of the Fey swears on his honor and his life to protect the women of the Fading Lands from harm. Any one of you could have sent me a warning. I could have arrived in time to stop her. But you didn't. Which leads me to only one conclusion: You meant her to weave Azrahn. You hoped she would. Because that would give you the opportunity to banish her from the Fading Lands."

He seared each of the Massan with a glare so hot, it was a wonder they did not burst into flame where they stood. "You dishonor your names and your steel."

Venarra stepped closer to her mate. "*Aiyah*, we allowed her the opportunity to weave Azrahn," she said, "but we did not make her do it. She knew the danger. She knows the law. Yet still she chose to put the Fading Lands at risk. We all saw what will happen if we allow her to continue leading honorable Fey down the Shadowed Path. She is the Eld's creature, sent here to destroy us, and it is our duty to stop her." Venarra's traveling leathers became scarlet *shei'dalin* silks, and a scarlet veil covered her face. "Rainier vel'En Daris, your mate stands accused of weaving the forbidden magic. She will confess or be Truthspoken."

Even before he sensed Ellysetta's instinctive, horrified recoil, Rain's hands moved in a blur. Four red Fey'cha thunked hilt-deep in the dirt a finger span from the boots of the three Massan and the *Shei'dalin* Venarra. The other Fey's answering blades froze in midair—caught by the swift, masterful weaves of icy-eyed Gaelen and Bel.

"Touch her and you die," Rain stated coldly. "Consider warning given."

"She has bewitched you!" Tenn accused.

"She has led me back from death to life and opened my eyes to truth. She has saved us all and risked her soul to do it. If that is bewitchment, then the gods themselves are the sorcerers who taught her the spells."

"Rainier Feyreisen." Venarra seized his wrist and spoke, her voice laden with the resonant, irrefutable command of a *shei'dalin*'s compulsion weave. "Did your mate Ellysetta weave the forbidden magic?"

He could not resist, so he spat the truth defiantly. "*Aiyah*, she did and so did I! *And I would do it again*."

Silence fell over the plateau. The eyes of the Massan and the *Shei'dalin* went hazy as private Spirit weaves passed between them. A moment later, Tenn turned back to Rain and Ellysetta, his face a mask of unflinching stone.

"Ellysetta Baristani and Rainier vel'En Daris, you are guilty of weaving the forbidden magic, Azrahn. For your crime, the Massan declares that you both shall be stripped of your steel and banished for all eternity from the Fading Lands."

Rain laughed without humor. "Banish us? You overstep yourself, Tenn. The Tairen Soul does not answer to the Massan, and the Massan's will does not trump the Tairen Soul's."

"You are mistaken, Rain. The Fey vested the Massan with the power to override your will a thousand years ago to ensure that you, in your madness, did not lead us astray, as you are doing now."

The words struck Rain like a mortal blow. He turned in stunned disbelief towards Bel, and the knife slid deeper into his heart when his best friend looked away. All this time . . . all this time the Massan had not simply been wielding power in his name. They'd been wielding power *over him*.

And not even Marissya had ever told him.

Not even Bel.

Eld ~ Boura Fell

Elfeya lay panting on the stone floor, every finger span of her body bruised and bloodied. She sensed the instant Shan regained consciousness, and she reached out to him on the threads of their bond, desperate to give him what information she could before her tormentors began again. *"Orest and Teleon, beloved. They strike at Orest and Teleon."* That much she'd been able to pull from the High Mage's mind as she'd healed him. *"Tell her, Shan."*

"Elfeya . . ."

"Tell her to warn them."

She cried out as hands seized fistsful of her hair and hauled her to her feet. Rough hands slammed her hard against the stone walls of the cell, knocking the breath from her lungs. Glowing, red-hot metal filled her vision. She tried desperately to close her bonds to Shan before the scream was ripped from her lungs and the smell of sizzling flesh assaulted her nose, but she wasn't fast enough.

A terrible, wild roaring filled her dazed mind . . . her screams and Shan's mingling in an agony of madness and pain as again and again and again the Eld seared and scorched her.

The Fading Lands ~ Fey'Bahren

Fey and tairen stood in a tense ring, violence simmering beneath the surface. Rain struggled to gather his thoughts and find the breath Tenn's revelation had knocked out of him.

"Rain . . . " Bel's expression was desolate. *"Sieks'ta, kem'maresk. I should have told you, but once you came back to us, I never thought there would be cause. I never thought they would be so bold."*

"You would banish the Defender of the Fey when the Fading Lands stand on the brink of a second Mage War?" Gaelen challenged with cold fury. "You would banish the woman who brought life back to the tairen and the Fey? You would cast them out when the only reason they wove Azrahn was to save your miserable lives?"

"The reasons do not matter," Tenn said. "The law is clear. Those who weave the forbidden magic must be banished or slain. These are the ways of honor. These are the ways of the Fey."

"These are the ways of death and idiocy," Gaelen snapped.

"Feel free to join them in their exile, *dahl'reisen*," Yulan spat.

Steli growled. *"What is 'banish'?"*

Rain answered, speaking aloud for the benefit of the Fey. "Banishment, Steli-*chakai*, means these Fey say I am no longer the Tairen Soul. It means they intend to drive me and Ellysetta-Feyreisa from the lair and from all lands of the Fey."

Every tairen on Su Reisu roared. Flames shot from snarling muzzles, searing the morning sky, wings spread wide in a show of fearsome might.

Protective shields sprang up around the gathered Fey. Dozens of hands reached for red Fey'cha.

Rain flung shields around Ellysetta but none around himself. He glared at the gathered warriors. "And you call *me* mad? You would pull red against the pride?" He raised his hands to the tairen. *"Steli-chakai, my pride-kin, stop."* To all of them, he said, "We have enemies enough without turning upon one another. Stand down, Fey." When they did not move, his voice dropped an octave and boomed across the plateau. *"I said stand down!"*

Behind him, Ellysetta gave a choked cry, and an icy chill washed over him.

He whirled around and all the blood drained from his face.

She was shaking, every muscle clenched, every tendon pulled taut beneath her skin. Her hands were clawed and her eyes were endless black pits awash in whirling red lights, like a dead sky filled with bloody stars.

She threw back her head, her throat convulsing. *"Sal veli! Piersan veli ti'Teleon te Orest! Sala talothi!"* They're coming! The enemy comes to Teleon and Orest! Kill them!

The voice from her mouth was not her own. Low and throbbing, as if ripped from the throat of death itself, the sound scraped across Rain's senses like a serrated blade.

The Azrahn-filled gaze pinned him, and in a guttural voice, she cried, "Feyreisen! Defend the pride!"

Her legs folded, and she collapsed into his arms, and in

her own voice, urgent and agitated, she whispered, "Orest and Teleon. They are in danger. He's coming. You must warn them. Warn them, *shei'tan*. Let them know . . ."

Rain clutched her to his chest and raised stricken eyes to the others. "We must warn Orest and Teleon."

"Are you mad? Did you see her eyes?" Tenn pointed a finger. "She's Mage-claimed! The Mages are using her to draw us into a trap!"

"How can they be drawing us into a trap?" Rain snapped. "Our brothers are already there."

"Then they must be trying to draw *you* out," Yulan snapped when Tenn frowned in perplexed silence.

Gaelen sneered. "Considering you just banished him, what do you care?"

"It isn't a trap."

All eyes turned to Ellysetta.

Her lids opened, revealing eyes of bright Fey green, glowing and just beginning to whirl with the radiance of the tairen. "It isn't a trap. The Eld are coming. I don't know how I know it, but I do. Orest and Teleon are in danger." She rose to her feet, though her body continued to shake with helpless tremors, and her eyes held his in an unwavering gaze. *"Believe me, shei'tan. Our friends are in danger. We must warn them."*

Her urgent concern and unshakable certainty filled his veins first with ice, then with blazing fire. She had no doubt. And because she had none, he could not doubt either.

Rain flung his head back and sent the cry on the Warriors' Path. *"Fey! To arms! Orest and Teleon, prepare for war! Kieran! Kiel! Get the shei'dalins and Ellysetta's family to safety! Now, Fey, now! The Eld are coming!"*

"Belay that command!" Tenn shouted on the same path. *"By order of the Massan, you will fall back to the Fading Lands! Do not engage the Eld!"* To Rain, he shouted, "Even if she isn't speaking as the mouthpiece of the Mages, you have no right

to command the armies of the Fey! You are *dahl'reisen!* You are cast out!"

Later, Bel would tell him that at that moment, Rain seemed to grow half a manlength taller, his shoulders twice as wide, and that his eyes blazed like twin purple suns. But all he knew at the time was the rush of his tairen's power, hot as the raging Great Sun and just as furious, filling him until his body all but exploded with its wrath. In a voice so low and deadly that the very ground rumbled beneath his feet, he growled, "War has begun and still you would divide us?"

Tenn stood his ground, refusing to back down. "War has not begun! Whatever trap the Eld are waiting to spring, I will not let the Fey rush into it! I will not sacrifice what precious few Fey lives we still have left for the sake of Celieria!"

Rain could easily have ripped out Tenn's throat and danced in the shower of his blood. "The Eld aren't attacking Celieria, you fool. Teleon and Orest are the gateways to the Fading Lands. They're coming for us!"

He spun away and sent a second desperate shout on the Warriors' Path. *"Fey! My brothers, you must each make your choice. Those who would hide from the Eld and hope the Faering Mists will protect you, retreat as the Massan have commanded. The rest of you, prepare to fight!"*

He leapt into the air, summoning the Change. *"Fahreeta, Torasul! Take two of the pride and fly to the Garreval. Protect the Feyreisa's family. Steli, guard Ellysetta. The rest of you, follow me as quickly as you can."* He circled Su Reisu. *"Gaelen, Bel, I may no longer be your king, but as your friend, I could use your blades."*

Bel exchanged a look with Gaelen, then said, *"We would follow you through the Seven Hells, Rain, if you will but give us a ride."*

Rain swooped down. Bel and Gaelen leapt onto his back, shouting, *"Miora felah ti'Feyreisa! Miora felah ti'Feyreisen!* And death to the Eld!" With a whooshing rush of powerful magic, Rain raced east towards Orest and war.

Celieria ~ Teleon

The *shei'dalins* did not get to finish their last session of Lady Darramon's healing. Within chimes of Rain's warning, Kieran and Kiel were hustling them and Ellysetta's family out of Teleon and towards the Garreval. Behind them, the Fey who had chosen to stay and fight were rushing Lord Darramon's party to the safety of the hidden fortress.

"What in the name of the Seven Hells is going on, Kieran?" Kiel asked privately as they hurried across the mountainside. After Rain's cry to prepare for war, the Warriors' Path had resounded with Tenn v'En Eilan's commands to retreat, claiming that he and the Massan were in charge of the Fey armies and that Rain was *dahl'reisen*, cast out for weaving Azrahn.

"Scorched if I know. The Massan have gone mad. Right at this moment, all I care about is getting the Feyreisa's family and the shei'dalins to safety before the Eld unleash every demon in the Well upon us." Kieran glanced back at the small group behind him. *"Quickly,"* he urged them. *"And quietly."*

Lillis and Lorelle clambered over the rocks, shrubs, and tangled grasses. Small slings were tied around their necks, holding the kittens they had brought with them. In addition, each child carried a small bag containing the belongings she'd packed the previous night. Sol hurried after his daughters, his own, larger pack on his back.

Behind Sol, the five *shei'dalins* followed in swift and graceful silence, their long scarlet robes and veils exchanged for brown traveling leathers. Fifty Fey, silent and grim, surrounded the small group. Their eyes glowed with power, the elongated pupils lengthened and widened like a hunting cat's. A shifting dome of Spirit hid them as they made their way across the unprotected mountainside towards the Garreval.

Kieran kept the small party moving and did his best to hide his worry. Not one booted foot had emerged from the Mists since Rain's cry to prepare for battle.

Eld ~ Boura Fell

"Master Maur." The Primages of the Mage Council bowed low as he entered the war room, his ravaged face hidden by the folds of a deep-hooded robe. He knew better than to reveal how damaged his physical body had become. The moment he revealed such weakness, ambitious Primages would be after him like thistlewolves stalking an injured ram.

"Status?" he snapped.

The Primages turned their attention back to the war map. Sib Vargus, the oldest of the Mages, touched his fingers to the Celierian section and swept upward in a single motion, whispering the Mage spell as he did so. A dark, shimmering image of the Celierian map rose over the table, dotted with several dozen pinpoints of bright light. He waved again, enlarging the view of the northeast quadrant of Celieria, from the Garreval to Orest.

"The Teleon force is in position in the Well, as you ordered. The rest have assembled in Boura Dor, awaiting your command."

Vadim examined the map. "Tell the commanders to attack. Here." He pointed to one of the pinpoints of light, whispered a Feraz witchword, and the light changed from white to red. He touched several other pinpoints in succession. "And here and here and here." His eyes narrowed on the section that showed the Garreval. A cluster of white lights was moving south along the very edges of the map.

He smiled and touched a pinpoint of light just east of

them. "And here. Bring Ellysetta Baristani's family and the *shei'dalins* to me, alive."

Celieria ~ Teleon

The Eld appeared from nowhere. Thousands of them. They came without warning and seemingly from every direction: the guardhouse, the barracks, the watchtowers, the bailey, all the fields surrounding the outpost. They simply poured out of great gaping black holes in the air, preceded by a hail of barbed *sel'dor* arrows and blue-white balls of Mage Fire.

The first scores of Celierians to die didn't even have time to cry out. Their only sound was the thud of their bodies falling from the walls.

The others, the ones who lived long enough to see their brothers fall and hear the crash of stone and splintering wood as Mage Fire blasted away towers and barracks, raised the cry. "To arms!" they shrieked, lifting sword and crossbow. "To arms! We're under attack!"

From the shadows of the outpost and behind the invisibility weaves of Teleon, Fey warriors who had gathered after Rain's urgent call sprang from their concealment, steel flashing in the sunlight.

"I san, sheisan, te Liss!" For love, honor, and Light!

They screamed the Fey battle cry and dove into war.

Three miles away, near the Mist-filled pass of the Garreval, Kieran paused to glance back at Teleon. The outpost was ablaze. Flashes of Mage Fire and Fey magic exploded like lightning in the sky. Even from this distance, he could hear the muted screams and crashes of battle.

A shout—not so muted—rang out. Their party had been spotted. Dark shapes rushed across the grassy plain towards them, a scant mile away. Eld soldiers. And with them something else. Something on four legs rather than two.

One of the *shei'dalins* cried, *"Darrokken!"*

The snarling, slavering beasts gained on the Fey with deadly ease. Red eyes gleamed with menace, and Kieran's blood ran cold. He'd never seen a *darrokken* before, but he knew the beast didn't need to bring down its prey to kill it. The yellow fangs dripped poisonous saliva, and the long, razor-sharp claws carried plague and putrescence. One bite, one slash of those foul claws and, without healing, a victim would die within half a bell.

"Run!" Kieran snatched up Lillis, while Kiel grabbed Lorelle. "To the Mists!" They began to run. They pelted over rock and scrub. The warriors fell back to the rear flank to offer what protection they could. *°Fey! Ti'Kieran! Ti'shei'dalins!°* He broadcast the cry on the Warriors' Path.

Behind him, Fey'cha filled the air like rain, but for every *darrokken* felled, another took its place, and the acid blood of the loathsome creatures ate at Fey steel so that each blade called back to its owner's sheath was pitted and brittle and smoldering with foul vapors that burned Fey eyes and skin.

Two Fey at the back of the line were the first to fall as the massive, leathery, slime-covered bodies of the *darrokken* tackled them to the ground and fangs ripped through Fey throats.

The pack split up, a dozen of the foul beasts racing to cut off the approach to the pass and herd the Fey back towards the Mages.

"Up! Go up! Run for the Mists!" Kieran changed directions, charging up the mountainside. It was beyond dangerous to enter the Mists on mountainous terrain, but that risk paled in comparison to the certain death posed by the *darrokken*.

Globes of Mage Fire pelted through the air. Sol stumbled and went sprawling. The warrior who paused to haul him to his feet died without a sound as Mage Fire took his head.

Larger spheres of the deadly blue-white flame showered

down. Earth exploded all around them. Rocks and trees—everything the Mage Fire touched—vanished in an instant, and great hunks of the mountainside tore away, tumbling down in an avalanche of falling debris.

"Gods have mercy!" Sol cried.

"Hang the gods," Kieran snarled. "Where are the jaffing Fey?" *"Fey! Ti'Kieran! Protect the shei'dalins! Fey! Ti'Kieran! Ti'shei'dalins!"* Lillis clung to him, her face buried in his neck, showering his skin with hot tears.

"Kieran!" Kiel shouted. "The mountain!" Another fearsome barrage of Mage Fire had dissolved half the mountaintop above their heads. The remaining rock and stone gave a rumbling shriek and collapsed, sending countless tons of dirt, stone, and wood rushing towards them in a deadly wave.

"Hold tight to me, *ajiana*," Kieran whispered to Lillis. He turned to raise both hands. Green Earth fountained inside him, wrenched up from the center of his soul, spinning in flows of extraordinary mastery and strength. He was Kieran, son of the Solande and Serranis lines, descended from many of the greatest and most powerful Fey the world had ever known, an Earth master of tremendous power.

Screaming defiance, he flung out the weaves.

The crumbling mountainside froze. Kieran gritted his teeth, feeding his power into the weave, holding up the weight of the mountain through sheer force of magic and strength of will.

Raising his voice, he shouted to the warriors behind him, "Five-fold weaves, *kem'jetos*! Keep that scorching Mage Fire off us!"

But the Fey were already locked in a desperate battle for their lives.

And they were losing.

Between the snarling filth of the *darrokken* and the fury of Mage Fire, the warriors couldn't protect themselves against the barrage of *sel'dor* arrows as Eld archers came within bow range. Weaves faltered, and Kieran screamed in helpless rage as his blade brothers began to fall. Acid seared his thigh as a barbed *sel'dor* arrow sank deep.

"Master Baristani, take the girls. Go with the *shei'dalins* into the Mists! Run!" Another *darrokken* crashed through the Fey, ripping and slashing warriors. Two of the *shei'dalins* grabbed Lillis and Lorelle and ran up the mountain towards the Mist-shrouded peaks. The other three screamed as Mage Fire, *sel'dor* arrows, and *darrokken* herded them back away from the safety of the Garreval and towards the waiting Eld army. "Kiel, scorch it, where are the Fey?"

Kiel slammed a furious Spirit weave towards Chatok and Chakai. *"Fey! Ti'Kieran! Ti'ku! Ti'Teleon!"* To me! To Teleon! Spinning blue weaves shot out from his fingertips, desiccating the *darrokken* pursuing Lillis and Lorelle.

Rumbling thunder shook the ground at Kieran's feet. *Krekk! More Mage Fire?* If the ground gave way beneath him, he was dead. He didn't dare divide his weave or the mountain would come down upon them all.

But this time, the rumble wasn't an avalanche spawned by Mage Fire.

The eastern army of the Fey charged out of the Mists, magic blazing, steel bared. Hundreds of them . . . a thousand . . . more. All of Chatok and Chakai had emptied and come rushing to the aid of their embattled brothers.

Two more arrows struck Kieran's back. His weave faltered, and he screamed with fury as the mountain fell.

Eld ~ Boura Fell

The collection of moving lights at the edge of Vadim Maur's display of Celieria winked out. He frowned and tapped the map of the Fading Lands, scanning the area near the Garreval, but the moving lights of the *chemar* didn't show there either. They were gone.

His brows drew together. *Scorch those fools!* They were supposed to capture Ellysetta Baristani's family, not destroy them and their precious *chemar* with Mage Fire.

He spun the display of Celieria into place. In Teleon, a new trail of *chemar* led away from the main grouping. The bread crumbs Den Brodson had left behind to lead the way into the hidden Fey fortress.

He tapped four more white lights around Teleon, turning them red. "Send in the second wave. Unleash the demons on the army in the Garreval." He tapped the line of *chemar* leading into the Fey's hidden fortress. "Send the Black Guard here and the Primages here." Last, he turned one final pinpoint red. "And here. Bring me Lord Darramon's wife."

"What about Lord Darramon, Most High?"

He glanced across the table and raised a brow. "Kill him. Leave no survivors."

Celieria ~ Teleon

The shouts of the Fey and the sound of booted feet racing were the first signs the Eld had breached the Fortress. Lord Darramon gripped his sword more tightly. Den moved towards Lady Darramon. He knew what was expected of him.

When it came, the attack happened with shocking speed. The gateway opened without a sound, a great gaping maw of darkness from which black arrows flew as thick in the air as a murder of crows. Lord Darramon rushed towards his wife and died, skewered on the barbed *sel'dor* blade of the High Mage's Black Guard. Lady Darramon screamed and fought like a madwoman until Den's fist clipped her temple. Then the silvery blue stone room ran red with blood, and demons howled as they rushed from the Well to feast on the dead and dying.

Eld ~ Boura Fell

"Victory at Teleon, my lord." Primage Rao bowed. "We have captured Lady Darramon, three *shei'dalins*, and two dozen Fey warriors. All are pierced and being brought through the Well. The hidden fortress and the outpost have been destroyed."

"The Fey?"

"They suffered heavy losses, my lord. Nearly a thousand slain before we drove them back into the Garreval."

"Excellent. Seed the Garreval with *chemar*. If the Fey come through again, we will be waiting for them." Vadim Maur turned his attention back to the illuminated vertical map display and scrolled to the section that showed Orest and the locations of the inactivated *chemar* there. He tapped fifteen of them. "Vargus, contact your commanders at Boura Dor. Begin the conquest of Orest."

CHAPTER TWENTY-FOUR

Celieria ~ Orest

On the ramparts and streets of Lower Orest, Celierians and Fey fought side by side. Axes, swords, and war hammers swung, cracking bone, severing limbs. Magic exploded from shining hands. Fey'cha flew with blurring speed and lethal precision until the pearlescent gray stone ran red with blood.

But still the Eld kept coming.

Devron Teleos swung his ancestor Shanis Teleos's *mei-cha* hard, blocking the downward slice of a *sel'dor* blade.

The blow rattled his teeth, but he merely snarled and slashed out with a red Fey'cha, angling the blade upwards, beneath the black scales of the Eld soldier's armor. His opponent screamed and dropped to the ground, dead in an instant from the lethal tairen venom forged into the *lute'cha* steel.

"Where the flaming hells are they coming from?" Dev shouted, whirling to battle another foe. Rain had warned him the Eld had learned how to use the Well of Souls to travel, but there'd been no whiff of Azrahn—nor warning of any kind—before the portals had appeared and poured twenty thousand Eld into their midst. The entire lower city was overrun.

Tajik vel Sibboreh swung his *seyani* long sword in his left hand and fired red Fey'cha with his right. "Scorched if I know, but so long as the maggots keep coming, I'll keep killing them." His red plaits swung about him like tails of fire, and his weapons moved at blurring speed. He fought like a demon. Nothing stood against him. His face was drenched in blood, his searing blue eyes an eerie sight in the mask of gore.

A tairen length away, a massive Eld soldier with biceps like tree trunks was sweeping a war ax like a scythe, sending gutted Celierian bodies flying.

Tajik bared his teeth in a savage grin, ran up a pile of rubble, and leapt across the melee towards the giant's back. Screaming, "*Miora felah ti'Feyreisa!*" he brought his sword down in a killing blow, severing the Eld's head with a single strike. The headless body remained standing for a moment, fountains of blood spurting up from its neck. Tajik turned his face into the shower and laughed.

All around him, Fey fought with lethal skill and eyes lit like savage stars. The sight filled Tajik with pride. Not one of the Fey had abandoned Orest, despite the nonsensical "retreat to the Fading Lands" *krekk* Tenn v'En Eilan had spewed across the Warriors' Path earlier in the day. Every blade under Tajik's command knew what his steel was made for, and it scorching well wasn't for retreating before the enemy even showed up on the field of battle!

A *sel'dor* arrow glanced off Tajik's shoulder plate. His eyes narrowed as he sighted a knot of Elden archers who'd made their way to the top of the city's inner wall. Magic blasted from his fingertips. Half a dozen archers burst into flame and tumbled off the wall.

Another wave of Eld came rushing around a rubble-strewn corner. Tajik greeted them with a clap of magic that brought a building tumbling down upon them. "You want death, Eld maggots? I'll give you death. This is for all the honorable and worthy friends you slaughtered! This is for my sister!" Ablaze with magic, he leapt into the billowing dust cloud and swung his sword in savage arcs, his Fey'cha flashing between each strike like bolts of lightning. "Come dance with the tairen, if you dare!"

Leaving Tajik to his slaughter, Dev ducked an explosion of Mage Fire that took out half a dozen less lucky fellows behind him and scrambled up a flight of stone stairs to the battlements of the outer wall to get a better view of the city. Lower Orest was in flames. Entire blocks of the city were burning with billowing clouds of thick, black smoke, and the screams and howls of battle rose from the conflagration.

From his vantage point, he could see Earth master Rijonn vel Ahrimor, the tallest Fey Dev had ever met, shaking a mile-wide swath of land like a carpet. He struck the ground with weave after pounding weave, sending huge shuddering ripples of earth racing out like waves on the sea, ripping buildings from their foundations, tossing enemy troops and massive siege weapons like flotsam. Nothing in his path could get through. Eld archers had turned the Fey's back into a damned pincushion trying to bring him down, yet the giant merely set his rock jaw and kept spinning his earthshaking weaves.

"Fey! Ti'vel Ahrimor!" Dev sent the order spinning across the Warriors' Path, then shouted to his commander in both voice and Spirit. "Take out those archers, men! Protect that Fey!"

"Lord Teleos! Get down!" A fist of Air slammed into his chest, knocking him to the bloody gray stone walk just as a massive sphere of Mage Fire shot past where his head had been.

Dev gave a grim wave to the white-haired, black-eyed Gillandaris vel Jendahr, Tajik's good friend, who was quite possibly even more savage and lethal than the red-haired Fey general. Magic blazed in Gil's hands, and with a heave, he flung his weaves over the crenellated stone. Dev scrambled to his feet and peered over the wall. Half a dozen Eld war barges floated in the middle of the mile-wide river, each carrying a full dozen blue-robed Primages who flung great balls of Mage Fire at the outer wall. Behind them, on the northern banks of the Heras, enormous trebuchets—where the Dark Lord had *they* come from?—launched explosive mortars against the outer wall.

Gil's weave hit one of the war barges, and his magic exploded with a concussive blast, sending shattered wood flying. *"Fey!"* Gil cried on the Warriors' Path. *"To the wall! Five-fold weaves to the river! Sink those barges and send those Mages swimming!"* He flung another weave of his own over the walls, hitting the same barge a second time, in the same spot. The hull cracked, and the Mages shrieked as the water of the Heras poured in.

Dev watched the screaming Mages in grim triumph. The Source-fed waters of the Heras burned Mages the way *sel'dor* burned Fey, which meant the rotting blue-robed *rultsharts* were bathing in acid. He couldn't think of a better fate for them. "Trebuchets!" he cried. "Aim for the river! Take out those barges!"

Gil grinned and gave a white-blond braid a deferential tug. *"I'll leave the boats to you, Lord Teleos. We'll take care of the*

Mages in the city." He leapt from the outer wall on an arc of Air, landing like a cat upon an abandoned wizard's tower on the inner wall. *"Water masters! Divide the falls! Let's make it rain!"* His laughter danced eerily through the smoke and sounds of war. Dense clouds of blue magic swirled over the city, and half the torrential falls of Maiden's Gate suddenly swept into the air and flooded Lower Orest.

A bell later, most of the Mage war barges had sunk, and Lower Orest was shin-deep in water. But the Eld kept coming. The trebuchets on the north banks of the Heras and the remaining Mages had made Orest's outer wall and its armaments their target. The wall went down, taking hundreds of men and Fey with it.

Dev abandoned the ruins of the outer wall and made an Air-powered leap to the crumbling walk of the inner wall. Reports were flying in from all over the city of new portals opening, delivering fresh enemy troops, demons, and *darrokken*, those foul, pestilential monstrosities created by the Eld.

The city's defenders were outnumbered, and even with the wild, murderous skills and magic of Fey sword masters like vel Sibboreh and his friends, the enemy was decimating them. The entire perimeter of Lower Orest was in flames, and the enemy was on the march west, towards the mountains. If the allies didn't retreat now, they risked being cut off and slaughtered.

The fight for Lower Orest was over. Aloud and in Spirit, Dev shouted, "Retreat to the mountains! Retreat to Maiden's Gate!" The series of stair-stepped walls that climbed the slopes of the Rhakis would be much harder for the Eld to conquer. The walls were thick, the armaments many, and the high ground gave the defenders the advantage. *"Retreat to Maiden's Gate! Retreat!"*

Wrapped in Gaelen's invisibility weave, Tajik raced after the retreating allies, slaughtering unsuspecting Eld as he went. But as he drew nearer Maiden's Gate, he began to realize the call for retreat might have come a little too late for him. The enemy was closing in, new, fresh, well-rested waves of them. Tajik began doing more running and less slaughtering.

Less than a mile from the fortified terraces of Maiden's Gate, a pack of slavering, filth-ridden *darrokken* burst out of an alleyway into the road in front of him. Though Tajik was still cloaked in Gaelen's undetectable weave, the beasts immediately turned and began racing towards him, red eyes gleaming, foul mouths dripping a froth of loathsome poison.

Tajik muttered a foul curse. *Darrokken* didn't sight their prey. They smelled them.

Though how the jaffing things could smell anything beyond the foul reek they exuded, Tajik could not begin to guess.

Red Fey'cha flew from his fingers. He spun north and took off running, his legs pumping as if his life depended on it. Which, he realized as the pounding footfalls of the beasts grew closer, it did. He dropped his invisibility weave and poured all his magic into speed and maneuverability, running faster than he ever had.

Behind him, the *darrokken* ran faster.

Just as the fetid breath of the foul beasts warmed the back of his neck and he felt the cold kiss of death draw near, a familiar Spirit voice cried, *"Vel Sibboreh! Duck! Five-fold weave!"*

He glanced up to see swooping darkness and a gaping, fang-filled maw filled with boiling flame. He dove for cover, shielding himself with magic as tairen fire enveloped the *darrokken*, incinerating them on contact.

The shout rose up from Maiden's Gate: "Feyreisen!"

Two black-leather-clad shapes leapt off Rain's back and landed near Tajik, blades unsheathed and magic blazing. Bel and Gaelen ran to his side, grinning like fiends.

"You're getting slow, my brother." Bel smirked. "The darrodogs almost had you."

Tajik dusted himself off and tossed back his braids. "Me? Ha! You're the ones late to the fight." His cocky grin melted to a sincere welcome as he clasped their forearms in a tight grip. "*Meivelei*, Fey. You're a happy sight. But come, let's hurry. Teleos has called retreat to Maiden's Gate."

"We arrived just in time, then." Gaelen brandished his steel. "I wouldn't want you to have all the fun."

The three of them ran for the western city, weaves blazing and swords flashing as they protected the flanks of the retreating allies. Behind them, Rain swooped across the ruins of Lower Orest, plowing the enemy lines with row after row of incinerating flame.

The battle of Lower Orest continued to rage. Rain's flame granted cover to the wounded and trapped allies struggling to reach the safety of Maiden's Gate. He flew as he had not flown since the Mage Wars, diving, soaring, twisting his lithe tairen's body through the sky with the sinuous ease of a sylph.

His nostrils filled with the scent and heat of his flame, the smell of roasting flesh and magic. Rage was there, pounding beneath the fury of his flame. Memories flooded him. Memories of the Wars, of Eadmond's Field. The voices of the dead grew loud once more, battering his mind with the fresh screams and bitter death of every Eld who fell to his flame.

But despite the wildness that hovered so near, a sense of peace he'd never known before anchored him to sanity. Ellysetta.

Their bond was not yet complete, yet she was there, singing across its threads. Weaving her love, her faith in him, across the distance. *"I am here, beloved. I am with you. Together we are strong."* Her song was a shining light in his soul, a brilliant golden-white sun that warmed the icy grip of his ancient demons and cooled the heat of his Rage. The beacon that kept his soul from plunging towards Darkness. *"Fly, shei'tan. Fly for us both."*

And he did.

Again and again he swooped and he soared. Again and again his roar ripped the skies over Orest, mighty, triumphant.

His presence gave hope to Orest's champions. From the ramparts of Maiden's Gate, archers fired flaming arrows whose hollow shafts were filled with intensely flammable, sticky fluid that burned hot enough to melt leather and skin. Along the last inner walls of Lower Orest, Water masters continued to funnel the waters of the Heras towards every spark of Mage Fire, while Fire masters amplified each blast of Rain's tairen flame and the archer's fire arrows, incinerating rock and stone, flesh and bone. Earth masters, shouting with effort, ripped great ravines across the ravaged sections of the city, swallowing entire legions of Eld before closing up again.

But for every portal Rain seared shut, another four opened. He couldn't understand it. There couldn't possibly have been that many *selkahr* crystals buried in Orest undetected. Yet portal after portal opened, and legion after legion poured out of them.

Sel'dor arrows filled the sky like swarms of locusts. His swooping attacks drew more of the enemy's fire with each pass, and despite Air masters' spinning whirlwinds and sharp downdrafts to knock the arrows from the sky, scores of acid black metal shafts pricked the membranes of Rain's wings like the thorns of a *kaddah*.

Exhaustion, blood loss, and pain finally drove him from the sky to the shelter of Upper Orest. He landed in Veil Lake with a clumsy splash. Panting, exhausted, he lay there, letting the *faerilas* wash over him, too tired to swim ashore.

Bel, Gaelen, and Dev simply plunged in and swam to his side to hack the barbs off the *sel'dor* arrows that pierced him and cut the poisonous black metal shafts from his hide. Freed from *sel'dor*, his wounds turned the waters around him red.

He closed his eyes, breathing hard as the *faerilas* seeped into his wounds. Its magic burned like cauterizing fire, healing and searing all at once. He bent his head to drink the restorative waters as his blade brothers tended his wounds.

"You should let Teleos's hearth witches tend you," Bel said. "Some of these wounds are deep."

"There are others in greater need. I will be fit to fly again in half a bell, and the Change will heal my wounds. What news of Teleon?"

Bel's eyes went dark as midnight. "Lost. Teleos got the word while we were in the Mists. The *rasa* are dead. More than a thousand of them. Teleon is destroyed again. Lord Darramon is slain and his wife missing. The Eld hold the Celierian side of the pass."

"What of Ellysetta's family? The shei'dalins?"

"Gone," Bel gave him the news bluntly. When it came to sorrow, warriors preferred their news served on a sharp blade. A clean cut hurt just a little less. "Kiel and Kieran, too. Dead or captured or lost in the Mists."

Rain flung his head back and roared in anguish. The Change swirled around him, burning with pain as the *sel'dor* barbs still embedded in his flesh twisted magic to agony. He embraced the pain, welcoming the acid burn. The roar became a scream that tore his Fey throat raw.

Gods. Ellysetta could not lose her father and the twins. Not after everything else. "Has anyone told her?" He didn't need to say her name.

"Nei." Gaelen's eyes were dry but haunted. "None of us had the courage to break her heart."

They'd been waiting for him to do that. "How long ago were they lost? Could they still be in the Mists?"

"If they entered the Mists, it wasn't through the Garreval," Bel said. "One of the few survivors of the battle says he saw them running up the mountain, trying to escape Eld and *darrokken*."

Hope left him on a low, pained groan. Traversing the Faering Mists was a journey fraught with danger even in the best of times. The Garreval was the preferred path because the pass was flat and wide, unlike the treacherous cliffs of Revan Oreth behind the Veil. Those caught by the illusions of the Mists were unlikely to fall down a cliff and break their necks in the Garreval. The Rhakis mountains, though, were precious little *but* cliffs.

"I will tell her. She deserves to know the fate of those she loves." He swam to the shores of the lake and pulled himself out. He dried off with a simple weave of Fire and Water, and then there was nothing left to do but spin the news to Ellysetta across their bond threads.

She answered instantly, as if she'd been waiting for his call, but though Bel had served the news to him on a sharp knife, Rain could not bring himself to tell her so bluntly. Instead, he told her about Orest, about the battle and the never-ending supply of enemy troops.

"The Eld are here in force. More than I dreamed they would send. Orest and Teleon are just the beginning. Warn Marissya. Have her get word to Eimar and Loris. They will listen when Tenn and the others will not. The Fey must prepare for war."

"They know, Rain. Sybharukai sent Xisanna and Perahl to fetch Marissya and Dax. Venarra controls the shei'dalins, but Marissya is going to Orest. The tairen are, too. Steli says the pride will reach Kiyera's Veil within two bells. Wait for them."

"I wish I could, kem'reisa, but the Eld will insist on making war." He tried to infuse his words with dry amusement.

"Rain . . . " The warmth of her presence dimmed slightly as worry cast a chill shadow. *"Have you news from Teleon?"*

He hesitated. There was no putting it off. She had to

know the truth. *"There is word, beloved . . . but it is not good."* In a halting voice he told her. All of it. Everything, because she would want nothing less. Because despite the heart he could feel breaking in her chest, she was a strong, fierce, brave woman. A Tairen Soul.

"Lost?" Her voice trembled. *"Papa and the twins? Kieran and Kiel?"* Her voice caught on a sob, and silence fell between them. A moment later, in a firmer voice, she said, *"Nei. Nei, if they were gone, I would know it. Half my heart would be dead, but it is not. They are not gone. They cannot be. I will not believe it. Nei."* He could almost see the tilt of her chin, the spark of defiance lighting her eyes. *"Someone saw them running for the Mists. That's where they must be. We just have to wait until they make it through, just as you and I did."*

If they found their way out at all. If they did not fall from a cliff and break their necks. If they weren't already captives of the High Mage of Eld. He left the possibilities unspoken. What Fey would rob his mate of hope? *"May the gods will it so, shei'tani."*

Bel, Gaelen, and Dev were wolfing down a quick meal and poring over a map Dev had produced. The sounds of battle were growing louder and the calls across the Warriors' Path more numerous. Without him in the sky, the Eld were on the march again, and gaining ground. *"I must go."*

"Light keep you safe, shei'tan, and please . . . please, Rain . . . wait for the tairen. Give them two more bells."

He would not make a vow he could not keep, so instead he gave her the vow he would never break. *"Ver reisa ku'chae. Kem surah, shei'tani."*

By the time Rain and the others returned to the fight, Lower Orest was black with thousands of Eld troops. In just the brief half bell he'd taken to rest and restore his strength, trebuchets had been positioned in a semicircle around the lower levels of Maiden's Gate, each protected by half a dozen bowcannon aimed at the sky. The Fey had thrown up five-fold shields to protect the defenders, but *sel'dor* rained down in a ceaseless barrage, and their shields had begun to fail. The trebuchets launched massive hunks of rock and exploding mortars into each breach.

Protected by airborne missiles and magic shields, an entire company of Mages lobbed sphere after enormous sphere of Mage Fire at the defenders. Hundreds vaporized in instants. Half of the first three levels simply disappeared, as if scooped out of the mountainside by the hand of a god.

"Fey!" Rain cried on the Warriors' Path. *"Twenty-five-fold weaves! Hold off that Mage Fire."*

He took to the air, twisting and turning as the air around him went black with *sel'dor* arrows and great barbed spears catapulted from the bowcannon. The arrows were a nuisance.

The massive spears, however, were tairen killers.

"Rain! Bank left! Left!" Bel's scream tore through his mind. Instinctive trust in his oldest friend sent him rolling left, and the bowcannon spear that would have ripped through his chest tore a gaping hole in one wing instead. He barely made it back to Maiden's Gate before his ripped wing gave out. He fell from the sky, crashing right into the center of an Eld attack force.

Fortunately, tairen didn't need wings to breathe flame. The entire level went up in a boiling sea of fire. Screaming Eld leaped from the walls and fell, burning, to their deaths.

Rain Changed and finished off those left with his swords, fighting with delirious fury and roaring in triumph as blood filled the air like hot scarlet rain. His teeth flashed in a savage grin. Bloodlust rose high. Tairen Souls killed with fire at a distance. But this close, intimate dance of death brought the savage predator in him screaming to the surface.

Dead allies were scattered like leaves across the ruins of Orest. Too many of them wore Fey faces. Friends' faces. This battle must stop. Here and now. No matter what.

He Changed again—his wings re-forming whole and untorn—and leapt back into the sky. This time when he dove for the Mages and *sel'dor* filled the air, he didn't try to dodge the missiles. This time he simply Changed into formless mist and let the spears and arrows fly through him.

The burn still hurt. Some sentient part of Rain scattered to the rainbowed gray cloud of the Change felt the acid brush of *sel'dor* against each tiny droplet of his being, but the foul black metal passed through him without doing harm.

When it was gone, he Changed back into the midnight black tairen with death in his eyes, and dove towards the knot of Elden Mages, spewing a furious jet of flame that incinerated everything in its path. The Mages' shields lasted a scant three chimes before crumpling like seared kindling, leaving the hot, fierce licks of tairen fire to consume the vulnerable red- and blue-robed sorcerers beneath. He screamed in triumph, put on a burst of speed, and raced into the sky.

Rain used the same tactic to destroy three of the trebuchets and their flanking bowcannon, but when he swooped down upon the fourth, the Eld had adapted to his attack. Their *sel'dor* barrage came in a continuous stream rather than a single, dense burst, so that he emerged from the Change into a stream of arrows and took a dozen of the barbed missiles in one side. His flame burned the rest, but as he dove to set fire to the trebuchet, portals opened on every side, revealing bowcannon targeted directly at him.

His body twisted, and four *sel'dor* spears raked deep cuts in his side as he swept by. *Sel'dor* nets fired from another two portals, and the weighted wire mesh wrapped tight around him and dropped him to the ground. His attempt to Change to escape the net ended in writhing agony as dozens more *sel'dor* arrows thunked into his side.

Eld surrounded him, brandishing black metal pikes and barbed blades.

A deafening roar drowned out the cacophony of battle. Bright, boiling clouds of flame burst from the Faering Mists, heralding the arrival of eight great tairen. With screams of fury, they dove towards the battlefield of Lower Orest. Steli led the way, white and fierce, and on her back she carried a slender, shining figure clad in studded scarlet leathers.

Flaming cyclones of Air and Fire shot from Ellysetta's fingertips, driving back the Eld circled around her mate.

Rain closed his eyes as tairen flame poured over him in searing jets. The heat and fire enveloped him, burning the *sel'dor* net and barbed ends of the arrows from his body without raising so much as a blister on his tairen hide. Moments later, he sprang into the sky. *"You should not be here, Ellysetta,"* he chided as he circled close to Steli's fierce form.

"Where else do I belong if not by your side?" Ellysetta tossed her head and gave him a blinding smile. *"Tairen do not abandon their mates. Tairen defend the pride."*

He gave a snort and blew smoke. Stubborn woman. Headstrong woman.

His woman.

And he would have her no other way.

"You bring pride to this Fey." He set every thread of their bond singing with the vastness of his love. *"In truth, I can use your help at the Veil. There are wounded in need of a shei'dalin's care."*

She didn't hesitate or argue. *"I will go."* Her eyes narrowed on the blood-soaked arrows quilling his side. *"Finish this, and join me, shei'tan. I will be waiting for you."* She stroked a hand down Steli's neck, and the white tairen wheeled towards Upper Orest.

"What shall we do with the Eld?" asked Pella, one of the other seven tairen, as Steli winged towards the mountain city.

Rain glanced down at the battlefield where so many had been lost. From this height, the Eld looked like nothing but ants scurrying across an anthill. *"Burn them,"* he commanded. *"Burn the Eld and scorch the ground. Leave no finger span unscathed."*

CHAPTER TWENTY-FIVE

With the reenergized Fey forces keeping the bowcannons, archers, and Mages busy, the nine tairen made short work of scorching Lower Orest.

Most of the Eld broke ranks and ran for the nearest portal when the pride fired the battlefield. Those who did not died ablaze and screaming. To Rain's great relief, blanketing the entire battlefield in tairen flame seemed to destroy both the portals and whatever had enabled them to open. No more gaping holes in space opened. No more foul armies of the Eld poured out. Lower Orest was left a barren, smoking wasteland, as was the fortified Eld village across the river, but he and the pride did not stop burning until they'd scorched every last remnant of the Eld army from the soil.

Rain sang the same instructions to Fahreeta and Torasul in Teleon, and they burned the Garreval, and the mountainsides, and the valley around Teleon to the edge of the Mists.

When they were done, the Fey in both Orest and the Garreval walked the smoking battlefields to collect the *sorreisu kiyr* of their fallen brothers. Many had been stripped and stolen by the Eld during the battle, but the rest were gathered, to be sent back to the families and loved ones left behind. Among them were dozens of *kiyr* from sixty *lu'tans* who had died defending Orest. Ellysetta packed their *sorreisu kiyr* in a silk-lined pouch and asked the tairen to take them back to Fey'Bahren, to be placed with honor alongside the *kiyranis* of the pride.

Leaving Rain and the Celierians to begin the process of cleaning and repairing the city, Ellysetta spun healing on the wounded. Sadly, there weren't nearly as many as she'd expected. Mage Fire, like demon touch, killed rather than maimed. She spun *shei'dalin* healing on those in direst need, and by the time Marissya and Dax arrived on the back of Xisanna, most of the remaining wounded needed little more than rest and a hearth witch's care.

To Rain and Ellysetta's surprise, Marissya and Dax had not come alone, nor empty-handed. Xisanna's mate, Per-ahl, bore the Massan Air master Eimar and his mate, Jisera, on his back, and Dax had strapped a large trunk behind Xisanna's saddle.

Dax slid to the ground on a cushion of Air and set the trunk on the ground.

"I don't understand," Rain said as Dax lifted the trunk's heavy lid to reveal the shining golden armor of the Fey king. "The Massan banished me for weaving Azrahn. I am *dahl'reisen*. I no longer have the right to wear that armor or lead the Fading Lands in war."

"Apparently, you do, my friend," Dax said with a smile. He nodded to the white tairen crouched at Ellysetta's side. "Talk to her."

Steli sniffed and ruffled her wings. *"The golden steel does not belong to the Fey-kin, Rainier-Eras,"* she said in Feyan. Her blue eyes scanned the gathered Fey as if in Challenge, and a low growl rumbled in her throat. *"It is not theirs to give or take. The golden steel is pride-made. It belongs to the Tairen Soul."*

"But I am no longer the Tairen Soul, Steli-*chakai*," Rain

said. "The Massan stripped me of my crown when they made me *dahl'reisen*."

The white cat snorted. *"Fey-kin do not choose the Tairen Soul. Only the pride can choose."*

"The pride never chose me," he reminded her gently. "I was Tairen Soul because I was the only one left."

Steli lowered her head and fixed him with her great, whirling blue eyes. Wisdom swirled there. Much more wisdom than most Fey realized. *"We chose, Rainier-Eras. We chose a thousand years ago, when we would not let you die."*

Silence fell over Upper Orest. Even the thunder of the Veil seemed to hush.

"What Tenn did will not stand, Rain." The Massan's Air master, Eimar v'En Arran, stepped forward to stand at Steli's side. The chimes in his hair tinkled in the breeze off the Veil, and his wintry eyes were hard and steady. "No Fey ever swore allegiance to the Massan," he added. "But we did swear allegiance to the Fading Lands and to our king, Rain Tairen Soul. You have my oath that Loris and I will see this set right. Until then, know that we stand where we always have: at the side of our king." He bowed low. *"Miora felah ti'Feyreisen."*

Rain looked into the faces of the gathered Fey, seeing the same acceptance, the same belief. In him.

He turned to Ellysetta and saw the pride shining in her eyes. And this time, for the first time, the Fey he saw shining back at him was the Fey he knew he was.

"Will you wear the armor, Rain?" Bel asked. "Will you be our king?"

There was only one possible answer. Only one true answer.

"Aiyah."

Eld ~ Boura Fell

Vadim Maur sat in silence. Frost crackled on every surface of the Mage Council's war room. The room was so cold his breath should have formed vaporous clouds around him, but the chill of his fury was too deep, freezing him from the inside out.

Victory in Teleon and Orest had been snatched from his grasp. Lord Teleos, the strongest ally of the Fey in Celieria, still lived, and both passes into the Fading Lands remained in Teleos's control. He and the Fey would move quickly to rebuild his defenses, and the Fey would continue to move freely in and out of the Mists and interfere in Vadim's plans for Celieria.

Today's unexpected defeats had been a costly miscalculation. Already, he knew, the whispers had begun in the Mage Council.

He would now need a victory, swift and complete, to silence the enemies in his ranks. Celieria must be turned, the Fey's main supporters slaughtered or silenced, and then he must find a way to bring down the Faering Mists and beard the tairen in their lair.

He brought up the display of Celieria and began to plan his next move.

Celieria ~ Upper Orest

The roar of Kiyera's Veil drowned out all other sound, and torches burned bright around the lake, turning the billowing mist off the falls to clouds of red-orange flame and illuminating the faces of the tairen and the Fey who had gathered as Rain's witnesses.

Wearing her studded scarlet leathers, the Fey'cha belts full of bloodsworn blades criss-crossing her chest, Ellysetta stood straight and proud and watched with unblinking eyes as her *shei'tan* shed his leathers and steel. Her bloodsworn quintet surrounded her, and Steli crouched behind them, wings spread in a show of protection and might.

The air was chill against Rain's skin, the magic of the waters of the Heras strong. Each breath drew clouds of magic-laden mist into his lungs, making his power hum.

Naked, he turned and walked down the slope to the lake and waded in.

The current was swift, and fought his progress as he swam towards the base of the falls and plunged into the torrential downpour of Kiyera's Veil. The water was icy from snowmelt and rich with potent magic from the ancient Source at Crystal Lake.

He turned his face up, letting the water pound down upon him. Invigorating magic engulfed him in clouds of billowing mist, and the icy streams of water cleansed him like the sharp, ruthless edge of a knife, stripping away the shadows of fear and doubt.

He stood there beneath the flow until the Veil had filled and scoured him, until every powerful branch of his magic awoke and surged up with desperate force, straining against the bonds of his control, fighting for release. His Fey skin grew brighter and brighter, and the water cascading down the Veil shimmered into mist and swirled around him in a silvery-white aura, like light from a star.

A voice, deep and resonant, like no voice he'd ever heard before, sounded in his mind and his soul and every illuminated cell of his body, as if the gods themselves were speaking to him.

You are ready, Rainier-Eras. Let yourself be king.

Tears mingled with the falling magic-bright mist. Peace stole over him. He breathed again, deeply, and filled his heart with courage and determination.

"I am Rainier-Eras!" He shouted it to the heavens, sending the affirmation spinning upwards in Spirit and thought and tairen song. "Feyreisen of the Fey'Bahren pride, king of the Fading Lands, Defender of the Fey."

The Fey and tairen echoed his cry. "Rainier Feyreisen! King of the Fading Lands! Defender of the Fey!"

Rain swam back to the shores of the lake. As his feet sank into the thick moss lining the bank, the star-bright magic continued to swirl around him, swathing him in veils of energy. He lifted his arms. Earth spun out in blinding whirls, enveloping the Fey king's armor, dissolving it in flows of green-hued magic that merged with the bright light spinning about him.

He continued to walk, setting one foot firmly before the other. With each step, the veils of magic flowing around him darkened to shades of red and black and gold, and he could feel the hundreds of Fey kings who had come before him brushing against his mind, whispering words of encouragement.

The sun-bright magic faded, leaving Rain clad in the armor of the king. He spoke a summoning word he'd never known before, and the king's gold blades settled snugly in their sheaths. The name-symbols etched into the armor flashed like a galaxy of stars before fading to simple gold and silver.

And there on the left breastplate, in a spot over his heart, a new king's symbol now shone: the sigil of Rainier-Eras, etched and encircled in gold.

Bel handed him the golden helm. Rain took it, remembering the Fey's brave cry of "To victory or death!" as Johr led them to war. He looked at his brothers, committing their faces to his memory, knowing many of them would not see another year. Knowing they would embrace their deaths so those they loved could live. He would not cry, "To victory or death!" That was not why he fought. That was not why they fought.

"To victory, my brothers." He caught Ellysetta's hand and raised it high. "And to life."

"To victory and life!" the warriors cried.

Rain summoned the Change, took Ellysetta on his back, and shot into the sky, leaving his plain warrior's leathers where they lay, the skin of his old life, now shed forever.

Celierian Language / Terms

bell—hour

chime—minute

dorn—a furry, round somnolent rodent. Eaten in stews. A "soggy *dorn*" is an idiom for someone who is spoiling someone else's fun. A party pooper.

Lord Adelis—god of light. While Celierians worship a pantheon of gods and goddesses (thirteen in all), The Church of Light worships Adelis, Lord of Light, above all others. He is considered the supreme god, with dominion over the other twelve.

Lord Seledorn—god of darkness, Lord of Shadows.

rultshart—a vile, smelly, boarlike animal. The term is often used as an insult.

Elden Language / Terms

Primage—master mage

Sulimage—journeyman mage

umagi—a mage-claimed individual, subordinate to the will of his/her master.

Fey Language / Terms

In Feyan, apostrophes are used in the following ways:
• Meaning "of." *Kem'falla*…my lady, literally "lady of mine." *E'tani*, literally "mate of the heart." *Shei'tani*, literally "mate of the truth/soul."
• In lieu of hyphen, and to indicate emphasis for words combined of multiple root words.
• Sometimes used to replace missing letters/vowels. *Ni v'al'ta!* (literally *Ni ve al'ta*.)

aiyah—yes

ajiana—sweet one

Azrahn—common name of Azreisenahn, the soul magic

bas'ka—all right

beylah vo—thank you (literally "thanks to you")

bote cha!—blades ready! (weapons at the ready!)

Cha Baruk—Dance of Knives

cha'kor—literal translation is five knives. Fey word for "quintet."

chadin—little knife; literally "small fang"; a student in the Dance of Knives. Each student is paired with a mentor who guides their progress through four hundred years of training in the school. It is an apprenticeship of sorts, though many teachers will contribute to the actual education.

chakai—First Knife or First Blade. Champion.

chatok—Big Knife (mentor, leader, also teacher in the dance of knives.)

chatokkai—First General (leader of all Fey armies, 2nd in command to the Tairen Soul). Belliard vel Jelani is the *chatokkai* of the Fading Lands

chervil—a Fey expletive. Bastard, as in, "You smug *chervil*."

dahl'reisen—Literally "lost soul." Name given to unmated Fey warriors who are banished from the Fading Lands. They either seek *sheisan'dahlein* or serve as mercenaries/assassins to mortal races.

deskor—bad

doreh shabeila de—so be it (so shall it be)

e'tan—beloved / husband / mate (of the heart, not the truemate of the soul)

e'tani—beloved / wife / mate (of the heart, not the truemate of the soul)

e'tanitsa—a chosen bond of the heart, not a truemate bond

faer—magic

falla—lady

Felah Baruk—Dance of Joy

Fey'cha—a Fey throwing dagger. Fey'cha have either black handles or red handles. Red Fey'cha are deadly poison. Fey warriors carry dozens of each kind of Fey'cha in leather straps crisscrossed across their chests.

Feyreisa—Tairen Soul's mate; Queen

Feyreisen—Tairen Soul; King

jaffed—a Fey expletive. Used as in, "We'd be jaffed if that happened."

jita'nos—sister's son

kabei—good

ke vo'san—I love you

kem'falla—my lady

kem'san—my love/ my heart

krekk—a Fey expletive

ku'shalah aiyah to nei—bid me yes or no

las—peace, hush, calm

liss—light

lute—red (also blood)

Massan—the council of five powerful Fey statesmen who oversee the domestic governance of the Fading Lands. They do not convene without the *Shei'dalin* and the Feyreisen except in times of extreme need.

Mei felani. Bei santi. Nehtah, bas desrali—Live well, love deep. Tomorrow, we (will) die.

meicha—a curving, scimitarlike blade. Each fey warrior carries two *meicha*, one at each hip.

miora felah ti' Feyreisan—joy to the Feyreisa (literally "Joyful life to the Feyreisa")

nei—no

parei—stop

sel'dor—literally "black pain." A rare black metal that painfully disrupts Fey magic.

selkahr—black crystals used by Mages. Made from Azrahn-corrupted Tairen's Eye crystal.

setah!—enough!

seyani—a Fey warrior's longsword. Each Fey warrior carries two *seyani* swords strapped to his back.

sha vel'mei—you're welcome

shei'dalin—Fey healer and Truthspeaker; capped when referring to their leader.

sheisan'dahlein—Fey honor death. Ceremonial suicide for the good of the Fey.

shei'tan—beloved / husband / truemate

shei'tani—beloved / wife / truemate

shei'tanitsa—the truemate bond

sieks'ta—I have shame (I'm sorry; I beg your pardon)

sorreisu kiyr— Soul Quest crystal

Tairen—flying catlike creatures that live in the Fading Lands. The Fey are the Tairenfolk, magical because of their close kinship with the Tairen.

Tairen Soul—also known as Feyreisen; they are rare Fey who can transform into tairen. Masters of all five Fey magics, they are feared and revered for their power. The oldest Tairen Soul becomes the Feyreisen, the Fey King.

teska—please

Ver reisa ku'chae. Kem surah, shei'tani—Your soul calls out. Mine answers, beloved.

Naming Syntax

Truemated men go from vel to v'En. Mated men go from vel to vel'En.

Truemated women go from vol to v'En. Mated women go from vol to vol'En.

For example:

• Marissya and Dax v'En Solande are truemates.

• Rain vel'En Daris and Sariel vol'En Daris were mates (*e'tanitsa* mates).